An Echo of Hope

Also by Dianna Crawford
in Large Print:

A Home in the Valley
Lady of the River

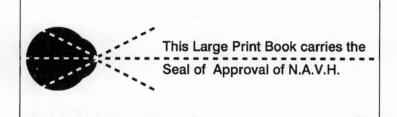

An Echo of Hope

Dianna Crawford

Thorndike Press • Waterville, Maine

Published in 2006 by arrangement with Tyndale House Publishers, Inc.

Thorndike Press® Large Print Christian Historical Fiction.

The tree indicium is a trademark of Thorndike Press.

The text of this Large Print edition is unabridged.
Other aspects of the book may vary from the original edition.

Set in 16 pt. Plantin by Al Chase.

Printed in the United States on permanent paper.

Library of Congress Cataloging-in-Publication Data

Crawford, Dianna, 1940–
    An echo of hope / by Dianna Crawford.
        p. cm.
    Originally published: Wheaton, Ill. : Tyndale House Publishers, c2003. (Reardon Valley ; bk. #3).
    ISBN 0-7862-8357-2 (lg. print : hc : alk. paper)
    1. United States — History — War of 1812 — Veterans — Fiction. 2. Women pioneers — Fiction. 3. First loves — Fiction. 4. Tennessee — Fiction. 5. Widows — Fiction. 6. Large type books. I. Title.
PS3553.R27884E28 2006
813'.54—dc22   2005031438

This novel is dedicated to my daughter,
Megan,

and her very own Promise Keeper,
Chad.

National Association for Visually Handicapped
serving the partially seeing

As the Founder/CEO of NAVH, the only national health agency solely devoted to those who, although not totally blind, have an eye disease which could lead to serious visual impairment, I am pleased to recognize Thorndike Press* as one of the leading publishers in the large print field.

Founded in 1954 in San Francisco to prepare large print textbooks for partially seeing children, NAVH became the pioneer and standard setting agency in the preparation of large type.

Today, those publishers who meet our standards carry the prestigious "Seal of Approval" indicating high quality large print. We are delighted that Thorndike Press is one of the publishers whose titles meet these standards. We are also pleased to recognize the significant contribution Thorndike Press is making in this important and growing field.

Lorraine H. Marchi, L.H.D.
Founder/CEO
NAVH

* Thorndike Press encompasses the following imprints: Thorndike, Wheeler, Walker and Large Print Press.

I would like to acknowledge my two critique partners for always giving their best; and Sue Lerdal, my editor, whose insightful edits greatly improved the manuscript.
I would also like to thank Helen Moore, who traveled with me throughout her native state of Tennessee;
and Louise Cox and the other gracious librarians at the Nashville Library.
I would also like to extend my appreciation for the hospitality and tour guidance of Bob and Faith Murray,
Bill and Opal McCoy,
Stan and Connie Melhorn,
and Roger Lowrance.

Chapter One

April 1815

"Are you sure? That's downright amazin'!"

Standing outside the Bremmers' home, Hope Underwood knew it wasn't polite to eavesdrop on conversations, but from the excitement in the voice of her friend Liza Dagget, she couldn't help herself.

"And after all these years!" another friend, Belinda Bremmer, added, sounding equally astounded. "I'm surprised Max never mentioned it in one of his letters to me."

The words breezed out the parlor window, along with the hem of the ruffled print curtains. Something unusual must have happened to Reardon Valley's militiamen, who were serving with Andrew Jackson's army down in New Orleans.

Hope, on a porch step of the rough-hewn house, removed her second mud-caked shoe and scraped it across its match to knock off the worst of the muck before

9

going inside to join the Friday afternoon sewing circle. Leaving the footwear behind, she picked up her basket of supplies and hurried toward the entrance in her stocking feet on this first sunny day in a week. She was curious to learn what her friends found so astonishing.

"What all did Howie say about —"

"Shh!" someone warned in an urgent whisper. "Hope's comin'."

Secrets? Were they keeping something from her? That wasn't like these women . . . her closest friends.

Hope gave the usual quick rap on the door, put on a smile as if she'd heard nothing, and walked into what was normally a cozy front room. Today, though, a large worktable had been set up in the middle of the polished plank floor.

The four women — Liza, Belinda, Gracie, and Delia — sat around it, needles piercing cloth. They all had their heads ducked, as if their minds were on nothing but stitching a set of tiny clothes for red-headed Belinda's expected baby. Then, one by one, they looked up with suspect smiles and greeted her.

"Sorry I'm late," Hope said, her returning smile probably no less stiff than theirs. "I had a hard time gettin' Timmy down for his

10

nap, and I didn't want to leave him until he fell asleep. Ma Tilly's joints are plaguin' her what with all the rain we've been havin'."

"Thank God the clouds are finally gone," the very pregnant Belinda said with fervor. "Our poor beleaguered men, havin' to trudge through miles and miles of mud to get back to us."

"Not to mention they could all come down with the ague or one of them awful Louisiana swamp fevers." A natural response from sad-eyed Liza — her grandmother was the valley's only healer.

"Does that mean the men are on their way back from New Orleans?" Hope asked, wondering if that had something to do with the secret they were keeping from her. Perhaps they didn't want to remind her that her own husband would not be returning with them — now or ever. Ezra had been killed during the battle at Mobile Bay seven months ago. Hope set her sewing basket on the table and took the empty seat next to Belinda.

Hope's older sister, Gracie, who unlike Hope had inherited the height and blond hair of their tall, Nordic father, broke into a happy grin. "I stopped off at Bailey's store, and there was a letter from my Howie. It was dated no more'n a month ago, and he said they were leavin' New Orleans in a few days, headin' back north to Nashville. But he wrote it would be slow goin' this time of year, haulin' all the army equipment and supplies, not to mention transportin' the wounded."

Hope was almost as thrilled as Gracie. She reached across the table and squeezed her sister's hand. "That's wonderful. I miss Howie's jokin' and singin' as much as you do. It'll be a pure pleasure havin' the men home again."

"We should be thankin' God every day that our army had so few casualties in that last battle," Delia, Howie's sister, remarked as she looked across the table with those dark expressive eyes. "You know it had to be a miracle from God when you think that the British had two thousand casualties whilst our American boys had only eight dead and thirty-seven wounded."

"My, yes, a pure miracle for sure," Belinda said, struggling to her feet and stretching her back. Due to give birth any day, the poor woman looked hugely uncomfortable. "And we must always remember to be grateful. After three years of having our valley's men off fighting at least half of the time, we've lost only two of the valley's brave soldiers. We need to keep the

12

Wallaces in our prayers." Her bright gaze then settled on Hope. "And you, of course, and Ezra's parents."

"Yes," Hope agreed. "It's been especially hard on Titus and Tilly. Titus is really too old and feeble to be out plowin' like he was doin' when I left the house. . . . And all the while as his youngest son dawdled on the porch."

"They spoiled Joel, that's for sure," Liza added. "From what I see, that yahoo's only got one thing on his mind — chasin' after a purty skirt."

"And at the moment," Delia laughed, "he seems to think Hope is the purtiest."

Delia's remark hit a sore spot. "Well, it won't do him one bit of good," Hope snapped back. "Not only is he four years my junior and lazy as an ol' dog, but he hasn't had the decency to respect my widowhood . . . not from the day seven months ago he heard his older brother was dead. If it wasn't for Ma Tilly bein' so sickly, I would've moved back home months ago." Hearing the ring of her own bitterness, Hope quickly returned to the prior topic. "This is much too fine a day for my personal peeves. The men are on their way home."

Belinda sat down again, supporting her belly. "Do pray they come quickly. This baby isn't going to wait much longer. And

I've never birthed one without Max being here with me."

"Of course we'll pray." Hope turned to her sister. "Gracie, did Howie mention in his letter how his foot was healin' from the cannon shrapnel?"

Gracie's deep blue eyes clouded, despite her attempt at a smile. "He just said it was comin' along. But if his foot was still on the mend more'n two months after that last battle, I have a feelin' his wound was worse than he let on."

"That big brother of mine is such a baby," Delia said to Gracie. "If it was really bad, he'd be carryin' on like a bawlin' calf."

Delia and Gracie and their respective husbands, Jacob Reardon and Howard Clay, were as close now as they'd been all their growing-up years, intermarrying the two families. The two young couples had even built their homes facing each other on either side of the road separating the Reardon and Clay lands. But the reason Delia could be so flippant about her brother's injury was because *her* husband had won the coin toss and remained behind to look after both families while Howie went to fight against the British and their Indian allies in what was now dubbed the War of 1812.

On the other hand, Hope's husband,

Ezra, had been more than happy to go — escape, would be more like it — even though Hope herself had been expecting a child at the time. And worse, she'd been just as glad to see him go. Their marriage had been a mistake. They never should've let their parents push them into what had been deemed the perfect solution to their separate sadnesses. It had only compounded each of their private sorrows. One good thing had come from their union, though — their son, two-and-a-half-year-old Timothy. She could never regret having Timmy. He was the single joy of her life.

Liza glanced at Hope across the table as she pulled a needle through a seam in a nightgown of dimity. "Hope, dear, have you heard any news from the soldiers that we haven't?" Her voice sounded too casual. Hope wondered again if the others were keeping a secret from her.

Gracie, sitting next to Liza, halted mid-stitch. "Of course she hasn't." Gracie lent Hope a sympathetic smile. She alone knew the depth of Hope's unhappiness . . . the long lonely years of waiting for one man before finally agreeing to wed another, only to become a widow within three years. Gracie looped her needle through the material in a couple of finishing stitches, bit off

15

the thread with her teeth, then held up a tiny long-sleeved blue gown. "Here's another finished one."

So tiny. Hope found it hard to believe that her own son had ever been small enough to wear a garment that size . . . her orphaned son who'd had his father at home for only a few short lulls in the war. She looked from the soft muslin gown to her older sister. "How long did you say it would be before the men return?"

"The way we figure, they could come marchin' back home in another week, maybe two." Tucking a flaxen strand behind her ear, Gracie grinned. "And if I know my Howie, we'll have us the biggest ol' party you ever did see. You know how he loves to play his music."

"And we know how much you love to sing along," Delia laughed. "It'll be like old times again."

Old times . . .

It had been ten years since Hope had felt like singing. Back before her loveless marriage . . . back when Ezra still had his Becky and she her Michael. Back when life had seemed so full of promise for all of them . . . before Michael had been chased out of the valley by vile accusations, and before Ezra's Becky died in childbirth. For all Hope

16

knew, Michael was dead, too. It had been nine years since his last letter.

As the other women started chatting about parties and frolics, Hope forced herself to concentrate on their words, on the baby blanket she hemmed — anything to keep her mind from falling into that well of pain that was always there waiting for her.

"Hush!" Delia suddenly demanded. She raised a hand for silence and turned toward the window. "Something's happenin' out on the street."

She was right. The shouting of a male voice came from the direction of the general store.

More yells. The church bell started clanging.

Hope and the other women sprang up, their chairs screeching back across the wood plank floor. They rushed out the front door.

Danny Wilson, a lad who lived just above the river, came riding past the church. He pointed toward Caney Fork. "The men! They're comin'!"

A thrill shot through Hope as she heard her friends cry out with joy.

Schoolchildren ran out of the church house as if it were on fire, shouting and jumping with excitement as they made a dash for the ferry landing.

17

The Wilson lad reached the Bremmer gate and reined his sturdy brown mare to a halt. He whipped a floppy hat from his strawlike hair. "Ma'am." He addressed Belinda up on the porch, then Gracie. "You, too, ma'am. Your men is crossin' on the ferry this very minute. The militia's a-comin' home!"

Hugging and laughing, Hope's friends bounded down the steps and out the walk while she stopped to retrieve her shoes.

Gracie turned back. "Come on, Hope."

"Don't let me stop you. I'll catch up."

As Gracie took off at a run, her cheeks beaming with lively color, guilt seized Hope. She never could've welcomed Ezra with a fraction of that gladness. Surely now, though, his happiness, his joy had been restored by his reunion in heaven with Becky and their stillborn baby. And the relief Hope felt at that thought was tangible.

Folks had poured out of the smithy, the leatherworks, the general store, and all the homes lining the road, filling the muddy way with excitement as they rushed down to greet the returning heroes.

After banging the last of the muck from her shoes and slipping them on, Hope lifted her black wool skirt above the muddy street and ran after all those hurrying down to the ferry landing. Reaching the splintery surface of the dock, Hope bemoaned as she often did that she was so tiny. Her head rose no higher than most of her neighbors' shoulder blades. She couldn't even see the river, let alone the raft being pulleyed across.

Amid the excited cries of greeting, one shout stood out. "They're halfway!"

Those just ahead of Hope stretched up on tiptoe to see, bobbing their heads back and forth. At least a score of adults and three dozen schoolchildren pushed and jostled, vying for a better view on the crowded quay.

Gracie — sweet Gracie! — broke past the cheering crowd and grabbed Hope's hand. Her cheeks still aglow, she sported an unstoppable grin. "Come on, little sister. Put on a smile. Be happy. Our men are comin' home!"

Holding tight, Gracie pulled Hope with her as she wedged back through the crowd until they reached Delia, Belinda, and Liza.

At this vantage point, only children stood in front of them, giving Hope a clear view of the approaching raft being drawn ever closer along a thick rope. Carrying a full load of men and horses, the flatboat dragged low in the water, swells lapping over the logs. The militiamen aboard all looked grimy and ragged, attired mostly in worn-out hunting clothes. Small wonder the British had called them "dirty shirts." Scraggly beards made many of them look even more unkempt. Hope couldn't discern one from another.

"There's Max!" Belinda shouted, laughing. "Can't miss that blond hair." Holding her belly, she thrust her other arm above her head and waved wildly.

Hope's heart swelled, sharing her dear friend's joy. Max would be here for the birth of Belinda's baby.

The shouts coming from the raft and those from the landing collided in a deafening roar as the ferry banged against the dock. A couple of overeager passengers lifted the front rail from its slot and carelessly tossed it into the water, freeing everyone to converge even before the mooring lines had been secured.

Belinda's husband, Max, moved with great speed for his hulking size. Tears streaming into his golden beard, he reached his wife and buried his face in her curly red hair.

Max's father, the valley's pastor, shoved forth with his own German bulk to reach his son. The silver-haired old gent engulfed both Max and Belinda in a burly hug.

Not to be left out, Max's youngsters grabbed on wherever they could.

Other militiamen scooped their own children up into their arms — schoolchildren who'd been fortunate to be in town at the right moment, along with Hope's sewing circle and a few folks who had come in on other business. But it didn't matter whether or not a man's family was present — no one lacked for a hug.

Gracie's brown-eyed Howie wore his usual cocky grin. He rode a sleek bay instead of walking off the raft, since one of his feet was swathed in bandages. But he didn't remain astride long. His wife and sister together pulled him down into their arms, while his and Gracie's school-age children grabbed his sleeves and shirttail, tugging and squealing. The boisterous cluster half carried him up the embankment.

In the distance, a lone regular army soldier in a blue uniform strode off the ferry and collected the abandoned bay's reins, adding them to those of the other horses he led.

Hope, having remained behind on the dock, took in the whole picture of Reardon Valley's returning heroes as they moved up the slope surrounded by the happy throng. She smiled as she heard a multitude of words spilling enthusiastically over each other in an unintelligible jumble of joy. Gracie had her Howie . . . and Liza was

21

clinging to her baby brother, who looked years older than when he had left to join the militia last summer. And Belinda —

Feeling someone's gaze upon her, Hope suddenly noticed the uniformed soldier. With his string of horses, he was the only one remaining on the quay with her.

She turned and looked up into eyes that were an unusually light shade of brown. The *exact* shade of her long-gone beau's. She searched the soldier's face. This man was several years older, his features more chiseled. But . . . no, it couldn't be. "Michael? Michael Flanagan?"

"Yes, ma'am."

His quiet affirmation slammed into her, knocking the strength from her legs. Her vision fuzzed.

Hands gripped her arms. *His* hands.

Hope's vision burst out of its fog. Michael Flanagan was staring at her. Intently. After all these years.

After all these years . . . Weren't those the exact words she'd overheard Belinda saying not thirty minutes ago? Michael must be the secret her friends had been keeping from her.

But why?

Michael Flanagan squeezed her arms. "Hope? Are you all right? You're white as a ghost."

Chapter Two

"It's been a long time," Michael was saying, his voice much deeper, smoother, than Hope remembered.

"It has." She couldn't believe how much he'd changed . . . taller, broader shouldered, with a military rigidness to his stance, to his mouth. His leather-gloved fingers had yet to release her arms.

Had he, this stranger, come back for her after all these years?

From behind, another hand clapped onto her shoulder. "Hope," a gruffer male voice said. Brother Rolf.

Michael released her, and she turned toward her lifelong pastor and grandfather-like friend.

"Has da sergeant told you?" Even after decades in America, the oversized preacher's German accent was still evident.

"What?"

"Max, he tells me dat Sergeant Flanagan has a delivery to your husband's family."

"To Titus and Tilly?" Her mind

couldn't make sense of it.

"*Ja.* Max says Ezra gives a packet to da sergeant here right before he dies."

The news shot through her like fire, then ice. Michael Flanagan had a delivery from her husband. Was it a message or more of Ezra's personal items? She'd received a letter from Ezra's commander shortly after his death, informing her that he'd died bravely in service to his nation. A few weeks later, a package arrived with Ezra's belongings — but there'd been no mention of anything more. And most definitely nothing about Michael.

"Hope?" Brother Rolf leaned down with concern in his Bavarian blue eyes.

"Yes?"

"I t'ink maybe I ride *mit* you and da sergeant out to your place. I am t'inking I might be needed."

This man — her beau of so long ago — was coming to her house? Ezra's family's house? She couldn't imagine how the Underwoods would react if they recognized him. They'd surely remember that Michael was the one she'd pined for all those years even after she married Ezra. That he was the notorious barn burner's son and had been accused himself of setting fire to her father's gristmill.

She turned back to the soldier. "Perhaps it would be best if you gave the packet to me here. I can deliver it to the Underwoods."

"I'm sorry, ma'am," he said with the same remoteness. "But my instructions were quite specific. I am to deliver the packet personally and wait until after the contents have been distributed."

"Ezra told you this himself? Before he died?"

"Yes, ma'am. Corporal Underwood lived for two days after he was hit by the fragments of a cannon explosion. He sent for me and handed the packet to me already wax-sealed and bound. I was not to send it by post or give it to any of his friends to deliver. He said it could wait until I found the time. I gave him my pledge, and I'd like to fulfill this duty as soon as possible. I've had it for seven months."

What could possibly be in it? Hope became even more uneasy. She'd never fully trusted Ezra, even though she'd shared a home — and a child — with the man. What dire message could he be sending now from beyond the grave? She shuddered involuntarily.

"Sergeant Flanagan." Brother Rolf spoke as Hope continued to stare dumbly at Michael. "You are *mit* young Undervood at da end?"

"Yes, sir. Me and Howie Clay. Colonel Coffee gave me leave to stay until Ezra passed over. We were friends back when I lived here in the valley." He said "back when" to Brother Rolf as matter-of-factly as if the ten years he'd been gone were inconsequential. "The surgeon plied Ezra with plenty of opium, so his passing was easy." Michael shot a glance at Hope. "Beggin' your pardon, Mrs. Underwood, if I've upset you with talk of your husband's dying."

Mrs. Underwood. A moment ago, he'd addressed her by her first name. What was she to make of that? And he'd spent time with Ezra. How much did he know about the two of them, their marriage? She felt layers of herself stripping away; yet Michael stood there, cloaked in mystery.

Had he wed? Did he have children of his own?

Again Brother Rolf filled the silence for her. "Max, he says our militia arrives home early because you give da loan of dese horses." He nodded toward the string waiting behind Michael — two with saddles, three loaded with boxes and bundles.

"The army leased my stock for the Southern Campaign. When Reardon Valley's militia requested to leave the regiment at Franklin to cut across to the valley instead of going the extra miles on to Nashville, the commander allowed me to retrieve my horses to help out with the wounded and supplies."

"*Ja,* ve are grateful to you. Especially Max *und* his family." Brother Rolf pointed up the path with a huge slab of a hand, but his son and daughter-in-law, Belinda, had reached the street above and were now out of sight. "You stay *mit* us. Now dat mine Inga is gone to be *mit* da Lord, Max *und* his family live *mit* me."

"I was purely sorry to hear of your wife's passing." Michael's tone was filled with genuine sympathy.

Rolf took in a ragged breath. *"Ja.* It vas hard. . . . Come. I help you unload *und* put da horses to pasture behind mine smit'y. Dey look like dey could use a few days' rest. Den ve go to da Undervood place. *Ja?"*

"That would be greatly appreciated. It has been hard on the stock with all the rain and mud."

Michael would be here for a few days. Hope shivered with apprehension, then caught herself before a relieved sigh slipped out. She'd have enough time to learn if he'd come merely to deliver the mysterious packet — or to see her. "I'll collect my sewing basket and my horse and meet you in front of the smithy."

Stepping out ahead of the men, she grazed Michael with a last glance. For all the questions she wanted to ask him, her fear of his answers coupled with the thought of making a fool of herself had paralyzed her tongue.

Hope felt even less comfortable as she traveled north on horseback along the valley road, dwarfed between the two much taller men. Worse, she still couldn't manage to think of anything casual to say — even something as seemingly innocent as a remark about how lovely the first fragile blooms of spring were. And they were. They'd shaken off the days of rain and now stretched above the new grass toward the sun. As Hope and the men passed through a pasture, the delicate splashes of color re-minded her of a stroll she and Michael took that last spring before the terrible incident.

She could still envision the humor in his eyes as they'd attempted to immortalize the beauty of these very woods and meadows in a sonnet. But mostly she remembered his searching high and low for a flower that would capture the "illusive depths of her sheer blue eyes," as he'd called them. After a childhood spent with the painful nickname of Ghost Eyes, to know that Michael thought her eyes beautiful instead of strange had been his highest compliment to her.

Wondering if he still thought her eyes or anything else about her attractive, she straightened the slump from her shoulders and raised her chin in an attempt to look her best, considering the fact that she was no longer an innocent-faced girl of nearly sixteen but a woman of twenty-six. Had he even noticed? Did he care?

Then her most embarrassing fear surfaced again. Had Ezra or one of the other men told him that she'd waited almost seven years for his return? Most likely, by then he'd dismissed all thought of her — particularly considering that her father had not only told her about and then refused to give her the letters Michael sent that first year but had refused to even tell her from whence they'd come. She'd never been able to reply, to assure Michael she didn't believe the lies about him, that she was waiting for his return as she'd vowed.

The wagon road narrowed as they rode into the shadow of the newly leafing woods, causing Michael's long-legged black mare to almost rub shoulders with her gray, dappled Arabian.

She caught the soldier stealing a glance at her but pretended not to notice. Still, if nothing else, he must be wondering why she hadn't extended even the merest courtesy of a polite inquiry. She simply had to engage him in conversation. She took a breath. "I apologize for my rudeness. Your arrival took me by surprise. Do tell me, how is your family faring?" After the words were out of her mouth, she realized his answer might include a wife and children.

He looked straight at her, his eyes ever so familiar in an otherwise unexpectedly mature face.

She did her best to remain composed while he stared.

Finally he spoke. "My ma is livin' with Duncan and Paddy and their families on a place halfway betwixt Nashville and the big Muddy. As far as I know, they're doin' fine. I've only received a couple of letters since I swung by to see 'em a couple of years ago." He seemed to relax his shoulders a bit. "I've been in the cavalry for the past four years, since . . ." His gaze faltered a second. "Never mind. From what Max and Howie said, I trust all is well with your folks, too."

"Yes. God has blessed my family with good health. And, of course, my brothers

30

and sisters are as rowdy as ever when we're able to get together."

His firm lips gentled, curling up slightly at the corners. "And just how is that rascal Wesley?"

Remembering what a scamp her younger brother had been whenever Michael had come calling, Hope chuckled. "Believe it or not, Wes is as tall as you now. And he's puttin' all that energy of his to good use. He and Spencer and some of their friends packed up and moved out to Missouri Territory as soon as land there opened up for settlin'. They've founded their very own Reardon Valley."

"I like hearing that. Young men with a dream and following it." Michael looked away then, his concentration returning to a particularly damp and puddled stretch of the wagon road.

Hope was grateful that he did. After he'd mentioned Wesley and Spencer following their dream, her throat had closed. She knew how it felt to be denied a dream.

But she'd long since given up waiting and praying for hers. And now, after she'd finally left her dream behind, Michael had reappeared.

"Ve turn off here," Brother Rolf stated, nodding toward the connecting path that led beneath some leafing hickory and black gum trees.

Hope's chest tightened even more as her gray gelding turned onto the path without any prompting. The Underwood clearing lay just ahead, and they — and Ezra's packet — would soon be exposed.

She shot a glance at Michael's saddle-bags. *Lord,* she prayed, *please let Ezra's words bring comfort, not pain.*

Hope's arrival home, earlier than expected and in the company of the pastor and a uniformed soldier, brought Ma Tilly and Joel from the house and Papa Titus from the barn.

Tilly removed a faded apron from her thick waist while tucking strays of gray hair into her bun as she started down the porch steps on unsteady feet.

By the time Hope and the men brought their mounts to a halt in front of the hewn-log house, the Underwoods had intercepted them.

"Goot afternoon, folks. I am happy to bring da news dat our militia is home. My Max is home."

"Glad to hear it." Titus brushed the dust and straw from his rumpled clothes and tufts of white hair, then extended a hand up to Brother Rolf.

"Sergeant Flanagan, here, he comes *mit* da boys." Brother Rolf nodded toward Michael, then dismounted. "He is bringing a packet for you. From Ezra, may da goot Lord rest his soul."

Tilly's eyes widened, and her age-veined hands went to her plump but sagging cheeks.

"After all this time?" Titus's scrawny frame and slumped shoulders testified to every day of his sixty-nine years. "It sure has taken a long spell a-gettin' here."

Hope demurely swung down from the Arabian, displaying a minimum of leg as Michael also dismounted. She felt apprehensive yet curious, knowing Ezra's parents would feel freer to ask far more questions than she had. And she was doubly glad Brother Rolf was here, just in case. . . . A few years older than Titus, the minister would know the right words no matter what the packet revealed.

Michael reached into a bulging saddlebag and pulled out a large deerskin envelope. Wax showed at the edges of the flap, and a leather thong secured the whole package. He strode directly to Titus and presented it to him. "Shortly before your son passed on, he instructed me not to entrust this to anyone else, but to deliver it to you personally once the fightin' ended."

Titus looked particularly vulnerable as he stared at it with faded blue eyes. He smoothed his bony fingers over the soft leather. "Ezra gave it to you with his own hands?"

"Yes, sir."

"Open it, Pa," Joel, his curly headed youngest, urged, eying the packet as if there might be gold in it.

Undeterred, Titus asked Michael, "You were there when Ezzy died?"

"Yes, sir. Me an' Howard Clay. We kept him company till he passed on."

Ma Tilly moved beside her balding husband. "Howie was there? With my Ezzy? That's comfortin' to know." A soft sigh escaped. "Now, y'all come on in. We'll have us a cup of coffee, and I'll see if we can't scrounge us up a cookie or two."

"Dat sounds real goot, Tilly," Brother Rolf said, lumbering toward the porch steps, with the others following.

Although Hope was grateful that none of the Underwoods recognized Michael, she knew she had little time left now to steel herself before the nebulous packet was opened. Closing her eyes, she summoned all her courage before following a few paces behind.

Once inside, Hope kept busy as the men-folk congregated around the simple oak table at the hearth end of the living room. She set a brown crockery cup before each man, making an effort not to pay Michael any more or less attention than she did the others, especially as she stood next to him, pouring the leftover noontime coffee from the large enamel pot. Joel squinted at her with a prurient look in his eyes, and she shuddered in response, almost sloshing the hot liquid on Michael's arm. She hastened to complete her task.

Meanwhile, Tilly moved quickly on her stiff joints to pile two plates with the applesauce cookies Hope had baked that morning. She spaced them down the center of the table, then returned to the worktable to crush enough granules from the hard sugar cone for their coffee.

"Hurry up, Ma." The usually lackadaisical Joel was growing more impatient as he sat beside Michael, at the end of the table closest to his father. His freckled hands were within easy grabbing distance of the packet.

Hope took a seat across from them and next to Rolf, while Tilly took her usual place opposite her husband. All eyes centered on Titus.

He worked off the thong ties and slid his finger beneath the flap, breaking the wax as he went. Turning the envelope upside down, he jiggled it until a leaden toy soldier fell onto the table with a clunk, followed by several folded letters. A different name was written on each outer fold. One had Hope's name scrawled across it.

Titus dealt out the letters as if they were playing cards, then passed Hope a second one that was addressed to her son, Timothy. And for the first time since they had arrived home, the thought occurred to her that her tot must still be upstairs napping.

More hesitant than the others to unfold the one addressed to her, Hope held on to both envelopes and watched as Tilly read her own letter.

Within seconds, the aging woman's face crumpled into a teary smile. She handed the letter to Titus, who also read it, his usually gruff demeanor melting away.

Rusty-headed Joel put his letter down first. With no sign of what the message had been, he folded it and dropped it down the neck of his belted overshirt.

Ma Tilly glanced up at him. "What did it say?"

He grunted. "Same old thing. Take care of Ma and Pa. Work hard." Grabbing a cookie, he scraped back his ladder-back chair, got up, and walked out the door.

As she watched him go, Hope had the idea that Ezra hadn't been any more gentle with his spoiled baby brother than he had been with her. More frightened than before of what her own letter would say, she took a deep breath and spread it open. She hoped no one was watching her now.

To my kind, long-suffering wife, it began. She caught her breath and continued.

I do not believe there are many unsaid words between us. We were not the closest of friends, and I know I should have treated you better. I'm sorry. But my biggest regret is that I left the care of my parents and my son to you alone. Do not mourn my passing. I joyfully go to join Becky and our daughter.

Tell Timmy I am looking forward to the day when I will see him again on the other side. And for you, Hope, to make up in a small way for the unhappiness I brought to your life, the messenger is my gift to you.

The messenger? His gift? Hope slanted an astounded glance up at Michael sitting directly across from her. He was politely

37

studying his cup of coffee.

Michael had said he didn't know what was in the packet. But did he know why he'd been the only one Ezra would allow to deliver the letters? Surely he must have guessed. He'd even been instructed by Ezra to wait until they were read.

Yet what could she possibly say? She didn't know his heart. Michael had chosen to stay away all these years after he'd promised to return for her. She couldn't shame herself by offering herself to him now. Besides, could she trust him? He easily could've changed as much on the inside as he had on the outside.

And what about the Underwoods? Tilly, with her many ailments, couldn't manage much by herself lately, and Titus was getting slower every day. She knew they counted on all she did for them.

Tilly made a muffled sound.

Spotting tears freely flowing over the old woman's cheeks, Hope placed a comforting hand on her shoulder.

"I'm fine." Tilly swiped at the wetness with a trembling hand, while crushing the letter to her breast with the other. "It's a purely beautiful letter. Purely beautiful. My boy even wrote the words large enough for these old eyes to see." Pushing her chair back, she rose. "If you folks'll excuse me, I'd like to be alone with my son's words for a spell."

Hope's own eyes grew moist as she watched the dear woman hobble up the stairs. *Thank You, Jesus,* she mouthed silently. Ma Tilly had a sweet remembrance from her son to treasure. And she would never need to know that he had been a less than admirable husband to her beloved daughter-in-law. Hope glanced at Titus and caught him sleeving off his own wet eyes as he read his letter.

A second letter still lay unopened before her. Were there any more surprises from Ezra? She unfolded Timothy's letter and with relief saw that Ezra had given his son a last gift of love and the regret that he wouldn't see his child grow up. He'd also sent Timmy the metal soldier to hold on to whenever he missed not having his papa around to take him hunting and fishing.

Hope picked up the sturdy leaden figure and turned it over in her hand.

"Is that for your little one?" Michael asked quietly.

Her gaze met his and found there an unexpected warmth. "Yes. Something to remind Timmy that he once had a papa."

"Tell your son that his father fought

bravely and died with great dignity. A man any son would be proud to have for a father."

Her own eyes threatened tears. "I will."

"*Ja,* ve all keep his memory alive for da tot. Ezzy vas a —"

Brother Rolf's words were cut short by the door banging open and Joel striding in. He stopped directly across from where Michael sat. "I thought you looked familiar. You're Michael Flanagan, that thievin' barn burner's son." His voice rang strident, accusing. "But then, you prefer burning gristmills, don'tcha? I heard they hung your pa for murder a few years back."

Was that true? Hope's gaze swung to Michael.

His fists were knotted. A vein bulged at his temple, and muscles bunched at his jaw. He rose from the table like a tightly coiled spring.

She feared he would lunge across the table for Joel.

But he didn't. He picked up his white leather gloves, then turned to her father-in-law.

Titus stared back unspeaking, his mouth slack.

"Do thank Mrs. Underwood for her hospitality." Pivoting on his boot heel, Michael strode toward the wide-open door.

Hope flew from her chair and started after him. Someone needed to apologize.

Joel caught her arm in a viselike grip. "Where do you think you're goin'?"

She swung a frantic glance back at Titus and Brother Rolf.

Brother Rolf was already on his feet, his expression a stern reprimand. "Joel, da man vas da invited guest in your house." He then turned to Titus. "If you are not needing me, I ride back home *mit* da sergeant now."

Looking out the door, Hope saw that Michael had reached his mare and was mounting.

Without a backward glance, he rode away.

Chapter Three

Hope had never seen such an outburst from Joel. He glowered out the door of the Underwood house until Michael and Brother Rolf rode out of sight. Breathing hard, his face was flushed with rage.

And he had yet to release Hope's arm.

Normally Joel cared only about how quickly he could finish a chore — if he couldn't talk his way out of it entirely — so he could ride into town and wile his time away with friends.

"Please," she urged, trying to peel his rigid fingers from her arm. "You're hurtin' me."

He glanced down at her captured limb, then up into her eyes. "You're not to see Flanagan while he's here."

How dare Joel presume to order her about! "Let go." She jerked free, her own anger building. Without glancing back to gauge her father-in-law's reaction, she stalked to the stairs that climbed the back wall from the parlor end of the room.

Reaching the floor above, she passed the entrance of the elder Underwoods' bedroom, relieved that Tilly had been spared Joel's outrageous behavior, and walked straight to her private quarters at the end of the hall. She eased the door open, careful not to disturb her two-and-a-half-year-old son. Deftly, she moved to the small alcove that held Timmy's crib, half expecting the dark-headed tot to be awake from the loudness of Joel's outburst.

But, thank goodness, Timmy slept peacefully on his side, his long lashes splayed across his rosy cheeks, his chubby hand clutching his stuffed lamb. Her adorable treasure. His fine cap of hair feathered across his brow, and she yearned to feel the dark, silky softness. Instead she pulled the quilt up a bit. Sunny as the day was, the air in the closed room still had the bite of cold.

Hope turned back to the room that held much finer furniture than the Underwoods' simple homemade pieces. As always, they were a reminder that her mother had given up a life of riches with her family in the East to marry her father. Walking with light steps to the cherrywood rocker by the window, she smoothed her palm over the gentle curve of the shiny arm, then glanced around the room at the other familiar pieces: the wardrobe, the tester bed, the four-drawer chest with its large-framed looking glass. Her Baltimore family had sent the ensemble for her fourteenth birthday . . . one of many gifts that testified to the fact that her mother's relatives had eventually accepted Jessica's marriage to Noah Reardon.

Noah Reardon, who'd always seemed such an understanding husband and father, yet had refused to extend the same compassion to Michael . . . Did her father sense something she couldn't?

Dropping down to the cane seat of the rocker, Hope moved aside a lace panel and looked down at the wagon path below. Mere moments before, Michael Flanagan had left on it. Michael Flanagan, after so many long and dreary years, had just as suddenly come again and gone.

Yet, remarkably, the first time he rode into her life eleven years ago was still as clear in her mind as if it happened yesterday. Hope rested her head against the back of the rocker and closed her eyes, letting the picture come to mind.

Unlike today, the weather had been warm and sticky that unforgettable afternoon, much the same as most days in the last of July.

★ ★ ★

While the rest of the Reardon clan had gone down to the swimming hole, Hope and Gracie sat on their family's front porch, complaining about the lack of a cool breeze, as they stitched seams of costumes for the patriotic play Hope had written. They had only a few more days to finish the old-fashioned clothing while the lads built the stage at the parade ground and painted the sets. A lot of work for the young people of the valley, but Hope was sure their efforts would be worth it. Howie Clay, Gracie's beau, had even written special music that he and Gracie would sing.

Hope swelled with pride and gratitude at the thought that all her friends admired her stage play enough to pitch in and turn it into an event the whole valley would be coming to see. Shoving the needle through a red-and-white-striped gown with her thimble, she started humming one of the lively jigs.

Gracie, the older and taller of the two sisters and blonde with golden skin and deep blue eyes, commenced harmonizing with her angelic voice trilling an octave higher than Hope's mellow alto. Folks were often surprised by the depth of Hope's voice, given her almost childlike features, but she didn't mind. She'd always found the blend of their two voices quite restful.

The rapidly growing pounding of racing horse hooves interrupted the melodious moment.

She and Gracie exchanged puzzled glances, then dropped their work into sewing baskets beside their chairs and rose.

"What fool would be gallopin' a horse like that in this heat?" Gracie started down the steps, her hands on her hips.

Before Hope could follow, two riders rounded the side of the house, reining in their mounts in a clod-kicking stop.

Howie whooped as he swung down, his rich brown eyes sparkling with merriment. Reaching Gracie in three vaulting steps, he caught her up and swung her and her pink-checked skirts around, then set her down, facing the horse he'd just dismounted. "Ain't he purty? All gold with a blond mane just like yours. It's one of them Spanish horses."

Despite being lathered with sweat, the animal was a beauty, Hope noted from her position at the top of the landing.

"Now when we go to play our music at the other settlements, we'll be ridin' up in fancy style . . . thanks to Flanagan here."

Howie nodded toward the other horseman.

A fellow Hope had never seen before sat bareback, his naked feet dangling from a white-stockinged black mare. The lean-faced lad swiped a strand of nut brown hair from his tanned brow. His eyes, though, were unusual — almost as light as the amber stone in her father's dress-up ring.

"Michael Flanagan, meet Gracie Reardon." Howie pulled Hope's sister to his side. "Like I said, I got me the purtiest gal this side of ol' Smoky."

The young man's gaze moved to Gracie, and he nodded politely.

The pink gingham, which complemented the delicate color in her cheeks, only added to Gracie's beauty as she smiled up at him. "You're the new family that took over the Colton place. Papa said you folks was in the horseflesh business."

"That's right, miss." He spoke so quietly, Hope scarcely heard the words.

"And Michael here made sure his pa gave me a fair price," Howie said, still excited.

The ginger-gold gaze of the nice-looking fellow drifted up to Hope on the porch.

She held her breath, waiting for the usual startled reaction to her almost colorless eyes.

None came. No change in his expression whatsoever as he nodded.

"Oh yeah. I forgot," Howie said. "That there's Gracie's little sister, Hope. She's the bookworm of the family. She's the one what wrote the play me an' Gracie's starrin' in." His glance then scanned the three Reardon homes, the grounds, and the outbuildings. "Hey, where is ever'body?"

"Down to the swimmin' hole," Gracie supplied. "Even the grownups. Hop down, Mr. Flanagan. Rest yourself on the porch while me an' Howie go water these poor hot horses." Returning her attention to Howie, she continued. "Hope, why don't you get us all somethin' cool to drink?"

Hope wasn't fooled by her sister's eagerness to water a couple of smelly animals. Gracie wanted a private moment with Howie.

With a sincere light in his amber eyes, the tall lad took a step toward Hope as the lovebirds left him behind. "I'd be pleased to help with the drinks, miss, if I'm not bein' too bold."

"Are you sure? It's cooler out here on the porch."

"I just need to wash up." He glanced down at his open hands.

"There's a washstand beside the back door. Then, if you'll fetch the jug of lem-

48

onade up from the cellar, that would be a pure help. It's on the top shelf beside the stairs."

As he started around the house, she ran inside, wishing she'd tied back her sable hair with a prettier ribbon. In the gilded oval mirror near the entrance, she took a quick perusal of her work apron and lace-trimmed indigo muslin dress. Thank goodness, she looked tidy, if nothing else . . . though she didn't know why she ever bothered. With a sister as comely as Gracie, no one ever gave her more than passing notice, even if they adjusted to her palest of blue eyes.

Still, Hope couldn't quell a quiver of anticipation as she rushed about, furnishing her mother's very best silver tray with a matching plate piled with cookies, lace-edged napkins, and four crystal goblets — accoutrements she knew would have to be washed and put away before Mama and Papa returned from swimming.

Hope had just finished when she heard Michael Flanagan's footsteps on the back porch. In a flash, she ripped off her calico apron and tossed it over a hook next to the door.

"Is this the right jug?" he asked as he stepped inside. He stared at her with such sincerity, her own sureness faltered.

"Yes, thank you." She took the thick earthen container from him. Uncorking it, she poured a portion into each fragile glass with both hands, careful not to drip any onto the tray.

"You sure do have dainty little hands," he remarked quietly.

"I know." Unsure of his motives, she avoided looking up as she placed the jug on the worktable beside the tray. "They're not at all adequate for most farm chores."

"Neither is that figurine sittin' on your mantel, but it sure is a pleasure to look at."

Laughter came echoing through from the front of the house. Gracie and Howie were back.

Hope shot the young man a guilty glance, though she knew they'd done nothing inappropriate. Looking away, she took hold of the tray handles. "Sounds like they're back just in time for refreshments."

Gracie and Howie monopolized the conversation for the remainder of the visit. Hope felt Michael Flanagan's gaze upon her from time to time, just as hers stole to him, and after the fellows rode away, she couldn't help daydreaming about the quietly handsome horse breeder. He hadn't flinched at her eyes, nor had he been bothered by Howie calling her a bookworm. And instead of treating her as if she were treading in a man's territory by writing a play, he'd looked at her with admiration.

And he thought her hands were pretty.

Hope remembered watching for him at church the next day, but he didn't come. The following afternoon she spotted him walking out of the saddler's. She'd been standing on the church steps saying good-bye to the schoolchildren she helped teach three days a week.

He must have sensed her eyes on him. His own gaze immediately sought hers, followed by a flashing smile and a wave.

Praying that her expression didn't give away too much of her pleasure, she returned his greeting.

With a couple of bridles draped over his shoulder, he strolled toward her.

Her heart skipped a beat, and her hands itched to free her hair from its practical but unflattering bun.

The last two youngsters banged past Michael at a run, thrilled to escape the constraints of education on such a warm day.

"What a pleasant surprise," Michael said, doffing a floppy brimmed hat as he stopped before her. Though he stood two steps below her, his eyes were level with hers.

"Yes, isn't it?" Hope had an inkling their meeting was no mere accident — most likely Howie had told him she was the schoolmaster's assistant. Still, the fact that she was a teacher's helper, a bookworm, and a female playwright didn't seem to bother his male sensibilities in the least, which added to her own confidence. "It gives me a second opportunity to invite you and your family to the play performance Saturday. In case Howie didn't tell you it's starting at four — if nothing unforeseen happens." She pointed toward the parade ground across from the church, where a stage had been built.

Michael glanced in that direction. "I'll ask my family. But whether they come or not, I'll be there. In the meantime, Miss Reardon, if there's anything I can do to assist you with the production, I'm at your disposal. Are there any last-minute chores that need doin'?"

Everything that came out of his mouth pleased her. "You're such a kind gentleman. I wish I did have something left undone. But I do believe every chore has already been assigned."

His expression fell almost imperceptibly.

But she'd seen it and knew. Michael Flanagan was truly disappointed. The thought emboldened her. "There is one small chore you could do — that is, if you haven't already promised all your dances to others. You could maybe save a reel for me." She wanted to request all of them, but, of course, that would have been much too bold.

"I wish all my chores could be that pleasurable." The words could have been construed as flirtatious except that his voice held no trace of impudence. Then his gaze faltered. "I'll come early, just in case you need help at the last minute."

Without thinking, Hope reached out and touched the back of his hand. "Thank you, Mr. Flanagan." Just as quickly, she retrieved it.

"No, I thank you for showin' such kindness to a newcomer to the valley. To even let me know it will be all right to ask you for a dance, when I'm sure a gal with eyes as amazingly beautiful as yours will already have a long line of beaus wantin' to partner with you . . ."

As he replaced his hat and bid her adieu, she knew he couldn't have said anything more perfect if she'd written his dialogue for him.

In the hectic days preceding the play, her mind kept wandering to musings about Michael. She'd even been caught just standing there, staring into space, daydreaming, by no less than five of her friends. But there'd been no helping it. Hope was falling helplessly in love.

Timmy whimpered and rolled over in his crib, bringing Hope back from the world of her memories. She glanced out the window and down to where Michael had disappeared into the trees.

He was back in Reardon Valley.

But was he still the Michael of her dreams?

Chapter Four

Hope settled back in her rocker again and relaxed. If Michael had changed, it would be for the better. He had been so handsome today, so manly in his uniform. She was reminded again of another day and another military uniform. The day of the play . . .

"Hope, it's too hot for this coat," her tall, towheaded older cousin complained as they stood behind the outdoor stage. "Couldn't I just go in my shirtsleeves?" Jacob Reardon fanned the blue uniform jacket away from him.

She'd been running in every direction all afternoon — if anyone should be hot, it was she. But she tried not to betray her impatience. "Jake, George Washington would never go into battle without being properly dressed. Go splash some cool water on your face. The play is starting in ten minutes."

More concerned that her cousin was developing stage fright more than anything else, Hope sought out their closest neighbor, Delia Clay. Delia and Jake had been mooning over each other for the past three years. If it were possible for anyone to calm his nerves, she could.

A score of other youthful players, all costumed in the period of the 1770s, milled about looking just as nervous. Fortunately, many of the lads' fathers and uncles had loaned the actors their old uniforms from that era. Everything seemed to be falling into place . . . and if Michael Flanagan would've come early, as he'd promised, all would be quite perfect.

Hope spotted the dusky-featured Delia bringing a pitcher of water from the well at the back of the parade ground. Attired in a white mobcap and half apron over a star-studded Federal blue gown, she truly looked the part, as did Gracie, with a ruffled cap and half apron topping her red-and-white-striped gown.

From opposite directions, two of the company called out to Hope just as she started toward Delia.

Narrow-faced Ollie Hamm intercepted her first, coming to a running stop directly in front of her, all the while hanging on to his tricornered hat as if there was a high wind. He was out of breath. "Jim Bob sprung his ankle and can't do the announcin'. His brother wanted me to tell you."

Trying to remain calm, Hope asked, "Did he send the signs with Francis?" It had been Jim Bob's chore to make the announcement signs preceding each scene.

"Oh, that's what them was for. He gave me some boards nailed to sticks. But there ain't no writin' on 'em. I left 'em over by the stage steps."

Hope shot a frantic glance in that direction. "Ollie, run over to the smithy and fetch me a good piece of charcoal. One that'll write black and bold. Hurry!"

As Ollie took off toward the big blacksmith barn fifty yards away, Hope's gaze followed him until it landed on Michael Flanagan.

Her heart gave that strange flip-flop again.

Michael rode past Bremmers' smithy, heading toward the parade ground along with the twenty or thirty valley folk who would likely fill all the remaining vacant benches in front of the curtained stage.

He'd come after all, though much later than he'd promised.

Bringing his black mare to a halt at a hitching rail in front of the church, his gaze found hers, and he waved. He hadn't sought out Howie first or anyone else — only her. The starched white shirt against his tanned face made his smile seem all the brighter.

She lifted her own hand. But their private moment was cut short as she suddenly re-membered that she still needed a person to carry the signs across the stage before each act. Catching sight of her younger but much taller brother, she snagged Wesley's blue-coated arm. "You're gonna have to tote the signs between scenes. Jim Bob sprung his ankle."

Wesley grinned, one of those scampy grins of his. "Really?"

She eyed him sternly. "Just walk across the stage. Nothin' more."

"Aye, aye, little sister." But the grin didn't diminish one whit.

"I am your big sister." It galled her even more to have to look up at the string bean as she scolded him. She whirled away, her wilted pastel blue skirts wrapping around her legs . . . just as Michael Flanagan reached her, his shoes polished and his rich chestnut hair neatly slicked back.

"Sorry I'm late." His voice still had that restful quality to it, more noticeable in the midst of all the backstage hubbub. "We had a mare foalin', and I couldn't leave till I knew they was both fine." He glanced up at the back side of the platform, then down to the excited young people waiting anxiously for the play to start. "Anything left that needs —"

Someone shoved Hope from behind. She slammed into Michael. Catching her arms, he steadied her.

"Beggin' your pardon, Hope," Ollie blustered as she turned to face him. "I didn't stop quick —" He glanced from her to Michael. His eyes widened, and he thrust out his open hand. "Here's the coal," he blurted just before making a hasty retreat.

"Thank you." Amused and curious, Hope peered behind her. Though she didn't glimpse the scowl that must have crossed Michael's face, it had certainly frightened the long-legged Ollie. Had Michael displayed protective anger? she wondered hopefully. His expression was now one of admiration as she spoke. "Mr. Flanagan, I do have something you could do to assist me, if you're still willin'."

"Anything."

She placed the chunk of coal in his hand and led the way to the stage steps and picked up the signs. "Please print ACT ONE on the first one and ACT TWO and ACT

THREE on the other two in really bold letters — big enough for everyone in the audience to see them."

As she handed the signboards to him, she heard Howie shout her name. "Excuse me a moment," she managed before reluctantly turning from Michael. "Yes, Howie, What is it now?"

Delia's dark-featured brother was as handsome in his uniform as Jake had been in his. But at the moment, frustration marred his expressive umber eyes. "Sammy just knocked into one of the braces. The backdrop is sagging."

Her gaze snapped to the set. One of the bracing logs was missing. Her eyes narrowed at Howie's younger brother, standing beside the fallen timber.

The kid just shrugged and rolled his big brown eyes.

Why had she ever thought putting on a play would be easy? She swung back to Michael.

He hadn't moved from where she'd left him. He stared down at the signboards and coal in his hands as if they'd caught fire.

In an instant the realization dawned. Michael Flanagan couldn't write. Or read either, most likely. Mayhap that was why he'd particularly admired her creative abilities. She hurried back to him. "If you don't mind, I'll do this. I need you to help Howie get the timber back up."

"Timber?" He looked to where she was pointing, and the worry smoothed from his face. "Right away."

Short minutes later, the church bell chimed the hour, signaling the start of the play. Almost magically, as if they hadn't just been doing a fair imitation of a stirred-up hornet's nest, the cast and crew took their places.

Hope took a calming breath and rushed to the stage steps. "I know you'll all be wonderful."

The lively "Yankee Doodle Dandy" reached them from the front, played by two lads on flutes and one beating a drum.

Gracie and Delia picked up their skirts and sprinted up to the stage to take their places for the first scene.

Hope turned and found Michael next to her. With every pretty young miss in the valley here this evening, he was beside her. Only her. "Shall we go watch the play out front?" she asked, as if they had already planned to do so.

A hint of surprise was quickly replaced by a smile. "I'd like that."

Taking his arm, she strolled away with

him, feeling quite mature for fifteen. The whole valley had come to see her play, and she had a beau of her very own. Of that she was almost sure.

In the long shade of late afternoon, Hope led Michael to the back row of benches on the grass, finding a vacant spot at one side. Since everyone in the valley probably knew she'd written the play, which she'd entitled Molly Pitcher after the play's heroine, she'd rather sit behind them and watch their reaction than have them see hers.

A couple of youngsters drew the canvas curtains aside for the first scene of the reenactment of the heroine at the Battle of Monmouth in New Jersey.

Gracie played the heroine and Delia portrayed her friend. They sat near the front of a set of Molly's home, shelling peas, and began to speak. Hope was relieved when the girls remembered to raise their voices enough for the dialogue to carry to the rear. The two characters commented on the war and their fears for their soldier husbands.

Then, on cue, Howie burst through a prop door for a brief reunion with his wife, explaining that General Washington and his soldiers were passing by on their way to intercept the British army.

Gracie, as Molly, valiantly offered to go with him to help wherever she could.

Howie looked quite grown-up when he, playing his character, refused — as any caring husband would. A kiss good-bye, and he marched offstage as the musical prelude to the first song began.

Gracie, her striped skirts billowing out behind her, rushed toward the exit, lifting her soprano voice in an emotional farewell song.

From offstage, Howie returned the same loving words in a strong tenor.

Hope glanced about her. Even the youngest children in the audience seemed absolutely spellbound. And the thunder and roar of the battle scenes were yet to come, not to mention the rousing victory song at the finale.

After the last refrain and the applause, Gracie ended the scene with Delia by dramatically telling her, "Help me rip cloth into bandages to take with me. Whether John wants me there or not, I'm going to the battlefield to help him and the other brave patriots wherever I can."

As the two boys pulled the curtain closed, everyone sitting in the rows of benches clapped with great enthusiasm.

Hope's chest swelled with pride. So far

the production was a grand success.

Then Michael leaned close and whispered, "I can see why Howie's so taken with Gracie."

His words stung more than a slap on the face. All the joy that had been building in Hope evaporated. Michael was interested in Gracie, not her. It was always Gracie.

"The way they sing," he continued, "them two just naturally fit together like hand in glove."

What? Had she been mistaken? Mayhap he wasn't mooning over her sister after all. Hope flushed and turned to see Michael's expression.

His attention was not on the stage but on Hope's hands folded in her lap.

Her confidence was returning; she sensed he wanted to glove one of her hands in his own. But he didn't, of course. That would have been much too forward.

To her immense pleasure, Michael stayed by her side for the remainder of the evening. It was as if they already had an understanding. Throughout the rousing congratulations after the play, while being introduced to her extended family, and especially whenever other young misses strolled up wanting introductions to the handsome newcomer, not once did he waver in his loyalty to her.

Hope and Michael danced every round and every reel together, their hands at last being given the opportunity to fold around each other publicly without compromising propriety. During the final and only true dance of the night — a waltz — she'd been almost as dizzy and exhilarated by whirling in his arms as having him near all evening.

The magical interlude came to an end as they bid each other good night in the deep shade of a beech near her family's wagon. With only the stars and a distant lantern or two for light and without benefit of a dance, Michael now took her hand again. "Miss Reardon, I can't tell you what an honor it has been, bein' allowed to be your partner all night, an' to know that you forsook all the other fellas just to make me feel welcome on my first outing here in your valley. You've made this the most enjoyable evenin' of my life."

"For me, too," she managed, wishing she could see more of his face in the dark than merely a distant lantern's reflection in his eyes.

"Truly? Could that possibly mean if I was to come a-callin' sometime, you wouldn't mind?"

"No. I surely would not."

Unexpectedly, he released her hand. "There's somethin' I need to tell you, though, before you agree. I don't want my silence to deceive you into thinkin' I'm somethin' I'm not."

Her breath stopped. Had he done something shameful or unlawful? Was this handsome young man's interest in her too good to be true?

"I can't read or write. What with Pa needin' me around the place so much and us movin' so often, I never been to school more'n a few weeks in all my growin'-up years. So you see, I'm not nearly worthy of —"

Hope pressed her fingers to his lips before he denigrated himself any further. "Now, isn't it a pure blessin' then that you and I will be keepin' company! As you know, I assist the schoolmaster at school. It would be my pleasure to teach you to read and write in our spare time. I'll not have one as high-minded as you ever callin' yourself unworthy again."

He did forget propriety then and took her by the arms. "You would do that for me?"

"Yes," she replied, laughing out loud.

"But in secret. You must teach me in secret. I'd just as soon folks didn't know how ignorant I am."

"Just put yourself in my hands. I'll have you readin' and writin' odes to the flowers and fields in no time."

Releasing her arms, he took both of her hands into his. "Or perhaps a lovely sonnet to an angel called Hope."

Timmy emitted a loud sigh, bringing Hope out of her reverie.

She peered between the wooden slats and saw that her son's eyes were still closed. With a slow smile stealing across her lips, she rested against the rocker's spindled back again.

The love of her life had returned. If that's indeed who he was.

Chapter Five

"I vant to apologize for da Undervoods," Brother Rolf said, reining his mount closer to Michael's as they neared the settlement.

The old man's gravelly words intruded on Michael's thoughts — the memory of the moment he first saw will-o'-the-wisp Hope and her see-forever eyes.

"It is hard for dem dat you, of all people, are da one to bring dem da letters. Dey know Hope is vaiting for you many years before she agrees to marry Ezra."

"I understand. Ezra told me about him an' Hope." Michael shrugged. "In the Underwoods' place, I probably wouldn't act no better. Besides, I got used to bein' unwelcome real early on. My pa saw to that."

Riding in the shade of leafing hickory and black gum trees, the elderly minister's expression sagged into one of empathy. "I should haf asked sooner. How is your family faring? Are dey vell?"

"I ain't seen none of 'em for quite a spell now, but I'm sure they're doin' a sight better than they ever did when Pa was alive." He'd tried to sound casual, but bitterness had crept into his voice.

"Bantry Flanagan, he has passed avay like Joel says?"

"That's one way of puttin' it. He was hanged by the neck till he was dead. His 'vengeance is mine' finally caught up with him. The last barn he burned had an orphan lad sleepin' up in the loft."

"I am sorry."

"Me, too. The poor kid didn't deserve to die."

Brother Rolf grunted. "Sure. But I am sorry for you, too. *Und* da rest of your family. Vhere are dey living now?"

"After Pa was executed, we moved farther west, where no one knew about Bantry Flanagan. Ma's livin' on a homestead with my younger brothers and their families. My two sisters are both married and settled roundabouts, too. Pa's dyin' was the best thing ever happened to all of us."

"Hmm." The preacher didn't sound pleased. "Did your papa make peace *mit* da Lord before he dies?"

The question caught Michael by surprise. "I-I don't think so. He spent all his time claimin' he was innocent, right up to the very last."

Brother Rolf's thick chest heaved with a sigh. "I vish da vords I say to him had been strong enough to reach his heart."

"You talked to Pa about God?"

"*Ja.* Several times. But he don't listen. His heart, it vas in rebellion; his ears, dey vas closed. Ever since dat last time, I been praying for him *und* you *und* da rest of your family. It pleases me to see you grown up into a fine-looking military man. You come to church *mit* Hope vhen you live here before — you are still going?"

The trees and brush at the road's edges seemed to be closing in along with Brother Rolf's questions. "I've gone off an' on. The army expects us to 'tend chapel if we ain't got other duties. I been goin' more regular the last year or so. What with death starin' us in the face day in an' day out, even the rowdiest soldiers took up prayin'."

In a swift move, particularly for a man Brother Rolf's age and size, he reached for Michael's mare's bridle and pulled the horse closer. The minister's round blue eyes narrowed as he glowered at Michael. "How is dis? You say you is praying, *und* you still haf hatred for your papa in your heart?"

Startled by the minister's sudden burst of passion, Michael stared back at him, confused by the old man's anger. "Bantry

70

Flanagan was a vile, unscrupulous scoundrel. He deserved ever'thing he got and a whole lot more."

Brother Rolf released the mare's bridle, but the intensity of his expression did not ease. "You know da Lord tells us dat ve are to forgive dem dat trespass against us."

"Well, there's trespassin' and then there's tramplin' under ever'thing good that comes your way. If you knew one-tenth of what he did, you'd —"

Brother Rolf blocked the rest of Michael's words with his hand. "Ve are still called on to forgive even our vorst enemies. Da Lord says ve are to hate vhat is evil but forgive da evildoer. Da Bible says da man, he don't know vhat he is doing."

"Rest assured, Pa knew exactly what he was doin'. Or else he wouldn't have sneaked around doin' his worst in the dead of night."

"Dat may be true, but he didn't know vhat terrible judgment from God vas vaiting for him, or he vould never haf done dem bad t'ings. He vould haf been down on his knees, begging for mercy." The preacher sighed again. "It is too late for him. It is you I am vorried about now. You must forgive your papa *und* get right *mit* God. If you don't, I vill not be able to bless any union between you *und* Hope Undervood."

After that last surprising statement, the minister kneed his horse into a faster pace, leaving Michael to stare openmouthed after him. Had he been that easy to read? Michael had thought he'd kept all emotion from his features, from his stance and his demeanor.

But he hadn't fooled Brother Rolf one whit, and certainly not Ezra's younger brother either. Joel had acted as if Hope belonged to him, not to his dead brother. Did Joel Underwood and Hope have an understanding?

Michael shook the thought from his head. He still didn't completely understand why Hope had married Ezra in the first place. Ezra himself had admitted there had been no affection between them. And Joel? He couldn't imagine that she would ever be involved with Joel. He'd just seen his love again after all these years, and nothing was going to steal from him the wonder that had been in her eyes. Not even the niggling thought that she'd been another man's wife.

When she had first recognized him at the river dock, her expression had been comparable to that of an evening long ago . . . an evening when the two of them had been invited to the Underwoods', of all places, for a cornhusking party.

★ ★ ★

After only a few weeks of the youthful Michael dropping by the Reardons' place for an evening of reading lessons and sitting with her during church services, folks in Reardon Valley had started thinking of them as a couple. A freckle-faced lad everyone called Ezzie had even invited the two of them to his corncrib for the party.

Michael could hardly contain his enthusiasm as he and Howie Clay rode to the Reardon place to fetch Hope and Gracie. He'd heard of cornhuskings and knew that if he found a red-dyed ear, he'd win a chance to kiss Hope. Slowing as they reached the front of the house, Michael first caught sight of Hope's formidable Nordic-looking father, Noah Reardon, as he stood with her uncle Ike in front of the barn.

Neither man gave more than a passing glance to Howie. The stern glower hardened each of their lean faces, though, when they nodded a greeting to Michael. No doubt they knew all about cornhuskings and were sending him a silent warning.

Michael returned their humorless greeting with what he hoped conveyed a sincere reassurance that no harm would come to Hope.

"Good. the girls are ready," Howie re-marked as he reined his palomino stallion to a stop at the front of Hope's house.

"It's about time you two got here," Gracie hollered from the top step of the porch. A cluster of blonde ringlets with the bounce of old wagon springs spilled down from her crown. "Jake left to fetch Delia a half hour ago."

Beside Gracie, Hope looked as re-freshing as a cool morning with her ebony hair cascading across her shoulder in one smooth, shiny lock.

"Sorry, pet," Howie returned. "Pa wouldn't let me leave till I finished plowin' under the early corn."

Bringing his black mare to a halt beside Howie's horse, Michael swung down from his saddle to fetch his lovely, though he did his best not to look too eager. He removed his brown felt hat. "Afternoon, Miss Reardon."

"Afternoon, Mr. Flanagan." Her gaze fal-tered, ever so slightly.

Had she, too, been thinking about the possibility of a kiss?

Wesley, their younger straw-headed brother, tromped out the front door, looking stormy. "I don't see why I can't go. Hope's only two years older'n me."

Shooting him an angry scowl, Gracie bounded down the steps. "We don't have time for his nonsense." She reached a hand up to Howie. "Help me up. We gotta get to the Underwoods' before all the red ears is gone."

Hope's porcelain complexion deepened to a rosy red . . . she had been thinking about the kiss, too.

Michael walked to the bottom step and reached up to her. "Shall we go?"

As warm as her gaze was when she came down to him, it was nothing compared to the emotion in her fathomless eyes when later that evening she actually found one of the first red ears.

They'd been at the Underwood place about a half hour, sitting on the lower floor of the corncrib along with a number of other young couples, surrounding a large pile of unshucked ears. Split into two teams, all were frantically ripping the outer leaves from the cobs with a number of prizes in mind — the least important prize, a boiled icing cake that would be presented to the team that husked the most corn. The other, more sought-after prizes were the ten red ears buried within the pile.

Good-natured jokes and teasing got

tossed back and forth almost as fast as the husked corn was tossed into opposing piles. Then, without warning, Howie started warbling a taunting, impromptu ditty.

Not to be outdone, Gracie began another, encouraging Hope and their friend Delia Clay to join her.

Hope seemed a bit shy as the other two sang, "The higher up the cherry tree, the sweeter grows the cherry," but she became emboldened as they started the next phrase and joined in, looking straight at Michael. "The more you hug and kiss a girl, the more she wants to mar—"

Her words came to an abrupt halt as her gaze fell to her lap.

She'd just pulled from the pile a red ear.

Her amazingly light eyes widened, and a startled cry flew from her mouth.

"Who ya gonna kiss, Hope?" everyone around her and Michael chanted. "Who ya gonna kiss?"

Michael could clearly see the pulse throbbing at her alabaster throat. But then his dark-haired beauty began scanning the circle. A slight teasing smile curled the edges of her lips, as if she hadn't decided. When at last her gaze returned to him, her smile suddenly turned shy. "Well, I reckon you are the closest . . ."

That was all the incentive he needed. He rose to his knees and cupped her delicate heart-shaped face in his hands . . . and almost fell headlong into the love that shone from the deepest reaches of her eyes. After a long gold-spun moment, he slowly — lest he ever forget this moment — lowered his lips to hers, touching their softness and their warmth, hearing her sigh ever so softly . . . knowing the kiss meant as much to her as it did to him.

Michael's horse stumbled over a root, wrenching him from the past. He quickly glanced at Brother Rolf to see if the perceptive preacher riding a few yards ahead of him had discerned his thoughts.

Instead of looking at Michael, the reverend had his big hand raised in greeting to a man herding in his milk cow with a long stick.

Glancing past the minister, Michael saw the smithy, and beyond it, the white spire of the church.

The church.

Even if the Underwoods wouldn't welcome him at their place, they couldn't prevent him from seeing Hope at Sunday services the day after tomorrow.

Michael's spirits rose up to meet the late-afternoon sun. The care of his horses, of his clothing, and some badly needed personal grooming would fill the hours tomorrow. And the very next morning he would see her, maybe even touch her hand. Time enough then to find out if she could forgive him for not returning for her as he'd promised so long ago. Or if any love for him still glowed within her . . . any spark that could be rekindled.

Chapter Six

"Can you just imagine?" Ma Tilly exclaimed in her shaky voice, a sweet grin warming her tired face. She sat across from Hope at the table, a pile of seed packets between them. "My Joel is out there, furrowin' the garden for us without me even askin'. I do believe my baby is becomin' a man."

Had it been anyone but this dear old lady, Hope would have contradicted her. At twenty-two, Joel should have long since taken on adult responsibilities. And the unseemly way he looked at her sometimes . . . Dodging the thought, Hope threw herself into the task at hand: separating the various packets they'd saved from last year's vegetable garden. "Timmy loves watermelon. Would you mind if we plant a few more vines this year? I know they take a lot of space, but . . ."

"If my grandson wants more watermelon, then that's what he'll have." With gnarled fingers, she picked up a paper pouch with the melon's name written across it. "Let me see how many seeds we got. By the by, where is that young'un? I ain't heard him in a while."

"Joel is lettin' him ride the horse while he plows."

"Now, didn't I just say my boy is startin' to put on his manhood? Takin' the time to give Timmy a treat. And this bein' Saturday an' all."

Ma Tilly was right about one thing. Joel wasn't anything like he'd been before Michael came here yesterday. Last night he'd been quiet — not his usual gabby self. With a deadly serious expression on his face, he'd spent the evening hours watching every move Hope made — unnerving, to say the least. And today? Normally, he couldn't wait to get his Saturday morning chores done so he could ride into the settlement and be waiting when any of his friends showed up. This was the day most folks took care of their town business, along with a good deal of their visiting — the women at Bailey's General Store and the men on the porch of the saddler's. And Hope had no doubt who'd be the prime topic of conversation today — Michael Flanagan.

The approach of a carriage outside interrupted their concentration. She recognized her father's deep voice, followed by lighter, female laughter. Her mother must be with him.

"Well, I'll swan." Ma Tilly braced her hands on the sturdy table and stood up. "That sounds like your folks. You didn't mention nothin' about them fixin' to drop by. I best get out the makin's for tea. Do we have any bread puddin' left over from last night?"

At the thought of her parents' visiting, Hope brightened, but her pleasure lasted no more than a second. They were not the sort to simply drop by without reason. "The puddin' is gone, but there should be a few applesauce cookies left in the crock. Ma, you go on out and invite 'em in. I'll take care of the tea."

The withered old woman turned back. "You are a blessin'. That's for sure. I don't know how I got along before you came."

As Hope watched Tilly hobble out, she felt guilty that she'd ever thought of leaving the old dear to try to run this household by herself.

But Tilly wasn't her flesh-and-blood mother, Hope's selfish side argued. Titus and Tilly had other children who could take care of them. Even Joel could, if he would truly become a responsible adult and take a wife. Just as long as the wife wasn't her, that is. She'd had enough burdens with his brother.

But now there was no time for such musings. Hope glanced out the kitchen window and saw her mother and father leaving their tiny shay behind and walking toward the house. Irritation gripped her. She had no doubt as to why they were making this surprise visit. They'd heard Michael Flanagan was in the vicinity. She busied herself preparing a pewter tray with saucered cups and Tilly's good pink ceramic teapot. She knew that her mother-in-law always wanted things nice when neighbors came calling.

Hope watched her father and much smaller mother as she carried the tray to the parlor end of the large room. Their smiles and greetings to Tilly had a strained quality to them. She just hoped her mother-in-law didn't notice. From what she could tell, neither Titus nor Joel had informed Tilly that the soldier who brought the letters yesterday was Hope's Michael.

Placing the tray on the tea table, Hope snapped up a couple of Timmy's wooden toys from the colorful Turkish rug her parents had given her when she married Ezra. She dropped the toys into her apron pocket just as the door opened.

Her mother, Jessica Reardon, entered

first, greeting her with another stiff smile . . . this tiny woman whom Hope alone had taken after, right down to the wide-set pale eyes.

Following behind Ma Tilly, Hope's long-boned father peered at her from over the old woman's cotton white head. As virile in his late forties as he'd been from her first memories of him, Hope could see in his set expression that he wasn't happy.

Hope's chest tightened. *Dear Lord, please don't let him make a scene in front of Tilly.*

"Oh, I see we've arrived not a moment too soon," her mother said in her cultured English accent. Instead of moving toward the parlor end, she walked to the kitchen table. "We came by with some garden seeds Hope's Uncle Ike sent." Glancing back to Tilly, she handed her a small envelope. "The seeds are for growing eggplants, which are squashlike vegetables in the shape of large eggs with such a deep purple color they're almost black. I have no idea what they'll taste like, but they should be fun to watch develop."

"Now, ain't that nice of you to drive all the way out here just to carry us these seeds." Ma Tilly plucked another packet from the table. "We got more okra seeds than we need this year, what with Joel bein' the only one left that's partial to it." She handed the seeds to Jessica. "I know your boys like fried okra as much as my Ezzy did. Did I tell you I got a letter from him just yesterday?"

"No, you didn't. But I thought he was . . ." Jessica sounded genuinely interested but a bit perplexed.

"Y'all come sit a spell and have some tea, an' I'll read it to you."

"Is Titus about?" Noah asked, speaking for the first time since crossing the threshold.

"Titus, he'll be plumb put out that he missed y'all. One of Harland's horses is down with the colic this mornin'. Titus took some of his tonic and went over to see what he could do."

Hope was glad Titus was at the neighbor's and even more glad that the Underwoods' garden plot Joel was plowing lay directly behind the house, blocked from view of the path leading to the front. If he and Timmy had seen her parents arriving, they would've come running.

As the four of them sat on the homemade but pillowed parlor furniture having their tea, Tilly read her poignant letter from Ezra, which brought tears to all their eyes, even

Noah's. He'd been fond of Ezra from the time Ezra was an affable, freckle-faced kid. After hearing the letter, they each, in turn, related some remembrance of Tilly's son. Hope waited till last, but was careful to mention an incident from their childhood, not wanting to bring up details from their marriage or give her father an opening to mention Michael in front of Tilly.

When Hope finished, her father huffed a breath. Then, placing a palm on each knee, he rose. "Jessica, dear, it's time we were off. The day's a-wasting."

"So soon?" Ma Tilly complained.

Jessica squeezed the woman's hand. "Afraid so. I need to get home and start dinner for my boys."

"But you haven't seen your grandbaby," Tilly argued. "He's out with Joel, plowin'."

"We'll say our how-dos on the way out," Noah said, making way for his wife to precede him out the door. "Hope, would you mind coming along and fetching Timothy for us?"

"Of course." She walked out with her parents, grateful her father had held his tongue, though she knew once they were alone he would not. Away from the house, she turned to face what she knew would be an unpleasant exchange.

"You know why we're here." Her father's politeness and subtlety were gone. "We know Michael Flanagan rode into the valley yesterday with the militia. And at the blink of an eye, you rode out of town with him."

"*And* Brother Rolf." Refusing to be cowed, she lifted her chin. "And I'm sure whoever told you about Michael also told you that just before Ezra died, he gave the sergeant a packet of letters, along with specific instructions to deliver it to the Underwoods personally. Tilly read you one of them." Oh, how she wished she was as tall as Gracie at times like these!

Her father shifted his weight. "I seriously doubt Ezra insisted Flanagan deliver the packet himself."

"That's what Michael said. But since I wasn't privy to that conversation, I cannot say for a certainty. Max and Howie were. I suggest you ask them."

"Sweetheart," her mother interceded, "your father and I merely want to save you from further pain."

Noah wasn't deterred. "Whether or not Ezra asked Flanagan to come here, he should've had the decency to stay away."

"*Decency.* How many times must I tell you? Michael was with me when your precious gristmill caught fire." She wasn't sure yet what she thought of the man Michael had become, but she wasn't about to let her father denigrate the memory of the young lad she'd known him to be back then.

"Whether it was he or his father matters little. He was raised in a thieving, vengeful family, and no one in this valley wants him here." Suddenly, the resolve in Noah's expression turned to lines of worry. "I beg of you, please don't grieve us or that already grieving family in there by taking up with a Flanagan again." He waved toward the house. "Think of your son."

A gasp escaped before Hope could silence it.

"Darling." Jessica spoke in quiet warning to her husband. "I do believe you've made your point." She turned to Hope with searching eyes, took her hands, and kissed her cheek. "I know this is a difficult and confusing time for you. We will keep you in our prayers."

Hope's throat started to ache as tears threatened.

"Thank you, Mama. And I'll keep you both in mine." She tried to sound daughterly, though she felt quite adamant about the fact that if anyone needed prayer, it was her judgmental father.

★ ★ ★

A shaft of morning light coming through the Bremmers' parlor window exposed a speck of lint on the blue uniform sleeve Michael had just given one last brushing to before donning the coat. Reluctant to take his attention from the arriving churchgoers, he swiftly removed a white glove and plucked off the speck. Never before had he wanted to be so immaculately groomed, to appear absolutely respectable and acceptable by this community — and most particularly, by the Reardons. Any chance at a life with Hope depended on it — this chance that Ezra had handed him.

He twitched slightly at the remembrance that Hope had married Ezra first, but he quickly suppressed the thought. How could he have expected her to wait for him when he'd lost all hope himself? Besides, there were more important things at hand to ponder. When Michael had first run into Max Bremmer and Ezra Underwood at Jackson's Fort down in Mississippi Territory, they'd informed him he had more to overcome than his father's reputation. He — not his pa — had been blamed for the blaze that destroyed the Reardon gristmill the night he and his family left the valley . . . another of Bantry Flanagan's legacies.

Brother Rolf expected him to forgive his father, though he'd been paying for his father's misdeeds his whole life — and, most likely, today would be no different.

Except perhaps for the one person who knew the truth.

Michael rested his hand over an inside coat pocket, reassuring himself that he'd slid the note into it. No matter what else took place today, he would somehow get the missive to Hope. *If* she came to church.

He glanced at the tall clock near the stairs, then continued to search each arriving conveyance that rolled to a stop in the field between the Bremmer house and the church, but the Underwoods had yet to come.

Considering the noise upstairs, it was obvious that the Bremmer children weren't ready yet, either.

From behind, a hand clamped onto Michael's shoulder. "Sit up front with us this morning." Max. Solid as the earth, just like his pops. "I want to publicly thank you for making it possible for our men to return home a week ahead of schedule. With folks so happy to have their menfolk back, it should go a long way in having them accept you."

Only Max and Howie Clay had any notion of how very vital that was to him.

The church bell started clanging, and abruptly all the noise above converged as Max's youngsters thundered down the stairs like a herd of galloping horses instead of four children, the oldest not quite ten.

"Papa!" the second-oldest of the three boys of stair-step heights shouted. "We gotta go. Mama says we're gonna be late."

"When were we ever on time?" Max quipped. With a shake of his shaggy white blond head, the big-boned man turned back to Michael. "I can't count the number of times we've had to walk all the way up to the front pew a good five minutes after the singing's started. And with us living right next door here with Pops for the past four years."

"Since your mother passed."

"Yep. Pops is too old to live alone, and with the smithy on one side and the church on the other, it seemed more practical than having him live across the river with us."

Last to descend, Belinda made the trip down the stairs with much more care than the children had, considering her condition. With her cheeks flushed from the strain and a hand at her back, she attempted a smile as she moved past her four squirmy children. Lifting a black bonnet from off a hall-tree hook, she dropped it over her piled mass of red curls and ran an appraising scan over her brood, then took her three-year-old daughter's hand. "I reckon we're ready to go."

But Michael wasn't. He'd yet to see the Underwoods arrive.

Nevertheless, he walked to the door behind the noisy Bremmer family.

Ahead of him, Belinda spoke sternly. "Quiet, children. I'll not have you running over there like a pack of wild animals."

Just as Michael reached the porch steps, he caught sight of another wagon rolling past from the north road. He immediately recognized the curly rust-colored hair poking out from beneath the driver's hat. Joel Underwood. Beside him, crowded on the jockey box, sat his elderly parents. They were dressed in coarse dark hues.

For a panicky second, he was sure Hope hadn't come, but reason took hold. He knew they couldn't all ride up top. She was probably sitting in the wagon bed.

Joel shot him a menacing glower.

Sure that the young man would have the presence of mind not to cause a disturbance at Sunday services, Michael nodded a greeting, then looked away and started down the steps.

"There's that nice soldier who brought the letters," Mrs. Underwood said and waved.

Managing a friendly smile, Michael tipped his tall military hat. Then, as the wagon came abreast of the house, he saw Hope.

She sat on a crate behind the driver's seat, holding firmly on to a toddler with the same shiny, dark hair. The little one stood on the box beside her, blocking Michael's view of her face. He waved wildly at everyone he saw, including Michael. His eyes were only a shade darker than Hope's and sparkled with excitement. Hope's child. If Hope had waited for him, would they have had a child that looked like this one? Would they ever?

Michael couldn't resist waving back.

The wagon continued on, giving him a clear view of Hope. And her of him.

Their gazes locked, holding him in place, sapping his breath. But the wagon was now too far away for him to read what was in her eyes.

Please, Lord, let it be a look of gladness to see me.

Chapter Seven

There was no denying it, Hope admitted. Michael Flanagan was looking astoundingly handsome this morning in his military uniform. Better than she'd ever let herself imagine.

"Hope."

She tore her attention from Michael striding toward her in the church hitching area.

Joel stood at the rear of the wagon, waiting to help her and her son off the back of the bed, his blue eyes brittle, his square jaw set. She'd neglected to notice that the vehicle had come to a stop between two others and Joel had already set the brake and climbed down.

She lifted Timmy off the toolbox, and he scampered to the rear, looking darling in the blue plaid outfit she'd just finished making. As he launched himself into Joel's waiting arms, she rose and smoothed the wrinkles from her black gabardine skirt and jacket — her dreary widow's weaves.

Stepping to the rear, she noted that her brother-in-law's demeanor hadn't improved. Determined not to be upset by it, she put on a pleasant, if distant, expression before placing her hands on his shoulders, all the while totally aware of Michael's approach.

Joel's hands were as rigid as his scowl as he swung her to the ground. Noticeably lacking were his usual flirtatious remarks.

"Thank you," she said politely. She watched Michael draw near.

Joel scooped up Timmy and caught her arm. "Come on. We'll be late."

Startled by his abrupt behavior, Hope had no choice short of making a scene but to allow him to hurry her to the church steps. The Carver family, who hadn't entered yet, were staring. They knew as well as she did why Joel was rushing her. At no other time in Joel's life had he cared whether or not he was late for services. Or for much of anything else. At least, that had always been her impression of the young man . . . *before* Michael's return.

Not bothering to greet the other members of the laity or even wait for his parents, Joel ushered Hope down the aisle and into the family's pew located about halfway to the altar. He followed with Timmy. Lagging behind, Titus and Tilly finally joined them, and Hope noticed that Tilly was huffing for breath.

Hope set aside her anger at Joel long enough to listen until Tilly's breathing became normal again, then resumed fuming over his despicable conduct. He'd prevented her from the merest exchange of greetings with Michael or with anyone else, for that matter. Snubbing a new visitor at Sunday service was grossly impolite.

As she sat there trying to regain her composure, she prayed that Michael wouldn't think she'd become a judgmental snob like her father.

Then, gradually, she became aware that her neighbors were glancing at her, whispering as they settled into their own pews . . . everyone, that is, except her parents, who sat closer to the front. But she had no doubt they wanted to look, too.

Abruptly all the whispering stopped, and the sound of lone footsteps coming up the aisle echoed to the high ceiling of the whitewashed interior. It was Michael, for a certainty.

Refusing to give anyone the pleasure of seeing her turn and gawk at him, Hope kept her gaze trained on the large brass cross that hung on the wall behind the pulpit. Soon, though, she caught sight of his soldier's uniform as Michael took his place in the front pew among the Bremmer brood.

Belinda's mother, the wispy Mrs. Gregg, began playing the pump organ, which she should have been doing all along.

Brother Rolf lumbered up from a chair behind the pulpit and announced a song in his loud, gruff voice.

Everyone rose to join in.

Little Timmy stood on the bench between Hope and Joel and happily did his best to sing along.

Hope, too, did her utmost, but if anyone had asked her later, she wouldn't have known which hymns were sung that morning. So many conflicting thoughts raced around in her brain, she felt as if she were caught in a whirlwind.

After the last hymn, the black-clad preacher raised a hand for silence and the congregation retook their seats. "O sing unto da Lord a new song," he recited from his big dog-eared Bible, "for he has done marvelous t'ings. His right hand and His holy arm haf gotten Him victory. Da Lord has made known His salvation: His righteousness has He openly showed in da sight of da heat'en."

The silver-haired man then bowed his

bulky head. "Lord God Almighty. We do sing Your praises today, for out of da mout' of a mighty enemy You haf snatched our men *und* give dem a great victory at da battle at New Orleans. Da kind of victory I haf not heard about 'cept in Your Good Book. Da fighting is over, *und* peace again reigns. Today ve come toget'er to especially t'ank You for bringing our sons and brudders and fadders and husbands home to us. Dis is a time of celebration *und* t'anksgiving. Yet in our time of gladness, ve must not forget da sorrow visited on da Vallaces *und* da Undervoods for da loss of deir brave young men. My prayer for dem is dat deir hearts, too, vill be lifted, dat dey may share in our joy today, as ve share deir sorrow. Ve ask dis of You, Lord, in da name of Jesus, da Son You gave up to deat' for all of us."

Hope couldn't help but be stirred by such poignant words. She pulled her own son onto her lap. Just the thought of seeing him go off to war one day was chilling.

Max, the pastor's son, left his pew and walked to the front. Standing beside his father, he began to speak in a voice almost as deep and gravelly as his father's. "I would also like to express the thanks of this community to Sergeant Michael Flanagan. As

I'm sure many of you already know, the sergeant asked his cavalry commander to release his string of horses back to him so that we could use them to transport our goods and our wounded home. Otherwise, we would've been required to traipse on up to Nashville first." He looked straight at Michael. "Stand up, Mike. Turn around, so we can thank you proper."

Hope held her breath, eager for the opportunity to study Michael unhindered.

He seemed reluctant, but after a second or two, he complied.

At that instant, the newly returned militiamen all stood up. "Hear, hear!" they shouted, thrusting fists into the air.

And for one brief moment, Michael's gaze locked with hers, before he discreetly peered past her. Unsmiling, he nodded and took his seat.

That's when she realized no one else had joined the returning men in their salute to Michael.

As Max returned to his pew, Hope noticed several people lean their heads close and whisper words she couldn't hear — words she dreaded, if Joel's behavior and her father's were any indication of the valley's mood.

The pastor's message was on forgiveness

. . . an utterly timely one. He began with the story of the prophet Hosea, who married a woman God told him would be so unfaithful some of her children would not even be Hosea's. But no matter how many times she sinned against Hosea, God asked him to forgive her and accept her back, the same as God had forgiven Israel's repeated adulteries against Him.

"Da same as Jesus tells us to do. He forgives our trespasses, as ve forgive dose who trespass against us." Brother Rolf glanced down at his Bible. "But if ye forgive not men deir trespasses, neither vill your Fadder forgive your trespasses."

As Brother Rolf looked up, Hope desperately prayed that every person in the congregation was listening.

"God calls on us to forgive da enemies who invaded our shores, just as He calls on us to forgive our neighbors. *Und* dose in our own household. Dis is not a request to be taken lightly. Dis is a command from almighty God. No matter how justified you tink your condemnation is, remember it is for God to judge. Vengeance is da Lord's. Not mine. Not yours. Ve are called to be merciful, to be peacemakers. T'ink of forgiveness as da vater dat cleanses our souls. I know some of you are t'inking dat da Lord tells us it is right to hate evil. Dat is so. But as for da hapless fools Satan tricks into doing his bidding, Jesus said — even vhen He is hanging on da cross — Forgive dem, for dey know not vhat dey do."

Hope let out a relieved sigh. Even her father should have been touched by that last statement. Michael deserved none of Noah Reardon's enmity or that of anyone else in this valley. At least the Michael she had known in her youth did not. What kind of man had he become? Certainly he had never deserved being left to wonder when she didn't answer his letters. Somehow she should've found a way to get word to him.

Would Michael be able to forgive her for not trying harder? Did it even matter to him anymore? Small wonder he had never returned for her. In that first moment she saw him, the day before yesterday, she should have welcomed him back to the valley.

Ma Tilly, sitting on the other side of Joel, muffled a coughing fit, which reminded Hope of her mother-in-law's presence, and a disturbing thought dawned — one she would've realized long before now if she'd been thinking rationally: with all the people here who recalled the whole Reardon/Flanagan saga, one of them was sure to blab to poor, sickly Tilly this latest, juicy tidbit.

This certainly was a fine kettle of fish.

And to add another fish to this morning's kettle, Timmy started squirming to free himself from Hope's lap, which drew more attention to them.

Reaching into her drawstring purse, she retrieved a wooden horse Ezra had carved for Timmy the last time he was home. Putting a finger to her lips for quiet, she handed it to her silky-haired son. He curled his stubby fingers around the toy and started galloping it up one of her arms as she tried to corral him.

At last Brother Rolf gave the benediction. Folks started gathering their hats and Bibles, then rising.

"Over?" Timmy asked, his eyes round with delight.

"Yes." Hope set him on the floor, and he frantically scrambled past his elders and out to the center aisle. This was her son's favorite time, when he could romp freely on the grass with the other little ones.

Joel rose, catching Hope's hand and bringing her up with him. Without looking at her, he dragged her out of the pew behind his parents.

How dare he! She wasn't his property. She tried to pull free, but his grip tightened.

Rather than lodge a protest while surrounded by the entire congregation, she demurred and went quietly with him until after they'd greeted Brother Rolf at the door and were outside in the glaring midday light.

They'd scarcely reached the bottom step when someone called to her from behind. Gracie and Delia waved from the top step to get her attention.

Joel let out an exasperated groan. "We don't have time for your silly sister. We need to get right home. Ma's feelin' poorly."

Hope glanced up in disbelief at the normally callous young man. Regardless of his freckles and curly hair, he seemed much older — almost dangerous. She wrested her hand from his and straightened to her full height. "I shall speak to my sister." Aware that she was blocking the walkway, she stepped to the side to allow others to pass.

Joel shoved his wide-brimmed hat on his head and his hands into his brown trouser pockets, moving with her. He continued to hover.

The girls, dressed in their Sunday best, reached Hope. Gracie was wearing her ruby red velvet suit and Delia, her moss green.

Hope glanced behind Gracie for Howie. Not seeing him, she inquired about his injured foot.

"Oh, it's much better," her sister said in a rush. "Since Ma Smith drained off the poison and put on a proper poultice, it's a-healin' up right fine. Ma said them army doctors don't know nothin'. She said it was a plain miracle his foot didn't putrify."

Gracie turned to Joel. "Lester Johnson wants to see you. He said he'd meet you over by his wagon."

Joel's sun-bleached brows crimped. "What for?" He didn't look happy.

"Lester didn't say exactly. Just that it was important."

Joel's expression turned suspicious, one brow arching. "Why didn't he just come an' tell me hisself?"

Gracie gave an exasperated huff. "Land o' Goshen, I wish he had."

"Oh, all right." Joel centered his attention on Hope again. "I'll be right back."

As he left them for the lot of parked wagons, Delia stepped closer. "What's got into him all of a sudden? He's stickin' to you this mornin' like pine tar."

"I know. I wish he'd leave me alone." Hope sighed. "He wouldn't even go into town yesterday. On a Saturday. You know what a sacrifice that must have been."

Her sister lowered her voice. "I reckon Michael's causin' more of a stir than

103

anyone would'a thought."

"Didn't I tell you?" Delia added, her dark eyes flashing. "Joel's smitten with you. Has been for years. What did he do when Michael showed up?"

"And what was in the packet Michael brought?" Gracie pried.

"Is Michael staying?"

Their questions tumbled over each other as curious passersby slowed to look.

"Delia, Gracie, not now," Hope pleaded. She felt like a lamb being nipped at by a bunch of herd dogs. "I'll tell you what I can Friday at sewing circle. I need to fetch Timmy. Tilly's not feeling well."

Leaving them behind, Hope hurried toward several little tykes chasing one another around the trunk of a tall elm. Timmy ran, stumbling and giggling after the others, having a marvelous time.

Hope stopped several yards short to watch them play. She hated to tear her son away, but she couldn't imagine a more volatile situation than the one brewing behind her — one that might explode from any of several sources. Most disappointing, though, was that she saw no possibility of having even one private second with Michael. His sudden reappearance had caught everyone, including her, by surprise, and she had many questions for him that needed answering.

She glanced back at the church as the last parishioners came out onto the landing — the Bremmers, along with Michael. After the message in today's sermon, she couldn't imagine anyone being obviously rude to Michael, especially not in the presence of brother Rolf. That thought was a dubious blessing, at best.

Becoming aware that her father and mother, standing with the elder Clays, were staring at her, she turned to watch her son play.

A few seconds later, Belinda ambled toward her on Max's arm, calling to her. Michael followed a few steps behind.

Hope's pulse quickened. She felt light-headed. Michael. She had to drag her attention back to Belinda. "Yes?"

"If you get a chance, come by one day this week for a chat." She gave Hope's hand a meaningful squeeze.

Hope knew Michael was staying with the Bremmers. Was Belinda attempting to facilitate a meeting between them? Did that mean he'd be staying the week? "I'll try."

"If not, we can talk on Friday," Belinda said much too casually.

Oh dear . . . had Hope misread her?

"Well, see you later," Max said, escorting his awkward wife on by. "I want to get Belinda home. Her feet are swelling."

"I'm just glad you're home, Max, to look after her." Then suddenly, Hope came face-to-face with Michael. Her breath caught in her throat. She had no doubt that every eye in the churchyard was on the two of them.

Michael removed his tall, braided hat quite formally. "Again, Mrs. Underwood, I would like to extend my condolences to you and your family for the loss of Ezra. He was a good friend and a brave soldier."

"Thank you, Sergeant Flanagan," she answered in little more than a croak.

Bowing slightly, he took her hand in a parting gesture. She felt something small scratch her palm.

He closed her fingers over the item. "Good day, Mrs. Underwood."

Before she could discern exactly what she held, he strode away toward the Bremmer home.

Again, Hope felt the heat of staring eyes. Her father's.

And Ma Tilly's. The usual warmth in the old woman's expression was missing as she and Titus stood with the Reardons. Obviously, Tilly now knew who Michael was and reckoned something was afoot.

Brassy in the noonday sun, Joel's rust-colored hair caught Hope's attention as he strode fast toward her.

She gulped and drew a deep breath, her insides churning. Joel always made her feel that sense of panic. And although Hope knew she didn't have a single thing to feel guilty about, she slipped what she'd now discerned was a small square of tightly folded paper into her skirt pocket without looking at it . . . or the words written on it.

Chapter Eight

On the ride home from Sunday service, Hope spent her time entertaining her son to get him laughing again after he'd been wrenched so abruptly from his playmates. Actually, she was grateful for the diversion of playing a hand game with Timmy as she and the rest of the Underwood family drove through the fragrant and gentle April warmth.

All the while, the three up on the driver's bench maintained a thick silence.

Within a quarter mile from their cutoff, her brother-in-law startled her by abruptly speaking. As he drove the wagon team, he addressed no one in particular. "Lester Johnson cornered me into sayin' I'd go over tomorrow an' help him build another bedroom for his kids." Joel didn't sound the least happy about the prospect.

"As you should," Pa Titus bluntly stated.

Relieved that the topic was unrelated to her, Hope continued to pat her little one's hands.

Her father-in-law drawled, "Lester brung his team over and helped us pull them stubborn stumps out last fall. So you make a good showin' of yourself over there tomorrow. Folks won't come an' help you iffen you don't return the favor. An' you know, Son, I'm slowin' up more ever' day. This place is gonna be all yours to work right soon, so —"

"Mine?" Joel seemed astounded. "But I thought the place was passin' from Ezra to his son."

"That's nonsense," the old man snorted, leaning past his wife. "Timothy ain't nothin' but a baby. You'll be responsible for him, too. Fact is, if we was livin' back in Bible times, you'd be honor-bound to offer marriage to your brother's widow."

"Is that so?"

Hope stiffened, fearful of the lascivious glint she might detect in Joel's eyes if he was facing her, and turned toward Titus and Tilly. How quickly the conversation had moved from helping a neighbor to Joel marrying her.

Joel's mother, sitting next to him, patted his knee in obvious agreement with her husband.

Feeling as if they were all in consort against her, Hope dreaded Joel's response.

109

"You're right, Pa." His tone was much more enthusiastic. "Ma, wake me real early tomorrow, so I can get my chores done and still put in a full day at Lester's."

"That's the spirit." Titus reached across his wife's lap and gave Joel's arm an approving squeeze. "I'll go with you. If Les has already got the wood cut to size, we should be able to get 'er up 'fore nightfall."

Hope turned back to her son, relieved the topic had returned to the Johnsons' new bedroom, and even more relieved that Joel would be gone all the following day. Her hand slipped down to her skirt pocket, where the folded paper from Michael was tucked away. She longed for a private moment when she could take out the note and read it.

"Mama, Mama," her tot urged, scrabbling for her hand. "Patty me. Patty me."

With a smile at her son, who looked more precious than ever in his blue plaid dress suit, she did as he bade, knowing that as soon as they arrived home she'd take him upstairs to change out of his Sunday clothes . . . and get that private moment she sought. She couldn't wait to read that note.

The next day was cool and cloudy. Michael, astride his black mare, broke out of the woods and into a patch of land he and his younger brothers had cleared when he was a lad. He pulled Ebony to a halt and surveyed the clearing. The log house they'd built still stood at its center. The barn, of course, had been replaced by another one — built, most likely, by the next occupants. His father had burned theirs in a scheme to blame the Reardons and force them to buy him out at a profit. And the scoundrel had succeeded.

Renewed anger surfaced. Pa had never missed a trick. And as a parting gift, he'd burned the Reardons' gristmill.

Surveying the property, Michael noticed that the place lay abandoned. None of the fields had been plowed for spring planting, and no livestock roamed the pasture. Saplings sprouted hither and yon. Nature was taking back the land.

His throat tightened with sadness at the lonely sight. He'd worked so hard on the land when he was a lad — especially after he had met Hope, vowing that henceforth this would be the Flanagan home.

He grunted out a bitter laugh. Such a naive young fellow he'd been back then. To think he'd actually believed his father when they stood in that very pasture. He glanced at the one to his right. In the middle of that meadow was where he'd extracted a promise from Bantry Flanagan to honor all his deals with the men of the valley, honestly and aboveboard — to do nothing to shame the family or get them run out.

"Sure, boy." The promise had spilled so easily out of his father's mouth.

Michael could still see his wiry father's lean, leather-skinned face as he grinned knowingly, displaying the tooth that was missing from a time when he hadn't been able to outrun his misdeeds.

"I know what it's like to be sweet on some li'l gal, wantin' to be with her ever' minute of the day."

Bantry had just returned after months on the road, trading horses — months when life at home had been peaceful, when Michael had been free to dream and make plans. But now his pa was back, taking over again with his loud talk. And someone had told him about Hope.

In retrospect, Michael had come to realize that his father had singled out the Reardons just to show him who was boss. A mere fifteen months from the time the Flanagans had taken up residence in the valley, Bantry again ruined everything for them, destroying whatever trust Michael had built with the Reardons and forcing him to leave Hope behind.

Now Michael's gaze landed on the tree. Nudging Ebony forward with his knees, he rode farther into the clearing, then halted at a split-rail fence surrounding the north pasture. Swinging down from the saddle, he vaulted over the top rail and headed toward a particular beech tree that had provided a circle of shade for the stock in years past . . . this tree that had meant so much to him.

He walked straight to its smooth gray trunk, and upon seeing that the carving was still there, tears sprang to his eyes. No one had marred it or added anything else to the bark. The words, etched in black against the gray, stood alone. Swiping away the wetness that blurred his vision, he ran his fingers across the letters he'd so painstakingly gouged with his knife. He'd written them one month to the day after Hope gave him his first lesson in reading and writing. The words had been meant to be a permanent vow to himself and to his beloved — words he'd once thought he'd be able to look at every day until they came true. *HOPE Flanagan.*

He frowned slightly. She was Hope Underwood now, wasn't she? Another man had gotten to her first, had had the privilege of giving her his own name. But perhaps there was still a chance to change her name to Flanagan. If they could retrieve what the years had taken from them . . .

Michael pulled a plain timepiece from his pocket: 12:10. His chest swelled with anticipation. Less than an hour, and he would meet with Hope. If she came.

Please, Lord, don't let anything prevent her from meeting me. You know I gave up hoping for a future with her when Pa was hanged. For so long, I felt such shame. As if I had nothing worthy to offer her. Especially not my sullied name. But the army has given me the chance to restore honor to my name. Now I do have something to offer. If it's not too late . . .

I'm sure You heard Brother Rolf preach an entire sermon yesterday directly at me. He's fixed on me forgivin' my pa, too, if I'm to be in Your good graces. But surely You can see how impossible that is. Please, Lord, don't hold it against me. Don't let Bantry Flanagan reach up from the grave and drag me down again. Please, God, let her come.

From the moment Hope read Michael's note yester's eve, her spirit had been soaring. Still, she felt as if she was suffocating every time one of the Underwoods

114

smiled at her, especially Joel. She could scarcely believe the rapidity of his change since Friday — from flirtatious blade to jealous suitor to heir of all he surveyed. Including her, or so he assumed. Thank goodness, he and Titus had left for the Johnsons' shortly after breakfast.

But now she had another problem . . . the four women who happened to drop by sat doggedly in the parlor end of the common room with Tilly. The Underwoods had certainly become popular all of a sudden. This was the second set of visitors since Michael's arrival last Friday. And their visit couldn't have come at a worse hour. Hope had just gotten Timothy down for his afternoon nap, and instead of getting that slice of free time she'd counted on, she was standing at the worktable near the hearth, hurriedly preparing a tea tray for Tilly and her elderly friends.

She shot a glance up to the mantel clock: 1:11. She fingered the note in her pocket. The note from Michael.

Mrs. Skinner's raucous laughter, followed by the titters of the other women gathered in front of the Franklin stove, started Hope moving again. Soon, she was sure, the conversation would turn to questions about the reappearance of Michael

Flanagan, and she wanted to be well away from the house before it did.

Lifting a tin of tea leaves off the shelf beside the fireplace, she crumbled several into Tilly's ceramic pot. As she poured steaming water over them, she let her mind's eye once more rove the missive Michael had sent her.

My cherished tutor,
I do apologize for the need for secrecy, but I am aware that my presence in the valley is not welcomed by certain factions. I shall await you in the woods behind your barn tomorrow from one o'clock until nightfall. If you are able to come and if speaking with me is not offensive to you, I would be honored to have a few moments of your time before I return to Nashville.
Forever your servant

Michael hadn't written either of their names on the note. For her protection, she was sure, in the event the note fell into another's hands. Cherished tutor. If nothing else, he had remembered that she was the one who taught him to read and write. His thoughtfulness endeared him to her, and despite her apprehensions about this man

116

who was now a stranger, the very notion of his imminent departure caused her distress. She needed to make that meeting.

Carrying the tray across the room to the women, she glanced once again at the clock: 1:22. She could feel his very presence out there. So close.

"My, don't you look purty today," Mrs. Dagget, Liza's busybody mother-in-law, said. "You look like a girl again in that light pink blouse. Don't she, Martha?"

Mrs. Jessup, the worst gossip in the valley, smirked, the husky woman's small gray eyes raking over Hope as Hope placed the tray on the tea table. "Too purty a blouse for just any ol' day." Obviously an opening foray.

"Now, ladies," Ma Tilly intervened, "it ain't as if she don't have no apron on over it. 'Sides, our li'l gal is pleasuresome to look at ever'day. Even in the black she wears out in public now. Which reminds me . . . Hope, will you be a dear an' fetch me Ezra's letter? It's up on the mantel. I want my friends to hear the last thing my boy had to say to me."

Hope gladly retreated as Tilly leaned forward in her straight-armed rocker and told her silver-headed, yet much sprier, cronies how much the letter meant to her.

Prune-faced Mrs. Skinner, who always

117

had a tendency to take over, started pouring the tea. "Hope," she hollered from across the room, "you forgot a cup for yourself."

Returning with Tilly's coveted letter, Hope made sure to keep her expression bland. "I don't need one. You ladies enjoy your tea. Titus asked me to check on Luzzy from time to time while he's gone today."

"Luzzy's our milk cow," Tilly explained as Hope handed her the letter. "She's due to calve anytime now."

Not waiting for any further objections, Hope walked straight to the back door, snatched her crocheted shawl from the hook, and threw it across her shoulders.

"Speakin' of birthin'," Hope heard Mrs. Bailey, the storekeeper's wife, contribute as she started out the door, "did you take a good look Sunday at how *big* Belinda Bremmer has got? I wouldn't be a bit surprised if she don't have twins."

Hope lifted the hem of her gray wool skirt and bounded down the back steps, not slowing until she reached the pungent-smelling interior of the straw-strewn barn. She didn't want to make a liar of herself, so she did take a second to check on the barrel-bellied cow — the only animal confined in a stall.

The animal stared back with liquid brown

eyes and continued to calmly chew her cud.

Hope started for the rear entrance. Michael was just beyond the north meadow, waiting for her. Michael.

Realizing she still wore her apron, Hope tore off the faded garment and tossed it over a pile of straw, then checked the tightness of the pins holding her chignon in place and adjusted the fringed shawl, with fingers that were beginning to tremble.

She took a calming breath. Hoping she truly did look pretty in the shell pink silk blouse, she headed out the rear door of the barn. She kept the large structure directly between her and the house as she walked swiftly across the sprouting grass, then climbed over the split-rail fence to reach the dense tangle of shadow-shrouded woods, which were even darker today because of the cloudy sky.

Holding the gathers of her skirt close to avoid catching the weave on any thorny bushes, she made her way in as straight a path as possible. Once the farm structures were no longer visible, she stopped and searched in every direction for Michael. Disappointment taunted her when he wasn't right there waiting for her.

Perhaps he'd been delayed. Perhaps he'd had a change of heart. Perhaps —

Michael stepped out from behind the thick trunk of an old oak.

She stopped, with several yards still separating them.

"You were able to come," he said quietly, unsmiling.

She desperately wished he would smile. She was starting to wonder how wise it had been to come here alone to meet this stranger. "I had to. To tell you why I never answered your letters." She clasped her hands tightly together. "I was told when each of them arrived, but they were never given to me. Nor would my father tell me from whence they'd come. And after your family left under such a cloud, I . . ." Her excuse sounded too inane to go on. What could she really say, except that she'd cried every night for years?

"I was pretty sure you never received 'em, Hope. It was harder, though, after I mailed one to Howie, thinkin' he'd get it to you for sure."

"You sent a letter for me to Howie? I never got it." Fury swept through her. "*Howie.* I thought he was my friend."

"He is." Michael, wearing plain work clothes, took a couple of steps closer. "Howie loves you like a sister. Not givin' you the letter was real hard on him. His pa was with him when they picked it up at the store. Mr. Clay convinced Howie that he was honor-bound to give it to your father instead of you. It's ate at him all these years."

"As it should." She couldn't believe Howie had never even told her about the letter.

"When we met up again last fall, that was the first thing Howie told me." He took another step toward her, handsome as ever, sincerity evident in his eyes. "He also told me you waited years for me to come back."

She almost choked on his last remark. Her cheeks started to burn hot.

"But you stopped waiting, didn't you? Why did you marry Ezra, Hope? I never stopped loving you, you know."

"You didn't . . . ? Then why did you leave me waiting all those years? Why didn't you come back?"

"I intended to. But I couldn't return empty-handed. I was savin' up. Ever' penny I could get my hands on. Doin' whatever horse-tradin' I could. Any odd job I ran across." He paused, closed his eyes a second. "But when Pa got hisself hanged, I figured, well . . ." His gaze faltered.

"Then it's true." Moving closer, she reached out and touched his arm. "I'm so sorry. That must've been terrible for you."

He sucked in a breath. His hand covered hers. "The way I figured it, what woman would want to marry a fellow with an old man like that? You obviously didn't. An', well, I signed on with the army over to Fort Pickering."

His hand felt astoundingly warm over hers. "Michael, I'm sorry! My . . . my marriage to Ezra . . . it wasn't . . . it wasn't what you think. There was no love between us. It was . . . it was very lonely. He wasn't the kind man you all knew him to be." She sighed deeply. Michael remained silent, his hand still on hers. "If it weren't for Timmy . . ." She paused again. Her unhappy marriage was not something she wished to belabor. "You . . . you do look splendid in your uniform." The words had just slipped out.

"Thank you." He glanced away briefly, but she could tell he was pleased. "I'm sorry about you and Ezra, Hope . . . I didn't know. As for me, the army's been real good to me. They judge me on my own merit, not my pa's doin's. They've always respected my know-how with horses and my sharpshootin'. It's been a good feelin'. But then I come back here, and pretty much all I run into is the same old suspicion and hatred. The Bremmers have been kind to me, though, and Howie dropped by, but . . .

122

The horses are rested, and Max and me finished reshoein' 'em this mornin'. I really ain't got no more excuses to stay."

"You're leavin'? So soon? Michael, you can't." She flung herself into his arms. *"Please."*

He drew her close for a long-spun moment; then she felt him take a ragged breath.

Finally, he spoke. "You know I'm not welcome here. Especially by your pa. He watched every step I took at church yesterday. And I understand. If I was in his place and thought my daughter was consortin' with a lawless family, I'd be just as worried."

Hope pulled back far enough to study Michael's golden eyes. "But you're not — you're not —" Tears choked off her words, blurred her vision; more spilled down her cheeks.

"Don't cry." Gently, he brushed his lips across one eyelid, then the other. "Don't cry," he whispered again, kissing the wetness from her cheeks.

Time seemed to float away, taking her with it. Eventually though, she discovered that her arms were around his neck, her own lips kissing his beloved face . . . then meeting his in a firm yet tender touch.

When at last they drew apart, Michael took her by the shoulders and in a breathless rush urged, "Come to Nashville with me. Leave with me tomorrow. Pack whatever you need, and I'll come for you. We can say our vows before the army chaplain at the camp."

"But I —"

He cupped her face in his hands. "Please. Say yes, Hope. Just say yes."

Chapter Nine

"I cannot simply ride away with you, Michael." Hope studied his face to see if perhaps he jested. "I have responsibilities. You forget, I have a small child and —"

"I didn't mean for you to leave without him. He's a part of you." Michael's gaze roved her face. "He has your incredible eyes, your hair. I fell in love with him the first second I saw him."

That, of course, melted her heart. How very much she wished she could forget everyone else in her life and escape with him. Gently, she took his hands from her face and wove her fingers through his. "Dearest Michael, there's also my period of mourning. It's still almost five months before my year is up. To disrespect Ezra's memory would break Titus's and Tilly's hearts. And you know they're gettin' old and feeble, especially Tilly. I cannot leave them until I've made other arrangements for their care. And to rip Timmy from them without warning? I-I can't. Please, understand. I need time, time to prepare them. And hopefully my folks."

The light in his eyes diminished. "They didn't mind causing us great suffering back then."

"I know. They thought we were too young to know our own minds."

"It's been ten years."

"I know."

"And you want more time." He removed his hands from hers.

Had she lost him? Panic knotted her insides as she saw despair in his eyes.

Closing them, he expelled a long breath, then looked down at her again. "Very well. I waited this long. I reckon I can wait awhile longer." Reaching for her, he caught hold of her arms. "*If* I know you'll eventually be mine."

"Oh yes." Her joy was unstoppable as she sprang up on her toes and gave him a quick kiss. "Bless you, bless you."

He wrapped his arms around her, his own relief evident in how tightly he held her. "I need to report to my commander. While I'm in Nashville I'll request a leave. Because of the war, I have a lot of time coming to me. Then, to give you extra time to start preparin' your folks, I'll go ahead and travel on to my family's farm — it's about sixty miles west of Nashville. See how my ma and my brothers are gettin' on. I should be gone six or seven weeks. Then I'll be back." He held her at arm's length. "I *will* be back."

During the thirty-minute ride back to the settlement, Michael wasn't nearly as elated as he would've been had Hope agreed to leave with him tomorrow. Nonetheless, he was happier than he'd been in a decade. With a little more patience, Hope would soon be his.

Hope Flanagan. Mrs. Michael James Flanagan.

Passing the last field of furrows before reaching the settlement, his mare stumbled over a root. When she regained her leisurely stride again, he patted the sleek black coat on her neck. "Good girl."

His hand lingered on the horse, recalling as he often did that first afternoon he met Hope. He'd been riding a black mare that day, too, and had every day since, in remembrance of her. Besides, Hope's hair was naught but one shade lighter.

Entering a grove of mostly pines, Michael inhaled the fresh scent. He took another breath while remembering the aroma of lilac water that had surrounded Hope.

And her eyes . . . they'd told him everything her words had not.

More than anything during the long lonely years, he'd missed gazing into those eyes. They'd always invited him to commune with the person that lived within . . . the loving, caring Hope who had never judged him, never looked down on him.

He should've known she'd be incapable of abandoning her sickly mother-in-law. His beloved Hope . . . he wouldn't have her any other way. And hadn't she introduced him to another Father? Their good and loving heavenly Father, whom they both could share.

She'd also given him the gift of literacy. Every time he took pen in hand or picked up a newspaper — or heard a church bell, for that matter — he couldn't help but think of her. Every time he saw a meadow a-bloom with spring flowers or patted his horse . . .

Yet Hope had said that her husband, Ezra, had not loved her. That would explain a lot, including why, to Ezra, her eyes had evoked a reaction very different from his own. Michael recalled the evening Ezra had mentioned them, that night when Jackson's army was camped near Pensacola.

Michael had come upon the Reardon Valley boys sitting around a campfire swat-

ting mosquitoes that rose up in clouds from the marsh behind them, and scratching at the fleas crawling out of the beach sand upon which they'd rolled out their blankets.

As usual, Howie and Ezra were happier than the others to see him, since the three of them had been fast friends when they were lads. Howie made room for him on his blanket while Ezra poured him a cup of chicory coffee.

Howie had changed little through the years, still as ready to laugh and just as quick to whip out his Jew's harp to entertain them with a tune. Ezra, though, no longer had that wide-eyed, something-good's-coming-my-way look about him. His round freckled face had lost its youthfulness. Losing his first wife, Becky, in childbirth had been hard on him — as hard as or maybe harder than Michael's never returning for Hope. And, although Ezra was now wed to her, he never seemed the least jealous of Michael's past courtship of Hope.

That evening, Michael would understand why.

The sun had just set in the west, and the gently lapping water of the hay shimmered an inspiring silver with a hint of its depths in the dark shadows.

"The sea," Michael said as he sipped his coffee, "reminds me of Hope's eyes."

Ezra brushed a hank of sandy hair from his eyes and glanced toward the water. "You're right. Looks kinda eerie." He shot a sheepish glance at Michael. "Not that I ever held her strange-lookin' eyes against her, mind you. Don't know what my folks would do without her carin' for 'em."

"Specially," Howie piped in, "since that brother of yours ain't worth the spit to polish my boots."

Looking back on Ezra's words now, Michael wondered if Ezra had indeed held it against her and if he thought his son's eyes were eerie, too. Would he have been capable of loving Timmy as a father should?

An unanswerable question now.

Then Ezra had said, *"Don't know what my folks would do without her"* — Ezra's long-ago confirmation of one of the reasons Hope said she couldn't leave the Underwoods yet.

Not yet, maybe, but soon.

The pines gave way to the corrals flanking the big blacksmith barn belonging to the Bremmers. He'd reached the settlement.

Just as he reined Ebony in the direction of

the rear stables, tall, sinewy Noah Reardon stepped out of the wide-open doors, followed by the much bulkier Max Bremmer and another man. Older now, Mr. Reardon's face seemed all the leaner, without even a semblance of a smile to give it breadth.

"Where have you been?" Hope's father demanded. He marched forth, intercepting Michael as if he were a court-appointed prosecutor. As a part-time lawyer, the man had no lack of experience questioning folks.

Refusing to let Reardon rattle him, Michael took an extra second or two to answer while he dismounted. "I've been out looking — for old time's sake — at the place where my family used to live. Before I leave tomorrow." Though he had ridden by the abandoned horse farm, he neglected to mention that his true old place was with Hope . . . always with Hope.

The hard lines on either side of Reardon's mouth eased. "You're leaving tomorrow. Good."

"And the farther, the better. Right?" Michael ground out, unable to mask his bitterness.

Reardon crossed his arms, looking quite sure of himself. "I can't deny it. My daughter means the world to me. Of all my children, she's the only one who is the image of my wife, and I can't — I *won't* — stop myself from protecting her. From keeping her safe. Do I make myself clear?"

Michael's first instinct was to wipe that smugly pious sureness from Reardon's face. His second thought was to let the man know he already had Hope's promise to marry him, that after all the years Reardon had kept them apart, her heart still belonged to him. *I may be leaving tomorrow,* he wanted to say, *but I'm coming back for her.*

But, for Hope's sake, Michael swallowed his pride. He gathered the mare's reins and strode past Noah — his greatest obstacle.

As he did, he noticed that Max and the other man still stood in the yawning entrance to the smithy. Loyal friend that Max was, his broad brow was crimped into a frown that had the look of real concern.

The other, however, a balding man with a large belly drooped over his belt buckle, lounged against the doorjamb, grinning at what appeared to be Reardon's triumph over Michael.

That made it all the harder to simply walk away. But for Hope, he kept moving and looking straight ahead, toward the day the two of them would be together.

★ ★ ★

Timothy banged his spoon on the table. "More."

Hope sat next to him within the light of two oil lamps, darning one of the men's old socks. "More, *please*," she corrected.

"Pease," he repeated, giving her one of his dimpled if manipulative grins.

"Such a good boy." Tilly, knitting a new stocking at the end of the table, treated him to a grandmotherly smile.

Timmy had made quite a mess of his mashed potatoes, but Hope didn't care in the least. She was much too happy. There would be problems to overcome before she and Michael could be together, but tonight she just wanted to savor the joy. She did wish she could see Michael one more time before he left for Nashville, but . . .

Rising from the table, she picked up her son's bowl and went to the hearth to scoop more potatoes from one of the footed pots, over which she ladled a bacon-flavored gravy. She didn't usually feed Timmy his supper before the rest of the family, but Titus and Joel had yet to return from helping the Johnsons, and it was fully dark outside.

Returning Timmy's bowl to him, Hope noticed that Ma Tilly was having to hold her knitting directly under the lamplight and still squinted to see.

"Ma, you really need to send for a pair of those reading glasses the next time someone goes downriver to Nashville." Too bad Hope hadn't thought of that when she spoke with Michael today. If he'd return with a peace offering such as that, it would endear him to Tilly for sure.

"I reckon I do need 'em. I tried on some spectacles Martha had with her, and I could see ever' vein an' age spot on my hand. Whew, what an ugly sight." She grunted a laugh. "Come to think of it, maybe them readin' glasses ain't such a good idea after all."

Hope caught the creak and crunch of a wagon rolling in. "Must be the men."

"Take some light on out to 'em. Dark as it is, it's a good thing that ol' horse knows the way home by heart."

Walking out with the long-handled lantern, Hope set it on a barrelhead near the barn door and wrapped her shawl more tightly around her shoulders. "Supper will be on the table by the time you two come in," she said as Joel reined the horse to a stop within the circle of light.

"That's my girl," he said cheerily as he hopped down from the rig.

His tone sounded more like the old Joel, but what did he mean by "That's my girl"?

With a raised brow, Hope hurried to the house, wishing she'd already eaten so she could go upstairs with Timmy.

As soon as she had bowls of savory-smelling food on the table and her son's dodging face and hands washed, she untied him from his tall chair and kissed the top of his feathery hair, putting him down. "Here's a cookie," she said. "Go over on the rug and build me a house with your blocks."

Timmy didn't get halfway there when the door opened and Joel burst into the room. "There's my boy," he shouted. Scooping Timmy up, he swung the tot around.

Her little one squealed with laughter.

Laying down her knitting, Tilly clapped her hands, as delighted as her grandson.

Hope wasn't nearly so pleased. She pressed her lips together, lest an unkind remark slip out. It wasn't that she didn't appreciate Joel giving Timmy special attention, though it was always rather slapdash, according to his mood. In the past few days, she'd especially come to suspect Joel's every kindness to her child.

Titus lumbered in, looking mighty weary. He walked stiff-legged to the table to take his usual seat at the head.

"Hard day?" Hope asked as she moved to his side and poured the old man some herb tea.

"Sure was," Joel answered for him. He lifted Timmy to his shoulders and brought him along to Joel's chair. "But we did get the walls up and the roof shingled. Ain't that right, Pa?"

"That's right, Son. An' Joel here did more'n his share," he said directly to Hope. Though his voice was shaky, a father's pride rang in his words. "He took up the slack for these tired ol' bones. Sit down, girl, so we can get the blessing said. I'm fixin' to eat an' go right on up to bed." He nodded his fuzzy balding head to Joel. "You do the honors tonight. I'm plumb wore out."

Joel's blue eyes widened in surprise, but for only an instant. Swinging Timmy down to the floor, he bowed his head.

Hope was equally amazed. Never before had Joel been asked to say grace. Sitting across from him, she belatedly remembered to lower her own eyes — but not before she spotted a contented smile round out Tilly's sagging cheeks.

"Father in heaven, I want to take this opportunity to thank You for the wonderful family You've given me."

Even in his prayer, Hope couldn't help

being irritated by Joel's assumed possession of her and her son.

"Thank You," he continued, "for this food spread before us and for the lovely hands that prepared it. In Jesus' name, amen." Joel looked across at Hope and sent her a cocky wink.

He was back to his old flirtatious ways, but Hope sensed that a new, serious determination lay just beneath the surface.

Bowls and platters were soon passed around and plates filled.

Timothy, not wanting to be left out, ran around to Hope's side and tugged on her skirt. "Up, Mama. Up."

Normally she would've tied him into his own chair, but she felt the need for a buffer and set him on her lap. Busying herself by breaking a piece of bread in half and buttering it for her son, she tried to avoid looking across at Joel, but she felt his eyes on her. She finally glanced up and saw him ripping off a bite of fried rabbit with his teeth.

Joel wiped his mouth on the sleeve of his homespun shirt. "Hope, you know them peaches of Mrs. Thompson's you was so partial to last fall? Well, I'm gonna see that you have two of them trees for your very own."

"Oh, really?" She couldn't ignore him, not in front of his folks.

"For a fact. Arny was over with us helpin' to build Lester's room. And when I told him how much you liked 'em, he said if I'd come over in the next day or two an' help him put together a cane mill, he'd dig me up a couple of them saplin's him an' his pa's been nursin' along."

"Now, ain't that sweet of you, Son?" his mother cooed. "Mighty considerate."

Hope thought *mighty, considering* . . . would have been more like it. The implication of his working to acquire something just for her was deliberate enough. But to have the gift be young trees that wouldn't bear fruit for another two or three years . . . surely that spoke of his intent to keep her on this farm long enough to eat their bounty.

Lord, she beseeched while trying to recapture her earlier joy, *why do matters always have to be so difficult?*

Soon, very soon, she would have to find the right words to tell Titus and Tilly of her recent decision to leave them. *If* there were any right words to be found.

They would just have to get by without her help, wouldn't they?

Chapter Ten

The next few days were increasingly trying for Hope. To get her household chores accomplished and the vegetable garden planted while attempting to avoid being caught alone with Joel had proved almost impossible. He seemed to be hovering, whether he was out in the field plowing or sitting across the dinner table from her.

Then there were the many private conversations Titus and Tilly kept having with her, commenting on their relief and pride in their youngest son's new industry. Her one compensation was that Joel was at long last relieving his father of the heaviest tasks . . . particularly since she planned to add to their burden by leaving them.

Soon, she knew, feeling a goodly measure of guilt, she would have to tell them. Soon.

Only during her quiet time alone in her room at night or upon awaking in the mornings was she free to relive her last conversation with Michael.

When on Friday the mantel clock struck

one, Hope could hardly wait to get out the door and ride alone to Belinda's house for their sewing circle. As she came into the settlement, practically blown in on an erratic breeze, she marveled at how much her life had changed since the prior Friday — or would be changing, she corrected, when she left the Underwoods and married Michael.

Dismounting in front of the Bremmer house and showing as little leg as possible to any passersby, she wrapped the reins of her stylish gray Arabian around the hitching rail outside their fenced yard. Patting Burns on the neck, she recalled why she'd named her horse after the poet Robert Burns. The fine-blooded animal had been presented to her on her twentieth birthday by her father, and in silent defiance of him, she'd determined that this gift would always remind her of Michael . . . something she'd shoved to the back of her mind these past few years.

Now, feeling just a touch giddy and wanting to share that feeling, she recited, near the animal's ear, that treasured portion of "A Red, Red Rose."

Till a' the seas gang dry, my dear,
And the rocks melt wi' the sun!
And I will luve thee still, my dear,
While the sands o' life shall run.

And fare thee weel, my only luve,
And fare thee weel a while!
And I will come again, my luve,
Tho' it were ten thousand mile!

"And Michael did come, Burns. He did."
Instilled with that infusing joy, she pressed
her hand to her heart and thanked the Lord,
as she had so often this week. Then, remembering where she was, she unhooked her
sewing basket from the saddle horn and
started up the walk at a fast pace. She fervently wanted to share with her old friends
the words that had passed between her and
Michael . . . the precious fact that he loved
her now as much as he ever did and of her
plan to wed him after her mourning period
ended.

Hope slowed her steps as caution returned. She'd better tread slowly and carefully until she was certain they'd keep her
confidence until she found the right
moment to inform the Underwoods and her
own parents.

Nonetheless, as she knocked at the door
and walked in, the mere thought of dis-
cussing Michael with the girls caused her
cheeks to grow warm with excitement.

All four usually gabby women went silent
and dropped their gazes to the sewing in

their hands, just as they had at the prior meeting.

Another secret? Hope didn't bother with a greeting as she scanned them. "Whatever you were keeping from me last week and whatever has got you all lookin' so guilty now, you will speak up and tell me this instant, or I'm walkin' back out the door." She waited where she stood, her basket in hand, while those seated glanced around the worktable at one another.

Belinda spoke first, looking particularly uncomfortable as she rubbed her lower back. "I don't blame you for being upset. We shouldn't have kept the truth from you." She turned to Gracie across from her. "You tell her. It was your letter."

Hope hiked a brow. "Yes, sister *dear.* Do tell me."

Gracie opened her mouth as if to defend herself but didn't. Instead she clamped it shut for an indecisive moment before finally speaking. "Hope, I can't tell you how surprised I was — we all were — to learn that Michael Flanagan was in the cavalry attached to Howie's regiment. And had been since the men returned to duty last fall. Howie had thought it best not to mention it. You know, with you bein' married at the time and all. But then later, when it looked like Michael might be comin' home with the men —" she gave Hope a helpless shrug of her slender shoulder — "with a packet from Ezra, Howie thought maybe he should mention it."

"Yet you took it upon yourself to keep it from me."

Gracie's deep blue gaze dodged from woman to woman, obviously seeking help.

Delia spoke up. "We didn't want to say anything unless we knew for sure. We didn't want to start you wondering . . . you know. And then be disappointed again."

"Disappointed?" Liza popped in. "Hope's a grown woman now. She's too sensible to still be mooning after some beau from her youth."

Both Gracie and Delia pinned Liza with flabbergasted glowers.

Hope wasn't satisfied by any of their answers but decided to move on. "All right, so what about today? What are you keeping from me today?"

Gracie picked up her sewing again. "Nothin', really. Howie an' me was just sorta hopin' that . . . never mind."

"What?"

"For goodness sake, Hope, sit down." Liza motioned to a lone, empty chair. "Don't pay any attention to Gracie and all

143

her romantic foolishness. Besides, he's gone now. It's time to move on."

Was that how folks thought? Something a little messy had happened this past week. But did they now consider it in the past to be swept out the door and forgotten?

"Do sit down," Delia also urged, but more gently. "Gracie was hopin' you and Michael might somehow get together. I suppose it was silliness considerin' . . . everything."

Gracie lunged to her feet, her cheeks flaming, her chair toppling with a bang. "If it was just silliness, Papa wouldn't have done what he did."

Hope, gripped by panic, moved quickly to her sister. "What did Papa do?"

Quick-tongued Liza spoke in Gracie's stead. "Your father merely dropped by the smithy's Monday afternoon and told Sergeant Flanagan he wasn't welcome here, which, of course, is the sentiment shared by pretty much ever'body in the valley."

"Not *nearly* everybody," Gracie defended fiercely. "We're not all as small-minded as you."

"Ladies!" Belinda rebuked, glancing around with an accompanying scowl on her freckled features. "I know firsthand what it's like to not feel welcomed. Have you forgotten? It wasn't until my family and I came to this valley that folks went out of their way to befriend us. You girls have lived in this community your whole lives. You have no idea what it's like to be alone with no folks around who are not just willing but eager to help wherever there's a need."

"As I remember," Gracie remarked, "things changed for you mostly because of Max."

"Yes, my dear persistent Max. Even back before my parents learned that we had to keep strictly to ourselves . . . back when we were still living in South Carolina and we knew mostly plantation folk . . . if a body could get the women to stop gossiping long enough to notice someone needed help, they'd simply send over one of their slaves. You girls have no idea what a special place this is. You're right, Gracie — not everyone in Reardon Valley is small-minded."

Hope relaxed a mite as Belinda continued. "Papa Rolf, I think, is the reason. He set up a high spiritual standard in the very heart of this valley, and woe to the person's conscience who tries to tear it down."

"Aye," Gracie agreed, sitting up straighter. "I sure did feel convicted durin' his sermon last Sunday. Remember? It was all about forgivin' others. Well, I have the hardest time musterin' up any charity at all toward Mrs. Skinner. You know, because of her infernal accusations about Howie's music — which reminds me, Howie's foot is almost healed now, so soon as you've had this baby and are up to it, Belinda, he wants to invite all the veterans over to celebrate the men's homecomin'."

Belinda chuckled. "Good old Howie. My goodness, but we've missed his enthusiastic spirit."

Hope cleared her throat, determined to return to the former topic. "Liza, are you one of those who would not welcome Michael back?"

"All I meant before," Liza said, lowering her attention to the baby item she'd been stitching, "was that it made me nervous the whole time Michael Flanagan was here, you know, wonderin' if somethin' was gonna just happen to catch on fire."

Appalled, Hope knew if she didn't walk out this second, she'd say something deplorable, or more likely, break down crying in front of Liza, and that would never do. Heart pounding, throat aching, tears threatening, she managed, "If you'll excuse me . . ."

Belinda let out a groan, blanching, until her freckles were the only remaining color on her face. She covered her swollen belly with one hand and grabbed the table edge with the other. "Liza!" she practically shouted. "Quick, ride out to your mother's place and get your grandma. And tell Max at the smithy. It's time."

Hope's anger fled. "What can I do to help?" she asked as Belinda emitted another long groan. Her friend was known for having her babies fast and furiously.

"My mother," Belinda managed between clamped teeth. "Someone needs to go across the river to fetch her."

Delia, her large brown eyes wider than usual, instantly volunteered. She'd always been squeamish at the sight of blood.

Leaving their sewing scattered across the table, Liza and Delia headed out the door, slamming it resoundly behind them.

The grimace on Belinda's face eased, and she glanced up the stairwell near the entrance. "If the chair banging didn't wake little Inga, that surely will." Then she let out a sigh. "Thank goodness. That was one fine pain." She stretched her back. "I've had small ones off and on all morning. They were irregular, so I thought maybe it was just some more false labor. But that one was a real whopper."

Gracie hurried around the table to

Belinda. "We need to get you upstairs before the next pain hits."

"And I'll put some water on to heat." Hope tossed her basket on the table and headed for the kitchen. She swung back. "Where are the towels and sheets you want to use?"

"I have them up in my bedroom," Belinda managed as Gracie helped her up from the chair. "There's a bucket by the door and another on the back porch. They'll probably need filling. And bring up my smallest tub. It's hanging on the outside wall." Waddling slowly toward the stairs, she added, "I think that'll do it."

After Hope emptied water from one of the buckets into the suspended kettle and stoked the fire, she quickly grasped the wooden container and the one on the back porch and sprinted out to the well, keeping Belinda's past birthings in mind. Every second counted.

As she cranked the well bucket down into the deep stone-sided hole, she caught sight of Max coming across the field in a limping run. Years before, Max had received a severe leg wound during his frontiersman days, but usually it was barely noticeable.

Waving her free hand, Hope gained his attention, then beckoned him to her.

"How is she?" he shouted as he veered in her direction.

"If you'll fill the second bucket, I'll run the first one up and find out."

"You know she had Inga within five minutes of her first hard pain," he gasped, out of breath as he came to a halt before her.

"That fast?"

Picking up a bucket, he tipped the well water into it and shoved it at Hope. "That fast."

She ran for the back porch. Lifting the tub off the wall, she raced on and reached the second floor of the house in a fraction of a minute. Banging through the bedroom doorway with her awkward burdens, Hope saw that Belinda's bed had been stripped of its usual bedding and replaced with an old quilt.

Gracie was helping Belinda, stripped down to her chemise, onto the corn-husk-filled mattress.

Just as Belinda lay back on her pillow, her water broke and another hard pain hit. Her belly wrenched, and she grabbed the bedposts above her head.

It couldn't have been more than three or four minutes since the last contraction.

"Towels!" Gracie hollered.

This was much too fast. Hope set the

bucket and tub on the floor. "Where are they?"

"I think it's coming," Belinda gritted out.

"In the cradle," Gracie again shouted as she hurried to check Belinda.

As Hope gathered the toweling, Gracie called, "I think I see the head. Push, Belinda! Push!"

In the midst of Belinda's horrifically long groan, Hope layered terry cloth in the strategic spot, as she stretched across from the other side of the bed.

Max's footsteps came pounding up the stairs.

Before he could've reached the bedroom door, though, it swung wide. The Bremmers' three-year-old stood in the doorway, her strawberry blonde hair looking as wild as her wide eyes. "Is Mama hurt?"

Coming from behind, Max caught her up in his free arm and burst into the room, slopping water across the floor. "Is she all right?"

Hope blocked his path. "Belinda's doin' just fine. Great, actually. I wish everyone had babies this fast."

"Mama's having the baby?" Inga leaned to the side, trying to peek past her papa's arm.

"Max, quick, take Inga over to the school," Hope ordered. "Your older kids can watch her. Then bring up the water that's heatin'. I don't care if it's not boilin' hot yet. And hurry. The baby's not waitin' —" Hope stopped talking. Max was already halfway down the stairs.

"That's good," Belinda said as her breathing eased to normal. "Keep him busy a few minutes more. *Oh no.*" She sucked in another gulp of air. "Here we go again." She grabbed the bedsteads, her body going rigid.

But she'd just finished with the last pain.

Gracie, at the bottom of the bed, yelled, "The head's out! It's comin'! Towel, Hope, a clean towel."

Another second or two, and a squirming, whimpering baby lay in Gracie's arms. Laughing, she wiped its nose and cleared its mouth. "Thank You, Jesus. Hope, the scissors. They're on the washstand. Come cut the cord."

As Hope complied, she glanced up to Belinda's moisture-beaded face. "You are amazing. Just three hard pains, and we're sayin' 'how do you do' to a whole new —" she glanced down at the baby Gracie was wiping clean — "baby boy."

"Another boy?" Belinda already had three

and only one daughter. "Make sure he has all his fingers and toes." She rose on an elbow to check for herself.

"He does," Gracie assured her as Hope rinsed out the basin on the washstand. "Now, lie back down till you've delivered the afterbirth. And Hope is right. You are a *wonder*."

Belinda dropped onto her pillow. "No, you girls are. Thank you so much for all you are doing for me. Like I said before, it's such a blessing to be around women who are not just willing but eager to help in a time of need."

Gracie smiled. "We wouldn't think of bein' anywhere else." She handed the baby to Hope and laid an extra layer of toweling down.

Another, much lighter pain, and Belinda had delivered the afterbirth.

Gracie worked fast to dump the towels in the tub, then continued with the remainder of the cleanup.

"Neither would I." Breathing easy again, Belinda smiled weakly, giving her that rare beauty only new mothers had, and nestled back into the pillow. "This valley is where I met my Max."

"Speaking of which," Hope said, carrying the baby to the threshold and looking down the stairs, "just where is your Max, anyway? I need warm water to wash off the baby." She rocked the newborn gently in her arms.

As if in response to her question, she heard the front door bang open.

"I'm back," Max shouted from below.

"Hurry up with the hot water," she returned from above. "Your *son* is anxious to make himself presentable."

"My son?" Pride mixed with the excitement in his voice. "Right away."

Conversely, sorrow swept through Hope. Ezra hadn't been within two hundred miles when Timothy was born. To him, their son hadn't been much more than a fulfillment of his duty to his parents.

"Oh, by the by," Belinda said, quite chatty now that the ordeal was past, "Max and I decided that if the baby was a boy, we'd name him Michael James after Michael Flanagan. If the sergeant hadn't so graciously supplied the horses, Max would still be out there somewhere between Nashville and here."

The thoughtful gesture so overwhelmed Hope that tears began to swim in her eyes. But it wasn't only Max and Belinda who were grateful to Michael — the other returning men had seemed just as thankful at church last Sunday. And they had parents and wives and children who should be just as grateful. Perhaps more people than she'd thought felt obligated to Michael. Folks that might very well welcome his presence.

Now, if she could convince her father Michael wasn't a menace, perhaps Michael might consider settling here. She wouldn't have to uproot herself and her son to travel to some faraway military post. Wouldn't have to take Timmy away from his aging grandparents. Or leave all the good people she loved and for the first time realized she'd always taken for granted.

Then Liza's words came pouring in again, full force. After the terrible things her father must've said to Michael, would he even bother to come back? He'd promised to return before — and didn't.

Chapter Eleven

As Michael neared the river port of Nashville leading his string of horses, he passed a
steady stream of militiamen, mostly on foot,
traveling in the opposite direction.
Tramping along the mud-slicked road,
they'd been discharged from military duty
and were on their way home. Though
ragged and dirty, one and all were in a merry
mood. They waved and called out greetings.

"We sure whipped them British," one
shouted up to him while banging his caked
shoe against a jutting slab of Tennessee
sandstone.

A little farther along, another raised his
rifle and called out, "Them redcoats'll think
twice before messin' with us hunters from
up Kentucky way."

And another — "Or the boys back in
Franklin County."

It did feel good, Michael knew, to be returning to their homes after a string of victo-
ries, ending with one so resounding, he
doubted the British would ever want to

tangle with these overmountain boys again.

The small farms behind him, he now rode past much more prosperous plantations with wide expanses of cleared fields being worked by the landholders' own private armies of slaves. If a body didn't know better, one would believe this fertile river valley was in Virginia or the Carolinas instead of mostly hilly Tennessee.

Just before reaching the first buildings of the port city, Michael turned off the road, where several companies of Regular Army and the remaining soldiers of 7th Military District were temporarily camped. In a plowed-under field surrounding a large barn, several rows of canvas tents had been pitched. Over one of the larger ones, their regimental flag flew.

Headquarters.

He knew he needed to report in, but first there was a question he needed answered . . . a question that had been nagging at him since he left Reardon Valley four days ago.

Skirting the makeshift village, Michael headed for the barn and its adjoining corrals.

Thorpe, a young corporal from Pennsylvania's hill country, came from behind a long-legged bay with a curry brush in hand. The toothy lad broke into a wide grin.

"Sarge, you're back." He swung open the gate to let Michael and his horses inside.

Michael scanned the other stock penned in the corrals. "They all look fit."

"Just got the last of 'em reshoed this mornin'," the corporal answered, then shot a doleful glance at Michael's string.

"Don't fret. I took care of mine while I was in Reardon Valley." Michael searched the grounds without success. "Do you happen to know where Sergeant Stover is? I'd like a word with him before I report in."

"He came by a little while ago to check on me. Then he headed on over to the mess tent, I reckon to see about the boys in there."

"Right." He glanced toward the largest canvas structure. "Take good care of my horses. They'll need waterin'. And they could all use a rubdown."

"Sure thing, Sarge."

Weary after three and a half days in the saddle, Michael walked toward the tent where all the food stores were kept and meals prepared, glad he'd reached the rank of sergeant. At this moment, his rank gave him the privilege of turning over his horses to the corporal, though he usually tended his own personal stock. Still, he felt slightly guilty about making extra work for Thorpe.

But he had questions for Sergeant Stover that couldn't wait.

Reaching the oversized structure with a number of blazing cook fires with pots suspended over them, Michael searched past the tied-back flaps. He spotted the soldier he sought among the crates and sacks and barrels of food stores.

Sergeant Stover, a man of no more than medium height, always maintained a posture of authority in the crisp movements of his powerfully built frame. Off duty, however, a keen sense of humor could dance in his quick brown eyes. But at the moment, he stared down at a ledger book in one hand, while holding a slate in the other. He was obviously taking inventory.

Two cooks in greasy aprons stood to one side, looking nervous.

Stover glanced up from his inspection. "Flanagan. You're back." A friendly welcome was in his crusty voice.

"Just rode in," Michael said, stepping inside. "When you get a couple of minutes, I'd like a word with you."

Stover eyed his subordinates, then set the paperwork on a nearby barrel. "You two get on with peeling potatoes. I'll be back in a few minutes." Turning sharply on his highly polished heel, he walked toward Michael with the precision of a parade-ground marcher.

Michael exited before him and waited for Stover upwind of the campfires and away from any passing soldiers. This conversation was for the sergeant's ears only.

"What's the problem?" Stover asked, the chiseled squareness of his features as void of emotion as his at-ease stance.

"Not a problem, really. It's just that you're the only noncommissioned officer I know who had a wife with you at Fort Pickering."

"That's right. And the sooner I get the supplies in order, the sooner we'll be returning. It's been eight months since I seen my li'l gal. And my son."

"Not that I want to pry into your private affairs, but I was wonderin' how Mrs. Stover's farin' as an army wife. What with you comin' and goin', leavin' her there in a fort teemin' with bachelors, and the only other wives there are married to officers and outrank her."

A slow grin dimpled one cheek. "So, you're thinking of taking a wife. I didn't know you was courting anyone."

"A war widow I've known since my youth."

"Well, I'm sure my Polly would be purely

159

pleased to have another sergeant's wife at the fort." His grin broadened. "Someone she outranks for a change. I know it's been mighty hard on her, not having the companionship of any other sergeants' wives. Specially these past couple of years with me gone so much because of the war." His expression turned serious. "It can be a real lonely life for a woman. It don't suit most of 'em that's tried it. In fairness to your lady, you need to tell her what to expect. Being away from her family and friends for years, maybe. Or being with them and away from you. That's where most of the wives end up — back home — with their husbands only seeing them on their yearly leaves. If at all."

This was not what Michael wanted to hear, though he'd come to wonder about the lack of sergeants' wives, considering marriage was permitted for that rank.

"Then, what with the war," Stover continued, glancing off into the distance, "there was the possibility of the British coming upriver to attack the fort or sending some of their Indian allies to do it for 'em. Fact is, I'm surprised Polly has stayed with me this long. But we stopped 'em good, didn't we?"

"We sure did," Michael agreed with force.

"And my Polly stayed there the whole

time. Never went home even for a short visit. She's got real starch. I'm purely blessed to have her."

"Well, I thank you for your brutal frankness. You've given me a great deal to consider."

"Sorry, lad, but it would be wrong of me to tell you some rose-colored fairy tale."

Michael exhaled with a heavy heart. "Reckon I better go report in."

Still, he knew he had to come to some decision before he saw his commander. His five-year enlistment had expired several months ago, with him signing only a temporary field extension until war's end. He'd never before given a thought to not reenlisting. He'd made a fine place for himself in the military where order, respectfulness, and honorable conduct were not the exception but the rule. Where, when he asked an honest question, he'd receive a forthright answer, as Stover had just provided.

But if Hope defied her family to come with him, they probably wouldn't welcome a visit from her if Michael ever needed to send her out of harm's way. Nor would he want to feel obligated to them by taking their charity. And could he expect Hope to give up everyone she knew and loved to partake of the hardships and loneliness of being

161

a military wife? Just to be with him . . . some of the time? Could he ask that of her? She really was such a delicate-boned creature. She still looked like a young girl . . . a young girl who'd waited almost seven years for him to return.

Whatever his decision, he would not leave her waiting again.

"Sir," he later said to the cavalry's Captain Causey after reporting on the completion of his prior orders and being given leave to speak. "I would like to request a six-month leave before deciding whether to re-enlist or not." Hopefully, it wouldn't take his love that long to say farewell to her past and her widowhood, but if she needed that much time, he could do no less than give it to her.

Three days later, wearing everyday work clothes, Michael rode out of the woods and into the clearing of his family's farm, which lay halfway between Nashville and Fort Pickering. He was immediately disappointed by what he saw. His two younger brothers hadn't cleared a single additional acre since his last visit. Worse, of the few farmable acres, only one quarter had been furrowed and seeded. And April was half gone. With the afternoon warm and sunny, they should have been out there this very minute plowing and planting.

But not a soul could be seen in the fields surrounding the two cabins and outbuildings. Instead, a cow and a few horses wandered across the unplowed stretch, eating the weeds of spring.

Riding closer to the crude dwellings, Michael spotted four ragged little ones running about barefoot between the facing cabins.

A man stepped to the edge of one of the shaded porches. He watched as Michael rode toward him.

Though the man's dark brown hair and beard were longer and shaggier than the last time Michael had seen either of his brothers, he was sure it was one of them. Either Patrick or Dennis.

With a sudden grin, the man waved in greeting, then turned back and yelled something into the house. The voice was Pat's.

Between the cabins, hogs rooted through a scattering of rotted garbage while chickens darted between the larger animals, snatching tidbits, unmindful of his approach. The children, though, had dashed like frightened bunnies up to the porch — they were obviously not used to having visitors. Before Michael reached the yard, a foul odor assaulted his nostrils.

A second bearded man came out. Denny. He jogged down the steps right behind his brother to greet Michael. Their grins and their frolicking brown eyes hadn't changed a bit.

"Howdy, Mike," Denny called out as Michael reined Ebony to a halt.

No matter how run-down the place looked, Michael was glad to see them. "Thought I'd drop by and see how y'all are gettin' along."

Two young women emerged from the one cabin with youngsters hanging on to their legs. These were the Applegate sisters Pat and Denny had married a year or so before Michael joined the army. They'd kept themselves poorly back then but looked far worse now . . . dull brown, unbrushed hair, wearing soiled aprons over shapeless home-spun, and both soft-looking, as if they didn't do much but sit around on their behinds.

His mother walked out behind them, looking no better. Her hair was caught back in a sloppy night braid, and it tore at his heart to see several missing teeth when she smiled in recognition.

She held out her arms to him. "Get down, boy, and give your mama a big hug." At forty-five, she looked easily ten years older.

Dismounting, Michael's memories from his growing-up years came flooding back. His mother had always blamed her husband for the slovenly way they lived. Michael had thought that once Bantry Flanagan was out of their lives for good, she'd change, become the tidy person many of his friends' mothers were. He wished he could remember some good times, times of laughing and joking. But all he recalled was the shame he'd felt and the vague excuses he'd given his friends, and especially Hope, about why he never invited any of them to his place. With or without her husband, his mother had remained the same. And his sisters-in-law fit right in.

His mother was upon him now. With tears swimming in her hazel eyes, she grabbed him in a tight hug. The stench of sweat and chewing tobacco assailed him as she reached up with both hands and kissed him on the mouth.

It took all his willpower not to recoil. He gently pulled away to arm's length. "You're lookin' fit, Ma," he lied.

"An' ye're handsome as a town dandy."

Michael turned to his brothers. "You're a little late gettin' your crops in, ain'tcha?"

Their smiles vanished.

Dennis cocked his head to the side.

"Naw. We're plantin' only a few rows of corn ever' two weeks. That way the crop don't come ripe all at the same time, an' we can take our time distillin' the whiskey."

"Whiskey?"

"Sure. Why bother with anything else? Whiskey brings in the biggest profit. An' it's sure a lot easier to transport. Ain't that right, Pat?"

"But you haven't even put in a vegetable garden."

Pat stepped next to Dennis and draped an arm over his younger brother's shoulders. "We don't go outta our way, thinkin' up chores to do now that you're gone. All we mess with is a milk cow for the young'uns, and —" he spread his arm toward the pigs — "a few pigs and chickens when the huntin' ain't good. We jist trade the whiskey for anything else we need."

His mother crowded closer. "There's time for all that man talk later. I want Michael to come inside, whilst me'n the gals, here, rustle him up somethin' to eat."

The thought of going into that house did little for Michael's appetite. After being gone for a while, he always forgot just how unclean his family was. Still, he didn't want to hurt his mother's feelings. "Sure, Ma, if it ain't no bother."

"Bother? It'll be a real treat, gettin' to fuss over my firstborn again. Are ye home for a spell or jist passin' through?"

"Just passin' through." Michael knew he'd never spoken truer words. Any fool thought he'd entertained on the ride from Nashville about his quitting the army and bringing Hope here to live with his family had been just that — foolishness.

Chapter Twelve

On the following Saturday, Hope paused from pressing the wrinkles from Tilly's black Sunday gown. The iron had grown cool. Taking it from the tall workbench she'd brought inside for the task, she set the iron on some hearth coals to reheat.

She stretched a kink from her shoulder as she enjoyed the quiet patter of rain on the roof. The sound, she surmised, should help Tilly and Timothy sleep all the longer. And with Titus and Joel out in the barn sharpening tools, she was being given a much desired respite. She'd been working especially hard this past week, helping with the spring planting, and once the downpour stopped, more awaited her.

Yesterday, she hadn't even been able to manage a few hours to go visit Belinda and her new arrival, Michael James. Hope smiled, knowing every time she looked at the baby she would think of her own Michael.

Then that sense of panic she'd felt all

week overtook her. Would he come back? That niggling doubt had caused her to delay informing the Underwoods of her plans — plans that she feared might be nothing more than fanciful dreams, if she didn't stand her ground. Or if Michael didn't return.

She reached for a cup, assuring herself he would most definitely honor his promise to her.

Movement outside the window caught her attention. Joel.

He ran from the barn toward the house as large droplets pelted his wide-brimmed hat and shoulders.

She groaned. Just when she was about to enjoy some coffee along with a rare moment of private leisure . . .

With no one else on the ground floor, Joel would prove a problem. It had been bad enough working out in the fields all week, feeling his eyes following her every move. She'd had to bite her tongue every day to keep herself from telling him that under no circumstances would she ever marry him. But she needed to wait until after the crops were planted, after he'd done at least that much work for Titus. Then she'd tell him. Not even for her beloved Titus and Tilly would she put up with his attentions too much longer. He'd always made her uneasy, but lately he'd been insufferable.

She snatched Titus's Bible off the mantel shelf. If anything would keep Joel from trying to swarm all over her, it would be to see her reading it. Dropping into a seat at the table, she let the big book fall open where it might and pulled the dining lamp closer.

Moving Titus's ribbon marker to the side, she began scanning the fifth chapter of Second Corinthians.

As she did, she heard boot steps, then scraping, just before the door swung open, blowing a draft of cold air; then Joel appeared.

He removed his hat and held it outside to shake off the moisture . . . a thoughtful gesture that wouldn't have entered his mind two weeks ago. He headed for the fireplace, hands extended, with a suspiciously happy smile. "It's a might nippy out there today."

"Hmm," she said, trying to sound distracted. She rendered a brief smile before returning her attention to the words before her.

"Aye. Just finished sharpenin' the big plow. It oughta slice through that mud now. Like a hot knife through butter."

She kept her gaze trained on the words a second before answering, to give the impression he was interrupting her. "That's good." Pricked by guilt for using the Bible to fool him, she stood up. "I just made coffee. Would you like some?"

"Yes, ma'am," he said with more enthusiasm than Hope would've preferred.

Then she realized that fetching the pot would put them both at the fireplace together. "Take a seat. I'll get it."

But he didn't. He merely moved over a step as she reached for two cups. Though he continued to rub his hands together, he watched her every move as she bent to hook the metal arm in the fireplace from which the blackened pot was suspended.

She had to walk around him to retrieve a towel from a nail in the mantel board.

He turned to face her as she did. Far be it from him to be the least bit subtle.

Doing her best to ignore him, Hope poured him a cup and thrust it at him to occupy his hands. After pouring some for herself, she returned to the table and sat before the Bible again.

He followed, but instead of taking a seat, he stood close behind her. "Whatcha readin'? Must be real interesting."

Since she had yet to actually digest a single word, she picked the first verse that her eyes landed on, hoping it would be one that harnessed any carnal notions he might be having. " 'Therefore,' " she read, " 'if any man be in Christ, he is a new creature: old things are passed away; behold, all things are become new.' "

He grabbed a chair and swung it in the opposite direction and placed it next to hers. "I know just what you mean. Ever since Pa said the place was mine, I felt like a new creature." Hooking a leg over the chair, he straddled it to face her, his smug expression much too close. "Now ever'thing on this place is like it's all brand-new. I mean, just think about it . . . I own the chairs we're sittin' on, the cups we're drinkin' out of. An' ever'thing else I lay my eyes on." His gaze made a presumptive sweep of her, as if wedding her were a foregone conclusion. "Ezzy never saw things around here the way I do. No, sir, he surely didn't."

Feeling like a cornered animal, Hope shot up from her seat . . . and, thank heavens, spied Titus coming up the porch steps. "Here comes your pa. I'd better get him some coffee, too."

Joel groaned, then uncurled himself and returned his chair to where it belonged.

"Come warm yourself at the fire," Hope said as the old man came in, brushing off the rain. "I'm gettin' you some fresh brew."

"I thought I smelled it," he said.

"Later on, we'll be havin' plenty of stick-to-the-ribs squirrel stew for supper. In the meantime, I'll cut you two off a slice of bread to hold you," she added in an attempt to keep Titus in the house.

"You are a *pure* blessin'," Titus said on a sigh, repeating the words his wife often used.

"Yes, sir." Taking his regular seat, Joel grinned up at her. "Our very own private blessin'."

As soon as she set a plate of sliced bread and butter before the men, she returned to ironing Tilly's dress at the long-legged bench. On her feet was the safest place to be with Joel in the room.

"I see you was readin' the Bible," Pa Titus said as he pulled the open book to the end where he sat.

"Aye, I've felt a particular need of late," she said in dire earnestness.

"Looks like you took up right where I left off."

"Yes, I thought I would whilst the iron was heatin'. If you're of a mind, it'd be a real treat if you'd read to me while I finish up here." If anything would run Joel off, that would. She suppressed a grin.

With a pleased smile, Titus cleared his

throat, took a sip of coffee, then moved the Bible farther away and focused his old eyes. "I'm right here at chapter six. 'We then, as workers together with him, beseech you also that ye receive not the grace of God in vain. For he saith, I have heard thee in a time accepted, and in the day of salvation . . .' "

That's all it took. Joel was up and heading for the door. "I best go put the cover on the wagon for church tomorrow. I don't think this rain is gonna let up."

"Ain't that boy takin' hold?" Titus said as Joel walked out, the pleasure in his hoarse voice clear as a crystal bell.

"Yes, he is," Hope agreed politely while sliding the heavy iron along a wrinkle in the skirt of Tilly's wool gown. She then quickly redirected the old man's thoughts. "Do go on reading."

As he did, she didn't pay much attention until he reached a verse that was exceedingly familiar. " 'Be ye not unequally yoked together with unbelievers: for what fellowship hath righteousness with unrighteousness? and what communion hath light with darkness?' "

Glancing up, she latched onto the words, repeating them in her mind as Titus continued reading further Scriptures. Joel had never shown any sign of discipleship to the

Lord. His baptism as a child, she knew, had been at his parents' insistence, and he went to church only because he lived in their house. Everyone in the valley knew this for a fact. No one could fault her for refusing to wed him on the grounds provided in that verse. Even Titus and Tilly would have to understand.

Her own father, in particular, would have no argument upon which to make a stand. Hadn't he and Mama told the story of their own courtship often enough . . . about how he'd been mightily attracted to her and had mourned the fact that he couldn't marry her because she was a heathen? Then in church one bright sunny morning, he'd seen the glow of Christ on her face as she received Jesus into her heart, and Papa knew at that moment she was God's choice for him as well. It was a lovely story Hope and her siblings had never tired of hearing while they were growing up.

After the dreadful banishment of Michael, though, she had resented the fact that her parents had had their happy ending while depriving her of hers.

Now, at long last, Hope, too, would have a happy ending. Michael would come back for her. Her chest swelled at the thought . . . then deflated at the next disturbing one.

What if he's fallen away from the Lord?
That is, if he had ever truly believed. He'd
never been to a Sabbath service until the
morning he went with her. After he left
Reardon Valley, had he returned to his family's heathen ways? Or had he kept Jesus in
his heart with the same love and hope that
he'd held for her there? The answer to that
question might very well bring great re-
joicing — or an end to her every dream.

On a sunny Thursday afternoon three and
a half weeks after Michael left the Reardon
Valley, he drove down into it on a wagon
loaded with supplies and his small herd of
horses strung out behind. He felt slightly
apprehensive about the choice he'd made.
But mostly, he felt good.

A mile or so through the gently rolling
landscape of mostly cleared land, he happened upon another rig coming from the
opposite direction. He exchanged a nod and
a howdy with the fellow guiding the other
farm wagon, but the older man's flabbergasted stare of recognition remained with
him long after they'd passed. Michael
doubted it would be twenty-four hours
before every man, woman, and child in the
valley knew he'd returned, when the only
one he truly wanted to know was Hope

Reardon Underwood — soon to be Mrs. Michael Flanagan, only four months from hence. Her mourning period would be over in September.

This Sunday, he'd see her for sure, if not before. The one thing he could count on in this valley was people's dedication to attending church. They'd stayed true to the Baptist principles upon which the valley had been established, and from what Max had told him, there'd never been a drinking establishment allowed to set up shop here, or even a whiskey still. The original deeds had stated as much.

Michael remembered his pa bragging about how he'd be hoodwinking any of his enemies who might be hunting him. *"No one will ever expect Bantry Flanagan to be livin' smack in the middle of a bunch of crazy church folks."* He'd won the land in a card game from a foolish young hayseed who'd just stepped off a raft in Nashville to file his deed. Michael knew, though, that his pa had had a habit of keeping a few extra aces up his sleeve.

Whatever had transpired before, this time the deed folded in Michael's shirt pocket had been gained honestly by using a portion of his ten years' of savings to purchase the farm from the land office. The latest owner had been killed in a farm accident, and his wife had abandoned the place to return to her family in the East. It had taken several years to clear the title, but now it was his alone, free and clear, for the price of the unpaid taxes.

Traveling between trees that mostly edged the road, Michael passed only one more man riding horseback before reaching the cutoff to his place. He was glad the property was in the north quarter of the valley and that he hadn't been required to drive through the more heavily populated central area.

Within a few minutes of dodging potholes along the wooded path, he came upon the clearing. Pulling his team to a halt, he felt an unexpectedly strong surge of joy. Unlike last month when he surveyed the structures and fallow fields, it no longer seemed neglected and lonely to him. In a few minutes, his horses would be grazing on tall green grass, every blade of which he owned, and he'd be sleeping under his own roof.

His gaze gravitated to the tree where Hope's future name was carved. One day soon, after he'd gotten the place spruced up a bit, he'd bring her here and show the etching to her . . . and prove to her that his long-ago promise, her years of waiting, had not been in vain.

He scanned his small kingdom again, gaining more confidence with each second. He'd made the smart decision to come here and stay while he waited for her to be free to come to him. Trying to pressure her into abruptly leaving with him, leaving everything she'd ever known for a life even he couldn't predict, would not have been wise. Yes, this felt right.

Lord, I know You're a God of miracles. You showed all of us that at the Battle of New Orleans. All I'm askin' is just one more little one. That You'll make the way smooth for Hope an' me.

He breathed deeply of the welcoming scent of meadow flowers and pine needles, then hopped down from the wagon to go check the fences before turning his stock into one of the enclosures.

My, but it did feel good to know that the rich loam he walked on was his. And soon, very soon, Hope's.

If certain folks in the valley relented and didn't make it impossible for them to stay.

"Mama! More!"

Sitting in the parlor of the Bremmer house, Hope looked up from the triangle

179

she was cutting out of a scrap of daisy-print calico.

"More." Timmy sat on a pallet beneath the stairs, eating a noon meal Hope had brought for him to share with three-year-old Inga. He picked up his spoon and pounded his metal plate.

"Say *please*," his Aunt Gracie prompted from beside Hope at the sewing table.

His luminous eyes narrowed into a scowl. "Please," he said begrudgingly, being a typical two-year-old boy.

Or were she and his grandparents doting on him far too much, as they had Joel? "Stop banging," Hope commanded as she laid down her scissors, "or I'll take you home right now." She stared pointedly at her son until he ceased; then she rose to fetch him and Inga more of his favorite — mashed potatoes and gravy — from the kitchen.

She'd probably made a mistake letting her boisterous child come with her today. But after three weeks of spring planting with Joel, she'd simply refused to wait until after she'd fed Timmy and put him down for a nap before coming to sewing circle.

"There are some c-o-o-k-i-e-s," Belinda spelled out from where she sat rocking her three-week-old babe. "On the shelf above the worktable for when they've finished."

"You'd think Liza would be here by now," Delia said across the table. "We're piecin' this quilt for her brother's marriage bed."

"And your sister-in-law's," Gracie laughed as Hope walked through the doorway into the kitchen.

"And your cousin's," Delia returned, her tone now much merrier. "I'll swan, but it won't be long before ever'body in this valley'll be related to ever'body else."

Not if I get my way, Hope wanted to call back as she slid the bowl of potatoes out of the warming niche beside the fireplace. One fine day, she'd be marrying someone without a single blood relative within a hundred miles. *If* he came back for her . . . another two or three weeks of waiting, and she'd know.

Returning with the serving bowl and two dried-pear cookies hidden in her skirt pocket, she spooned another dollop of gravy-slathered potatoes onto the little ones' plates.

Fluffy-haired Inga grinned with her mouth of tiny baby teeth. "T'ank you," she lisped sweetly.

Hope reached down and tousled her fine red-blonde locks, fervently wishing her own next child would be a girl — another of the possibilities Michael's arrival had brought with him last month: the dream of a baby girl she could hold as close as Belinda held her newborn . . . a baby girl who would one day gaze up at her with Michael's golden brown eyes.

"Hope!" Delia was requesting her attention.

"Yes?" She set the bowl on a side table and sat down.

"I was just sayin', I'm downright amazed that your Joel is still workin' hard ever'day, just like a real farmer. You did say he plowed and furrowed all your acreage hisself, without Titus havin' to get out his horsewhip even once." The dark flair of her brows danced playfully.

But Hope didn't see the humor in her words. "Oh, he's full of himself, all right. He even offered to keep Timmy for me this afternoon . . . one more strand in that web he keeps tryin' to weave around me."

"Pshaw. He's never stuck with anything before," Delia pooh-poohed, while stitching two opposite-hued triangles together. "Specially not somethin' that's raisin' blisters on his hands. Mark my words, that kinda gumption won't last much longer."

"I don't know." Gracie wagged her head. "What with the prize danglin' right there in front of him ever' day *and* night, just a room away, that's a powerful incentive for any young buck in his prime. And, don't forget, he always did want ever'thing Ezra had." She turned to Hope beside her. "Most particularly you, little sister."

"Don't remind me. I can almost see his mind a-workin'. It's as if he has a battle plan. Last Sunday at church, he sidled up to Papa, tellin' him how he wanted to clear the knoll behind the east pasture and asked for advice on how to furrow it to keep the soil from washin' down in a storm. And, of course, Papa couldn't have been more pleased. He invited Joel over to look at how he plowed his hillside. 'Course, if that was all Joel was interested in, he could've ridden up to the Dillards'. They're usin' the same method, and their place isn't half the distance." She shrugged. "It really doesn't matter what he does, though. After church Sunday, I plan to come right out and tell him he's wastin' his time. I figure all the hard springtime labor should be finished by then."

"Well, you know, Hope," Delia said, "maybe you shouldn't be so quick to look this gift horse in the mouth. Joel may be three or four years your junior, but he ain't half bad to look at. Anyway, that's what all the young misses at church seem to think."

"If Hope chooses to remarry . . ." Belinda, who'd been quietly rocking the baby with her eyes closed, surprised Hope by speaking. ". . . I think this time it should be to someone she could love."

"Thank you," Hope said with definition. At least one person thought as she did.

"Oh, here comes Liza." Gracie pointed out the front window.

Remembering the children under the stairs, Hope decided their little ears had heard more than enough women talk for one day. And considering Liza's opinions of late . . . She hurried to the children with a cookie in each hand. "Take these and go up to Inga's bedroom. Don't fight. Play nice."

Seconds later, Liza burst through the front door, her face flushed, her down-slanted, honey-colored eyes burning with excitement. She quickly scanned the room, her gaze stopping on Hope. "You don't know, do you?"

"Know what?" She held her breath. Joel must have done or said something he shouldn't have.

"He's back. Michael Flanagan is back."

Hope's quick intake of breath nearly

choked her. Impossible. Michael said he'd be gone six or seven weeks. It was less than four. Knees weak, she dropped down beside Gracie.

"He's out at his old place. Old Man Wallace saw him ride in yester's eve with a wagon all loaded down like he was plannin' to stay. So Mr. Wallace took it on hisself to drop by this mornin', pay him a visit. And would you believe? Michael Flanagan has up an' bought his old place again."

Gracie elbowed Hope. "Sounds to me like he's back an' he's diggin' in. And there's only one reason, or should I say, one *person* he'd ever want to live here for."

"Quit grinnin', Gracie," Liza scolded. "This is not funny. This is very serious. Can't y'all see all the trouble a-brewin'?"

But Hope could hardly contain her joy. All those lonely, neglected years as Ezra's wife were as good as forgotten, because Michael had returned. For her. Just as he said he would. She bent down to her basket on the pretext of rummaging through for some interesting scraps of fabric until she could calm the exultation that surely must show on her face. He hadn't merely returned; he'd come to stay. She would not be required to leave her lifelong friends, her family, or her church after all.

After restoring her composure, Hope rose from her basket. "Better get back to work, ladies. Time's a-wastin'." Still, she couldn't keep herself from glancing out the window, on the chance that Michael might be out on the street this very minute.

When she saw that he wasn't, the white-washed church building caught her attention. Certainly Michael would be there Sunday — even if his only reason for coming to a house of God was to see her.

That last plaguing thought tempered her joy.

Chapter Thirteen

Michael Flanagan rode into town two hours before any of the other folks would be coming in for Sunday service and reined Ebony around to the rear of the Bremmer place. It wasn't that he was afraid to encounter the neighbors, he justified as he strode to the back steps — he'd just prefer his first public appearance since purchasing the farm to be in the company of friends and, hopefully, supporters of his cause.

Besides, he figured he had some explaining to do.

He heard talking in the kitchen, but before raising a gloved hand to knock, he straightened the fall of his uniform coat. Wearing his military attire had been another deliberate act. Until he made a final decision about whether to reenlist or not, he still considered himself in the army.

Or had he worn it as an extra layer of protection? To a degree, he did feel duplicitous. When he'd parted from the Bremmers almost a month ago, he hadn't actually stated that he'd be returning — implied, maybe, but never actually said the words.

Filling his lungs with nippy May morning air, he knocked.

"Come in!" Max yelled along with a couple of his young boys.

Removing his braided blue hat, Michael did as they bade, walking into a warm, cozy hearth room filled with the smell of bacon and freshly brewed coffee.

Looking surprised, Max sprang up from the big kitchen table and extended a hand. "Sorry, we thought you were one of the neighbor kids." He did look pleased to see Michael, and so did the rest of his family.

"I just wanted to drop by to let you know I've returned. I didn't want to spring myself on you sudden-like by just showin' up at church." He nodded a greeting at Belinda, then broke into a grin of his own. "I see you and your family have been blessed by another little visitor."

Belinda sat to the side of Max with a tiny baby nested beneath her chin, patting its back. "Yes, we have. A new baby and a new neighbor, it would seem. We were mighty surprised to hear you've taken up residence at your old place."

"I vasn't." Brother Rolf, in a stiff-collared white shirt, lumbered up from his chair at

the far end. He offered a rough and cal-
loused hand. "Pleased ve are to haf you for a
neighbor."

Michael hoped the minister's words were
sincere.

"Sit down, Michael," Belinda urged.
"Take my seat." Handing the baby to Max,
she rose and picked up her used dishes and
three-year-old Inga's beside her. "I was just
about to take the children up to get them
ready for church. Have you had your breakfast yet?"

"Yes, ma'am," he said, taking her place.

"You will have a cup of coffee, though."
Placing the dishes in a water-filled pan on
the drainboard, she hooked her finger
through a mug on the shelf above and set it
before Michael as Max passed the blackened coffeepot to him. She eyed her three
older sons across the table. "Boys, stop your
dawdling. Put your plates in the dishpan
like I told you and get on upstairs."

"Aw, Ma," Rolfie, the oldest, complained. "Sergeant Flanagan just got here."

"Up, boys," Max ordered gruffly. "The
sooner you're dressed, the more time you'll
have to pester the poor man."

Brother Rolf lifted his black frock coat off
the back of his chair. "Is time I go over *und*
start da fire in da church stove. *Und* check

189

mine sermon notes." Walking past, he clapped a hand on Michael's shoulder. "You stay for Sunday dinner. Ve haf nice talk."

Seconds later, Max and the baby were the only souls left in the room with Michael. "Well, I sure can clear a room in smart order."

"Yep, looks like it's just you and me and Michael James here," Max said, moving the sleeping babe to his other arm.

"So, it's a boy. And did you say his name is Michael James?"

"That is your name, isn't it?"

"Yes. Are you saying . . . ?"

"Well, you did get me home in time for the birth. But, let me tell you, Belinda has her babies so fast, I don't know why she even bothers to send for the midwife. Luckily Gracie and Hope were here at the time."

"She was — I mean, they were? What did they think of the idea of you namin' a baby after me?"

Max grinned. "Yes, Michael, Hope looked real pleased. From what Belinda says, she's been real closemouthed about you, but when Liza told the girls you were back, Belinda said she fairly glowed."

"She did?" That made Michael feel so

good he was sure a glow of his own was starting to show.

"I wouldn't get myself all worked up just yet." Max leveled a stern gaze on Michael. "You still got some mighty big mountains to climb hereabouts before you can even drop by her place without causin' a row."

"I know that."

"And what's this about you buying your old place back? You never mentioned nothing about that before you left. I thought you planned to stay in the military till you retired."

"That was the plan when I rode out, but I got to wonderin' if an army fort was the best place for a wife and family."

"The wife being Hope?" Leaning away from the tiny bundle, Max took a sip of coffee.

"That's right." Michael wrapped his hands around his own cup and eyed Max. "I plan to marry her, no matter how long it takes. No matter how many mountains I have to climb. Whether as a soldier or a civilian. I took a six-month leave to see how things go. And for Hope's sake, I'm going to do everything I can to establish a horse-breeding farm and regain her father's trust. I don't want her to have to give up everyone she loves in order to marry me."

"Do I take it, you two have some sort of an understanding?"

"We spoke briefly."

"I'm surprised she didn't mention it to Belinda. Well, good luck. I'll keep you in my daily prayers."

That disturbed Michael more than he wanted to admit, even to himself. Had Hope changed her mind?

Hope had been sitting in the back of the wagon with Timmy for a good ten minutes before Titus and Tilly came out of the house. As anxious as she was to get to church this morning, they seemed just the opposite. But then, Hope had little doubt they knew Michael had returned to the valley. They'd probably found out even before she did, since Joel had interrupted her sewing circle to fetch her home on Friday. He'd said Ma Tilly wasn't feeling well, yet Joel was the one who'd looked feverish, agitated. After that, a lot of nervous glances had passed between him and his parents, a lot of sudden silences whenever she walked into the room.

Hope realized now how unwise she'd been by not making her position clear from the start. All the excuses she'd given herself about waiting for the right moment, waiting until the fields were planted, were just so many cowardly delays on her part. She already had a note prepared to give to Michael, asking his forgiveness for procrastinating instead of preparing the way for him. Today, once she and the Underwoods returned home from church, she would show them Ezra's letter and tell them what was in her heart.

Even so, just the thought of the hurt she would cause Titus and Tilly made her chest tighten. And Joel? As a youngster, he'd always been quicker to fight, even, than to laugh. There was simply no telling what he would do.

As Titus half lifted and half pushed Tilly to the driver's seat, the sweet woman gave Hope an apologetic smile. "Sorry I'm late," she said, straightening her skirts, then the gray-feathered bonnet on her head. "These ol' bones just didn't want to move this mornin'."

"I think we'll still make it on time," Hope assured her, then swung her attention to her son standing near the rear of the bed. "Timmy, stop runnin' your hand across the wheel. You'll get yourself all dirty."

He shot her an impish grin. "I not dirty." He wiped his palms down his blue plaid trousers before she could stop him, then held them out for inspection. "See?"

"Where's Joel?" Titus grunted out as he painfully hoisted himself up to sit beside his wife.

"Barn," Timmy answered for his mother and pointed in that direction.

At that moment, Joel strode out the wide doors, his rusty brows shelved over his eyes, looking as grim as the day Michael brought Ezra's packet to their home. He carried a long rifle with a powder horn dangling from its barrel.

"What's that for?" Titus demanded as Joel came toward them. "You ain't goin' huntin'. You're goin' to church."

Joel cocked his gaze toward Hope, then shoved the rifle onto the floorboard of the driver's seat. "Heard there was wolves on the prowl."

Titus snorted. "Ain't been no wolves hereabouts for twenty years."

Muscles bunching beneath his jacket, Joel vaulted effortlessly onto the seat. "You never know."

As he unwrapped the reins from the brake stick, Hope realized she'd been underestimating Joel, still seeing him as merely Ezra's kid brother, someone to be handled. The truth was, he was a fully grown, powerfully built man.

Fear for Michael's safety took hold of her. Her first instinct was to tell Joel to put the rifle away or she wouldn't go. But she realized that was exactly what he wanted, to cow her into submission. To keep her from Michael. She fiddled with the chin bow of her black bonnet to cover her fear.

Joel slapped the reins over the team's backs, and the wagon jerked forward.

Jarred into remembering that they were on their way to the Lord's house, the house of the Prince of Peace and Almighty Power, Hope recalled the years of Brother Rolf's preaching that to walk in fear was to deny the sovereignty of the Lord. She searched her mind for some verse she'd memorized as a schoolgirl that would help her face this day.

Finally one came that she knew she could latch on to. Slowly, silently, she mouthed the words from Psalm 91 to herself. *"I will say of the Lord, He is my refuge, and my fortress: my God; in him will I trust. Surely he shall deliver thee from the snare of the fowler, and from the noisome pestilence. He shall cover thee with his feathers, and under his wings shalt thou trust: his truth shall be thy shield and buckler."*

She repeated them many times on the road to church, praying that Jesus truly would be Michael's shield and defender on this day.

A half mile from town, Hope heard the distant church bell clang several times, calling people to worship. Then it ceased.

As she and the Underwoods drove into the parking area, it was empty of people. Obviously, they were the only latecomers. Hope wasn't surprised. Everyone else in the valley would know that Michael Flanagan had returned, giving this day the excitement of uncertainty.

Leaving the rifle where it lay, Joel hopped down, came to the back of the wagon, and helped Hope and her son off. With Timmy propped on one of his arms and a hand at her elbow, he wasted no time leading them up to the entrance.

The final strains of a congregational hymn beckoned them with, "O god, our help in ages past, Our hope for years to come; Be Thou our guide while life shall last, And our eternal home."

Hope sang, "Amen," along with those inside, ardently praying the Almighty would guard them all today.

Joel held the door open for her, and she entered in the lull.

People turned to watch them as they

started down the aisle. Their movement was accompanied by a hum of whispers.

Hope was again the center of speculation, but her eyes had their own search to make. Almost instantly, her gaze landed on a coat of military blue. He was present, not ten yards ahead of her, as she allowed Joel to usher her into the Underwood family pew. Whatever else happened today, Michael truly had come back.

On the dais, Brother Rolf rose from his chair with an open Bible in his hand. "Goot morning to you all. I am reading dis morning from Colossians t'ree, twelve to seventeen." Placing the big book on the unadorned pulpit before him, he began in his guttural voice. "Put on derefore, as the elect of God, holy and beloved, bowels of mercies, kindness, humbleness of mind, meekness, longsuffering: Forbearing one another, and forgiving one another, if any man have a quarrel against any: even as Christ forgave you, so also do ye . . ."

As Brother Rolf continued, Hope knew exactly why he'd picked that particular passage: he was making a plea to the people of this valley to be kind to Michael. She made her own silent plea that Joel would listen to those holy words and be convicted. But from the tension she glimpsed in his jaw, the hardness of his mouth, she doubted it.

Up front, Michael seemed quite unconcerned as he sat between Max and the Bremmers' oldest boy.

Taking her cue from him, Hope settled comfortably against the back of the long bench. Surely the Lord hadn't brought Michael back only to have him killed because of her.

Timmy, standing on the seat beside her, leaned close and started blowing on the short black feather tucked in the band of her rounded bonnet. Giggling out loud, he reached for it.

She caught his hand, then put her index finger to his lips. Opening her drawstring purse, she withdrew a top-knotted cluster of undyed yarn strands that she'd braided partway down their length. Sitting Timmy beside her, she demonstrated how to weave sections one over the other. Then she laid the ends across his lap, fervently hoping his attempts at plaiting would keep him busy and allow her to concentrate on Brother Rolf's sermon.

But neither her mind nor her gaze would depart from Michael for long, as unbidden, unwanted questions resurfaced. Was Michael listening to Brother Rolf's words with a true and believing heart? Would he have chosen to come to the Lord's house today even if she hadn't been expected?

And there was still the matter of the rifle in the wagon.

Chapter Fourteen

At the conclusion of the church service, Joel wasted no time scooping Timmy up and catching hold of Hope's hand. His thumb pressed painfully into her flesh as he turned to drag her out.

Tilly's slow rise from her seat blocked Joel's path. "Oh, dear," Hope's mother-in-law said while struggling to bend down between the pews. "I dropped my purse."

"Move, Ma," Joel ordered impatiently. "I'll fetch it for you." He stood Timothy on the seat and stooped to look for it.

Timmy took that chance to escape by running along the empty pew bench to the aisle. Wishing there was room for her to do the same, Hope took the opportunity to search out Michael. Her attention was caught, though, by Titus. Instead of leaving his end seat for the entry doors, he worked his way toward the front, past those exiting.

"Ma, I don't see no purse," Joel said, craning his neck up at her.

"I'm sure I brought it." But Tilly's voice

sounded doubtful as she shot a guilty glance toward her husband, drawing Hope's attention to him again.

Titus now stood talking to Hope's much taller father — Tilly had deliberately delayed Joel for her husband. Hope could think of any number of reasons why Joel should be slowed up, but which one had led Titus to her father?

Noah shot a glance to where Hope stood.

"Well, Ma," Joel said, rising to his full height and blocking Hope's view. "You must be gettin' addlepated. Now, move along. I wanna get outta here." He caught hold of Hope's arm.

On Hope's part, she couldn't think of anywhere she might step that wasn't wrought with conflict . . . conflict she'd allowed to escalate. If only she'd confronted the Underwoods and her father from the start.

But, she defended, her own thoughts hadn't always been clear, bouncing back and forth like a rubber ball. The only thing she knew for sure was that she wanted to speak to Michael. Joel's rifle in the wagon and the threat it represented prevented her from exacerbating the situation by going to him. She took one quick look at Michael standing in the front with Max and Belinda, then let Joel pull her away.

With Joel walking directly behind her exceptionally slow mother-in-law, Hope finally reached the front doors and Brother Rolf. She jerked away from Joel and grabbed hold of the pastor's big strong hand as if it could somehow bring her into a safe haven. "Brother Rolf, if you have time, I'd like to drop by and speak with you one day this week."

His old blue eyes warmed with a wise smile. "You know you are velcome anytime. Until den, know dat God is *mit* you."

The dear man's words did enfold her like a cozy blanket on a cold day. She walked out into the pleasant sunshine, reminded that God, who knew all her weaknesses and faults, still loved her and would not forsake her.

Her calm lasted only until she reached the steps and saw that Joel had left her far behind. He hurried past those ahead of him, briskly walking toward the family's wagon.

The rifle.

Hope lifted the hem of her widow's skirt and raced down the steps. Reaching the bottom, she spotted her father moving fast, closing in on Joel. The still formidable man stepped in front of Joel, blocking his path. She stopped and watched, a little relieved, as he took Joel by the arm and forcibly led him toward some maples behind the parking area.

"Your pa'll settle him down."

Hope saw that her mother-in-law had come alongside her.

Tilly took Hope's hand in her pale and shaky one and patted it. "Put on a smile. Here comes your mama."

Lovely in a finely woven jacket and skirt of silver gray, Hope's mother joined them, her pale eyes showing concern. She took Hope's face into her kid-gloved hands and pecked her cheek. "I know today must be incredibly difficult for you."

That brought the threat of tears, and tears were the last thing Hope wanted the overly observant congregation to see.

"You're not to worry anymore. Titus just invited your father and me over for dinner this afternoon. And while we're there, I promise you, we're going to sort through this troubling complication and make sense of it."

Hope knew very well the sense her father wanted to make of it . . . of her entire life. But she'd reserve her comments until they'd left her curious neighbors behind. "If you two will excuse me, I need to talk to Howie's pa about making my Timmy a new pair of shoes. He's growin' so fast."

Scanning the milling churchgoers for Baxter Clay, the cobbler, her gaze found Michael first and paused. He did look splendid in his blue uniform coat and white trousers as he came down the church steps with Max.

Their eyes met, and he started toward her.

The situation was much too volatile. As unobtrusively as possible, Hope held a hand up in front of her to stop him.

He understood immediately and veered toward a gathering of three returned militiamen.

Knowing he would be welcomed by them, she relaxed slightly. But not for long. Crossing the grassy churchyard in the direction of where the elder Clays stood with Gracie and Howie, every soul she passed slid a glance her way.

Upon reaching the Clays, Hope was grateful for their welcoming smiles and greetings, though Baxter's didn't seem quite so friendly. But naturally, he would judge her dilemma from her father's point of view. Aside from being Gracie's father-in-law, the dark-eyed man with graying umber hair had been close friends with Noah for years.

His Dutch-looking wife, though, reached out and pulled Hope into a spontaneous hug and whispered in her ear. "Don't fret, darling girl. God is seeing you through."

Hope knew Sabina spoke from experience. When she first came to live with the Clays, the Lord had seen her through some of her own harrowing moments. Hope kissed her rosy cheek. "Thank you." She then turned to Mr. Clay. "Timmy's shoes are already too tight. I was wonderin' if you could size his feet today and have a pair made for him in the next week or so."

"Sure thing." The thin-built man's expression was more jovial now, more like what one would expect of the father of Howie. He glanced around. "Where is your little whirlwind?"

"He's playing on the Smiths' wagon," Sabina answered in Hope's stead. "Can't miss that blue plaid suit. I'll fetch him, Baxter, and bring him over to our wagon." Taking over Hope's duty as if she knew Hope had other business to tend, Sabina took her husband's arm and strolled away, leaving Hope alone with Gracie and Howie.

"We're havin' a gathering at our place Saturday night," Howie said, chipper as ever, despite the fact he favored his injured foot and pulled at his stiffly starched stand-up collar. "Considerin' the differences of opinion round about, we've decided to just invite the returnin' heroes and their wives or sweethearts." His brown eyes sparked with mischief. "You, of course, are invited, you bein' both a hero's wife and one's sweetheart."

"Howie, you seem to forget," she scolded, "I'm still in my mourning period. I probably shouldn't come."

"Of course you should," Gracie said. "I'm sure the men will want to say a few words to commemorate Ezra."

Howie bent closer. "And Michael will be there."

Obviously, Howie wasn't aware of the gravity of her situation. Hope glanced back to where Noah and Joel stood and saw that Titus and her Uncle Ike had joined them. Between the three of them, they would be able to handle Joel . . . for the moment.

She pulled a folded scrap of paper from her pocket — the note she'd written. "I need for one of you to get this to Michael. It's best that I don't hand it to him myself."

"Why not?" Gracie's voice rang with disappointment. "You've just gotta take a stand, Hope. I *know* you're still in love with him. Simply walk over and talk to him."

"Please, keep your voice down. There's

206

already enough trouble brewin' without me causin' more. Joel brought his rifle. He has it in his mind to shoot Michael."

Howie stiffened. "That scoundrel." Instantly alert, he quickly scanned the milling people.

Hope caught his arm. "Everything's under control. Papa and Uncle Ike are seein' to Joel." Feeling the muscle in Howie's upper arm relax, she turned to Gracie. "But you're right. I am gonna take a stand. Mama and Papa are comin' for dinner today, and I'm going to tell all of them together it is my intent to marry Michael once my period of mourning is past . . . if he still wants me." Merely talking about confronting both sides of her family at once turned her legs to mush.

"Good girl." Gracie wrapped an arm around Hope. "You're shakin'. Now, see here. I know it's scary, but you can do it."

"Pray for me."

"All the way home, dear sister. All the way home." Gracie gave Hope's shoulder a final squeeze. "Now, give me that note. I'll see Michael gets it before he starts gettin' itchy and does somethin' stupid."

As Hope deftly slipped the scrap into Gracie's hand, her sister cocked a smile. "It is a love note, isn't it?"

★ ★ ★

"My favorite time of da year," Brother Rolf said as he strolled leisurely up the walk of the Bremmer home with Michael and Max. As usual, he was the last to leave the church grounds after Sunday service. "Everyt'ing is green again *und* da vindow boxes is starting to bloom *mit* da petunias. Max, he knows to marry a *fräulein* dat loves flowers like mine Inga did."

"That's right, Pops," Max laughed as they stepped up to the wide and shaded front porch. "I married Belinda for her flowers. And speaking of my lovely wife, I'd better go see if I can lend her a hand, what with the new baby and all."

Michael took one longing glance up the north road, where Hope had disappeared several minutes ago, flanked by the Underwoods and the Reardons, then turned back to Max. "I can help, too. I know my way around a kitchen."

"No, you keep Pops company out here where it's cool — which reminds me. Before the hot weather sets in this year, I'm determined to build us a summer kitchen."

"I'd be glad to help you with it," Michael said. "Help pay you good folks back for all your kindnesses to me."

Max latched on to the door handle.

208

"Don't think I won't take you up on it. And from the way this day is heating up, it won't be none too soon. Have a seat. I'll send one of the kids out with something cool to drink in a few minutes."

Passing between the long containers of flowers suspended at the windows and along the porch railing, Michael chose one of the weathered rockers at the shadiest end. He knew that Brother Rolf had gotten exactly what he wanted — time alone to question him. Even though the note Gracie had slipped into his hand earlier remained unread, Michael's resolve was such that whatever Hope had written would not change his answers to the minister in the least. He was wholly committed to seeing his plan through.

Still, he very much wished for an unwatched moment to read his beloved's words. The strain in her eyes this morning had been unmistakable, not to mention the hostile stares he'd received from many of her kin. He couldn't help but worry about her. But he knew he had to be patient, though his heart told him otherwise. That was the vow he made to himself, moment to moment.

Brother Rolf lowered his bulk into a wide, pillow-padded rocker across from him. "So, you bought back your papa's old place." His statement begged an answer.

"Yes, sir, that I did. But I never really thought of it as Pa's. Me an' my younger brothers put in all the work there, buildin' and plantin'. Pa only stopped by from time to time, just long enough to get things stirred up again, what with his cussin' an' braggin' an' schemin'." Too late Michael realized he'd let his anger toward his father spew forth in front of Brother Rolf.

"Hmm." The pastor rocked forward, steepling his fingers to his lips and holding Michael in the grip of his gaze. "Da bitterness *mit* your papa, it is still burning holes in your heart. You *und* me, ve talk about dis before."

"I remember," Michael said as calmly as his inner rebellion would allow. He refused to look away. "I also listened to every word of your sermon this morning. When you convince the good people of this valley to forgive my father and forget what he's done, then I will too." The tone of hatred in his voice was unmistakable.

A hint of a smile lifted the old man's heavy jowls at the challenge. He thrust out his thick wide hand. "I have your solemn word on dis?"

Michael gladly offered his own hand. "As

they say, charity begins at home."

If Brother Rolf would assist him in winning the trust of the folk hereabouts, clear a path for him and Hope, he would gladly forgive even Bantry Flanagan. Gladly.

Chapter Fifteen

On the entire ride home from church, Hope knew both her father and the Underwoods were of one mind and she another. Her mother, though, she wasn't sure of. Jessica had always sympathized with Hope during the long years she'd waited for Michael. Still, when Noah and the Underwoods had concocted their plan to wed her to recently widowed Ezra, her mother had been the one to convince her that it was time to give up on Michael's promise to return and move on with her life.

While ladling chicken and dumplings into a large serving bowl from a footed pot at the Underwoods' hearth, Hope looked up at her mother.

Jessica stood at the worktable, all her attention apparently on slicing cheese and the German sausage she'd brought to supplement the meal that Hope had set to simmering on banked coals before leaving for church this morning. Tilly was doing her best just to set the table.

After the service, Hope's mother had seemed totally empathetic when she'd said they'd sort through the matter. But would she stand by Hope now, give Hope's feelings for Michael her respect and support?

Hope wished she could speak to her mother alone, to learn if she had an ally or not. But she couldn't very well ask Tilly to leave her own kitchen.

Then a disturbing realization surfaced. Jessica had told her after church that Titus had invited them to dinner only the moment before, yet her mother had brought food from home to add to the meal. What was this all about?

Placing the large crockery bowl on the table, Hope glanced out the back window.

Her father, Titus, and Joel stood near the Reardon wagon team, entertaining Timmy while they watered the horses from a couple of large buckets. Noah and Joel tossed her son back and forth. She couldn't hear, but it was obvious that the child was squealing with delight.

The men, however, as evidenced by the hard set of their expressions, were having a serious conversation. Hopefully they were reprimanding Joel for bringing a weapon to church.

"Looks like the food's all on," Tilly said.

Hope turned back to a room that was a bit too warm from the cook fire.

"Child," her mother-in-law continued while easing her old bones into an end chair, "if you'd pour some hot water in the teapot, I think we can call the menfolk in."

"I'll summon them." Her mother's English accent added an air of aristocracy to her words, and though tiny of stature, her elegant presence always drew notice. She placed the platter of cold cuts in the midst of the other serving dishes and walked to the door.

On the other hand, Hope wished she could disappear completely. Very soon now, she would have to muster the courage to tell them of her plans to marry Michael. Her hands began to tremble as she carried the hot water kettle to the teapot. How would she get through the meal hour, let alone try to eat, knowing the conversation that must take place at its end?

"Dinner!"

Hope jumped at her mother's yell out the back door.

"Hope," Tilly said, "you're spillin' the water."

Focusing on her task again, Hope gripped the pot handle tighter, taking more care. If she couldn't even manage her hands, how could she expect these people to take her seriously about managing her life?

"Dumplin's! Like dumplin's!" Timmy shouted as he rode Joel's shoulders into the house ahead of the older men.

Joel swung Timmy down into the tall child's chair and looped the strap around him, securing the tot as if he did it every day.

That was enough of a performance to refuel any of Hope's lost indignation and prop up her resolve. "Mama, why don't you sit by me?" she suggested. "And, Papa, you sit across, next to Joel."

Once everyone was settled with the elder Underwoods at each end, the tabletop separating Hope from her primary adversaries, Titus cleared his throat. "Shall we pray. We thank You, Father, for the food You have set before us to nourish our bodies and the food of Your Word You give us to nourish our souls. In Jesus' name we pray. Amen."

Hope raised her lashes to see her father and Joel staring across the table at her, both men looking quite congenial and proper in their starched shirts and cravats, as if they had nothing of import on their minds.

"Dear?" her mother said, holding the bowl of chicken dumplings out to Hope.

She quickly took it and filled hers and Timmy's plates, determined not to allow the men to distract her.

Unlike his mother, Timmy had no problem eating with gusto. He immediately began shoveling in his food, his fist clenched around a short-handled spoon.

Hope pretended to concentrate on her own meal by slathering butter on her bread and stirring honey into her tea as she tried to glean courage from the nearness of her mother next to her.

Noah glanced up from his food, swallowing the last of a bite. "Excellent dumplings."

"Hope's turnin' into a mighty fine cook," Tilly said, bragging on her. "What with me turnin' into my crippled-up ol' grandmammy, I don't know how we'd get by without her."

"Joel's been takin' hold real good lately, too," Titus added. "Becomin' a right smart farmer. Ain't that right, Hope?"

Instead of scolding Joel for his dangerous behavior this morning, he was trying to get her to compliment his son's extremely belated demonstrations of his manhood. She couldn't resist leveling a sharp barb. "You're right, Pa Titus. This spring Joel didn't slack off the way he always did before, leavin' most of the work to you."

"I also noticed," her father quickly

jumped in, his voice trying to sound encouraging, "the place is looking better than I've seen it in some time."

Refusing to be party to praising a grown man for doing what he should have done all along, Hope gave Timmy half her slice of buttered bread.

Joel spoke to Noah beside him. "You know that knoll back yonder I told you I was plannin' to clear this summer? I been thinkin' on buildin' me a new house right on top of it with the best of the logs. That way, when I walk outside of a mornin', I won't have no problem a'tall lookin' out over all I own." His gaze now encompassed Hope. Was he including her as part of his personal property?

Her ire building, Hope set down her fork and picked up her cup of tea. No sense trying to get even a first bite down, since the men had no intention of waiting till after dinner to have their say. From above the rim of her cup, she narrowed a stare first at Joel, then at her father.

Noah shifted in his seat; he at least had the decency to appear uncomfortable. He, too, laid down his fork. "I don't believe Joel has mentioned anything to you about him coming by our place Friday afternoon."

"Friday?" Her sewing afternoon at

Belinda's? The day she learned Michael had returned? Hope shot a glance to Joel. "You mean the same day you came for me at the Bremmers' sayin' I had to come home at once because Ma Tilly was sick?"

A flush tinged Joel's freckled face.

"I reckon she couldn't have been all that sick," Hope continued, disgusted that he'd lied to her the other day, "if you felt you could ride all the way down to my folks' place for a little chat before fetchin' me and Timmy home." She shook her head, then took a sip of her tea.

"I don't know what's going on between you two kids this afternoon," Noah stated with fatherly authority as he looked from one to the other. "You can sort that out later. Your mother and I have come here today to tell you that Joel came to us like a proper gentleman, seeking your hand in marriage."

Hope gasped, choking on her tea, then erupted into a fit of coughing.

Her mother slapped her on the back until the episode began to subside.

"I see we caught you by surprise," her father went on as everyone else at the table continued to gawk at her. "But I want you to know that Joel says he loves you with all his heart, and that he'll provide for you and be a good father to Timmy."

"Better than Ezra ever thought of bein'," Joel blurted. Realizing what he'd just said, he shot a guilty glance at each of his parents.

"Yes, well . . . ," Noah demurred, then continued. "I have given my blessing. It seems the most sensible thing all the way around." He looked at the others, seeking support. "We all do."

Hope turned to her mother in disbelief. "You, too, Mama? *Et tu?*"

Jessica gave her a weak smile. "It did seem quite reasonable . . . and Joel did sound quite sincere when he confessed his love for you."

Rising slowly, deliberately, from her chair, Hope's gaze scanned those at the table, then settled on her father. "Was this plan hatched before or after you learned of Sergeant Flanagan's return this week? Or need I bother to ask?"

Noah's lean graying features hardened. "Daughter, you are a grown woman now, with a child to consider, and —"

His words were cut short as Hope spun away. "No. Not this time." And out the back door she slammed.

"Sit down," she heard her mother-in-law's warbly voice say to someone inside. "Give the girl a few minutes to cool herself off."

They might be giving her a few minutes, Hope fumed as she stalked out to the barn, but she wasn't giving them another second. Reaching the interior of the barn, she unhooked her horse's bridle from a wall hook, went to Burns's stall, and slipped it over his ears.

After having dinner with the Bremmer family, Michael rode home. Entering the clearing surrounding his place, he reined his black mare to a stop, taking a moment to read the note from Hope. Encouraged, he looked with joy at his finer-boned broodmares in one pasture with their stallion and the four recently acquired draft-horse mares and their massively built stud. Over the past several years, he'd been picking his stock with a careful eye, trading for the best bone structure and muscle tone his savings could afford. He patted Ebony on the neck, watching the horses swish their long tails and toss their manes as they gazed back at him.

"Don't they look beautiful, girl, against the green grass?" One day soon, he'd bring Hope here and show his herd to her. From her note, he knew she was still as sincere about wanting to be with him as he was with her. "Maybe she can direct me on what I could do to make the house more livable, too."

He glanced across the meadow to the simple two-story cabin . . . and spotted a two-wheeled shay in front.

Hope? His heart started pounding crazily.

But just for a second.

He identified the small carriage and bay hitched to it. Noah Reardon's. Michael searched the porch, the barnyard, yet saw no one.

Nudging Ebony into a slow pace, he continued to scan his surroundings, not the least keen on being ambushed, especially without either his rifle or his pistol.

As he neared the house, Mr. Reardon stepped out his front door, followed by the shorter, curly headed Joel Underwood, Ezra's belligerent younger brother. Hope must have already told them she planned to marry him, and they'd come to confront him.

"Afternoon, gentlemen." Michael made a point of not betraying any emotion in his tone or expression. "Sorry I wasn't here to greet you. I was havin' dinner at the Bremmers'."

"Afternoon," Reardon returned from the porch landing. "I see you've brought some fine-looking stock with you."

"Yes, sir. I think they'll make a fine start. Did you find what you needed in my house?" Michael asked, hoping to put them on the defensive.

"Just checking," Hope's father said, seemingly unruffled. "In case you didn't hear our knock. Your place is spartan, but quite neat."

The man had actually complimented him. "I like things tidy."

"If you did, you wouldn't have come here to live."

Reardon strode down the steps, which now gave Michael a clear view of the man speaking — Joel. A rifle dangled dangerously from one hand.

"Out huntin', are ya?" Michael asked, though he doubted it.

Joel's rusty brows ridged over his narrowed eyes, his expression one of pure hatred.

Michael stared back, immensely aware of his distinct disadvantage. Joel stood between him and his own weapons in the house. Silently, Michael vowed never to leave the place again without one, even to go to church. If he survived today.

"The last time we spoke," Reardon said, climbing up on his wagon, "you said you were leaving the valley."

"That's right." Determined not to appear concerned, Michael dismounted. "I left and now I've returned."

"You do know that everyone in the valley is going to be watching you." Reardon glanced past Michael to Joel. "Come on. Time's a-wasting."

Underwood started down the steps, then halted and looked at Mr. Reardon. "We can't just ride outta here." He then targeted Michael, the knuckles of his hands white as he brought the barrel of the weapon up, level with Michael's chest. "Where's Hope, soldier boy? Where you got her hid?"

"She's gone?" Despite the fact that Joel held a rifle on him, Michael took a step forward. She'd run away from them? His concern rose, wondering what had taken place at the Underwoods' today.

"Joel." Reardon's tone brooked no argument. "Climb on up here. *Now.* Most likely she's gone to visit Gracie. I'll drop by on the way home."

Young Underwood glared at Michael, a vein popping to the surface of his forehead, his desire to put a bullet in Michael obviously doing battle with Mr. Reardon's prudence. Michael remained still, not allowing any fear to show. Finally, Joel growled something unintelligible and trotted down the remaining steps and out to the wagon.

As Michael watched the two drive away and disappear into the woods, tenuous feelings of victory began to swell in his chest. Hope no doubt had followed through with what she wrote in her note — she had informed those two that she planned to marry him.

At least, that was what he chose to believe.

He glanced toward the barn, scanned around the other outbuildings, and searched beyond to the woods.

But where was she?

Chapter Sixteen

Furious and deeply hurt, Hope rode the entire way to Gracie's, almost an hour from the Underwoods'. Gracie and Howie's log house sat near the road that bisected the southern half of the valley. In the shade of maples and hickories, it faced Delia and Jacob's on the other side . . . within easy hollering distance.

As Hope approached, seeing again how close her sister and their dearest friends lived to each other, she felt all the sorrier for herself — more than she ever had since she left her parents' home, the one that sat just across Delia's back field — for marrying Ezra.

Both sets of young children romped and played between the two houses, just as she and the entire Reardon clan had when they were young. Her mood grew more morbid by the second as she thought of her own small son, who had no other children to play with and was left to entertain himself.

The youngsters saw her ride in and ran

toward her, waving and announcing her arrival in loud shouts.

Hope spotted Howie sitting on Jake's front porch with her tall blond cousin, who had always been on the serious side.

Jake did have a friendly smile, though, upon greeting her. "Hope, I didn't know you was droppin' by. Delia is over to the other place with Gracie, helpin' her with the dinner dishes."

Howie, his still-recovering foot shoeless and thrust out before him, leaned forward in his chair. "Don't forget about Saturday night."

She did her best to find a smile and a wave for him as she guided her gelding, Burns, past the children, none of whom were older than eight. Halting the horse in front of Gracie's log house, Hope slid off his back, an easy move since she hadn't taken the time to saddle him.

"Where's Timmy?" Delia's three-year-old son asked, looking up with those rich brown Clay eyes.

"Sorry, Kurt. Next time. I'll bring him next time. I promise."

As she started up the steps, the door swung open and Gracie stepped out, wiping her hands. No smile lightened her features, only concern. "Come in, little sister. Are you all right?" Gracie instinctively knew something was wrong.

Hope drew in a breath, willing herself not to cry, willing herself not to run into her sister's arms with the men and children watching. "No," she barely managed as Gracie moved aside for her to enter.

A mingling of food aromas greeted Hope, reminding her that the two friends always shared the chore of Sunday dinner.

Delia stood at the drainboard, drying a plate, her expression as empathetic as Gracie's. "You look like you could use a cup of tea." She tossed her muslin towel over the remaining dishes. "Sit down. I'll fix us some."

"Yes, do that, Delia." Gracie motioned Hope to a finely crafted birch dining chair near the hearth end of the large room and took one directly across from her. "Something's gone terribly wrong or you wouldn't be here. I take it no one was real pleased about Michael comin' back."

"Actually, the subject scarcely came up."

"But Gracie said —" Delia broke off speaking while pouring hot water into a blue-and-white porcelain teapot and shot a glance at Gracie.

"Papa had something else he wanted to drop on me." Hope turned to her sister.

"Did you and Delia know that Joel came down here Friday and asked Papa to give me to him in marriage?"

"No!" they both chorused, their mouths falling open.

"It gets worse. Papa said yes."

"He can't do that," Delia retorted, bringing the teapot from the worktable. "Aside from the fact that you're a grown woman with a child, you don't even live under his roof anymore. What on earth could he be thinkin'? That ain't like your pa."

"When it comes to keepin' me from Michael it is. And, of course, he made the pronouncement at the dinner table in front of Tilly and everyone."

Delia rested a hand on Hope's shoulder. "Here, dear," then placed a porcelain cup and saucer before her. "You've been havin' a hard time of it, ain'tcha? Ezra dyin', and now all this turmoil with Michael comin' back."

Hope couldn't help but be exasperated with straightlaced Delia sometimes. "Michael didn't just come back on a whim. Ezra sent him as a parting gift to me."

Gracie reached across, placing a hand over Hope's much smaller one. "Don't you think you're colorin' things a mite prettier than they purely are?"

"Not at all. Ezra was very specific in his last letter to me. The one Michael brought. He wanted to make amends for never bein' a husband to me."

"Don't say another word," Delia ordered, bringing two more cups from Gracie's birch china cabinet. "Not till I get there." She set one before Gracie and one for herself, then dropped into a chair.

Gracie poured. "Honey? Cream?"

"No." Hope picked up the fragile floral cup and took a sip of soothing India tea. While Gracie filled Delia's cup and her own, Hope continued. "In the packet Michael delivered, there was a letter addressed to me. Ezra wrote about the fact that he was dying, but that I shouldn't be sad because he would be with his Becky again, and he hoped his gift to me would make me just as happy. His gift, he said, was the messenger."

Delia gasped.

But not Gracie, her lips melted into a tender grin. "How sweet." Then, unexpectedly, she frowned. "Why haven't you mentioned this before?"

"When? We haven't had a single private moment since the packet arrived."

"At sewing circle, you could've told us

there the very next week," Delia pointed out.

Hope turned to her cousin's wife. "If you recall, Liza was too busy tellin' us all how scared she was of havin' her place set on fire. And then Belinda went into labor."

"And," Gracie contributed, "we didn't have circle durin' plantin'."

"Last Friday I planned to tell you. But again Liza came busting in, this time with the news that Michael was back, and all the rest of the silliness she spewed about fires breakin' out everywhere. And, well, I simply didn't want to . . . to cast my own private pearls out for her to trample underfoot. The letter from Ezra was too precious a gift."

Delia's expression crumpled at Hope's last words. "Ezra and Becky . . . it's hard to believe they're both gone."

"I know." With an empathetic smile, Hope touched Delia's cheek. She then took a breath. "I have much more to tell you. Michael and I met just before he left last month. He told me he never forgot about us and that he still loves me. He wants to marry me as much as he ever did."

"If that's so, then why didn't he come back years ago?" Gracie asked, a pinch of anger in her tone.

"You have to remember, because Papa never gave me his letters, I never had any to answer. Then when Michael's father was tried and hanged, that sort of put an end to his dreaming. He couldn't believe I'd still want to marry into such a family."

"He had a point," practical Delia said. "From what I heard about the rest of his family . . ." She raised a dark brow. "From what I could see, he was the only one of that bunch that was tryin' to better himself." Her expressive features softened into a smile. "And I think that was because of you."

"Maybe, partly. But Michael was full of integrity — and kindness — from the first day I met him. He was always appalled by the things his pa did."

Gracie leaned forward. "That's fine, Hope, but I'm interested in the here and now. When Michael said he wanted to marry you, what was your answer?"

Hope chuckled, a bit self-conscious. "Well, yes, of course. But —"

Startling Hope, Gracie came out of her chair and grabbed both of Hope's hands. "I'm so happy for you. And he's bought his old place back so you won't have to ever leave us." Then her golden blonde features turned solemn. She released Hope and returned to her seat. "But you've got Papa rantin' and ravin' and Joel threatenin' to kill Michael."

"There's more than that. My biggest problem is what to do about Tilly and Titus. It's about all she can do to get herself out of bed and dressed of a mornin'. And poor old Titus, he's gettin' slower by the day, too. I can't just leave them without knowin' they're bein' cared for. If you'll recall, the only reason Ezra and I even agreed to marry was so I could take up Tilly's chores and care for her."

"And as far as the Underwoods are concerned," Gracie chipped in, "you marryin' Joel is the perfect solution. You'd remain with them indefinitely."

Delia snorted. "That's all mighty noble, but Hope marryin' Joel? That's askin' too much. Like you, Hope, I'm not one bit fooled by his sudden spurt of industry. Besides, Titus and Tilly have other children. It should be their responsibility, not yours, to care for their parents."

"I reckon you've forgotten about the story of Ruth in the Bible," Hope reminded. "Ruth went with her mother-in-law and took care of her after her husband died."

"Yes, but Naomi didn't have anyone

else," Gracie countered, taking a sip of her tea.

"And she helped Ruth find a good upstandin' husband, too, not a *Joel.*"

"Delia, you can't blame Titus and Tilly for wantin' to believe the best of Joel. I can't tell you how many times they've bragged on him this last month for goin' out on his own and gettin' the fields planted."

"You gotta stop bein' so softhearted," Delia argued. "You need to get some letters off to Joel's older brothers and sister right away. I'm sure one of them will take in their folks. You really need to leave the Underwood place as soon as you can."

"If Papa and Uncle Ike had to stop Joel from shootin' Michael today, who knows what that scamp will try next," Gracie agreed.

"And you may have rejected his marriage offer today, but I doubt that'll stop him," Delia continued. "He's wanted you from the first day you walked into that house, and now that he thinks he has both families' blessings. . . . All I can say is, you better keep your bedroom door locked at night."

A chill ran through Hope. "I don't have a lock."

"Then you stop off at the Bremmers' on your way home," Gracie urged. "I'm sure they have a slide bolt or two on hand."

"While you're at it," Delia added, "it would be prudent, I think, to have Brother Rolf add his own message to the letters you'll be sendin' to Ezra's older brothers and sister. They'll put more stock in anything he writes."

"And in the meantime," Gracie said with her humor returning, "that note I gave Michael this mornin', was it to set up another meetin' between you two?"

"No, just to let him know I was finally going to tell the folks about our plans." Hope expelled a heavy breath. "But I didn't. Being the coward I am, I ran off."

Gracie squeezed her hand. "Your knowin' we're here to help however we can should make it easier now. So you listen to your big sister and do as I say. You and Brother Rolf get those letters written, then show Ezra's to Titus and Tilly and tell them what's in your heart. They're good people — they'll understand. Then on Saturday, you come early and help me get ready for the party, and just maybe —" her lips slid into a conspiratorial grin — "just maybe we can arrange for Michael to come early, too."

Hope used her time while traveling north across meadows and fields interspersed with woods to search for the right words to say to Brother Rolf. If she were persuasive enough, perhaps he'd not only write compelling letters to the Underwoods' older offspring, but support her cause by convincing Noah Reardon of how stubborn and wrongheaded he was being about Michael — had continued to be for a decade.

The thought of her father sitting at her noon table, telling one and all that she was to wed Joel, infused her with renewed rage. In every other area of his life, her father was kind and reasonable, but when it came to a Flanagan, he'd refused to budge since the night his gristmill burned.

No, before that. From the day Bantry Flanagan accused him of cheating, of having false scales for the weighing of grain, Noah's pride had taken over.

Her father had always been known for his honesty, even when he was lawyering, and when his integrity had been called into question, his resentment of Mr. Flanagan had spilled over to include the entire family. He had commanded her to have nothing more to do with any of the Flanagans, and he had added that Michael would no longer be welcome at their table.

As devastating as that decree had been, the next few days turned into a nightmare.

The Flanagan barn mysteriously burned to the ground. Bantry showed up at the church house the very next morning for his first and only time, accusing her father of setting the fire. He stood in front of the entire Sunday morning congregation and demanded that her father buy him out at a considerable profit.

And her father had. Gladly. Anything, he'd said, to get that lying dog and his whelps out of the valley, away from honest, God-fearing folk.

Bantry Flanagan made sure he had "the last say," though. On the night before Michael and his family were to leave, Michael had arranged a secret meeting with Hope in the woods behind the Reardon fields. And while they made their last tearful vows and promises, fire lit up the sky. The Reardons' gristmill had gone up in flames. And since Michael had been spotted on the road a short time later, he'd been blamed.

No matter how many times Hope told her father otherwise through the ensuing years, he'd never been fully swayed from his belief that Michael had sabotaged the mill out of spite.

Noah Reardon had been enraged when his own honesty had been placed in question by a relative stranger, yet he refused to believe the honesty of his own daughter, whom he'd known her entire life. To Hope, that was a far greater affront. He had betrayed the very person he should have known her to be.

Nearing the settlement, Hope topped a wooded knoll to see her parents coming toward her in their two-wheeled shay drawn by their bay. They were on their way home from the Underwoods'.

She tightened her grip on Burns's reins, her emotions swinging between betrayal and fury.

As they neared, Hope read empathy in her mother's expression, but her father sat tall on the seat beside her, as stony-faced as a statue.

She quelled a panicky impulse to gallop right by them. Straightening, she reminded herself she was a grown woman, not a child. Determined to ride past with dignity, she latched her gaze onto the church steeple in the distance.

Of course, there was nothing she could do about the crunching sounds of approaching horse hooves and wheels or the creak of the harness and shay springs.

Just as she moved her gelding to one side to pass, her father reined his horse across her path, blocking her progress.

She had no choice but to stop and face her parents.

"It was very childish of you," her father said in a matter-of-fact manner, "to run off like you did."

His statement added fuel to her fury. Gritting her teeth, she spoke with the same deadly calm. "When one treats another as if she were a mindless child, one should not expect an adultlike response."

Her mother quickly placed a stilling hand over her father's, then spoke to her. "Hope, dear, I really think the three of us need to sit down quietly and have a nice long talk."

"About what? The time for talking was *before* Papa blithely took it upon himself to usurp my life. *Again.* Do you have any inkling of how difficult it will be for me to live at the Underwoods' after this? Now, if you'll excuse me —" Hope guided Burns around their rig — "I have to go see about my future." Without a backward glance, she heeled her mount into a gallop.

Chapter Seventeen

"I see, I see." Brother Rolf nodded thoughtfully and sat back in his rocking chair on the Bremmers' front porch after Hope finished explaining the events that had taken place on this Sabbath Day. "I vas t'inking young Flanagan is da only one *mit* years of unforgiveness in da heart. But you, mine *kinder,* you are also keeping anger for your papa inside you for all dese years."

Hope shot to her feet. "Can you blame me? After what Papa's done to us? Is still trying to do. Think about it — he'd rather pass me off on lazy, selfish, quick-tempered Joel than allow me the chance for true happiness. And look at me. He didn't even have the decency to wait until I'm no longer in black."

Brother Rolf reached for her hand. "Sit down, Hope. Rest. Take some deep breaths. Your face, it is red as mine Inga's roses."

Feeling foolish, she did as he bade. Besides, she had some letters she still needed to convince him to write on her behalf.

Her minister sat back and rambled on. "I don't t'ink Michael has da hatred for your papa. His heart is much too full of malice for his own papa to haf room for yours. He blames Bantry Flanagan's evil deeds for turning everyone against him. *Und* so far vhen ve talk, Michael is not villing to give up his unforgiveness." Brother Rolf's bushy white brows dipped sternly. "So now I say dis to you, too. God is not listening to your prayers. *Und* as long as you are living outside of fellowship *mit* da Lord, I am not performing any vedding. First, you must go to your papa *und* forgive him. From da heart."

Why was she always the one expected to give in? Trying to remain calm, she asked, "Are you going to ask Papa to forgive me and Michael then? Even though there's *nothing* to forgive."

Brother Rolf surprised her by letting a long low chuckle rumble up from his massive chest. "Today it is your soul ve are talking about."

Hope studied her pastor a moment, then, despite all her indignation, made a supreme effort to comply. "Brother Rolf, I will do as you say. I will go to my father and forgive him." The words were out. She was committed. "But I also need something from

240

you. After today, it'll be too uncomfortable for me to stay with the Underwoods much longer, but both of them are getting weaker, and Tilly, in particular, is unable to care for herself. I intend to write their older children to ask them to make arrangements to either come back here to care for Titus and Tilly or take them to live with one of their families. I'd appreciate it if you'd also write three letters to send along with mine, explainin' the situation. Unless you have another idea."

Brother Rolf had kindly allowed Hope the use of his writing paper and ink to compose her half of the letters to the older Underwood children before she left his house. He'd also offered to send both their messages with the postman when he next stopped at Bailey's General Store.

While riding up the north lane to the Underwoods', Hope felt as if the day hadn't been a total disaster. Although she had yet to announce her intention to wed Michael once her mourning period ended, she'd at least taken care of the first step in making arrangements for Titus and Tilly.

But the bargain she'd made with Brother Rolf to forgive her father — speak the words to him — might very well be the hardest task

241

she would ever perform.

Father in heaven, I know I promised Brother Rolf, and I know Jesus forgave those who nailed His hands to the cross as well as those who ordered it done. She glanced up through the canopy of tree branches she passed beneath. *I do know this, Lord. I do.*

But her anger and resentment choked out every other thought whenever she considered her father. It even stole this quiet time when she would much rather daydream about Michael.

Halfheartedly she tried once more. *Lord, I don't know how to . . . I don't even want to ask You to . . . but would You please give me a love for Papa again? I ask this in the name of Your own sacrificially forgiving Son.* She'd made the request, said it out loud, and told herself to believe it would happen, though she knew it would take a miracle to change her feelings about him.

But God is a God of miracles, she reminded herself. *He is the giver of pure and unselfish love.*

At the thought, Hope pulled Burns to a halt beneath the shade of a gnarled and aged oak. Had the love she had for Michael been given to her by God? Or was it just her own selfish desire?

The almost imperceptible vibration caught her attention, and she glanced into the tangle of woods, guessing that the river cut through the forest not far to her left. It brought to mind a quiet half-moon cove that curved inland just south of the ferry dock . . . the spot where every new believer in Reardon Valley was baptized.

But none of the baptisms she'd witnessed over the years had meant as much to her as the day Michael had stepped into the water with Brother Rolf. She'd stood at the water's edge on a golden September afternoon, along with the entire congregation. The heat of the day warmed her even beneath an overhanging willow. . . .

Michael had never looked more hand-some than he did at that moment, with the sun streaming across his face, haloing his hair. The white cotton robe she'd made him for the momentous occasion shone brilliant against the emerald green swirl of waist-deep water, as did his straight white teeth as he smiled up to her. Only her.

His gaze reached all the way to her heart, tugging at her until her eyes blurred with tears.

For her, Michael, shy Michael, stood before all their neighbors, willing, even eager, to embrace the Lord they both worshiped.

Brother Rolf, in his full, richly accented voice, asked Michael the all-important questions, then buried Michael in the gently flowing water and brought him up again, symbolically resurrected into a new and eternal life.

"I introduce you all," Brother Rolf said, his heavy arm draped companionably across Michael's dripping shoulders, "to our new brother in Christ, Mr. Michael James Flanagan."

As the two waded toward shore, Hope forgot herself and slogged into the water to meet them. Her lavender skirts wet to the knees, she reached Michael and took both his hands into hers, gazing up into his golden eyes, unable to find the words to express her joy.

Michael had no such problem. "Now," he said quietly, for her ears only, "even death will not separate us. We'll be together for eternity."

"And it will happen!" Hope practically shouted, as much to convince herself as anything.

The cutoff to the Spencer place lay just ahead. A tremor coursed through her. The

Underwoods' lane would be next.

Dreading her return, she pulled her thoughts back to the day of Michael's baptism.

Afterward, she remembered, her family invited everyone to their place for a supper of cold meats and fresh apple pie to celebrate the momentous event. Normally the parents of a new child of Christ would have hosted the party, but the Flanagans had not even agreed to come to the baptism.

Papa, bless him, had stepped up to the mark for that occasion. The week before, when Michael had reluctantly admitted to her parents that his folks wouldn't be coming, Papa had clapped a hand around Michael's shoulder and said, "I want you to think of me and Mrs. Reardon as your godparents from now on."

Hope took a tear-clogged breath. That had meant so much to Michael back then . . . and to her.

The same love for her father she'd felt that long-ago day filled her now. Papa had always been such a dear before everything changed. Somehow she would have to cling to those earlier memories when she spoke to him. She trusted God to grant her, even now, a miraculous change of heart — her father's or her own.

The turnoff to the Underwood place came into view, and Burns eagerly veered toward it. Hope drew hard on the reins to halt him. She wasn't ready to face Joel and the Underwoods just yet.

Longingly, she gazed up the main road until it was lost at the top of a gentle rise. Knowing that it wasn't even a mile to Michael's place, everything in her yearned to go directly there to him.

She closed her eyes against the desire. Now was not the time. First she had to face her families with her decision.

Besides, the sun hung low, trimming the western hills. She needed to get home to Timmy.

Giving Burns his head, Hope allowed him to turn onto the cutoff, and moments later, she rode into the clearing and toward the barn. The lamps were already lit in the house, giving it a cozy glow on this spring evening. The place looked serene, peaceful.

Until Joel slammed out the door. Not bothering with the steps, he leaped off the porch, then took long strides, coming straight for her.

She refused to be intimidated by someone she used to teach at school. Sliding off the mount's back, she swung to face him.

He halted directly in front of her, too

close, his hands akimbo, his face flushed. "Where have you been?"

"I am not answerable to you." She side-stepped him. For all her bravado, she experienced a shiver of fear. And she'd just remembered that she'd forgotten to ask Brother Rolf about a bolt for her bedroom door.

He caught her arm. "As long as you're living under my roof you are."

She looked down at his hand, then up into his eyes. "You'd better be careful with your threats, unless you want to be left to do all the cookin' and cleanin' and washin' around here." Jerking free, she collected her horse's reins.

There was a stiff silence. Then, "Sorry." Joel actually sounded slightly mollified. "We was just plumb worried. You were gone so long. We was afraid somethin' happened to you."

"Mama! Mama!" Her baby boy came running as fast as his little legs would carry him. "You leave me." He flung himself into her waiting arms.

Scooping him up, she gave him a hug, then tossed him on the horse's back. "I just went over to your Aunt Gracie's for a while." She retrieved the reins and began leading Burns into the barn.

"You leave me!" her son complained more loudly. "I wanna go."

Although Hope didn't look behind her, she knew Joel followed. She made certain her next words were loud enough for him to hear. If he was going to protest, let him do it now. "Saturday. You may come with me Saturday. Gracie needs me to help her get ready for company."

"Goody, goody!" Timmy dove off the horse and into her arms, clinging to her with a stranglehold. "Yes'aday. We go yes'aday."

"No. In this many days." Peeling his fingers from her neck, she counted out the number on them.

Joel picked up the reins she'd again been obliged to drop. "Why don't you two go on in and get supper started? I'll put away your horse."

"Why, thank you." Surprised by his unexpected helpfulness, she stared after him as he walked Burns into the barn. Joel no longer seemed angry. Nor did he act the least like a rejected suitor.

An uneasiness overtook her.

The following morning, Hope served both men their breakfast. Titus ate his in the same stony silence as the night before. Joel, on the other hand, followed her every move with an unnerving smile. When they both went out the door to finish their chores, she was quite relieved. At least Joel still intended to work.

But now there was the matter of Ma Tilly, who had yet to come downstairs. Hope headed up to check on her mother-in-law, knowing she was as upset as Titus. Listening to Tilly trying to keep some sort of inane conversation going last night at the supper table had been almost too painful.

But this morning, Hope was determined to set matters right between them. Without knocking, she entered the room simply furnished with homemade furniture, patchwork quilts, and rag rugs. She found Tilly across in her rocker, staring out the window, tears streaming. The sight ripped at Hope's heart.

Quickly, Tilly wiped away the wetness. "My hands," she said, massaging her gnarled fingers, "is givin' me more trouble than usual."

Maybe so, but Hope knew the old woman had never before shed tears over a little pain. Moving to her side, Hope knelt beside her and took the worn-out hands into her own. "I think maybe the ache in your heart has found its way down to these."

"Think so?" Tilly's head drooped, and

her voice still had tears in it.

"I love you. You are my other mother. And I hope you think of me as your own true daughter."

Tilly looked up at her for the first time. "I do, I do."

"For always. Your very blood flows through my son's veins. And I want you to be assured of this — as long as I'm allowed to have a say, you and Titus will never want for anything."

With red-rimmed eyes, Tilly rested a hand on Hope's cheek. "You've always been a good girl."

Hope pulled the letter she'd received from Ezra out of her apron pocket and unfolded the thick paper. "I read you the missive Ezra sent to Timmy, and I think it's time I read the one he sent me."

"Only if you want to." Looking anxious, Tilly wrapped her bony fingers around the wooden rocker arms.

"I've wanted to since I received it. But the moment never seemed right."

Hope read slowly, giving Tilly time to absorb the news that Ezra had not been an ideal husband to Hope but that they could share the joy he had felt at the prospect of being reunited with Becky and their newborn.

Tears again ran down the old woman's tissue-thin cheeks.

Hope dabbed at them with the corner of her apron. "I love knowing that he's with Becky, too," she whispered softly. "She always was his one and only true love."

Tilly opened her mouth to protest.

"No, Ma," Hope said before Tilly had a chance to speak. "Ezra and I never loved one another that way. It's true — we were not the best of friends. But you needn't feel badly for me. Let me finish the letter. 'Tell Timmy I am looking forward to the day when I will see him again on the other side. And for you, Hope, . . . the messenger is my gift to you.' "

Tilly's thin brows crimped. "I don't understand. The messenger is a gift?"

Hope placed a hand over Tilly's nearest one. "He knew that Michael Flanagan was my one true love, as Becky is his. And in recompense Ezra sent him to me."

Her mother-in-law grew very still. Her gaze slid to the window again. "I see."

Staring at this old dear, Hope didn't think she did understand. "Because I hope to one day marry Michael doesn't make me love you any less. You're my Ma Tilly."

The old woman's worried gaze sought Hope again. "But Joel's countin' on marryin' you somethin' fierce. That's all he's talked about for weeks. Only the good Lord knows what he's gonna do now. You know the temper he's got when he don't get his way."

"Tell you what. Let's you and me make a pact. I won't go borrowin' trouble if you don't. It's months till my year of mourning is through. Let's just live one day at a time and let the Lord take care of the rest. And today, I say you need to come down and let me fry you some hotcakes. I made fresh strawberry syrup."

As she helped Tilly to her feet and out to the upstairs hall, Hope came face-to-face with Joel's bedroom door, which stood mere feet from hers.

How long, she wondered, would it take for one of Tilly's other children to answer her letters? How long before one of them would come and relieve her from living under the same roof with Joel?

Aware it could be weeks, a chill of apprehension ran the length of her spine. Last night she'd lodged a chair beneath the door latch. On her next trip into town, she had to buy that bolt.

Chapter Eighteen

Michael rode into town a little before noon on Saturday in a very good mood. Although he hadn't caught a glimpse of Hope since the prior Sunday, Howie had come by his place to inform him that she would be at their house several hours before the party . . . and if he was so inclined to also drop by early, he would be most welcome.

He smiled even now at Howie's understatement as he guided his mount to an empty space in front of Bailey's store. He had a few supplies to purchase before he saw Hope and all else was forgotten.

Dismounting, he noticed a movement on the porch of Hatfield's Saddlery across the street. In years past it had been the gathering place for the local men, especially on Saturdays, and from the number of young bucks lounging in the line of chairs and leaning on the posts, nothing had changed — except these fellows were taking inordinate interest in his arrival.

With a nod, he tipped his light gray civilian hat in their general direction. Considering this valley was several miles off the main road, he reckoned they didn't get too many new folks in town and rarely had new fodder for gossip.

Hopefully, the returning soldiers had put in a good word for him, displacing the past stories about his family — with the younger people, at any rate.

Among the sacks, barrels, and stacked crates inside the store, Michael caught sight of a young militiaman, Junior Smith. He stood at the back counter beside his father, Ken, the local wheelwright. Both men were as big and rawboned as Junior's older sister, Liza, was small and delicate. They were engaged in conversation with the proprietor, Mr. Bailey.

Michael noted that the storekeeper was getting on in years, though some copper color in his hair still showed through the gray. He had more girth beneath his work apron than Michael remembered, too. But the friendly smile he'd always had for everyone hadn't dimmed.

Junior must have sensed that someone had entered through the open doorway. He turned around, and upon recognizing Michael, both his cheeks dimpled in welcome as he hurried to the front. "Sergeant Flanagan. Heard you was back and settlin' in. How's it goin' out at your old place?"

Extending a hand, Michael shook the younger fellow's. "While I'm on leave, I'm just plain ol' Michael Flanagan. The farm has been neglected for quite a spell, so findin' somethin' to do ain't been hard."

"I know just what you mean." Sandy-haired Junior glanced back at his father. "I'll swan, but I think Pa went out of his way to save up jobs for me to do. Aside from havin' me fixin' a bunch of busted wheels an' axles, him and me built a whole wagon and a hay cart since I been home. And we still got a cabin to raise before my weddin' next month."

"So, you're gettin' married. Congratulations."

Junior's grin broadened until every tooth in his mouth showed. "Yes, sir. You are comin' to Howie's tonight, ain'tcha? I'll introduce you to Mary Jo then."

"I'd like that. And if you need help buildin' that cabin, just give me a holler."

"Thanks." Something out the doorway caught Junior's eye, and his buoyant expression flattened. "I heard some talk goin' around that a few no-account hotheads is thinkin' on tryin' to get rid of you. It probably won't amount to anything, but I'd keep my eyes open and my rifle loaded if I was you, livin' out there by your lonesome and all."

Michael glanced over his shoulder. The only people he saw were those same young yahoos over at the saddle shop.

Junior stepped closer. "If them boys over there start givin' you trouble, just give a holler. Every jack man what marched home with us'll come a-runnin'."

"That's good to know." He squeezed the young man's thickly muscled shoulder. "But I don't think it'll come to that." Still, Michael took a memorizing look at their faces. Perhaps he'd been wise to slip his pistol into his saddlebag.

As Hope rode south, with Timmy sitting in front of her happily jabbering, she no longer had any doubt that Joel was following her. Rounding a curve, she reined Burns in among the lower branches of a beech tree and waited no more than a few seconds before catching a glimpse of her brother-in-law riding into view about fifty yards behind her.

Amusement overtook her anger. He would sure be in for a surprise when she turned off at her parents' cutoff instead of traveling on to Gracie's. She wondered if he'd want to risk being caught spying by her father . . . to show himself for the sneak he really was.

"Burn tree! Burn tree!" Timmy bounced up and down upon spotting the old lightning-struck oak that marked the Reardon path. "Gramma, Grampa."

"That's right," she said, holding the excited tot more firmly. "We're goin' there first."

Riding through fields of young corn, they soon reached the large yard shared by three Reardon homes. Her youngest brother, Danny, came outside her parents' house to greet them. Coltish at eight, he'd inherited the long-boned Nordic looks similar to the rest of her siblings.

A big grin split his face as he ran out to meet them. He squinted up at them against the early afternoon sun. "Howdy. Didn't know you was comin' by. Timmy, I got me some pups. You wanna see 'em?"

Hope barely kept hold of her eager son as she lowered him to the ground and watched the two take off for the barn. Then, glancing back at the house, she wished she could be as glad to see her parents. But she must speak to them if she ever expected God to listen to her pleas.

She checked behind her to see if Joel had

followed her up the straight open path. Once she saw he hadn't, she dismounted, secured Burns to a post ring, and started for the door.

Her mother stood in the opening, wiping her hands on her apron. "I didn't expect a visit from you today, dear. I had planned to ride over to Gracie's to see you there."

"You did? Just as well I came by here first then. Is Papa around? I'd like to speak to him, too."

"He and Ike walked down to the gristmill after they ate." Her mother wore her hair in a neat bun at the nape of her slender neck, her gray-and-brown gingham dress looking equally tidy beneath the work apron. "They're inspecting all the parts in case they need to replace anything before the season starts."

"Probably just as well. You and I can talk first if you're not too busy."

"No, just finishing up the noon dishes. Come in. There's still coffee on the coals."

Hope lifted the hem of her own dreary black gown and mounted the steps. Walking into her family's large common room full of fine furnishings was a pleasant reminder that her mother's Baltimore relatives were prosperous merchants. They sent expensive gifts every year, most likely to atone for

Jessica's having been raised at wilderness trading posts and abused by her drunken, though educated, English father. Which reminded Hope . . .

"Mama," she said, taking a seat at the kitchen table, "if Papa had no problem marrying the daughter of a man given to lyin', cheatin', and drinkin', why can't he see that Michael is not like his father either?"

"Ly*ing,* cheat*ing,* and drink*ing,*" her mother corrected as she fetched the best cups from the china cabinet; her diction lessons had proved nearly useless over the years. She turned toward her daughter with fluted floral cups and saucers. "Darling, you know the story. He didn't allow himself to love me until he knew that God was truly in my heart."

She chuckled as she placed the dishes before Hope. "It is rather humorous. When your father first saved me from mine, I thought he was much too fine a person for me in my bearskin robe. Then when we reached my mother's people in Baltimore, he thought I came from much too fine a family for him. 'Tis fortunate for you we sorted through those misunderstandings. But as for your question, you must understand, fathers simply cannot be reasonable concerning their daughters. Noah still sees you as his tiniest of daughters in need of his fatherly protection." With a smile, she went to the hearth for the coffeepot.

"I know. And that's been the problem."

"I've been concerned about you this week," her mother said, returning with the blackened pot and a change of subject. "How have you fared at the Underwoods'?"

"It's getting a little less stilted with Titus and Tilly. I showed Tilly the letter I received from Ezra, and I think she's starting to accept the inevitable."

"Inevitable?" Her mother paused while pouring brew into Hope's cup.

"Yes. Ezra specifically sent Michael here to me."

Her mother straightened and studied Hope a moment. "That's very interesting." She took a seat at the end of the table. "Indeed."

"Joel, though, is an entirely different matter. Surprisingly, he's still doing his share of the chores, and he's still smiling at me all the time, as if he knows something I don't. He has started going visiting of an evening again though . . . which gives me a little time without the stress of having him around. But when he comes back he's cockier than ever. It's very unnerving." Hope shook her head. "I still can't believe

Papa would've ever considered him for a son-in-law."

"Yes, I know how immature Joel has been, but Noah's had a couple of long talks with him and felt that he'd grown up considerably and would provide a good Christian home for you and Timmy, particularly since Titus and Tilly are there to guide him."

That stiffened Hope's neck. "To begin with, Joel isn't remotely Christian. Every move he makes is only to further his own desires. I'm sure he told Papa whatever Papa wanted to hear. Michael, on the other hand, was the most honest and sincere young man I ever knew. And Papa's too stubborn to remember that. And worse, my father's known me my whole life and still doesn't trust that I have a brain in my head."

Her mother covered her hand. "Sweetheart, you have to believe your father truly feels your infatuation has always blinded you where Michael is concerned."

Suddenly remembering her mission, Hope took a calming breath and a sip of the burning-hot coffee as she recalled the words she'd rehearsed on the ride here. "Forgive me. This is not why I dropped by. I came to tell you that I did feel you betrayed me last week. But that I forgive you, and with God's

261

help, I am erasing my resentment. I know you love me. You simply do not understand."

Her mother's almost colorless eyes captured hers, but she didn't speak.

Hope smiled reassuringly, then stood. "I really should go find Papa now. I need to get to Gracie's. She's counting on me to help her this afternoon."

During the quarter mile ride to the gristmill, Hope prayed that she'd be able to sincerely forgive her father. She'd lost control for a moment with her mother. She couldn't afford to do that with Papa or they'd probably end up in a row.

She led Burns down the wagon path to a mill creek that fed into Caney Fork just beyond. When she reached the cool shade of willows and sycamores edging the water-powered mill, her long-legged father stepped outside. He'd obviously seen her coming. Her heart picked up pace, and she shot a silent prayer heavenward for calm, peace, love.

"Afternoon, Papa," she said to his stubbornly hard face while dismounting. She kept the reins securely in her hand, not ready to let go of her means of escape.

"Daughter," he greeted with a curt nod, stopping a few feet from her.

She felt her resolve start to crumble. "I think it's best if I get right to the point." She made certain her voice did not tremble. "I've prayed a lot since last Sunday, and the Lord has helped me to see you with more loving eyes."

His expression softened slightly, to one of puzzlement.

"As you know," she continued, determined not to waver, "I've resented your interference during these past ten years, and I've kept a distance between us. I've come to tell you that I forgive you. And I'm forgetting all you have done to keep Michael and me apart. With God's help, I'm determined never to dwell on any of it again."

He didn't respond. He just stood there, staring at her. Finally, he released his own ragged breath. "Thank the Lord. You've come to your senses."

Her anger sparked hot as ever. He'd discounted everything she'd said, crediting her confession to regaining her senses.

With supreme effort, she doused her indignation and went on. "Mostly, I'm trying to set things right by following Jesus' example. He loves me and forgives my every sin, and all He asks in return is that I love others and pass on that same forgiveness. So I love you, Papa, and forgive you. Past, present, and future."

His eyes had become misty. His chin quivered. Reaching for her, he pulled her close.

She could feel the warmth of being against him, the strength in his arms making her feel safe again, the smell that was her papa alone. Her tension began to evaporate.

"You can't know how much this means to me," he whispered hoarsely. "I've missed you so very much."

That brought tears to her own eyes. "Me, too, Papa." She held on to him a healing moment longer, then inhaled deeply and stepped back. "I really have to go. I'm expected at Gracie's, and I'm late." Finding the reins still in her hand and her horse mere inches behind her, she mounted her dappled Arabian and nudged him forward.

"In the end," her father called after her, "you won't regret this, sweetheart."

Feeling quite uplifted, Hope collected her son. But as she rode back toward the main road, she mulled over her father's words. He thought she'd capitulated, and that was the reason he'd held her close. He thought she'd given up Michael.

Hope hugged her own son for comfort, knowing her mother would tell Papa soon enough.

Nearing the main road, Hope wondered if Joel and his horse still lurked behind some brush. She glanced about while listening for sounds of his mount whinnying a greeting to her own or the shuffling of its hooved feet. Hearing nothing, she checked Burns's more sensitive ears to see if they were perked and turned toward a suspicious sound. But her mount simply pranced along, unaware of anything out of the ordinary.

She relaxed. Perhaps even Joel could deduce how foolish he was, how sneaky.

Then a delicious thought popped into her mind, and an unstoppable smile slipped across her lips. Michael would be at Howie and Gracie's, waiting for her.

No more than a couple hundred yards down the tree-lined main road stood the facing log homes of Gracie and Delia, and Hope's heart leaped with anticipation.

Timmy, excited himself about playing with the children, tried to throw himself off the horse. "Down! Down!"

Hope held her child fast until she spotted the youngsters playing behind Delia's house; then she lowered him to the ground to join them. Her little man took off as fast as his short legs could take him.

She herself would've loved to leap down and run straight into Gracie's house. But as a responsible adult, she knew she must ride around to the back to unsaddle and stable her horse, since she planned to spend the night.

And she was utterly rewarded. Howie came walking out of the barn carrying one end of a stack of boards, and Michael held the other.

Michael looked in her direction. Their gazes met and clung to each other, taking Hope's breath. He was here, and they would have time to talk. All the time in the world.

Chapter Nineteen

"Michael," Howie said, his expressive brown eyes roving over the two, "if you'll help me get these boards out front to the seating area, you and Hope can have the barn to yourselves for a few minutes."

Michael held Hope's gaze another second or two, reluctant, she knew, to leave her. "Sure. We'd like a little time to ourselves —" his attention returned to her — "if the lady so wishes."

"Yes, we'd appreciate that." It was hard to think with Michael looking at her as they stood in Howie Clay's barnyard. The rolled-up sleeves of his white cotton shirt contrasted wonderfully with his deeply tanned arms and, of course, his face and golden eyes. Belatedly, she remembered to dismount. "In the meantime," she said, modestly lifting her black-skirted leg over the horse's back, "I'll put Burns away."

She'd scarcely led the Arabian gelding to an empty stall and uncinched his girth when she sensed a change of light. Glancing up at the doorway, she saw Michael walking toward her in long, fast strides.

He stepped into the stall next to her. "Here, let me get that."

She moved aside, allowing him to lift the heavy saddle off the horse and toss it over the railing. Then she brought the thick wool underpad to drape it beside the rest of her tack, careful not to let the smelly, hairy blanket come within a foot of her black linen skirt.

Michael grabbed a rag from a nearby hook and quickly dried the moisture from where the saddle had rested on Burns's back. "This horse sure has fine lines. Too bad he's gelded. He would've made a fine stud for breeding."

"Yes," she agreed, assessing the Arabian. "I've always liked his shorter nose and back. And the way he holds his head high. But Papa wanted a gelding for me. One that wouldn't suddenly take off, chasing after some frisky mare." Unable to control the grin the imagery evoked, she glanced at Michael.

The corners of his mouth started to curl. But he quickly recouped. "Your father was absolutely right. Stallions are too unpredictable."

Hope became overly aware of how close

they stood and, smoothing down her wide lace collar, she thought it best to step out of the stall while searching for something less personal to say. "I was surprised to hear you bought land in the valley. I thought you planned to stay in the army."

"I still might," he said, closing the stall door after them. "If things don't work out here."

Did he mean between the two of them? "I'm not sure I understand." Was he backing out of their agreement?

Very serious now, he studied her a moment. "After I left, I got to thinkin' about what it was like for me growin' up, movin' from place to place, never gettin' to know anyone very well. Until I met you, I was always lonesome. Here in this valley was the only place I ever truly felt happy. And, well, I don't want to take you away from all your friends and your family if it can be helped. You would rather live here, wouldn't you? Or was I mistaken?"

She should never have doubted him, but still she experienced a great surge of relief. "It was sweet of you to worry about me. But I can't be happy if you aren't. I want you to be where you have the same respect you receive in the army."

He moved closer, touched her cheek with

the side of his hand, his gaze waxing tender. "You've never changed, have you? You always surprise me with your kindness. As long as I know we'll eventually be together, there's no rush. I've been given six months' leave to decide whether to reenlist or not." He stepped back and searched her eyes. "You haven't changed your mind, have you?"

"No. Never. No matter what else you might hear."

A line formed between his eyes. "Is anything else being said?"

"Not that I know of. But, please, promise me. Believe only what you hear from my own lips."

His expression relaxed, and he smiled. "And such lovely lips they are."

And without further warning, he lowered his to hers in a slow, agonizingly blissful kiss.

When at last he drew apart from her, she'd become breathless, dizzy, mindless. It took all her resolve to remember the things she wished to tell him. To aid her in this, she stepped back and held out her hand, putting some distance between them. "There are things I need to tell you, and I can't unless you stay over there."

The pleased look on his face didn't help.

"I've written to Titus and Tilly's older children and told them that one of them will have to come and see to their parents. I also spoke to Brother Rolf. He told me it was past time that I stopped resenting my own parents and to forgive them, especially my father."

Michael sobered, but only slightly.

"So I stopped by my folks' place before I came here. Mama was at the house and Papa at the gristmill. It was hard, but I told them. I told Papa I forgive him for the past, the present, and the future. That seemed to please him very much, but I doubt if it will change the way he thinks about you. I really don't think I'd put too much work into that place of yours."

Michael reached out and smoothed a hand over her hair. "Give it time. We've got time."

Reaching up and taking his wrist, she kissed his warm palm, then twined her fingers through his. "We should probably start back to the house."

He sighed. "Probably so."

As they started out into the bright flower-fresh May day, Hope remembered something else. "Brother Rolf told me he'd said the same to you. About forgiving your father."

Michael slowed to a stop. "He did. But I honestly don't believe I can. I reckon I could tell Brother Rolf I do, but it wouldn't be true. You see, there's a difference between your Pa an' mine. Yours is by nature an honorable man. He's just been tryin' to protect you. I could never fault him for that. But my pa deliberately and with forethought lied, stole, cheated. He took revenge even when he had no call to. Day after day, he ruined any chance we had for a respectable life. How do you forgive someone who wantonly destroyed everything you ever hoped for? Even now, years after his death, folks in this valley only hate me 'cuz of him. Not because of nothin' I ever did. Because of him."

She searched his eyes, wishing to somehow reach the deepest part of his soul. "All I know is, if you want God to hear your prayers, you must forgive."

He shook his head. "God's not stupid. I could say the words, but He'll know I don't mean them."

"I understand, truly I do. And so does the Lord. And He's also all-powerful and the Father of mercy. Ask Him to help you. Ask Him to wipe away the pain and anger and humiliation. The betrayal. For our own sakes, we need to get right with God."

Michael quirked a quick smile. "It sure would be nice to have the Lord on our side for a change."

"I can hear Brother Rolf now," Hope said, chuckling. "He'd be sayin' he'd rather have us wantin' to be 'on the Lord's side.' " She took his hand again. "Like you said, give it time. Right now, I need to go check with Gracie. See what she wants me to do."

Walking through Howie's back door openly as a couple, with Hope on his arm, felt almost as wonderful to Michael as when he kissed her in the barn. A number of different aromas mingled in the air: spices, meat juices, and fresh-baked breads.

Howie glanced up from his fancy dining table and raised what looked like a glass of cider. He grinned knowingly. "Come in. Have somethin' cool to drink before Gracie puts us all back to work again."

Gracie, standing at the drainboard peeling potatoes, shot her husband a withering look, and smiled warmly at Michael and Hope. It was so nice to know a few people who wanted him to marry Hope.

"Have you had your dinner?" Gracie asked Hope.

"Yes, before I left home." Hope left Michael's side and started toward the hearth end and Gracie. "What do you want me to do?"

Gracie laughed. "What do you think?"

Hope cocked her adorable head to the side. "Finish peelin' those potatoes."

Glancing past to Michael, Gracie's smile turned mischievous. "When we were girls, Hope hated peelin' potatoes more than anything. Specially when we were expectin' a big crowd." She raised her brows playfully at Hope, then wiped her hands on her apron. "But I think Howie's got the right idea. Let's all sit a spell. Catch up." The woman was obviously hinting that she wanted to hear the latest.

Michael pulled out a finely crafted chair next to Howie's.

"Grab us some glasses, Hope," Gracie said, "while I rinse the rest of this potato mess off my hands."

"I assume Delia's watchin' the young'uns at her place," Hope said as she moved gracefully to the china cabinet, "but where's Jacob?"

"I sent him in to the store for more sugar and lemons," Gracie supplied.

"I told you she was workin' us all to death," Howie piped in. "A body'd think we invited the king of England."

Once everyone had a glass of the cider

Howie poured from a thick earthen jug, he made himself extra comfortable by kicking back and crossing his legs as he eyed Michael, then Hope, who'd taken the seat right next to him. "So, did you two get things sorted out?"

Beside Michael, Hope stiffened. "We've always been clear about what we want. It's Papa and now Joel who are the problem."

"Just like Romeo and Juliet." Howie's wife certainly had a fanciful streak.

"I certainly pray not," Hope continued. "They're both dead at the end of the play."

"Maybe so," Gracie sighed, "but it's still all so romantic."

"I didn't think it the least romantic when I had Joel sneaking along behind me today. He followed me all the way to Mama's."

Michael's blood froze. "Joel followed you? What else has he done? If he tries to harm you, I'll —"

Hope caressed his clinched fist, her crystal eyes holding his. "You mustn't do anything that will give him an excuse to cause more trouble."

"More?" What had the bounder been up to?

"I'm sorry. I should have mentioned it. Without a word to me, Joel went to my father and asked for my hand in marriage.

Then, in front of Titus and Tilly, Papa told me he was accepting Joel's proposal."

Having a hard time maintaining his composure, Michael recalled the visit he'd had from Mr. Reardon and Joel the other day. "Did this happen last Sunday?"

"Yes." Hope added a lackluster smile. "Perhaps it was just as well. Now they all know my own intention. They may not have accepted it yet, but they know." Picking up her glass, his delicate but brave beauty sat back in her chair. "Please, could we not spoil the rest of this day with my problems? All week I've been looking forward to these few hours we can enjoy together," she added to the Clays, including them in a sweeping glance.

"She's right," Howie agreed, always one for having a good time. "Gracie'll have us all out totin' and haulin' them splintery ol' kegs an' barrels soon enough. Movin' 'em this way an' that. An inch here, a foot there . . ."

Gracie kicked up a brow and stabbed her husband with a pointed stare, then softened her blue gaze as she turned to Michael. "With all the food that's comin', we'll need two tables set up. Then I count twenty adults, maybe more, and at least that many young'uns plus ours. I want another six tables set up and enough kegs and benches for everyone to sit on." She shifted her attention to Hope. "And they should be put where I want 'em, shouldn't they?"

Hope grinned. "Absolutely."

Howie responded with a good-natured roll of the eyes. "And you can believe me when I say there ain't an extra board, keg, or barrel sittin' nowhere for a good mile around. This woman's had me out beggin' and borrowin' all up and down the road."

"You poor dear," Gracie quipped mockingly as she patted her husband's hand.

Michael heard Hope chuckling softly, but as for him, he was so moved by the teasing banter going on between a husband and wife who clearly adored one another that his eyes started to burn with unshedable tears. Sucking in a breath, he reached beneath the table and, capturing Hope's hand, laced his fingers through hers. Someday . . .

As Howie had predicted, Gracie stood out on the front lawn a short time later, directing exactly where each of the board-on-barrel tables was to be placed, only to change her mind several times.

Michael and Howie were moving the boards of one table for the third time when Michael heard his friend grumble something about it being time "to gag the woman."

Trying to keep a straight face, Michael glanced toward the house, where Hope had been left to finish peeling potatoes for a huge salad. She stood at a window, looking back at him so highly amused, she had a hand pressed over her mouth to literally keep from laughing out loud.

With no free hands to stop himself, the humor of this nonsense exploded from him.

Howie dropped his end on top of a barrel and joined Michael in a burst of guffawing, with Hope still at the kitchen window joining in.

Indignant, Gracie planted fists onto her hips. "Laugh all you want. But keep movin'. There's plenty more that needs doin' before evenin'." She glanced past them, her attention diverted to the road. "Here comes Jake. It sure took him long enough."

Jacob Reardon rode casually toward them on a plain brown horse, not hurrying in the least, which Michael had no trouble understanding why. Considering Jake was Gracie's cousin, he'd surely been in her indecisive clutches a number of times before.

"I just wish you would've let me go to the store instead," Howie complained to Gracie. "Please tell me you're outta somethin' else."

She swung back to her husband, the skirts

of her faded brown work dress swirling out around her, and cocked her chin. "If I need anything else, I'll go for it myself. I, too, could use the rest." Then she brushed a hand through the air. "The tables are fine now, right where they are. So I'm goin' back to the kitchen."

"We sure will hate to see you go, sugarplum," Howie shot after her.

"You needn't worry, dear heart," she returned just as mockingly. "I'll never be too far away that I can't shout more orders."

Howie sidled over to Michael. "Women get plumb crazy when they got company comin'. You'll find out soon enough."

"I hope so."

"Ah, everythin's gonna work out," his friend reassured as they started transferring the kegs to either side of the newly placed table. "Just give it a little time."

Jake nudged his horse to a faster pace once Gracie was out of sight, then reined the animal to a halt beside the men. Always a serious fellow, his facial features looked as long as ever as he swung a leg down. "I saw Joel Underwood in town," he said, joining them. "He was hangin' out at the saddler's with that bunch he used to run with. They all just purty much sat there an' stared at me the whole time I was in the store."

The same had happened to Michael.

Jake turned directly to Michael. "Bailey at the store says he's heard bits an' pieces, and he thinks they're gonna try to run you outta the valley."

Howie stepped alongside Michael. "They're just a bunch of lazy no-accounts. When the rest of the militia gets here this evenin', we'll come up with somethin' to nip this in the bud."

That didn't make Michael feel any better. He didn't want folks choosing sides over him, turning this peaceful valley into a battleground. He looked back at the house. There was nothing in the world he wanted more than Hope's happiness. But would he ever be able to give it to her?

Chapter Twenty

Michael had mixed feelings when the valley's returning militiamen began arriving with their wives and children shortly after Jake returned from the store. Although he was glad to see men with whom he'd fought alongside and made the long trek back to Tennessee, he'd hoped to have a few more private moments with his lady.

The first to arrive were loud-talking, curly headed Bill Jessup and his family. Michael didn't get to meet his wife or children, though. Mrs. Jessup, a thin, long-waisted woman, headed straight for the house with a large bowl while their four children ran for Jake and Delia's across the road. Everyone seemed right at home here.

"Kids didn't wanna miss out on anything," Jessup practically shouted as he strutted over to the men, with his usual jolly grin and hearty handshake. "Glad to hear you'll be stayin' on at your old place," he told Michael. Without being asked, he pitched in, laying boards for the reel across a large square frame they'd just hammered together near the front porch.

Then the others began to roll in, one after another, shouting "Howdy" and waving as they neared. The Dillards, the McKnights, Jim Johnson and his young family, all pretty much did the same as the Jessups had, as if coming to the Clays' was an everyday thing.

Michael could hear the women in the house, all talking and laughing at once. Glancing in the window from time to time, he could tell Hope was being teased quite a bit; her smile had that embarrassed look to it. . . . Hope surrounded by her friends. Part of all she'd lose if things didn't level out here and she came to live with him at an army fort.

Big-boned Junior Smith rode in with his gal, and he did make a point of introducing Mary Jo Reardon to Michael, as he'd promised earlier at the store.

Michael vaguely remembered her from years before — Ike Reardon's daughter. Seven or eight back then, she was still as blonde as the rest of that bunch . . . except for his own silky haired brunette.

When Junior said, "my betrothed," Mary Jo's round cheeks reddened, and she ran giggling up the porch steps in what was obviously a new blue dress to join the women.

Then Max and his brood rolled in.

Michael walked over to help the new mother down. "How you doin'?" he asked as he reached up to Belinda.

Instead, she handed him the new baby wrapped in a light blanket. "Here, hold Baby Michael. It's time you two got to know each other."

Too late to protest, Michael had the tiny squirming thing in his hands, hoping he wouldn't hurt it or drop it or . . . He couldn't remember ever being more apprehensive.

"Cradle him in your arm, Michael. Don't let his head bob all around."

"Oh, right."

Just about the time he began to feel comfortable holding his blue-eyed, thumb-sucking namesake with hair so blond and fine that he looked bald, Belinda walked up beside them, ready to take her son back.

Michael handed him to her, wishing he'd had just a moment longer before she strolled into the house with her babe.

"Men," Howie called over the shouts of the children chasing each other around Jake's house. He stood at the well, washing up from an afternoon of hard labor. "If you wouldn't mind moseyin' on over here, I got somethin' that needs sayin' away from the womenfolk."

A bit leery, Michael joined the others at the stone-walled well that had been dug near the road for the Clays and Reardons to share. He wasn't all that sure he wanted Howie to rally the boys to his cause.

"On the trip back from New Orleans y'all got to know Flanagan here for the straight-talkin', kindhearted fellow he is, even if you didn't know him when he lived here before."

"You bet," Jessup said, with a resounding slap to Michael's back, practically knocking him off his feet.

Howie grinned, seeming to think that humorous. "Glad to hear that. An' the way I figure it, we veterans ought to still look out for one another."

"Hear! Hear!" Junior Smith rooted.

"Wait a minute, Howie," Michael said, stepping in. "I'd rather you didn't. I didn't come to Reardon Valley to stir up more trouble."

"What trouble?" Short and fiery Duncan McKnight wanted to know.

"Mike's probably right," Jake said, taking his side. "He already has more than enough to deal with."

"Us pretendin' more's not on the way

don't stop it from comin'," Howie argued.

"Look," Dillard piped in, a frown marring his narrow face. "I live all the way to the other end of the valley, and I been busy gettin' my crops in. So what's been goin' on I don't know about?"

"We're purty sure," Junior Smith said, "Joel Underwood is gettin' his pals all worked up. We think they're gonna do whatever their pea-sized brains can come up with to run Flanagan off. Joel's had his eye on Hope from the time his brother married her. And just when he thought he had a clear field, some mighty stiff competition shows back up."

A slow grin widened young Johnson's already round features. "So that's why you left off soldierin' to come here."

"Where you been, boy?" Jessup bellowed. "I say, what's a few runty pups when we already took on them Creek Redsticks and the whole blamed British army? We'll wipe my mama's floor up with the likes of Joel Underwood an' his friends."

"No. Really, I appreciate the offer," Michael said. "But I'd rather try to handle the situation in a peaceable manner."

"He's right." Max, who'd been the commander of the small militia, spoke in a forceful tone. "Michael has enough to juggle right now without being the cause of the whole valley choosing up sides. Best thing we can do is keep cool heads, pray, and let the Lord handle it."

Michael wondered if the Lord would step in for the valley's sake and for Hope's, even if he couldn't get past the unforgiveness in his own heart.

"All right," Jessup begrudged, "we'll hold off. For now. But don't 'spect us to wait till them boys has got theyselves all worked up for a tar-and-feather party."

"Sneaky as some of 'em is," young Johnson added, "I'd say they'd be more into back-shootin'."

Michael held up a hand. "I appreciate your enthusiasm, men. But I got too much at stake here, so I'd just as soon keep a lid on things if I can."

"Well, you just give us a holler if you need us," Jessup said, "an' we'll come a-runnin'."

A couple of the wives brought pitchers of lemonade and glasses out for the men, then returned inside where the women did whatever they do to finish getting supper on. But with all the hooting and tittering coming from within, Michael was sure there was a whole lot more talking going on than anything else.

That wasn't to say that the men weren't enjoying themselves, too. They'd circled some of the kegs and sat within easy reach of the refreshment table. At the moment Duncan McKnight had launched into a tall tale of some extraordinary feat at the Battle of horseshoe Bend. Every time he stopped long enough to take a breath, bone-thin Amos Dillard inserted the plain facts, sending everyone into bellows of laughter.

Although Michael enjoyed the company of the men as the afternoon waned, there was only one person he yearned to be with . . . this one who was still bound by the dictates of her widowhood.

One of the older children, a towheaded girl in braids, came walking across the road, loaded down with Hope's little one. Without thinking, Michael rose to go help her.

"I think Timmy's plumb wore hisself out," she said, shifting the tot's weight. "He keeps askin' for his mama."

"Here, let me take him in to her." Michael reached for him, glad for any excuse to see Hope.

As dark-haired Timmy wrapped his arms around Michael's neck, he reared back, and with those same see-through-you eyes of his mother, he looked at him and blinked. "Who you?"

Michael smiled, hoping it would better his chances at being accepted as he started toward the house with the tyke. "I'm an old friend of your mama and papa."

Timmy's eyes popped wider. "Papa?"

"Yes."

Those same forever-and-beyond eyes as Hope's turned pouty. "I never seed my papa."

"You were probably just too young to remember. 'Cause he sure talked about you. A lot. Me an' your papa were soldiers together in the war."

Timmy brightened then, bouncing up higher on Michael's arm. "Me gots a so'dier."

"Oh yes. The lead soldier." The one that had been in the packet he'd delivered for Ezra.

"At my house. You come see."

"I'll do that, first chance I get," Michael said, starting up the porch steps. "I reckon everyone tells you that you got purty eyes just like your ma."

At that, Timmy squinched them, then rubbed one with a knotted fist. "Eyes tired. Don't tell Mama."

In a teasing gesture, Michael blew across the tot's long lashes, causing him to blink and giggle as they walked across the threshold of the Clay house.

The women all turned toward them . . . those just sitting and talking and those at the hearth or worktables performing chores. And every last one of them shot Michael a knowing grin — except Hope.

After a brief openmouthed moment of surprise, she laid down a bread knife and hurried to intercept him.

"Me not tired," Timmy stated vehemently, causing every woman in the room to laugh. "Me not!" The two-and-a-half-year-old tightened his grip at Michael's neck.

Sensing Timmy was about to throw a tantrum, Michael took the initiative as he drank in the sight of Hope. "I smelled cookies baking in here. I thought maybe me an' Tim here could go on upstairs with a cup of milk and one or two of them fine-tastin' cookies. I got a story I wanna tell Tim about his papa." Reluctantly, Michael tore his gaze from Hope and returned it to her son. "You wanna hear about how your papa fired guns so big a lad your size could crawl right inside the barrel? Of course, if it was time to shoot it, you'd better get back out, 'cause if you didn't, why, you'd go flyin' halfway to the moon."

Excitement began to dance in the little one's eyes. "Over the moon. Like the cow jump."

Michael realized he'd forgotten about their audience, until the women started chuckling. He glanced up to see them all ears.

Hope intervened. "You two go on up. I'm sure you have quite a store of tales to unfold. I'll bring up your cookies and milk."

Michael couldn't have asked for things to work out any more splendidly. In a matter of moments, he'd have Hope and her son all to himself.

Hope thought she loved Michael before, but watching him carry her child up the stairs reached a tender spot she never knew existed. Then to have Michael care enough for Timmy to tell him good things about his father . . . She wondered if Ezra would have done the same, had their roles been reversed. It was hard to imagine, since he'd demonstrated no affection for Timmy the two times he'd returned home during the war. For Ezra, the war had been his means of escaping an unwanted marriage. Her throat clogged with the emotion already blurring her vision.

"Ain't that just the sweetest thing you ever saw?" Gracie crooned.

Her sister came alongside her, reminding Hope that a number of other young women stood behind her. Deftly, she wiped the tears from her eyes with her black linen sleeve while pretending to brush aside a strand of hair.

Turning back to them, she saw that everyone except Delia wore a grin so wide, they looked like senseless children.

Sensible Delia's smile was tempered by worried eyes.

Gracie swept past Hope. "Delia, would you fetch a few cookies from the basket on the china cabinet. I'll pour the milk. We don't want to keep Michael and Timmy waiting now, do we?" Her musical voice was just shy of laughter.

"No, we sure don't," short and round Ruthie Dillard agreed before falling into a fit of giggles — giggles she attempted to muffle with a wad of apron.

The other women did no better at hiding their mirth, and Hope wondered what Michael must think of them, though nothing could diminish her own joy.

Polly Jessup stepped in front of Hope. "Your bun is crooked." With long thin fingers, she reached around and quickly straightened the large knot at the base of Hope's neck, then straightened the wide lace collar at her throat.

Mere seconds later, balancing a pewter

tray of milk and cookies, Hope found herself climbing the stairs so filled with anticipation at having a few private moments with Michael and Timmy, she could scarcely breathe past her pounding heart.

Chapter Twenty-one

Reaching the second-floor hall of Gracie's house, Hope heard voices coming through the open doorway of the nearest bedroom. She paused on the threshold with the tray of milk and cookies to find Michael, with his back to her, stooped before a corner rocking chair.

Timmy sat on the edge of the rocker while Michael wiped the grime from his feet with a damp washcloth. Such a thoughtful man.

"And them big cannonballs," he related as he scrubbed, "shot out over the water, makin' the loudest noise you ever did hear."

"Bang!" Timmy clapped his hands. He was so engrossed in Michael's story, he had yet to see his mother.

"Louder. Even the ground shook. But your pa wasn't scared. He just went an' got another one of them big ol' black balls and shoved it in the gun barrel, ready to shoot again."

Timmy spotted Hope then, as she listened at the entrance. Taking a big breath, he spread his arms wide. "Mama, Papa big like — like — Pepper."

"Maybe not quite as big as our work-horse," she corrected as earnestly as Michael turned and glanced at her.

Michael rose to his feet, bringing Timmy up with him, then took the seat, placing Timmy on his lap. "It might be best if I handle the milk for both of us. Your sister probably wouldn't appreciate us makin' a mess on her clean floor."

"Or havin' crumbs in her bed," Hope added, unable to stop smiling. "If you don't mind, I'd like to join you."

Timmy reached up. "Cookie."

She set the tray on a low mahogany chest beside the rocker and handed her son a small cinnamon-spiced treat. Then she brought a woven-seated chair from beside the four-poster and set it next to them, totally aware that Michael watched her every move. As soon as she sat down, she asked Timmy what he'd been doing at Delia's house, knowing he'd blithely jabber about his afternoon between bites, leaving her and Michael to quietly enjoy this time and repast together.

With Timmy tucked against his shoulder, Michael gently rocked back and forth, his eyes never leaving Hope's.

She did her best to pretend interest in what her son was saying, but her gaze gravitated to Michael's more often than not.

Within a few minutes, Timmy began to yawn between bites, his words becoming fewer, his eyelids droopier, until his little body gave in and his head lolled against Michael's chest.

Hope took a half-eaten cookie from Timmy's fingers, then lifted him off Michael's lap and laid him on the bed, propping pillows on either side, lest he roll off in his sleep.

When she turned back, she found herself in Michael's arms. Without her realizing, he'd come up behind.

Slowly, his mouth lowered to claim hers.

Giving in to this stolen, pulse-racing moment, she reached up around his neck, allowing her returning embrace to express all the love she'd been saving for him. She felt his own love for her in all its tenderness as one of his hands gently cupped the back of her head, just as he had Belinda's baby's earlier.

Something banged loudly downstairs, bringing Hope back to the reality of the moment. With reluctance, she pulled away and gazed up at her beloved.

His eyes seemed darker, the pace of his breathing quicker.

She was certain she looked equally enlivened — her face felt incredibly warm.

Taking Michael's hand, she moved quietly away from her son and toward the hall. "We must restrain ourselves," she whispered. "Surely you know people are watching every move we make."

He glanced past her. "Not here, they're not. Besides, you're just too beautiful." Upon reaching the doorway, he pulled her close again.

Exerting monumental willpower, she stepped out of his arms. "We mustn't." Her words fought against her own desire. "I'm still in mourning."

He shot her a disbelieving look and whispered back, "Every woman down there was thrilled to give us some time alone."

She couldn't help smiling at the truth of his words. The women had been encouraging them, to say the least. But that wasn't her concern. "We mustn't do anything that would look like we're courting. Especially in front of the children." She closed the door to the bedroom behind them. "If they think we're sweethearts, it would be easier to keep the lid on a pot of boilin' beans than to keep them from tellin' everyone they see."

"Sweethearts. I like the sound of that," he breathed absently while tracing the hair framing her face with his finger.

He wasn't making this easy. "I'm very serious. For the sake of Ezra's parents and out of respect for his memory, I won't be joinin' you in dancin' any of the squares and rounds. Even if everyone here thinks it's all right. I don't want to risk hurtin' them like that."

"That's fine with me. I never did learn all them newfangled steps anyway." He leaned closer, his finger now tracing the line of her sensitive lips. "I'd much rather sit off to the side with you and have you tell me a hundred reasons or so why you adore me."

"You're incorrigible." With a soft laugh, she slipped past him and to the landing. "Besides, I do believe that's the gentleman's chore."

Everyone talked at once as they lined up for a pass at the food tables on the Clays' lawn. The younger children ran back and forth shouting to their mothers which foods they wanted on their plates. Michael stood in their midst with Hope, reveling in the joy and energy all about them. He knew he was smiling like a simpleton, but he couldn't help himself. He was actually living one of the moments he'd dreamt about for a decade . . . surrounded by good friends and Hope at his side.

She moved just ahead of him along the serving tables, filling her plate with the same grace she did everything else.

With her so near, he paid little attention to his selection of food, merely spooning from the handiest bowls and platters.

Hope, a smile further decorating her incredible beauty, gazed up at him with those haunting eyes. "Timmy is going to be one fumin' little fellow when he comes awake and finds we've started without him."

Michael glanced up to the second story of the house. "Do you want me to go get him?"

"No. If he's awakened before he's ready, he's real fussy. If he doesn't come down by the time we've finished eating, I'll dish up his favorites for him."

Their plates filled, they started to look for a couple of places at the dining tables that hadn't been spoken for, when Max caught Michael's eye and pointed to the almost empty table where he and Belinda sat.

"Is sitting by the Bremmers all right with you?" Michael asked Hope.

She barked a laugh. "As long as those rambunctious boys of theirs stay at the kids' tables."

Michael surveyed the shorter, noisier setups where the children were bumping around, vying for the various spaces to land. "I know what you mean." He looked forward to the day when he'd have several of his own.

Upon reaching the Bremmers, Michael deliberately waited until Hope chose a seat; then he took the one opposite her. Though it was nice to sit beside her, this evening he'd much rather have her before him to look at as much as he'd like.

Jake and Delia soon joined them, followed by Amos Dillard and his wife.

"Hurry up, ever'body!" Max's oldest yelled from one of the children's tables. "So Pops can say grace. I'm hungry."

"Me, too!" was called out from a number of tables, and everyone started laughing.

"That means you, too, Gracie," Howie chastised.

With a pitcher of lemonade in her hand, she glanced up from pouring more of the tangy drink for some of the children. "I'll be right there," she said, eying her husband with a superior smile, "as soon as I hear *please*."

"Please!" was shouted from every direction.

"Well, if it's that important to everyone

. . ." Gracie began a slow meandering, teasing saunter to her seat beside Howie, then took an inordinate amount of time straightening her pink-and-blue plaid skirts, while ignoring every call for her to hurry up.

As soon as she was seated, Max stood, his gaze sweeping the children's tables. "Shall we put down our drinks and forks and fold our hands, please. We're going to talk to our Lord."

An incredible amount of clatter followed, as utensils banged onto plates. Needless to say, a number of children had already been sampling.

Michael glanced up to see Hope and Belinda exchanging looks and snickering.

Max cleared his throat, no doubt in hopes of regaining their attention. "Our dear heavenly Father, we come together as one to thank You for this bounty of firstfruits You have graciously provided for all of us, the swift as well as the slow. In Jesus' name we pray. Amen."

The agreeing amens were accompanied by more snickering. Michael was amazed that Max would say something meant to be funny while praying.

Max must have noticed. He wagged his fork at Michael. "Trust me, God has a sense of humor. He'd have to have one to put up with all our foolishness."

Michael glanced across at Hope. She gave him a smile and a shrug and commenced eating along with everyone else.

But Michael couldn't get Max's statement out of his mind. He'd never considered God to be all that friendly. It made Michael feel as if the Lord really was right here enjoying the fellowship of all these folks. The thought filled him with an unexpected warmth.

"Sergeant Flanagan." Jake Reardon, the only non-militia man there, put down his fork. He sat on the other side of Hope. "Howie tells me you were in charge of the cavalry's horses during the last campaign."

"Yes." The young man's question made Michael uneasy. He looked too much like his Uncle Noah not to. "That's one of my duties."

"Then you been around a whole lot more horses than me. I don't mean to put you out or anything, but if you have the time, one of my work team has a big bump on his back that I can't quite make out. I was wonderin' if you'd take a look at it — I mean, I'd pay you."

So, standoffish Jake needed something from him. "No sense talkin' money before we've even seen what we're lookin' at."

Plucking a slice of bread from a central platter, Michael turned to Delia beside him. "Would you please pass the butter?" He returned his attention to Jake. "Why don't we walk across to your stable soon as we finish. I'd prefer to examine the animal while there's still daylight."

Hope, beside Jake, sat back slightly, out of her older cousin's periphery, and sent Michael a nod of approval.

While buttering his bread, Michael came to understand that Jake had decided to give him a chance to prove himself. One less obstacle in his path to make Hope his bride.

It had been over a year since Hope had seen Howie bring out his harmonica to play. As the women cleared away the dishes and the men dismantled the tables and carried them back to the Clay barn, Howie, with that slight limp of his, stepped onto his porch, followed by Duncan and his fiddle. Taught by his father, Duncan could almost make that instrument talk. Jimmy Johnson wasn't so bad on the banjo either. The youngest of the trio vaulted onto the porch to join them. Before they'd gone off to war, they'd made some lively toe-tapping music together.

Carrying a load of plates to the house,

Hope bumped into Gracie coming out the door with a bucket of scraps.

"Is Timmy still asleep?" Gracie asked. "I haven't seen him runnin' around."

Hope glanced up the stairs that climbed the back wall. "He's only been down about an hour."

Gracie smiled as Duncan and Jimmy began tuning their strings. "If nothing else'll wake the busy li'l tyke, the music will. well, I'm off to feed the pigs. They sure are gonna feast tonight."

With so many dishes to wash, Gracie had placed a pad on her good dining table, then set two big washtubs on it, one for washing and one for rinsing. With women working from both sides of each tub, and several more drying, Hope knew they'd be done by the time the little band finished practicing.

Hope found another bucket for slop and was starting to scrape the scraps into it when Nancy, Jim's wife from up near Carthage, came to work alongside her. A strong, capable woman, she'd seemed an odd match for short, pudgy Jim. But he made the seemingly serious woman laugh, and after spending so many lonely years herself, Hope figured that was as good a reason as any to fall in love — probably better than most.

"Hope," the woman said, their heads close together as she wiped gravy from a plate with a piece of bread, "I just wanted to tell you I think your Sergeant Flanagan is a real fine fellow. It almost makes a gal wanna cry to hear as how you an' him has been pinin' after each other all these years, an' how you're finally meetin' up again. It's awful you having to lose your husband that way, but I'm just sorry there's folks here now that want to keep you and your sergeant apart."

Engaging the woman's steady green eyes, Hope realized how lax she'd been in her own neighborly duties. "Thank you. I appreciate that very much. I've been intendin' to come by and get better acquainted, and I'm ashamed I haven't." Hope straightened, stretching a kink in her back. "I'd like to set a date right now. Wednesday at about two. If that's convenient."

"That'd suit me just fine. With me bein' the quiet sort, I don't make new friends all that easy."

Finished scraping, Hope deposited her dishes on the table and returned to help Nancy with hers. "I reckon movin' away from your folks and all your friends would be kinda hard."

"Aye. But Jim and his ways . . . he just

swept me off my feet, and here I am."

Hope felt real empathy for Nancy. She, too, might easily find herself far from everyone she held dear. "Forget Wednesday. Instead, I'll pick you up Friday noon and take you to my sewing circle. From now on my friends will be your friends. Bring your needle and thread. We're —"

An unexpected silence brought Hope's head up. The musicians had stopped rehearsing and everyone else had ceased their talk.

Gracie came hurrying in from feeding the hogs, her face pale. "Hope, come here. It's Joel. He just rode up with two of his friends. He insists on speaking to you."

Hope heard more than her own gasp echo off the log walls. The other women understood the ramifications of his sudden appearance.

Grabbing Hope's hand, Gracie asked, "Where's Michael? Joel looks like he's spoilin' for trouble."

"He's still over at Jake's barn, I think." Her heart pounding, Hope took several deep breaths, then walked out to meet her brother-in-law.

Waiting just outside the door, Howie sidled up to her, taking her arm. "Think I'll just mosey on out there with you."

Joel, along with one of the Hatfield boys and Reggie Wilson, remained mounted at the edge of the grass, looking quite sullen as his gaze roved the crowd.

Hope walked directly to him, determined to show no sign that his presence was out of the ordinary. "Joel, what brings you all the way down here?"

Before answering, he glanced insolently at Howie standing close behind her. "Ma fell and hurt herself, and you need to come home."

His two young cohorts weren't very good at subterfuge. They both looked more surprised by Joel's report than Hope did.

"I'd hate to ride all the way home to find out you were lying like last Friday."

Joel frowned menacingly, though his freckles detracted from it. "I'm telling the truth." He scanned the gathering spectators once more — looking for Michael, no doubt.

"You know I promised Gracie that I'd stay the night and help clean up. If Tilly is truly hurt, you should've gone to fetch Ma Smith."

"Never mind." Ruthie Dillard stepped up. Only slightly taller than Hope, Amos's calm-spirited wife was considerably rounder. "We was fixin' to go home early.

We'll stop by your place on our way, and if Ma Underwood needs someone, I'll stay over."

"Are you sure you want to leave early?" Hope asked, hating that the Dillards would drive all the way down from the north end of the valley, then have to leave so soon.

"Yes. We left our Charlie and a neighbor boy home to look after the stock, but they acted much too happy to see us go. I think they're up to somethin'."

"I purely do thank you, Ruthie," Hope said, giving her a hug. As she did, she glanced across the road and saw that Michael and Jake had yet to reappear.

"That ain't what Ma wants," Joel retorted while removing his hat and swiping at the sweat beading his brow, even though it wasn't hot.

Ruthie, in her calm assurance, stared at Joel. "That's nonsense. Your ma purely loves it when I come a-callin'. Stop your fussin' and get on back home to her. I'll round up my young'uns and we'll be right along."

Joel glanced around again. "I was thinkin' on hangin' round here a spell."

Howie, still behind Hope, entered the exchange. "Any other time we'd be pleased to have you. But tonight's strictly for the boys

307

what fought the redcoats at New Orleans. 'Sides, you need to get on home to your ma."

Reggie Wilson reined his bay around. "Come on, Joel. Can't you tell when you're not wanted?"

Joel stalled, his attention returning full force to Hope. "We'll be havin' us a talk tomorrow. It's time you an' me got some things straight."

Howie draped an arm over Hope's shoulder. "After church. Me'n Gracie'll be seein' her home and checkin' on how your ma's farin'."

Max stepped up beside her. "Maybe me and Pops'll drop by and see how Tilly's doing, too. See what we can do to help."

Knowing he'd been outflanked, Joel jerked hard on his mount's bit, causing the blaze-faced horse to squeal and rear. Ramming his heels into the animal's sides, Joel galloped away with his friends trying to catch him.

Hope moved back from the dust kicked up by the horses, knowing that the secretive, smiling, biding-his-time Joel was no more. He had been replaced by an angry, determined man. Just the thought of going home to that made her stomach knot.

"Don't worry, li'l sister," Howie offered.

"I don't care if your pa's tryin' to marry you off to him. That snot-nosed pup ain't gonna be ridin' roughshod over you."

Turning back toward the house, Hope had the added embarrassment of seeing every man, woman, and child staring at her. They had, of course, witnessed the entire incident.

"Howie," Max said, "get on up there and get some music going again. No sense letting that hothead ruin our party."

"You're right." His voice upbeat now, Howie headed for the porch and his harmonica. "Gracie!" he yelled. "Come on, give us a song."

After that, the silence was broken, and everyone started talking again while the children resumed what appeared to be a game of hide-and-seek in these last moments of twilight.

Max put a sympathetic arm around Hope, giving her a squeeze, then started back with her. "You know we'll keep you in our daily prayers."

"I'm just grateful Michael was spared this."

"Yes," Max agreed, nodding his blond head absently.

Before they reached the house, though, everyone grew quiet again. Had Joel returned? Hope whirled around. But instead of Joel, Michael and Jake came walking across the road, immersed in a private conversation.

Then Michael slowed and scanned the group, a frown crimping his brow. His attention settled on Max and Hope. "Something's wrong. What is it?"

Chapter Twenty-two

"Here's the turnoff to our place," Jim Johnson called out.

Michael edged Ebony closer to the family's wagon and into the circle of light shed by their suspended lantern. "It's been nice keepin' company with you. I'll see you at church tomorrow."

"No," Jim said. "Follow us on in. I'll get my rifle, and we'll go to your place together."

Michael glanced into the deep shadow of the sided wagon bed to see if the slumbering babes had stirred. He didn't want them frightened. He moved still closer to Jim's side and lowered his voice. "I 'preciate the offer, but I can take care of myself. I have my pistol in my saddlebag."

"I insist. I won't take no for an answer."

Sitting up on the driver's bench with her husband, Nancy leaned across him. "Me, too. Shiftless ne'er-do-wells like Joel and his bunch don't make their kind of mischief when other folks is a-watchin'."

Even an owl added its own *"Whoo, whoo, whoo."*

Michael exhaled. "Well, I reckon I wouldn't mind the company." He was too weary to argue any further. Besides, it wouldn't put Jim out all that much. The Johnsons were Michael's closest neighbors. His path intersected the road just a quarter mile north of theirs. He nudged his mare onto their cutoff.

He'd already been obliged to swallow a cartload of anger and disappointment tonight. Joel's unwelcomed appearance had taken the fun out of the get-together at Howie Clay's. Folks started leaving shortly thereafter. When Jim had insisted he not ride home alone but leave with them, even Hope had agreed, concerned that Joel and his cohorts might be lying in wait somewhere along the night-shrouded road. Michael's time with Hope had been cut painfully short.

Upon reaching the Johnsons' house, he dismounted and helped get the two little ones up to their loft room.

Jim collected his rifle and fixings from above the mantel and walked out, grabbing the lantern off the wagon.

"That's not a good idea," Michael said. "If there is anyone at my place, we don't want to announce our arrival before we're ready to."

"You're right. How about I just hop up behind you? After we check out your place, I can ride your mare home, and you can drop by for her in the mornin'."

A scattering of clouds had rolled in from the west, blotting out any moonlight that might have drifted down through the trees. The going was slow until they reached the main road. From there, Ebony took over with her keen homing sense, and while the men strained to see or hear anything out of the ordinary, she soon carried them to the edge of Michael's clearing.

He reined her to a halt. "Jim, would you mind reachin' into the saddlebag and gettin' my pistol? There's a bag with ball an' powder there, too."

Obliging, Jim then slid off the horse and loaded and primed his own weapon, while Michael, still mounted, did the same. "Just to be on the safe side," Jim suggested, "why don't you skirt the meadow and come up on the back side of the house, an' I'll keep low an' move in on the front?"

"Good a plan as any," Michael answered softly. "But you keep that good-lookin' head of yours down. I ain't returnin' no shot-up husband to Nancy."

The moon slipped out from behind a cloud as Michael, edging the woods, rode parallel to the house. He quickly scanned the area and saw no lurking silhouettes, no saddled horses anywhere, only his.

A horse whinnied. Ebony answered. Michael listened for any others, his body tense. But all was quiet — a pretty good sign that no strange horses were about.

Dismounting, he approached the house with caution, his long-barreled gun at the ready. Hugging the rough-hewn wall, he circled around, listening for any movement inside the house.

Still nothing.

Once he was satisfied, he waited in front for his neighbor to join him. "Don't shoot. It's just me," he called when he spotted Jim coming from behind a nearby hickory.

Jim straightened and heaved a sigh. "It's better to be sure than sorry. I'll stand at the door whilst you go in and get a lantern lit."

Walking into the pitch-black of the interior, Michael took stock of where the sparse furnishings were, then started for the fireplace and banked coals at one end.

He stubbed into something on the floor. Something heavy, yet with a little give. His imagination heightened; a body was the first thought that came to Michael's mind.

Reaching down, he quickly realized it was a large, filled sack.

But what on earth was it doing there?

He stood still, listened. Nothing.

The palm holding his pistol had grown damp. He transferred the weapon to his other hand, wiped the sweat on his trousers, and took the remaining steps to the hearth. Finding a sliver of kindling, he scraped it among the banked coals at the rear of the fireplace until he uncovered some bright red ones.

In a matter of moments, the lantern was lit, and he spotted his pocket watch on the mantel — one of the few items of any value he owned.

His short but stout neighbor walked inside, closing the door after him. "That's an odd place to leave your flour sack," he commented.

"No more odd than how the chairs are turned." Holding high the lantern, Michael grimly nodded toward the center of the room. Both chairs had been turned around, their backs pushed flush against the rustic table.

Still holding his rifle, Jim glanced anxiously around the room, his boylike face marred with a frown. "Do you see anything missing?"

315

"Not so far. Not even my timepiece. But then it does have my initials etched on the back." Setting the lantern on the table, Michael lit a few candles with a wooden sliver as he further inspected the surroundings. Considering he'd been a man on the move for the past three years, he possessed mostly just the bare essentials in utensils and supplies.

In the corner where the flour sack should have been leaning, he spotted another strange thing . . . his tin coffee cup sitting on the floor. Obviously, Joel wanted there to be no mistake about his having been there. Still, nothing appeared to be stolen.

Upstairs in the one large space beneath the slanting roof, Michael again found everything as it had been before he left, except that his pillow lay at the opposite end of his neatly made bed. Then he noticed that his army coat, which had been hanging on a wall hook, had been switched with his work clothes, and his work boots were separated, one on each side of the room.

He hurriedly remembered the one thing of value in the room. Michael handed the lantern to Jim and knelt in front of the chest at the foot of his bed. Lifting the lid, he rummaged past his folded clothes to a tin box that held his important papers. He quickly shuffled through them. The deed to the property was still there. He released a pent-up breath.

"Well?" Jim asked, holding the lantern over the box.

"Everything's here."

Jim nodded thoughtfully. "You're bein' toyed with. Like a cat with a mouse."

Caught by a breeze, clouds skittered across the morning sky, and the sun sparkled off the dew dotting the leaves and grass. It was a lovely late spring day, Hope decided, as she walked back from the springhouse with a large bowl tucked in each arm. Her dowdy black skirts whipped at her legs, making the climb up Gracie's porch steps even more difficult since she had no free hand to lift her hem.

Reaching the landing, she turned back to stare down the road on which Michael had departed last night. Too soon. Too soon.

"Stop moonin'," Gracie yelled from inside. "We need to get the food ready to go so I can get me an' the kids ready for church."

"Go on," Hope said, walking across the threshold. "I'll finish up here. Timmy and I are already dressed."

"Bless you." Gracie whipped the apron

from over her long-sleeved nightgown. "It's sure lucky we got all this food left over from the party last night." She started for the stairs. "Don't forget what big eaters Max and Rolf are. I figure if they're going to ride up to the Underwoods' with us, we should feed 'em good." Her bossy older sister stopped halfway up and glanced over her shoulder, flipping her blonde night braid out of the way. "If you see Baxy, send that rascal on up."

Setting the bowls on the drainboard, Hope returned to the doorway and searched the area between Gracie's and Delia's across the road.

Like a monkey, Baxy, his grandfather's dark-featured namesake, swung down from a maple branch, hanging on by one hand. "Look!" he shouted to no one Hope could see. "Here come's Grampa an' Gramma."

From the direction he pointed, Hope guessed it wasn't Baxter and Sabina Clay. But just to make sure, she stepped out onto the porch.

Her own mother and father came riding in their four-seater with her baby brother, eight-year-old Danny, in the back.

Hope closed her eyes. It was much too early to have to make conversation with Papa.

Before the black carriage came to a stop, Danny hopped down and ran over to Baxy.

The boy dropped from the tree. "Guess what?" Baxy shouted to his young uncle loud enough for anyone within a mile to hear. "Joel Underwood rode in here last night with his friends, tryin' to look mean, an' he lied somethin' awful. Ever'body knew he was just tryin' to make Hope go home, 'cuz he's jealous."

"Baxy!" Hope spoke much too harshly. She softened her tone. "Your ma wants you upstairs right now to get ready for church."

"Oh, pooh," he grumbled.

"Now," she commanded.

"I'll come with you," Danny offered, and the two youngsters raced by Hope and into the house.

As she turned back, her father was helping her mother down from the carriage.

Dressed in her silver gray Sunday outfit, Jessica appeared as regal as ever as she descended, holding her skirt away from the wheel. "Sweetheart," she asked of Hope, "your father would appreciate a moment alone with you. I assume Gracie is upstairs."

"Yes." Hope's throat started to close as she shifted her attention to her father, looking distinguished and intimidating in his charcoal lawyering suit and striped cravat. Passing her mother, who gave her a warm smile, she walked down the steps.

"I take it Joel made a bit of a fool of himself at your party last night," her father said, strolling to her.

She really wasn't ready for this conversation. "Just Joel bein' — be*ing* — his true self."

Noah held her in his steady, gray gaze. "Tell me honestly. Wouldn't you have agreed to marry Joel after your mourning period was over if Flanagan hadn't shown up?"

Tell him *honestly?* Was he questioning her truthfulness again? "No. Never. He used to be merely a lazy no-account with no thought for anyone but himself. But lately, he's become a duplicitous, sneaky schemer. Is that truthful enough for you?"

She caught a flicker of a smile curl one side of her father's mouth.

He cleared his throat. "Yes, I do believe so. Your mother and I had a long talk yester's eve, and I shall no longer pressure you into betrothing yourself to Joel. But that does not imply that I've changed my feelings about Flanagan. I shall insist on having his actions checked out for the past decade and on getting to know him a whole lot better before I'll ever begin to trust him."

Hope felt encouraged that her father was finally giving some ground. "That's why Michael moved here . . . to this place where so many are eager to disapprove of him. He's here to regain your trust and win your approval."

Her father shook his head. "It won't come lightly, if ever."

"If it doesn't, so be it." She crossed her arms stubbornly but continued to speak as he had, in dispassionate, measured tones. "When my year as a widow is finished, we'll leave here. Michael is happy and successful in the army. There he's measured by his own deeds and conduct, not his father's. Now if you'll excuse me, I need to finish dishing up food for Titus and Tilly's dinner." She swung away, stalking toward the house.

"One more thing, Daughter."

Reluctantly, she turned back to face him.

"I love you very much."

His words caught her off guard. She felt her lower lip begin to tremble. "I love you, too, Papa."

Michael's eyes felt dry as dust as he dismounted at the back of the Bremmer house. He'd gotten precious little sleep the night before. Every creak and groan of the house, every hoot of an owl or screech of a wildcat, woke him. Climbing the steep steps, he stopped at the washbasin beside the door. Removing his white gloves, he scooped cold water over his eyes before knocking.

"Come in," came Max's gravelly shout.

Entering, Michael was relieved to find Max and Brother Rolf alone at the table. From the noise emanating from the floor above, he knew Belinda had her young'uns upstairs getting ready for church.

"Grab a cup of coffee and join us," Max said, nodding toward the hearth, his own feet propped comfortably on a nearby chair.

A body couldn't help but feel at home here.

The burly father and son waited before saying anything else until he had a steaming cup of very black brew and joined them.

"Max tells me you all haf some excitement at da Clays' last night." With his earthen cup in hand, Brother Rolf leaned back in his groaning seat and took a swallow, as if waiting for Michael to speak.

"I just got through telling Pops about Joel and his friends popping up last night," Max explained.

"That wasn't the only place they visited," Michael said, unbuttoning his blue uniform coat. "I came home to find things in my place moved hither and yon."

Max sat up straight. "Are you saying they were skulking around inside your house?"

"That's right. But from what I can tell, they didn't take nothin'. Nonetheless, they made sure I knew someone had been there."

"That doesn't sound good."

Michael looked from Max to Brother Rolf. "I'm more worried about Hope livin' in the same house with Joel. What's that old sayin' about a scorned lover?"

"Max, he vas already planning to ride home *mit* Hope after church today. But I t'ink maybe I better speak to Joel after da service mine own self."

Chapter Twenty-three

Although Hope vowed to forgive her father's past and any of his future endeavors to keep her and Michael apart, her old nature had reared its ugly head.

So now, all the way to the church service, she prayed for God to forgive her stubbornness for refusing her father's offer to go in their carriage with them. She'd known it would have been a friendly, reconciling thing to do, but she'd made the excuse that her horse needed to be exercised. And once committed, she'd been unable to make herself relent, to bend to her father's offer.

Even knowing all this, she'd rationalized by telling herself that if she hadn't gotten distracted so many times, she would have left early on Burns in the hope of getting a few private moments with Michael.

She did feel rather foolish, though, as the five-vehicle caravan carrying the Reardon and Clay clans rolled into the church parking area with her and Ike's sixteen-year-old lad the only two mounted. Even

Timmy had deserted her for Gracie's wagonload of youngsters.

Before dismounting on this unseasonable balmy day, Hope glanced across to the Bremmer house, where Michael usually went to visit first. But she saw no one outside.

"Hope," Gracie called from the front seat of her wagon, "the Dillards are over by the church steps."

Seeing Ruthie, for whom the term "pleasingly plump" must have been coined, Hope experienced a rush of love. No one had such a dear smile for everyone she knew or a more huggable body. And today Hope could surely use one of those hugs.

By the time she tethered Burns and reached Amos and Ruthie, most of her adult family were already gathering around the Dillards with the usual greetings.

Her father usurped her by asking the important question first. "I heard you went to check on Tilly Underwood last night. How was she after her fall?"

"I'm afraid we was misinformed," lean-as-leather Amos supplied, cocking his head toward Howie. "Mrs. Underwood was gettin' round as good as can be expected for an old woman with rheumatiz in her joints."

"She was real happy to see us, too,"

Ruthie added. "I gotta make a point of droppin' by to see them more often." Her gaze sought out Hope. "We stayed long enough to help 'em get through their evenin' chores."

"Thank you." Hope reached for Ruthie and got the hug she'd wanted, along with the fragrance of rose water. "And do come by anytime. Tilly does love company."

Moving away from the group, Hope climbed the first two church steps, hoping for a glimpse of Michael among the other arriving wagons and riders.

Her father stopped below the steps, the two of them now at eye level.

It gave her a sense of equality. "Joel lied, just as I suspected."

"And like I said, spurned young men sometimes act a little desperate. I'll have a talk with him. He'll settle down."

Just as the church bell rang to call the congregation to worship, Michael came walking out of the Bremmers' yard, along with Belinda's boys. He looked just as handsome as ever in his uniform.

Noah must have read the anticipation in her expression. He glanced over his shoulder, then returned his attention to her. "I'm counting on your good judgment this morning. Your *wisdom*," he said, as if he were arguing a case in court. "I know you would prefer to sit with Flanagan, but considering Joel's possible reaction and the further consequences, I strongly suggest you sit with us." Without waiting for her answer, he ascended the steps and, taking her by the elbow, ushered her through the open double doors.

Michael caught the briefest glimpse of his lady in black before her father whisked her inside. Disappointed, he slowed his pace, reckoning that it was preferable that she sit with Mr. Reardon than Joel Underwood.

He scanned the Sunday morning throng entering the building, looking for the freckle-faced rascal. But he found neither Joel nor the Underwood wagon and team.

Howie Clay came across the lawn to intercept Michael beside the church. "I wanted to be the one to tell you." Mischief sparked in his brown eyes and his smirk. "When the Dillards stopped by the Underwoods' last night, they found Mrs. Underwood in fine health."

"Does Hope know?"

"Oh yes. Her an' the entire Reardon clan. That oughta start shiftin' the holdouts to your side. Now I'm just waitin' for Joel to show his lying face here. If I know him, he'll show up late so he don't have to explain hisself. Unless he weasels outta comin' altogether."

With the bell in the tower continuing its call, Michael and Howie removed their headgear and followed the stragglers inside. About three-quarters of the way down the aisle, Howie stepped into the pew just behind Hope and her parents.

Michael couldn't resist his next move. Stopping beside the elder Reardons' pew with his tall, military hat tucked beneath one arm, he bowed to the waist. "Good mornin', Mr. Reardon."

Hope's father stared frozen-faced up at him, but for only a second. "Good morning, Mr. Flanagan." He had no choice but to respond politely, considering where they were.

Michael swept his glance across Hope and to her mother. "Mrs. Reardon. How lovely you look today."

"Why, thank you, Mr. Flanagan. You flatter me."

"On the contrary. Any stranger would be more likely to think you were sister to your beautiful daughter rather than her mother." He then let his gaze stray to Hope's fragile elegance and linger. "Mrs. Underwood."

A smile trickled across her generous lips.

"It's a pleasure to see you, too, Sergeant Flanagan. I do hope your ride home last eve was a pleasant one." Her voice had that enticing honey huskiness to it.

"Howdy!" In the row just ahead of Hope, her wide-eyed son popped up from among his cousins and stood on the wooden pew, facing him.

Michael grinned. "And howdy to you, too, Tim. You're lookin' mighty handsome this mornin'."

Timmy's small hands flew to his dark pate. "Unka Howie put good smell here." The tot clambered over a blond cousin to reach the end. "Smell," he said, leaning out and bending his adorable head.

Michael complied, knowing everyone seated nearby watched — except Noah Reardon. "You're right, Tim. That does smell fine. You can tell me all about it after church." Then bowing slightly to the lad's grandparents and after taking a last, lingering glance at Hope, Michael strode to the front to sit with the Bremmers.

During the service, Hope caught only snatches of the pastor's sermon. Every noise behind her became a distraction as she listened for the Underwoods to arrive. Not hearing any latecomers, she was kept guessing, because she didn't dare turn around to look — everyone in the sanctuary seemed to be watching her every move as she sat between her parents.

After what seemed like the longest service of her life, Brother Rolf finally concluded his sermon by referring to the first chapter of James. "Vhen you go home dis week, I vant you every day to remember dis. Be quick to listen. Slow to speak. *Und,* most important, slow to anger. Remember to pray you are doing da vill of God, not merely each man doing vhat he t'inks is right in his own mind."

He took what sounded to Hope like an exasperated breath, then continued. "Also remember to pray for little Benny Auburn. He falls from a tree yesterday *und* broke his arm. Da Undervoods are also not here dis morning. Pray dat one of dem is not bad sick."

Hope's first instinct was one of guilt. Suppose Tilly had actually taken ill this morning, and she wasn't there to help? But her suspicious side guessed that Joel, too embarrassed to show his face, had probably disabled the wagon so his parents would have no transportation — Tilly was much too feeble to ride horseback.

As the congregation rose to leave, Hope

wished she could lag behind to wait for Michael at the front but decided to delay their meeting until she wasn't surrounded.

At the entrance, her father shook hands with Brother Rolf, extending the usual compliments on the sermon, and walked out ahead of Hope.

Then Brother Rolf engulfed her hand in his. "Me *und* Max, ve are coming to your place today to check on Tilly, *und* I t'ink ve haf a talk *mit* Joel, too."

If anyone could talk some sense into Joel, it would be the old minister. "Gracie and Howie are coming, too. We've planned for you, so there's plenty of food. Ride out with us, and we can all have dinner together." As she walked down the steps, though, she dreaded the confrontation with her brother-in-law.

Hope, with her mother right behind her, stopped once they'd reached a grassy spot.

Jessica smiled warmly. "Speaking of Sunday dinner, sweetheart, I insist you and Timmy come to our place next week. I'll invite Gracie and her family, and we'll make an afternoon of it." She reached out, tucking a strand of Hope's hair beneath her dreary black bonnet. "It's been much too long, with you and your father at loggerheads. I've missed your cheery laughter immensely."

Hope returned the smile. . . . Her poor mother, always trying to make everyone happy. Hope hated to add another complication, but . . . "I'd love to come, but only if you invite Michael, too."

"Oh, dear," escaped as her mother glanced at her husband walking toward the wagons. "I'll have to discuss this with your papa first and let you know."

Jessica left her side to go speak with her husband, and Hope immediately searched out Michael.

Surrounded by friends, he stood a number of yards away with the younger Clays and the Bremmers. His gaze was already on her. He nodded with a hint of a smile, and the people milling between them seemed to fade away.

But just for a moment. Starting toward Michael, she tried to get a glimpse of her father's face while her mother spoke to him.

Paying scant attention to where she stepped, she practically bumped into the much taller and hardier Nancy Johnson. Remembering their conversation the evening before, Hope stopped for a second. "Don't forget Friday sewing circle," she reminded, then quickly excused herself, hoping she hadn't sounded too abrupt as she hurried on.

Hope began to slow her pace. Even though there was nothing stopping her from walking up and standing right beside Michael, an entire congregation was watching every move that Ezra's young widow made. She joined Michael's group but kept a safe distance by standing, not next to Michael, but across from him. Still, being this close to him, it took her several seconds before she even realized someone was talking.

"We'll ride up to the Underwoods', then, right after lunch," Max was saying to Gracie.

"We were hoping you and your pa could join us," Gracie said. "We packed up all the food left from last night. There's plenty. Isn't that right, Hope?"

She dragged her gaze from Michael's. "Yes. I already spoke to Max's father." Remembering her manners, she turned to Belinda, who was holding her tiny son. "You'll come, too, won't you?"

Maintaining a slow rocking motion as she cradled her baby, Belinda shook her head. "I've already prepared dinner. I'll ask my parents to stay and keep me company — which reminds me, Gracie," she said, swinging her attention to Hope's older sister, "Papa wants you to sing next Sunday. You'll need to get with Mama to practice beforehand. Why don't you walk along with me now to talk to her?"

As the two women departed, Hope's gaze darted once again to her own parents, and she saw the fury in her father's eyes as he glanced back at her.

Be brave, she told herself. *Don't back down.*

When Hope first walked up, Michael had glimpsed her gladness to see him, though she'd stopped several feet short of coming to stand at his side. He'd really hoped for more, considering the treasured moments they had had alone yesterday. But, he kept telling himself, he must be patient.

Now, as she turned back from watching Belinda and Gracie walk away, her entire demeanor had changed. Her eyes practically shouted her fear.

He swung his attention to where she'd been looking and saw the reason. Hope's father marched straight for them, his mouth hard-set, his fists clenched. Instinctively, Michael moved closer to Hope. She darted an anxious glance up at him.

"Be brave," he whispered. "It'll be all right."

His words chased the fright from her eyes. "Yes," she said. "Yes," just before her father was upon them.

"Morning," Mr. Reardon said, greeting Max and Howie with the curtness of a commanding officer. Then he turned to Michael, his features granite. "Sergeant Flanagan. If you would oblige me, I'd appreciate a word alone with you."

The last time Reardon spoke to him at Bremmers' smithy, he hadn't given Michael the courtesy of vilifying him in private. This, at least, would be an improvement. Michael nodded. "Of course. It would be my pleasure."

As he walked away from his friends with the older but definitely still formidable man, Michael shot one last glance back at Hope. The fear had returned to her eyes as she stood there, her arms akimbo, watching.

A dozen or so yards away, Reardon stopped with his back to Hope.

Michael did the same and turned to him. "Yes, sir. What is it you want of me?"

Reardon's gray eyes narrowed, his thick, sun-whitened brows shelving over them. "You already know what I want, *have wanted* for the past ten years. But that's not why I asked to speak to you." Closing his eyes, he butted his folded hands against his mouth, then sighed and studied Michael again. "I am to invite you to dinner at our house after church next Sunday."

"I'm sorry, sir. I must have misunderstood you."

That seemed to make him all the angrier. "No, you didn't. We'll be expecting you and our daughter."

Dinner at the Reardons'? With Hope?

With the precision of a West Point general, Noah Reardon made an about-face and stalked away, leaving Michael to stare after him, openmouthed.

Coming to, Michael closed his mouth and started back to Hope with a much lighter step than when he'd left her. Although the invitation had been begrudged at best, it was progress. Definite progress. And just one short day after Hope had humbled herself and forgiven her father.

If only Joel would make the same effort. A smile tugged at Michael at the thought of Joel ever making an unselfish gesture . . . one that didn't further his own purposes. He would never completely trust that scoundrel.

But then Michael remembered that he had his own failing. He wasn't the least ready to forgive his own father either.

Chapter Twenty-four

A crazy thought passed through Michael's head as he traveled along the wooded north road, and he chuckled. He actually found himself wanting to thank Joel Underwood.

"Did you see something funny?" Hope asked, riding horseback at his side.

"No, not really." Michael had been invited to accompany her, along with Howie's family, Max, and Brother Rolf, as far as the Underwood cutoff after the Sunday service. He and Hope now followed far enough behind their party to avoid the dust kicked up by the Clay wagon at the front and the Bremmer buggy just ahead. "I was thinkin' what a favor Joel unwittingly did for us by not showin' up for church this mornin'."

A slow grin trickled across her lips, and she guided her Arabian a little closer to his mare. "Now, that's somethin' to smile about."

He wished he could reach over and rip the dreary black hat from her head so he could see all of her face. But, of course, propriety dictated that he maintain a respectable distance from the widow.

"It's so lovely being here with you, I hate to spoil this time by asking, but I must." Her smile evaporating, she glanced ahead to the others in case they might be listening. "What did my father say to you? Did he threaten you in any way?"

"Why? Would you go charging after him if he did?" he teased.

"This is not a joking matter."

"No," he drawled, "I reckon not. Actually, I think you'll be pleased. Your father invited me to come to dinner at his house next Sunday. You could've knocked me over with a feather. I'm sure it wasn't his idea. He seemed real reluctant. But still . . ."

"Mama talked him into it." The expression in her lovely heart-shaped face brightened considerably. "You said yes, didn't you?"

He shrugged. "I'm not sure if I said anything. But, then, Mr. Reardon knew I wouldn't refuse once I heard you were gonna be there."

"All I can say is, you're a remarkable man." Her guileless eyes bespoke her sincerity as full sunlight fractured into a thousand dapples and played across her face as they rode into a grove of maples and black gum. "To move here knowing you would face such opposition, such hostility . . . I confess, even I wasn't sure about you when you first returned. But you never lashed back at anyone. If anything should prove your worth to my father, that should. If I haven't thanked you already for your infinite patience with Papa, I do so now."

She gave him far too much credit. "It's really not that hard, Hope, when I know the prize that awaits me. And I'm so glad you gave me a chance to prove myself; I hope he will, too. Your father is an honest man who cares deeply for his family. A man to be imitated."

"All except his stubbornness. Please, don't imitate that," she said with a playful lift of her slender brows. Then she grew serious. "I should warn you, he wants to have you investigated. See if you've been in any trouble since you and your family left here. I'm dreadfully sorry."

"Don't be. I have nothing to hide. If anything, having me checked out will aid our bid to remain in the valley."

"But as you said last week, we should leave our options open. So, just in case, what sort of things would I need to bring with me to Fort Pickering?"

Michael sensed Hope didn't believe her

father would ever truly relent. For her sake, he prayed she was wrong. He looked skyward, searching for the right words, then came back to her. "While I was in Nashville, I spoke to the only married sergeant I've served with at Fort Pickering, and I have to be honest with you. What he had to say wasn't promising. Stover said it's been real hard on his woman bein' the only enlisted man's wife at a frontier fort. With us gone fighting so much this past couple of years, and with the only other women at the fort lordin' it over her — they're officers' wives," he elaborated with a grimace. "Stover's amazed she's stayed. He said most of the brides pack it in and go back home within the first year."

"But the war's over now," she protested.

"We still leave on patrol or some other mission off in Indian country for weeks at a time. I'd have to leave you at the fort to wile away the days. But I'm even more set against us headin' out west on our own where you wouldn't have no woman friends a'tall. Settlin' on some uncleared piece of land where we'd have to build ever'thing up from scratch, and you'd be workin' yourself into an early grave." He shook his head. "I won't let you do that. So now you know why I'm doin' ever'thing I can to make a go of it here where you do have friends an' family you can count on. Where there's a store close by an' Nashville is just an easy three-day float downriver." He included a chuckle with his next words. "I'm trying to think of this as me tryin' to run one of them Shawnee gauntlets before I can be accepted into the tribe."

"Exactly what is a Shawnee gauntlet?"

"You don't know?" He grinned. "That's where a tribe lines up in two rows facing each other with sticks and clubs in their hands, ready to swing. And your job is to run between them from one end to the other without falling down. Falling down could prove deadly."

He didn't get the response he'd expected. Her lower lip began to tremble, and he thought she was going to cry.

Instead, she took a huge breath. "You never think about what's good for you. Just me, only me. It kills me to see you treated badly."

The love he felt for her swelled inside him. He moved Ebony closer and caught her hand. "I have to try. If I can't give you a happy life, I could never —"

She gripped his hand tighter. "Don't say it. The only place I will ever be happy is with you. Wherever that is. No matter how hard we have to work. Don't you ever give up on us. Promise me." Her voice strained with her urgency.

Without Michael noticing, the buggy just ahead had slowed considerably, and he and Hope were almost upon it. A hand reached out from the side and waved them forward.

The enclosing woods had given way to a meadow, and now there was plenty of room for Michael and Hope to move their horses alongside the leather-bonneted vehicle. Although Michael preferred the intimacy of just him and Hope, he couldn't very well ignore the request. Besides, Hope had already nudged her mount forward.

The hand had belonged to Brother Rolf. "Goot," he said, as they came alongside him and Max, who drove the horse and rig. "I am vanting to talk to you before ve reach da Underwood cutoff." His fatherly gaze centered on Hope. "I yust vant you to know I am proud of you. Your mama tells me before she leaves dat you go to your papa yesterday *und* make da amends. Dat you are forgiving him *und* starting new again. You are da goot daughter of bot' your fadders. Da one here in da valley *und* da utter One." He tipped his face skyward. "Da One in heaven."

"I'm trying," she said with a helpless expression. "But it's not easy."

"You asked for da vanting to do it, *und* now God, He vill give you da power and da love."

Michael noticed that Max, on the other side of the minister, was grinning, though he kept his eyes on the road ahead. Michael envied the enjoyment Max derived from being with his father. Though he'd never had even a hint of that with his own pa, he hoped one day he'd have that kind of relationship with Timmy.

"Michael." Brother Rolf's gruff voice snagged his attention again.

"Yes, sir?"

"I vas vondering how you and your own papa are doing *mit* dis forgiving business?"

Michael wished he had the answer the kind old man sought, but he didn't.

Too soon Hope saw the cutoff to the Underwoods'. Michael would leave her here, and most likely she wouldn't have an opportunity to see him again until next Sunday.

She gazed up at him, missing him even before they'd parted.

He returned the same look of yearning.

"I wish I could invite you to supper some evening this week. But with Joel being so difficult . . ."

"Are you sure you'll be all right there with him?" It was obvious in his tone, his expression, that he didn't want her returning to the Underwoods'.

"I'll be fine. Gracie reminded me to get a slide bolt to put on my door, just to be on the safe side. We'll mount it before they go home."

She could see the concern in his eyes and knew he wanted to say more on the subject, but he didn't.

Up ahead, Howie halted his wagon team and hopped down, then strode back to Hope and Michael. "Let me help you off, li'l sis," he said, raising his hands. "I think I'll ride on to Mike's for a few minutes. Take a look at all he's done to his place."

Wishing she could go instead, Hope came down into Howie's arms. She knew she couldn't go, of course. It wouldn't be proper without a chaperone.

As Howie adjusted the stirrups to his leg length, he and Michael exchanged odd glances.

Disturbing glances.

Had they kept something from her? Did they think Joel might be waiting there to ambush Michael?

Before she could ask, Michael nudged his black mare into a trot, leaving her behind.

The children in the back of the wagon all yelled, "Good-bye," and waved as the men rode over a gentle hill and out of sight.

Hope rode beside Gracie into the Underwood clearing, and with each revolution of the wheels, her chest tightened more. She had no idea how Joel would react after their confrontation the night before.

Gracie must have read her anxiety. "Don't worry. Joel will mind his p's and q's with Max and Brother Rolf here. And me an' Howie plan to stay until we feel good about leavin' you here."

Before Hope could reply, Timmy, in the wagon bed behind her, reached up and grabbed her neck. "Hugs."

She lifted him onto her lap and wrapped her arms around her warm, squirmy son, wishing she could've done the same when she parted from Michael.

Tilly and Titus came out on the porch as the two vehicles rolled to a stop just short of the house. Upon recognizing their visitors, both grinned wide enough to show a gap or two where they had missing teeth.

"Don't want you to panic," Gracie hollered in a tease. "We brought enough dinner with us for everyone."

"Well, get yourselves down and come on in." Cheery as ever, Titus summoned them with one hand while wrapping the other around his wife's waist. "Ain't had the pleasure of feedin' the minister for some time now."

As the children dropped off the back of the wagon to make a dash for the barn to see the new calf, Hope and the other adults climbed down more carefully and started for the house. Joel had yet to show his face.

"Hope," Tilly said as she drew near, "you ain't gonna believe this, but we had company last night, too. The Dillards dropped by on their way home from your party at Gracie's. Said y'all was havin' a real fine time."

"That was nice of them," Hope agreed, not wanting to tell them Ruthie Dillard had mentioned to her earlier that they would stop by.

"An' that sweet Ruthie," Titus added, "helped me an Ma finish up the dishes, too. Amos has got hisself one fine li'l wife there."

"*Ja,* he does," Brother Rolf chimed in as he lumbered up the porch steps. "I don't see Joel about. Is he sick? I get vorried when you don't come to church dis morning."

"No, Joel ain't ailin'," Titus said, stepping back to allow his guests to enter the house first. "But my wagon sure is. The hitch is split almost clean in two. Joel lashed it with some leather straps, but he still didn't trust it, so we had to stay home. Ma's horseback-ridin' days is long gone. Ain't that right?" he said to his wife at his side.

Tilly smiled apologetically to Brother Rolf as they came inside. "The rheumatiz, you know."

Hope glanced around the large room and out the windows. "Where's Joel, Ma? He promised to stay close till I got back."

"Oh, you know you can't keep that boy tied down. He rode on over to the Smiths' to see if Ken an' Junior could make us a new hitch 'fore next Sunday."

"So, he's not here," Max said, and exchanged another one of those odd glances with his father.

Hope's chest tightened. It was true. The men were keeping something from her. Something about Joel. And Michael?

As Michael rode into his clearing with Howie, everything looked as it should. The horses were peacefully grazing . . . just as they had been the night before.

Even so, Michael had an eerie feeling tingling up his spine. He reached into his saddlebag and pulled out his loaded pistol and cocked it, his eyes scanning in all directions — at the sides of the barn, the sheds, the house.

"Ain't you a might jumpy?" Howie asked, staring at the weapon. "I really don't think Joel's the ambushin' type. A little headstrong and jealous, maybe, but he ain't no backstabber."

Feeling a little foolish, Michael lowered the hammer and slid the gun back in the saddlebag again. "You're right. I reckon all that Indian fightin' we did has made me skittish."

"I see you got all your fences secure, and your buildin's look sound," Howie said, surveying the place.

"There's still some leaks here an' there in the roofs." Michael chuckled as he guided Ebony to the front of the house. "I found that out the other night when it rained. Got woke up to water drippin' in my ear."

"Still," Howie said, dismounting, "it ain't a bad start. Get yourself some chickens an' a few hogs. An' there's still plenty of time to plant a few rows of feed corn. Did you bring a plow with you?"

"One was left here. Needs sharpenin'."

Howie started up the steps. "Was much in the way of furniture left? If not —"

Michael, looping Ebony's reins over the hitching post, glanced up, wondering why

Howie had stopped in midsentence.

Howie was staring down at something on the porch.

A black cat.

A dead black cat.

Chapter Twenty-five

Michael picked up the dead cat and went for a shovel in the toolshed behind the house.

Howie followed. "What kind of a person kills some poor cat just to make a point?"

"It's the kind of thing my pa would've done." Michael looked down at the limp creature. "But I can't point a finger to the person I know did this, 'cuz I ain't got no proof. Besides it just looks like some schoolboy prank, like the last time Joel dropped by. He's craftier than a body would think."

"One thing Joel didn't count on, though," Howie said. "He didn't expect you to have a witness either time. He figured it'd just be your word against his, with you comin' off lookin' a might silly." He opened the shed door and brought out Michael's shovel. "I'll bury the cat. Why don't you check around, see if he did anything else."

"The horses!" Michael bolted toward the pastures, counting heads as he went. The stock was all out in the open, and they appeared fine. He then checked the barn and the house. Everything seemed as he'd left it. But he was still edgy.

As he walked up to Howie, his friend was patting the last of the grave dirt back into place with the back of the shovel. He glanced up at Michael. "Well?"

"Ever'thing checks out. Far as I can see." Michael took the implement from him and set it inside the shed again. "But tonight I'm bringin' the horses into the barn and stayin' out there with 'em. It's taken me years to acquire that string, and I'm not lettin' nothin' happen to 'em."

"You need to get yourself a good watchdog."

"I thought of that. Still, a barkin' dog can't warn me when I'm not here."

"Maybe so, but while you are here, you'd be able to sleep at night. You know, from where I stand, I'd say Joel's tryin' to bait you into callin' him out, not the other way around. He wants to either run you off or kill you, but look like the righteous one whilst he's a-doin' it." Howie started back for the front along with Michael.

"He ain't gonna find it that easy."

"But is stayin' here worth all the trouble? What if he threatens Hope? If I was you, I'd just sign on with the army again an' wait till

Hope's free — her year of mourning will be up in a few months, won't it? — then just come back long enough to fetch her outta here."

"I wish it was that simple." Michael stopped with Howie beside Hope's horse. He ran his hand along the animal's regal neck . . . a mount befitting his lady. "If you hear of a good dog someone would be willin' to sell or even loan out for a spell, I'd be much obliged."

"I'll ask around. Well, reckon I better get on over to the Underwoods'. I'll be real curious to see Joel's face when I come ridin' in fresh from your place," Howie said, chuckling lightly. He shoved his polished dress shoe into the stirrup. "You keep an eye out. Hear?"

Hope had already finished the breakfast dishes and had fires going beneath two of the three washtubs that she was now filling with water from the well. All the while, her mind raced through the words she planned to say to Joel. After dumping a bucketful, she stopped a second to catch her breath and wipe perspiration trickling toward her eyes. Her gaze went directly to Joel's upstairs window as it had several times before.

He had yet to roll out of bed. He'd managed to elude the Bremmers and Howie yesterday by staying gone until late in the night. And now he was avoiding her by lazing the morning away in bed.

Returning to the well, her resolve only strengthened. His staying in bed all day would not change what she had to say to him. He'd have to get up sometime.

Once she finished filling the tubs, she added some sticks to the fires beneath and returned inside to fetch the items in need of washing. Just as she did, she spotted Joel sneaking out the back door.

If Tilly hadn't been sitting at the spinning wheel and Timmy playing with his wooden horses on the floor, Hope would've yelled for Joel to stop. Instead, she strode across the room and followed him out the other side.

"Joel!" she called once she was a few yards from the house.

Heading toward the barn, Joel took a couple more steps before hesitating, then stopped. He turned around with an expression on his freckled face that rivaled the innocence of a newborn babe. "Do you need somethin'?"

She sent a fleet request to the Lord to give her the right words. "To talk to you." She'd used carefully modulated syllables, trying to keep any animosity out of her tone. While closing the space separating them, she was suddenly instilled with unexpected courage and decided not to mince words but to come right out with it. But before she could say a word, he started making excuses.

"I know I shouldn't have lied the other night. But when I found out Flanagan rode down to the Clays', too, I just couldn't help myself."

Hope clenched her teeth. "I think it's important that I say this straight out to you. I have never considered marrying you, and I never will."

Her statement scarcely fazed him. "That's just because you was older. But I'm full growed now. Plenty man for you." His own courage building, he took a step forward. "More man than Ezra ever thought of bein'. An' for certain more than some murderin' barn burner's pup."

Finding it hard not to dispute his words, Hope prayed for calm. "Joel, if you are set on marrying, there are two or three young gals who I'm sure would gladly say yes to a proposal from you. I simply am not one of them."

Joel stiffened, the muscles across his shoulders bulging beneath his work shirt. "You'd like that, wouldn't you? Have me bring in another gal so you can run off with that piece of trash. If anyone's been lyin' around here, it's you. You just been pretendin' to care about us."

Hope realized any further talk was useless at this point. She whirled away. "I have to get back to the wash."

"This isn't over," he railed after her. "You just wait an' see. I'll show him up for what he is. For the connivin' cowardly trash he really is."

Michael was sitting at his table that afternoon, trying to salvage an old harness he'd found in the barn when he heard the creak and crunch of an approaching wagon. Scraping back his chair, he dropped his awl on the table and strode to the door, where he retrieved the pistol from a shelf above.

Walking out, he shaded his eyes as he watched a man coming, driving a two-wheeled cart behind a single horse. Then Michael relaxed. The floppy hat and smile were none other than Howie's.

Michael sauntered out to meet his pal. "What brings you up this way again so soon?"

A dog began to bark and leaped up on the high side rails of the hay cart.

"Whoa." Howie reined in the big

chestnut farm horse. "Found you a dog," he said over the barking. "For the time bein' anyway."

Michael stepped closer to examine the animal. Tied with a rope, it looked like a longhaired sheepdog of some sort.

"That there's Napoleon." Howie hopped down from the cart. "Belongs to the Skinners. They said you could keep him here as long as you need him. You'll have to keep him tied, though, or he'll just run on back home." Dropping the back gate, he climbed aboard and retrieved the dog.

Once the animal was on the ground, Michael saw that the tricolored dog was well-built and had intelligent eyes. He glanced back at his friend. "I surely appreciate this. I didn't get much sleep last night. A lot of strange noises I never heard before. Speakin' of Joel Underwood, what did he have to say for himself yesterday?"

Howie raised his slash of dark brows and wagged his head. "He never showed his face the whole time we was there. And we waited until almost suppertime."

Michael didn't like the sound of that. "That means Hope was left to deal with him alone? And if he was mad enough to slit the throat of a cat . . ."

"He wouldn't dare touch her. He'd have

all the Reardon and Clay men down on him in a heartbeat, and he knows it."

That gave Michael little comfort. "I don't like this at all. Hope won't let me come visitin', and I have no idea what that rowdy will be up to next."

"It's hard, I know. I'll drop by on my way home. But first, let me tie Napoleon up so we can unload the grindstone I brung."

"Grindstone?"

"Yep. You did say you had a plow that needed sharpenin', didn't you?"

Michael smiled. "If I didn't know better, I'd say you was tryin' to turn me into a clod-hopper just like you."

"That's right." Howie's grin rivaled Michael's as he tied the dog to a porch post. "I brung you some corn seed, too. An' if you don't say thank you right quick, I'll bring you some real sweet-smellin' hogs to-morrow."

"Timothy, sit still!" Hope commanded as she tried to slick down the cowlick at her son's crown. On the settee at the parlor end of the big room, she held him with her knees as she dipped the comb into a mug of water again. She wanted him to look especially nice today. They'd be seeing Michael at church. Just the thought sent her mind to drifting.

"Me want smelly stuff." He squirmed, dodging from her next attempt.

"Just as soon as I'm finished." The clock on the mantel said 9:15. If they didn't hurry, they'd be late for church.

And she still hadn't caught Joel alone this morning to tell him her plans for the afternoon. She glanced up the stairs, willing him to come down. He'd been up there for the better part of an hour getting ready.

With the cowlick somewhat tamed, Hope picked up Timmy and took him to the hearth end. "So you want to smell good." Not wanting to waste time going upstairs for some of her lilac perfume, she lifted the lid off the tin holding her vanilla beans, then scraped one with her nail and held it up for Timmy to sniff. "Do you like that?"

"Uh-huh."

"Good." She rubbed the bean across the underside of his wrists and along either side of his neck.

As she did, Joel shot down the stairs and rushed out the back door without slowing.

Hope quickly set Timmy on his feet, then hurried after her brother-in-law. "Joel!" she shouted as she ran down the steps.

He stopped and turned. Dressed in his brown suit with a black tie, he really didn't look half bad, though she knew that what was inside the man was not nearly as nice. His expression was one of surprise.

She couldn't blame him. She'd spoken to him only when necessary all during the week. "I need to talk to you a minute," she said upon reaching him. "I'm having dinner today at my parents', and I'm taking Titus and Tilly with me, so you'll need to ride your horse to church this morning. Oh yes," she added, trying not to sound guilty, "you'll have to see to your own dinner. There's plenty of leftover food out in the springhouse."

His blue eyes narrowed. "So, what you're sayin' is I'm not invited."

Hope had no intention of telling him that Michael would be there. Still, her next words were not a lie. "It will be difficult enough dealin' with Papa without havin' you there, too."

Joel relaxed, a smug grin replacing his frown. "Your pa ain't no more of a fool than I am. He knows what's best for you. And that's me."

"I sure am sorry I'm so slow this mornin'." Tilly clung to Hope and Titus as she leaned forward, trying to hurry. "Just can't seem to get these hips to work proper."

Timmy slipped free from Hope's other hand and raced for the church steps. They were late again, and the music had already started.

"Take all the time you need," Titus said, patting Tilly's hand tucked in his arm. "You earned it, ol' girl."

Hope watched anxiously as her son dashed wildly through the open doors just as a congregational hymn came to an end. Even after he disappeared from sight, she could hear the patter of his new leather shoes across the floor. She cringed, wishing she could run after him, but Tilly would need full support this morning while mounting the steps.

As they reached the landing, Hope spied Timmy near the front, clambering over his cousins in one of the Reardon pews.

One of Delia's girls pulled him onto her lap, and Hope's mother glanced back and whispered something to him.

"He'll be fine there," Tilly said to Hope as they started up the aisle.

Satisfied that she was right, Hope's attention moved on to the front pew and the man in the royal blue uniform coat. She took a thrilled breath. Although she knew he'd be there, she always had to make sure.

Reaching their own pew, Hope stepped in

first, with Tilly following. But it wasn't until she was seated that she realized Joel was not there waiting. Yet he'd taken off from home at a gallop before they left. He should have arrived long before them.

"Where do you reckon that boy of mine got to?" Tilly asked as, up front, Brother Rolf announced the next hymn.

Balding Titus frowned and glanced back toward the entrance.

Yet, regardless of their concern, regardless of the fact she knew she shouldn't, Hope was glad Joel wasn't around threatening trouble. Mrs. Gregg at the organ started the prelude to the next hymn. Hope relaxed and prepared to sing on the beginning note.

Her sense of freedom ended with the following song when Joel came hurrying down the aisle, sweeping his hat from his curly head. Still, she was grateful for one thing. He dropped into the aisle seat instead of stepping over his folks to sit by her as he usually did. He did lean forward, though, and sent her a knowing look.

By the time the service concluded, Hope's stomach was in knots. Although she'd deliberately delayed telling the older Underwoods that Michael had been invited to her parents' for dinner, she feared Joel had somehow learned of it. She wondered what he would do.

But she shouldn't have.

The moment Brother Rolf said "Amen" at the end of the benediction, Joel leaned around his pa and gave his mother a peck on the cheek. "Gotta hurry. I'm off to a friend's place for dinner." Then with another mysterious glance Hope's way, he shot up the aisle.

By the time she helped Tilly down the outside steps, he was nowhere to be seen. But as she glanced behind her, Michael stood on the landing, looking at her only. Today he would be going with her to Sunday dinner at her parents'.

Please, Lord, let this be a day of reconciliation. Between Papa and Michael. And give Titus and Tilly a love and acceptance of Michael that Ezra, at the very end, would have wanted — that I so desperately need.

Chapter Twenty-six

Nearing her parents' rutted track, Hope pulled on the wagon team's traces, doing her best to bring them to a stop in a patch of shade. The black of her dress drew in the heat of the noonday sun.

"Why are we stoppin'?" Titus asked from the other side of Tilly, his own coat off, his shirt damp and rumpled.

At the church house, Hope had told those dining at the elder Reardons' she wanted to be last to depart because she would be driving more slowly for the sake of Tilly's painful joints. But she'd had another equally important reason. "I need to speak to you two before we reach Mama's."

Tilly raised a thinning white brow. This was obviously a strange place for a talk.

"I wanted to prepare you. Papa also invited Sergeant Flanagan to dinner today."

The grooves in Tilly's forehead deepened as she narrowed her red-rimmed eyes on Hope. "Have you known this all along?"

Hope felt even more duplicitous. "Yes.

And I see now that I was wrong not to tell you. Forgive me." Glancing across to Titus, she untied her chin ribbons and removed her suffocating bonnet. "I wanted you to be able to talk with him. He and Ezra became close friends during those last weeks."

Titus removed his own hat and wiped his brow. "You're basin' that on the letter Ezra sent you, ain't you?" His tone was almost accusing. "You know this Flanagan comes from bad blood."

This wasn't going well. She'd been a fool to wait until now to tell them. "From the letter and some of the things Howie and the sergeant have told me. But I should've respected your judgment enough to let you choose whether you want to come or not. Just say the word, and I'll turn this rig around."

Tilly's bony hand slid over Hope's. "You know we wanted you to marry our Joel. For us it was the perfect fit, thinkin' as how he might settle down for you." She inhaled a shaky breath. "But you've made your druthers plain enough. So if you want us to spend time with this young man, well, I reckon I'd like to hear what he's got to say about my Ezzy." She turned then to her husband. "Iffen it's all the same to you, Pa."

"You sure you're up to it?" he asked, searching his wife's face.

"This is 'bout as good as I'm gonna feel these days." She looked at Hope. "The biggest thing I'm gonna regret is the day you ain't our daughter no more."

"Ma, I'll always be your daughter," she defended with passion. "You're my son's grandparents. Nothin' can ever change that. I will never forsake you." Laying the traces over the front board, she wrapped an arm around Tilly. "Never."

Hope had scarcely gotten the team moving again when she remembered she'd already made plans to leave their care to others. She'd written letters to the Underwoods' older children, and any day now, she expected to hear word back from them.

Another thing she'd done behind Titus's and Tilly's backs. What had she been thinking to treat them as if they were her children?

Tomorrow. She'd tell them tomorrow. They'd had enough surprises for today.

"What's taking her so long?" Michael asked Howie. Looking down the road, he took off his cavalry coat and dropped it over one of the chairs clustered beneath an old sycamore. "I don't feel real comfortable bein' here as it is." Hope's parents had been polite — Mr. Reardon had handed him a tall glass of lemonade as soon as he and the Clays arrived — but he knew they'd rather he'd declined their invitation.

Howie straddled a chair. "Sit down. She'll be along any minute."

Michael felt too nervous to stay seated, but standing, he was more noticeable. Taking a sip of his drink, he shot a glance to Mr. Reardon.

For someone who had seemed so foreboding since Michael's return, Hope's father appeared much less so as he stood at the washstand near the well, helping his young grandchildren wash for dinner. Hope's Timmy was among them. Mr. Reardon was even laughing and talking with them as he swiped at their faces.

That was the man Michael remembered from his youth . . . not the one who had bluntly informed him he was not welcome in the valley. The words could not be taken back now, and there was no way Michael could feel comfortable around the man. For Hope, though, he'd stay, endure whatever came his way.

A random thought flitted through his mind: Had Hope's father known that Ezra had not been the best husband to her? Surely he did. Howie said Ezra had used any excuse to leave. In three years, they had never spent more than a few weeks under the same roof. Mr. Reardon had to know he'd treat Hope far better than that.

"How's that dog workin' out for you?"

Michael jumped at the suddenness of Howie's question. "Good. We've been sleepin' in the barn with the horses. The first night Napoleon kicked up quite a racket, and a few minutes later I heard hoofbeats fadin' off into the distance. After that, it's been real quiet."

Mrs. Reardon came out of the house with a large bowl for the long table set up on the other side of the big tree, and Gracie followed with another.

Michael lowered his voice, not wanting them to hear his next words. "It's Hope I been more worried about. What did Joel have to say when you went over to the Underwoods' last Monday?"

"That jasper?" Howie grinned. "Purty much what I expected. Fake apologies an' excuses. Acted as innocent an' harmless as a newborn lamb."

The women were too close now, fussing at the table.

Michael changed the subject, nodding toward Noah's older brother's house. "Where's the rest of the family?" It appeared empty.

Howie glanced in that direction. "Ike an' his bunch are over to the Smiths' for dinner, plannin' the weddin' betwixt Mary Jo and Junior. An' Hope's brother Caleb is off to his friend's." Looking back at Michael, Howie plucked a stem of grass to chew. "Ain't we enough for you?"

"Actually, I was sorta hopin' to lose myself in the crowd."

"Speaking of crowds . . ." Howie dismounted his chair. "Here comes Hope an' the Underwoods."

Michael and Howie strode to where Hope brought the wagon to a stop by the barn. Feeling the eyes of the Underwoods on him, Michael deliberately walked to Hope's side to help her down, letting Howie assist the old couple.

Meeting Hope's gaze didn't help as much as Michael had counted on. He saw uncertainty in her expressive eyes as she wrapped the reins around the brake and came down in his arms.

But that one brief moment of holding her, breathing in her lilac scent, reminded him why he exposed himself to animosity and possible retribution. "I love you," he whispered before setting her feet on the ground.

Her ethereal gaze roved his face, telling him the same.

Then from the other side of the wagon . . . "I don't need your help, boy," Mr. Underwood groused. "They ain't out diggin' my grave just yet."

Breaking into a grin, Howie spread his hands. "I'd let you help me."

Carefully, stiffly, climbing down on his own, the old man's round blue eyes twinkled. "You always did act like a sissy girl."

Howie clutched his chest. "Straight through the heart," he playacted. "You stabbed me straight through the heart."

"Stop yammerin', you two," Mrs. Underwood said from up on the driver's seat, "an' help this ol' sissy girl down."

Michael relaxed a bit as he took Hope's arm. If the Underwoods could joke, maybe they'd extend their geniality to him, too.

Mrs. Reardon spread an old quilt on the grass where Michael and Howie had been sitting and called the children. Hope joined the women, who started filling plates and setting them before the eager youngsters.

Standing with the other men and waiting for Hope to join him, Michael tried to come up with something of general interest to say, but nothing came to mind as Mr. Reardon and Titus continued to stare at him.

Howie was no help. He whistled some

little ditty as he edged ever closer to the food-laden table.

At last the women left the noisy children and joined them, Hope moving to Michael's side. Tendrils of ebony hair had fallen from her upswept coif and graced her slender neck, stealing his attention, before he remembered where he was.

Howie grabbed the closest chair, which happened to be near the end where Mr. Reardon sat down to preside. Michael staked out the place next to Howie, but first seated Hope on his other side, protecting both his flanks.

Gracie sat on the other side between the Underwoods as Mrs. Reardon took the chair at the opposite end from her husband.

Everything looked quite grand, from the fine china to the silver utensils, reminding Michael of a special dinner for army officers. He hoped he'd remember to keep his elbows off the table and his lace-edged napkin in his lap. The last thing he wanted to do was cause Hope any embarrassment.

Surprisingly, the first minutes went quite well, with folks getting their fill of the fried chicken dinner Gracie and Mrs. Reardon had prepared. Then Michael got the feeling someone was staring at him.

Looking up, he found the withered Mrs.

Underwood studying him.

He nodded politely.

"Hope says you an' my Ezzy spent a lot of time together."

Michael noticed the abrupt lack of any other movement at the table. He put his fork down and wiped his mouth on the fine white napkin. "Whenever we got the chance, ma'am. We was in separate units."

"I don't mean to pry, but I was wonderin' what you lads talked about. 'Sides the war," she added, picking up a piece of bread.

"Mostly about the pranks we used to pull," Howie popped in.

Mrs. Underwood glanced at Howie. "I'm sure you did." Then she addressed Michael again. "What else did Ezzy talk about? Did he miss his home?"

Michael felt uncomfortable speaking about Ezra's last days, but he sensed that was exactly what she wanted to hear. Still, he hedged.

Hope, next to him, didn't seemed disturbed by the questions as she loaded her fork with carrot rounds.

"Mrs. Underwood, Ezra talked a lot about his family and this valley. He thought you was the best ma he could ever ask for. And he felt the same about you, too, Mr. Underwood," Michael tossed the old man's way.

"What'd he say exactly," she continued to press, the intensity in her gaze pinning him. "Tell me everything."

Michael shot a glance to Howie, but his friend was looking skyward so deliberately, one would think it was his job to count sycamore leaves. There'd be no help from his quarter.

"Well, ma'am, the truth is, I was one of the few people there that had known Becky. So Ezra mostly spent a lot of his time tellin' me about the different things they did together after I left the valley. About their weddin' and the purty blue dress she wore. And a crown of yellow flowers. I — uh — that was purty much it."

He thought that would be the last thing the old lady or anyone else at the table would want to hear, considering Ezra's second wife sat straight across from her. Amazingly, she smiled warmly and looked at Hope. "Do you remember that, daughter? Felicity Gregg's yellow rosebush had just come into bloom, and you gals made that coronet for Becky with ribbon streamers to match her summer blue gown." Staring off into the distance, she smiled again. "An' there was just enough breeze . . ." She turned to Gracie beside her. "Remember?"

Hope's blonde sister wrapped an arm around the white-haired woman. "I sure do. Purtiest bride that year. Or any other."

Mrs. Underwood gazed into Gracie's eyes. "I hope she had them same roses in her hair when she went to meet Ezzy and take him to their eternal home." Her voice was now trembling with emotion.

"Why, that's the loveliest picture, Ma Tilly." Gracie gave her an extra hug. "An' that's just how I'm gonna think of the two of them from now on."

Although Hope gave his hand a reassuring squeeze under the table, Michael was sure he'd told them more than he should have. After that, not much more was said.

Eventually Noah Reardon rose from the table, signaling the end of dinner. The children ran off to go slide down the nearest haystack, and the women started clearing the dishes.

Michael picked up his plate. The least he could do after such a fine meal was help.

"No." Hope took the plate from him. "It's time. I want you to take courage and go strike up a conversation with Papa." She nodded toward her father and Titus, who were strolling toward the front porch of Ike Reardon's house, away from the bustle.

One would be difficult enough to talk to.

But both of them? Michael shot Hope a disbelieving look.

"Go on," she urged. Without giving him a chance to protest, she walked away, collecting plates as she went.

Michael scanned the area for Howie to accompany him, but his friend was walking around Noah's house, headed for the necessary. So, picking up his half-full glass to wet a throat already going dry, he started for the other porch.

"Have a seat," Reardon said, unsmiling, as Michael neared. Hope's father pointed to one of two empty rockers. "With the women occupied for a while, it's a good time for some real talk."

Underwood rocked back in his chair, not speaking, but obviously interested.

Michael took the chair closest to the steps — for a fast getaway.

"I'm not going to beat around the bush," Mr. Reardon said, as if he ever did. "You've come back here after a decade, expecting my daughter to still be sitting around, waiting for you."

Although Reardon paused and looked as if he expected an answer, Michael hadn't actually heard a question, and because of his military training, thought it wise to wait for a proper query. He took a swallow of his drink and set it on a small table beside him.

Mr. Underwood rocked forward, still eying him. "Did my son Ezra truly tell you that you could have his wife?"

That was a definite question. Sitting stiffly in his chair, Michael addressed the balding old fellow. "No, he did not. That would have been most disrespectful of Hope, and that Ezra never was. All he did was make me promise to bring you folks the letters he wrote when he knew his time was short."

Wanting to get the interrogation over with, Michael shifted to stony-faced Reardon. "But I will say that was not a hard promise for me to make." His heart started pounding anticipating the next words he would say. *Courage.* "Sir, the truth is, I love your daughter. I never stopped loving her. I owe who I am today to her. I don't know if she ever told you, but she taught me to read. She took me to church. She gave me my first Bible at Christmas. She changed my whole life. I know this don't please you, but I wouldn't know how to stop lovin' her."

Michael's palms were damp by the time he finished, but he refused to betray his nervousness by wiping them on his trousers.

The two older men exchanged looks; then Mr. Reardon turned back to Michael.

"Howie tells me you've got a nice pair of matching bays I should take a look at. He thinks I need to make a good impression, look successful if I'm to accept a candidacy for Congress."

Mr. Underwood grinned and slapped his knee. "Well, I'll be! I heard some of them fancy-dressers from Nashville paid you a visit last week. An' it's about time, too. Time one of our own had a say back East in Washington."

"One thing's for sure," Mr. Reardon said, lounging back in his chair, "I'd see to it that no foreign troops ever blithely march in and burn down our capitol again."

"After the lickin' them redcoats took in New Orleans, I doubt they'll be venturin' back anytime soon," the old man said with a confident grunt.

"There's been talk of nominating General Jackson for president." Reardon seemed to forget Michael as he continued talking politics with Mr. Underwood. The inquisition was over. For now.

His own gaze drifted to the sycamore tree and Hope. One hurdle jumped, but how many more to go?

Chapter Twenty-seven

Walking into the chill air of the Reardon springhouse dug into the side of a stream bank, Hope heard footsteps crunching on the path above.

Her pulse picked up pace.

Had Michael managed to sneak away from the other men talking on the porch to steal a few minutes alone with her?

Hoping he'd been discreet, she quickly set the two covered serving bowls she'd brought in the wooden trough, where a few inches of water from the spring flowed past. Then she reached up and tucked any stray hair, tightened her pins, and splashed some of the icy water over her cheeks, blotting them dry with the apron she snatched from her waist. Taking a deep, calming breath, she stepped out the low door.

To her vast disappointment, her father stood before her, the rocky streambed behind him.

She barely caught herself before venting a groan.

"Don't look too letdown," he said, making way for her to precede him on the upward path. "I've come bearing good tidings. Of sorts," he tempered. "I've come to tell you I won't stand in your way if you still want to marry Flanagan once your mourning period is past."

She whirled to face him. "You won't?"

"Not that I think he's the best choice, mind you. Not nearly."

"Oh, Papa!" Flinging herself into his arms, Hope gave him a big squeeze. "Thank you, thank you. You don't know what this means to me, to both of us. I can hardly wait to tell Michael." She picked up her skirts to run.

Her father caught her arm, a piece of a smile curling one side of his mouth. "Make sure I'm not with you when you tell him. It's one thing to be hugged by you, but I surely don't want him gushing all over me."

"Oh, Papa . . ." Stretching up on her toes, she pecked him on the cheek, then climbed the bank in search of her beloved.

Reaching the top, she scanned the large clearing for Michael. After a moment, she spotted him with Howie. They were with the yelling, squealing youngsters at a pile of hay stacked high alongside the barn. The two men were pitching the youngest ones to the top for a quicker slide down.

Howie swung up his curly top, Lulu, and sent her sailing. She ripped out a three-year-old banshee scream. Her skirts flying over her head, she came sliding down in a fit of giggles.

Michael held Timmy over his head, one-handed, twirling him around. A wild stream of laughter poured from her son before he was tossed onto the hay. Then, like the rowdy little tyke he was, Timmy threw himself off, rolling all the way down.

An arm went around Hope's shoulders. Her father had caught up.

She glanced up at him and saw he, too, was watching the horseplay with a goodly amount of grandfatherly pleasure.

He looked down at her and pecked her temple. "Howie seems to put a lot of store in Flanagan, too. Maybe the fellow's not so bad after all."

All afternoon Michael had looked for a moment when he could be alone with Hope. Lounging against the sycamore and surrounded by her relatives, he noticed that the conversation had diminished to a quiet drone. Timmy slept in his grandmother Tilly's lap while Hope picked straw from her son's pant leg. Shadows stretched long across the Reardon grounds, and, alas, Michael knew he had livestock to get in before dark.

He smiled apologetically at Hope, then rose to his feet, telling himself there'd be other days. Noticing he still had an empty glass in his hand, Michael stepped over a couple of drowsy children and headed for Mrs. Reardon's kitchen to return it.

Leaving the glass on the drainboard, he turned around to find Hope standing in the doorway, the slant of the sun's rays bathing her in a golden glow.

She moved straight toward him.

He glanced beyond her to see if anyone else followed.

No one.

"I've been wantin' to get you alone," she said in her silky low voice. As she neared, her eyes captured the amber light pouring into the room. "I have somethin' to tell you."

The instant she was within reach, he drew her away from the windows into a corner, his mouth capturing hers in a much awaited kiss. It lasted precious few seconds before she pulled away and glanced toward the door.

"I know," he said. "Sneakin' around like this reminds me of when I was a kid, tryin' to steal a spoonful from the honey crock."

She nodded with a chuckle. "I know what you mean. But here it is, nearly time to go, and I still have something to tell you that simply can't wait." Her beautiful eyes softened. "Papa has agreed to our marriage."

Stunned, Michael stepped back. "He has?"

Her eyes, her smile were effervescent. "He did." Laughing, she rushed back into his arms.

He couldn't believe it. He held her tight, breathing in the lilacs of her hair, never wanting to let go. She was really, truly, going to be his.

He stepped back far enough to see her face. "Next week. Is next week too soon to get married?"

The joy lighting her face faded. "You misunderstood. Papa said he wouldn't stand in the way if I still wanted to marry you *after* my mourning period is over."

Disappointed, he nodded. "I know. But I was hopin' . . . It's all right. We were already waitin' till then, anyway." Gliding his knuckles along the delicate curve of her jaw, he took her face in his hands. "Knowin' this will make it so much easier." He kissed the tip of her slightly upturned nose. "How are you doin' with Joel? Is he still botherin' you?"

"I'm doing all right. Don't worry about me."

"But I do. I can't help it."

"Truly. I'm fine." She squeezed his hand. "We really should get back to the others now."

"Actually, I need to be goin'. I have a few chores to tend before dark."

"So soon?" Her sadness endeared her to him all the more.

As Michael rode north toward the settlement, Hope's wonderful news remained with him. He wanted to stay longer. But because of the prowler problem he was having at his place, he couldn't. He needed to round up his horses and get them settled inside the barn before nightfall. She would have been more understanding about his leaving had she known the reason, but she had enough vexing her without his adding to her worries.

A pesky mosquito joined him, buzzing around his face and reminding him that the mugginess in the air meant he was nearing the river and the settlement.

A shot rang out.

Both he and his horse jumped, but his

well-trained mare quickly stopped prancing and settled into her easy canter again as he instinctively scanned his surroundings. He saw nothing suspicious, but he was extra watchful as he rounded the upcoming curve.

A lone wagon loaded with a family rolled toward town just ahead, probably traveling home after a Sunday outing as he was. He smiled at the sight. One day in the not too distant future, he'd be taking Sunday rides with his own family.

As he trotted past them, he tipped his tall military hat. "Good afternoon." They looked familiar, probably from church.

The bearded driver tipped his own wide-brimmed black hat. "Was that you shootin' back there?"

Michael reined in to match the speed of the rig. "No, sir. And the way it echoed off the river, it was hard to tell exactly where it came from."

"Probably just some youngster out huntin'."

"And on the Sabbath," his plain-faced wife rebuked in a censuring tone. She tucked her long chin. "Brother Rolf don't take kindly to folks breakin' the Sabbath like that."

"No, he probably don't." Michael

nudged Ebony into a gallop. "Nice talkin' to you."

Reaching the crossroad down to the ferry dock, Michael slowed his mount to a trot and turned her onto it, but toward the stores and steepled church. The town street was empty and lamplight brightened the windows of the few homes lining it. Folks were settling in for their evening meal on this day of rest.

He glanced past the church to the Bremmers'. Perhaps he'd stop by and tell them his good news. Just as quickly, he decided against it. Brother Rolf would probably start questioning him about whether or not he'd forgiven his pa yet — the biggest obstacle to his marriage, as far as the minister was concerned.

Still, he had to admit that one week and one day after Hope had forgiven her father, he agreed to their wedding. Was it God who'd softened Mr. Reardon's heart or merely his daughter?

A slow smile traveled to his lips. His Hope could never be thought of as *merely*. Never merely.

The pound of horses' hooves. Closing in.

Michael swiveled around. No one behind. His horse whinnied and reared. Michael clung to her back as other horses squealed.

A horse reared, hooves flailing. Another went down with its rider.

As the one still mounted managed to bring his horse under control, Michael swung down from his saddle to see about the other. "Where did y'all come from?" He reached out to give the one sprawled in the dirt a hand.

The young man slapped Michael's offering hand away. "Don't touch me, soldier boy."

Such hostility. As the unfortunate stallion clambered to its feet and shook itself off, Michael took a closer look at the fellow and the one still mounted. Both good-sized farm boys with faces browned from long hours in the fields. Not more than nineteen or twenty, they looked familiar.

"Your horse! He's limpin'!" the mounted one announced as if he wanted the entire town to hear. "The soldier boy crippled your horse!"

"Where in blazes did you two come from?" Michael asked again. The only possibility was from between two of the buildings lining the street. He became suspicious.

The riderless chestnut was definitely limping.

"You came racin' down the street like a

madman!" the other lad shouted as he came to his feet and dusted himself off.

Bailey, who lived next to his store, stepped out of his front door.

The one who'd just risen, a stringy-haired fellow, spotted Bailey and started shouting again. "You saw it, didn't you? He ran me down. Crippled my horse."

Michael did his best to maintain a calm voice. "I raise horses. Let me take a look at his leg."

"What for?" The younger man practically ran to his stallion. "The damage is done. See? The leg is already all swole up."

From years of experience, Michael knew an animal's leg couldn't swell that soon after injury. He stepped closer. "What sort of game you tryin' to pull on me?"

"You run Reggie down," the thick-browed fellow atop his horse said, his voice still raised, "and you're accusin' us of foul play?" He heeled his mount straight for Michael.

Michael sidestepped the attempt, then turned to the one called Reggie. He really needed to settle this matter before it turned into an incident. "I'll make you a deal. I'll pay you twenty dollars cash money for the horse."

The oversized lad's mouth dropped open. "You will?"

Michael dug into his pocket. He hated to give up so much hard cash, but he would to keep peace. Besides . . . he ran an appraising eye over the lame chestnut. Though a little large for a saddle horse, the stallion had good muscle tone and form that he could pass on. He'd make an adequate stud.

Dropping two ten-dollar gold pieces in the lad's outstretched palm, Michael strode to the horse. "I reckon you'll want to remove your saddle."

"What for?" Reggie's confused expression turned belligerent. "You ain't takin' my horse."

"I just bought him."

The rider used his mount to cut Michael off, then grabbed the lame stallion's bridle. "Now who's tryin' to get the best of who? You ain't buyin' this horse for no measly twenty dollars. That was just for damages. Come on, Reggie. Let's get outta here."

Reggie banged past Michael and flung himself up behind his pal. Before Michael could regain his footing, the two sped toward the river at a gallop, dragging the lame animal behind them.

Enraged that they'd made a fool of him *and* duped him out of twenty dollars, Michael snatched up Ebony's reins to give chase.

As he shoved his boot toe into a stirrup, he saw that Bailey's wife had joined her husband on their porch. Across the street, Hatfield had also come out of his house.

It took all Michael's restraint to merely tip his hat and smile at the spectators. His hand trembled from anger as he did. Mounting in an unhurried fashion, he sucked in his rage and reined Ebony toward home.

For Hope's sake, he kept telling himself. For Hope.

Chapter Twenty-eight

A thud awakened Hope.

Her pulse racing, she glanced toward the door but saw no movement in the dark or any unexpected shadow.

She remained still and listened. She was already jumpy at night because Joel had been acting so strangely of late, and she had never trusted him anyway. Regardless of the fact that she heard nothing more, she threw back her covers and padded quietly to the door. She knew she'd bolted it before she retired, but she couldn't stop herself from running her fingers across the cool metal to be sure it was still secure.

Something scraped the floor in Joel's room next to hers.

All her senses heightened. She waited there a few moments longer but only detected what sounded like Joel rolling over in his bed.

With her uneasiness quelled somewhat, she started back to her own bed, then decided to check the window first, to see if anything moved out there. All the while, she reminded herself that though some "valley of the shadow of death" might be lurking in the inky darkness, she should fear no evil for herself or her son. She was God's child.

Timmy, she noted as she passed his crib, seemed to be sleeping peacefully. His child-like breaths were soft and even.

Relaxing more yet now fully awake, she continued to the slightly ajar window and opened it wide. Perhaps dawn was approaching.

Fireflies sparked here and there against the velvety blackness — one of the lovely signs that summer had arrived. The breeze against her cheek and throat was cool but not cold.

And it would be Saturday morn soon. Joel had resumed going into town on Saturday afternoons. Without him around to monitor her every move, she just might ride on up to the Dillards', visit Ruthie awhile. And didn't Michael's place just happen to be on the way?

Any remaining fear was swallowed by her enthusiasm for this exceptionally pleasant idea. And the earlier she got started making soap, the sooner she'd be finished.

She leaned far out of her west-facing window to see if there was any hint of dawn.

There was. Except the glow wasn't coming from the east. It was coming from the south.

Impossible.

Fire! Near town!

Catching herself before she shouted the dreaded word and woke her son, she rushed to the door. Deftly, she slipped the bolt, then ran to Titus and Tilly's room. Not bothering to knock, she hurried to her father-in-law's side of the bed and shook his arm. "Wake up!" she said in an urgent whisper. "Fire!"

"What?" He sounded groggy. But for only an instant. He lurched up. "Fire? Where?"

"In town, I think."

Tilly rolled toward them, her white hair almost glowing in the dark. "How close?"

"A mile or so away," Hope assured her. "Don't worry. I'm gonna go see if I can help. If I'm not back before Timmy wakes up, please watch him."

"I'm going, too." Titus was already fumbling with his trousers. "Go wake Joel."

The threesome set off with every pail, bucket, and tub they could lay their hands on. Hope rode on the driver's seat with Joel and Titus as they drove south through the midnight darkness toward the fire's glow. By the time they reached the settlement and turned onto the town street, it became apparent that the blaze was centered just north of the ferry crossing.

Lamplight pouring from the windows of the homes lining the empty street lit their way. Everyone in town was up. When they passed the Bremmers' house, Hope spotted Belinda standing at her gate, clutching a fringed shawl tied over her nightgown.

"Where's the fire?" Hope called to her.

Belinda stepped out and pointed. "At the Wilsons'. Their barn. It's been burning more than an hour now. I can't go help because of the baby."

The Wilson farm lay behind the saddler's property with a path running between it and the river. As they passed the saddle shop, they spotted men down on the ferry dock, filling buckets of water from the river and pouring them into tubs in a wagon bed.

"Joel," Titus said, "soon as them boys is outta there, take the wagon on down. No sense goin' to the fire without fillin' up first."

Once their wagon was on the landing, they filled their own containers; then Titus ordered Hope to drive. "That'll be your job. When the buckets is empty, you load 'em up and get back down here for more water. Catch yourself a lad or two to help you fill 'em up."

When all three were back aboard the wagon, she slapped the reins across the nervous team's backs, urging them up the bank. Once they turned onto the path to the Wilsons', the hungry flames licking skyward were visible above the trees. The roar, the crackle all but drowned out the shouts of the firefighters.

The horses started prancing in place, balking. No doubt they, too, saw the danger and smelled the smoke as they tossed their heads, their nostrils flaring and twitching.

Joel reached across her and pulled the whip from its slot, cracking it in quick succession onto each of their backs. The horses jolted forward.

"You be the boss, Hope," Joel hurled. "Don't give them horses a chance to think." Leaning across her again, he slammed the handle back in its leather sheath.

Passing three other wagons, Hope drove around the house to see the barn totally engulfed in flames. At least fifty people ran back and forth in the eerie light, tossing buckets of water, beating out escaping sparks with sacks. The fire heated the air she breathed. Her cheeks burned.

Someone shouted, "Over there! The chicken coop!" The man pointed toward a shanty a number of yards from the barn. A small fire had started on its roof.

As Hope guided the team in that direction, men were already hauling water from her wagon to toss onto the coop.

"We're just tryin' to save the rest of the buildin's now." It was Mr. Wilson, the owner of the barn. Smudged with ash, his face red, he helped Titus down.

By the time Hope reached the rear of the wagon, all the water had been taken. She ran after the men, collecting the containers as they were emptied, then climbed atop again, and, taking a tight grip on the reins, snapped the frightened horses into moving. "I need help fillin' the tubs!" she shouted as she started back toward the river dock.

Two boys obliged. She made another trip, then several more, while the men and women of the valley valiantly labored to save the Wilsons' home and their other structures.

As she reached the landing for yet another load, the latest ash-covered volunteers who leaped off the back seemed to be having a conflict, though their words were spoken in hurried whispers.

Climbing down to help them, she realized the two were Joel and Reggie, Wilson's oldest son. She'd never thought of herself as the sneaky type, but something about the urgency of their secret conversation told her to stay behind the wheel and listen.

"Yeah, but you made it sound like it was nothin'," Reggie was saying. "Just give him a hard time. Let him know he wasn't welcome. You didn't say nothin' about him maybe comin' to burn my pa's barn."

The barn had been deliberately set afire?

"I purely didn't think he had the guts," Joel defended. "He should'a knowed every finger in the valley is gonna be pointin' right at him. Specially after you boys had your run-in with him right in the middle of town for all the folks to see. What does your pa have to say about it?"

Hope had a sick feeling in the pit of her stomach that they were talking about Michael.

"You think I'd tell him what we done?" Reggie raised his voice. "Pa knows that horse already had a pulled tendon. He would'a taken a strap to me if he knew I rode a lame horse like that. Besides, he would'a made me give back the money."

"Just how much did you get?" Joel asked angrily.

"I'd like to know that, too," Hope said, stepping out from behind the tall wheel. "After you two tell me what you're talkin' about. If I haven't already guessed."

Joel grabbed Reggie's arm. "Leave her outta it. She don't need to be bothered."

The good-sized fellow jerked away. "Why not? She's why Flanagan come back here." He turned a beefy-faced sneer on Hope. "Your lover burned down our barn."

Refusing to be intimidated by another lad she'd tutored at school, she stared hard at him. "That's nonsense. Michael would never do such a thing. He's an honorable man."

"Well, maybe he thinks this is his way of regainin' the honor we took offen him. We made a fool of him good and proper, me'n Benny Moore."

She swung to Joel the inciter. "And you put them up to it."

"Hey!" A woman shouted from a waiting wagon above. "Stop your yammerin' an' get your water. We need to get down there."

Grabbing a bucket, Hope started toward the edge of the dock angrier than she'd ever been. "We'll finish this once the fire is out."

Hot, dirty, and exhausted, Hope watched the morning glow trim the hills just as the last billows of smoke, the last sizzling embers were drowned. All that remained of the Wilson barn were a jumble of charred timbers and ashes, the strong acrid smell, and thin wisps of white rising from the rubble.

The rest of the firefighters stood staring at the destruction with the same weary, defeated look.

But none of the other buildings had been lost, she reminded herself, and started gathering up the Underwoods' buckets and tubs. As she did, she spotted Joel talking heatedly again with Reggie. But this time Mr. Wilson and a couple more men stood with them, listening, frowning, their postures going from the slump of tiredness to tense.

Even before the haze of smoke had disappeared, Joel was taking this opportunity to incite the men against Michael.

Hope climbed onto the wheel hub and searched the sooty men for Max or Brother Rolf. She easily spotted them with the Smith men because of the foursome's size. They stood with several others near the Wilsons' washstand, waiting for a bar of soap to be passed their way.

She ran to them. "You have to stop it," she said frantically even before she reached them. "Joel and Reggie Wilson are tryin' to blame the fire on Michael."

"That's just plain stupid," Junior Smith said. "Surely folks ain't gonna start blamin'

Flanagan ever' time they're careless with some fool candle."

"Reggie *und* Benny Moore, dey run into Michael *mit* dere horses last Sunday," Brother Rolf explained. "But dey are blaming him. Dat is vhat Bailey at da store says. I t'ink maybe Reggie is feeling guilty."

Hope felt a little encouraged that men as big and powerful as Junior and Brother Rolf were siding with her. She glanced at Ken Smith, then at Max. "Well, someone needs to do something. Say something. Please, go over there. Talk to them."

Her last words were scarcely out of her mouth before the four Goliaths walked, shoulder to shoulder, toward a gathering, murmuring crowd.

Following behind, Hope spotted Titus; the few curls on his balding pate were plastered down with sweat mixed with soot. He sat on the Wilsons' chopping stump, his elbows braced on his knees, his head drooping between his hands. He looked more haggard than she'd ever seen him. As concerned as she was about the accusations against Michael, she couldn't ignore her father-in-law's condition.

She walked to him and stooped before him to view his face. "How about a nice cool drink of water?"

His weary gaze lifted to hers. "I'd be obliged."

"I'll be right back with it." She shot a quick glance to the men congregated near the charred rubble, desperately wanting to be there to defend Michael. But a more pressing matter sat before her — an old man who'd given far more than he should have these past hours. She laid her hand on his matted head. "Then I'm going up to the Wilsons' house and get you a cup of strong coffee. I'm sure Mrs. Wilson has a big pot brewed. I'll put lots of cream and sugar in it, just like you prefer."

Once she'd seen to Titus's immediate needs, Hope went to join the men, praying to God for justice. Michael shouldn't have to endure this kind of slander. Not again. *Lord,* she asked, *have I been too selfish, wanting to keep him here where so many distrust him? Even I had a hard time trusting him when he first arrived.*

As she reached the group, the men started dispersing. She was too late. And their expressions were all grim.

Joel headed straight for her. "Come on, Hope," he ordered brusquely, then strode on by. "Get Pa, and let's get outta here." He was miffed for sure.

She hoped that meant he'd failed in his attempt to place blame where she knew it didn't belong. On Michael.

Intercepting Max as he came her way, she asked him what had transpired.

Short, feisty Duncan McKnight halted alongside Max. "We put a stop to them mischief makers. Reggie's dad made 'em hand over them two ten-dollar gold pieces, too. Them that they swindled outta the sergeant."

Max glanced back to where the Wilsons still stood with Benny Moore. "Yes, but I don't know if Carl Wilson is all that convinced Michael didn't revenge himself on the lads by burning his barn." He heaved a tired sigh. "But at least no one's riding off half-cocked. Not today anyway. Everyone agreed to take the time to look into things proper."

Duncan stepped closer. "Don't you worry yourself, lass. We won't let 'em ramrod Sergeant Flanagan." He wiped his blackened hands on his equally sooty pants. "Well, reckon I better get on home. Sun's already topped the hills."

As Duncan walked away, Max eyed her and opened his hand. In it lay two shiny gold pieces. "I'll be taking these to Michael later today, along with the news of this night."

"Come on, Hope!" Joel yelled at her, his impatience unmistakable.

She waved at him to acknowledge she'd heard, then turned back to Max. She had one more thing to ask. "Would you mind stopping by for me? I want to go with you."

Chapter Twenty-nine

Reaching the end of a narrow furrowed row, Michael rose from dropping carrot seeds in the narrow trough he'd hoed. He pulled a kerchief from a pocket of his work pants to wipe the perspiration stinging his eyes. He knew he was getting a late start with a garden, but if everything worked out and Hope was able to come here to live by fall, he wanted her to have plenty of fresh vegetables at her fingertips.

Stretching a kink from his aching back, he scanned the rows he'd already planted today. First thing after chores this morning, he'd started with rows of green beans and peas, tying string between thin poles as he went. Then came the beets and potatoes and onions, the mounds for cucumber and squash vines, and now carrots, with turnips and corn left to go.

He glanced up at the position of the sun. He still had another three or four hours of light yet. Enough time to finish if he kept after it.

Beyond the garden plot, he noticed the dilapidated chicken coop. Howie had been right, even if he had been joking. Hope would want some laying hens, some fryers, and a rooster. And it wouldn't hurt to fatten up a hog or two before winter.

Napoleon came to his feet from where he'd been snoozing in the shade of an apple tree. Ears perked, the shaggy dog stiffened and moved forward as far as the rope securing him would reach and started barking.

The house blocked Michael's view of the lane into the clearing. Moving to gain a better vantage point, he saw two riders coming.

And one rode a light gray Arabian.

Thrilled to have Hope pay him a visit, Michael jogged to the washstand near the back door and washed his face and hands. His clothes and boots were caked with mud, but he had no time to change. Drying his hands on a towel, he raked fingers through hair he knew needed a trim. And grinned. Hope was coming here to see him.

The dog kept up the barking as Michael walked around to the front to greet Hope. Timmy was perched in front of her, and the other rider, he now noticed, was Max Bremmer.

It would have been his heart's desire had she come alone. But if she required a chaperone, Max was a better choice than most.

But the dog's incessant barking he was sure they could all do without. "Stop, Napoleon!" he commanded, then walked out to the drive to meet his love.

"Mike! Mike!" Timmy yelled. He wore a bright red shirt and waved happily . . . her cute little miniature.

"Hi, Tim," he returned with a measure of the tot's enthusiasm. "This is a real surprise. Max, Hope." His gaze lingered there, mingling with hers as she brought her mount to a halt before him.

"Down! Down!" Not waiting for Michael to reach the side of the horse, Timmy dove into his arms, giggling.

Laughing himself, Michael lifted Timmy up to straddle his shoulders, then returned his attention to Hope, looking so pretty in a summery day gown of lilacs on gray . . . the lilacs reminding him of her fragrance anytime he was fortunate enough to get close to her. "Sorry but about all I have to offer y'all is some cool well water and a spot of shade. But you're most welcome to it."

"A shady place would be very nice," Hope said, lowering herself to the ground. No bonnet covered the long, shiny dark hair she'd casually pulled back with a lavender ribbon.

After always seeing Hope in drab black whenever she appeared at public gatherings, he simply could not take his eyes off her.

Max cleared his throat, and Michael discovered the man stood before him with an outstretched hand.

"Good to see you," Michael said, shaking Max's hand.

"Down." Timmy, riding his shoulders, dove forward.

Michael obliged by flipping him over and setting him on his feet, earning himself some more delighted giggles.

Timmy grabbed his mother's hand and shouted, "Dog!" He started pulling on her, trying to go to Napoleon.

Seeing this, the dog wagged its tail and strained against the rope in an attempt to reach the tot.

"That's Skinner's dog, isn't it?" Max observed.

"Yes."

"He's good with children." Max turned to Hope. "Why don't you take Timmy to see him a minute or so while Mike and me have us a little chat?"

"But I —" She stopped short. "Of course. But only if you'll do the same for me before we go."

The square-jawed German grinned knowingly. "Sure. I'd like to take a look at the new horses Michael brought with him this time."

She lifted her gaze to Michael and paused until her young son began pulling with both hands.

Even as Michael walked with Max to the porch and they sat down on the top step, Michael couldn't help following Hope and her youngster with his eyes.

"I want to get this said before she comes back with Timmy," Max began.

Max's tone gained Michael's full attention. "It's serious, isn't it?"

"Afraid so. There was a fire last night at the Wilson place. Their barn went up in flames."

A sick feeling crawled its way into Michael's stomach, a terrible reminder of years past. "I'm sorry to hear that," he said, hoping against hope that would be the end of it.

Max looked out across the meadow. "There was talk that you set the fire."

"Whatever for?" Michael came to his feet. "Surely I'm not gonna get blamed for every knocked-over candle or lantern."

"Of course not. But considerin' it was the Wilsons'."

"Wilson . . . I don't even know 'em."

Max stood up and opened his hand, revealing two gold coins. "You knew one well enough to give him these."

Michael looked up from the coins. "The kid with the lame horse. It was his family's barn that was destroyed?"

"Yep."

"I see." Michael heaved a sigh as Max handed him the coins. "It's all fallin' into place. The run-in I had with them lads Sunday makes a lot more sense now. I thought it was just some young bucks doin' their best to make me feel unwelcome. I figured Joel'd put 'em up to it. But for that lad to burn down his own barn . . ."

"Actually, it was his father's barn. But I don't think Reggie set fire to it. If it actually was arson, I'd figure Joel did it."

That was a great relief to Michael. He wouldn't have to defend himself to Max Bremmer.

"While we was putting out the blaze," Max continued, "I saw Joel and Reggie together, and they seemed to be at odds about something. Still, they were in full agreement when they accused you."

"Joel actually came out and said the words?" Cold anger turned Michael's jaw to stone as he envisioned the sight. "I'm surprised they didn't show up here with a rope and a noose."

Max watched Hope and her son pet the dog, then stepped around so she couldn't see his face. "Junior Smith and McKnight took your side."

"They were at the fire?"

"Everyone within the sound of the church bell or saw the fire glow came. Anyway, Storekeeper Bailey witnessed the whole thing last Sunday between you and the lads. And once Carl Wilson heard what his son had done, he made him give me the money Reggie gulled you out of. But even old man Bailey figured, if you was so inclined, you'd been given plenty reason to want to take revenge."

Michael smiled grimly. "They're never gonna forget, are they? That I'm Bantry Flanagan's son. Well, you be sure and tell that to your pa for me. He told me once that he would never bless a marriage between me and Hope as long as I harbored this hatred for my father. So I told him I'd forgive Pa *if* the rest of this valley would." Michael's gaze drifted to Hope. "And that ain't never gonna happen."

Suddenly Max gripped Michael's shoulders and spun him around. "What kind of fool are you? To play games with your spiritual life. Small wonder everything in your life is in such a mess. Until you put obedience to the Lord first, you're never going to have peace." He released Michael as abruptly as he'd grabbed him. "Get straight with the Lord."

Michael had never seen Max so passionate about anything, even when he was on the battlefield leading his militia into life-or-death situations. "I'm sorry, but I haven't been able to do it on my own. Pray for me. Pray that God will somehow free me from this hatred."

"You know I will." Max's expression slowly dissolved into a smile. "I always did think you had real promise."

Michael grinned then, too. "Did you, now?" A flash of color caught his eye, and he spotted Timmy in his red shirt running in the lower pasture.

Hope, in her long skirts, swung her legs over a section of the zigzag fence and chased after her son.

Only a couple of docile mares grazed in the enclosure and presented no threat to the tot. Nonetheless . . . "I need to go fetch Timmy."

Max chuckled. "He is a handful. I'll go check out your herd now. Give you and Hope the moment alone I promised her."

Leaving Max behind, Michael vaulted the fence and ran to catch up with Hope. He didn't want to lose a second of the little time they would have together.

She was play-chasing her son around the beech tree in the middle of the pasture, her warm, throaty laugh filling the air. Timmy dodged back and forth, his eyes dancing with delight and squealing with every near capture.

Just as he reached them, Hope stopped in her tracks, her laughter dying away. But she wasn't looking at him. Instead, she stared at the tree trunk, then touched it. "How long has this been here?"

He observed the words *Hope Flanagan,* then gazed at her again. "In a couple of months, it will be eleven years."

"What?" piped a high-pitched voice from below.

Michael picked up the imp. "This." He took Timmy's hand and ran the stubby fingers across the writing. "When your mama and me was a lot younger, she taught me how to write. And these are the first words I ever scratched into a tree trunk." He again beheld Hope. "Come to think of it, they're the only words I ever carved in a tree. Or ever wanted to. Somehow having them there, permanent-like, made everything seem possible." He traced his own fingers across the gouged and puckered scars turned black with age. "This tree is one of the reasons I bought the place back."

"Down. Me down." Timmy was restless again.

Lowering the squirming child to the ground, Michael let him run through the tall grass, while he never took his eyes from Hope. His attention was now captured by the dollops of light filtering through the branches to dance across her porcelain doll-like features and lending mysterious depth to her eyes of ice and fire.

"All the years you were gone," she said softly while smoothing her hand over the wood, "this tree was standing here, proclaiming our destiny. And I never knew." Her gaze changed then, clouded over. "But I've been placing our destiny at risk. It's been wrong of me to ask you to put yourself in danger for me. Enduring ill favor for my sake was bad enough, but if Joel will set fire to a neighbor's building and blame it on you, he's capable of anything."

Her confirmation of his suspicions was very disturbing. Michael enfolded her hands within his. "Do you know for a fact he did it?"

She gazed up at him with a steady stare. "I don't have proof. I didn't actually see him do it. But the way he acted all last night . . ." She shrugged a slender shoulder. "I know he did. I want you to load up your goods, take your horses, and ride out of here. Today. I'll come to you when the time is right."

"I can't —"

Her finger covered his lips. "If Max and Brother Rolf hadn't been there this morning to stop Joel, I truly believe you'd be hanging from this very tree right now."

He pulled her to him. "But I'm not, am I? In fact, things couldn't be finer at the moment." He breathed in her flowery scent. "I'm holding my beloved in my arms."

She reared back. "But —"

He smothered her next words with a kiss.

But the tension did not leave her neck and shoulders.

Easing back from the embrace, he dropped a quick kiss on a crease her worry had caused just above her perfect nose. "Tomorrow after church service, I'll have Brother Rolf call a meeting. We'll bring everything out in the open and see what happens after that."

She looked up at him with some of her assurance returning. "Yes, for the most part, they're all good people. I suppose we should give them a chance."

Then the thought of her leaving here to go back to the Underwoods', to Joel, turned Michael deadly serious. "I couldn't let you go home if I thought you were in any kind of danger. Whatever happens, under no circumstances are you to let Joel guess that you suspect him."

Chapter Thirty

"Max, it broke my heart," Hope said as they rode south from Michael's. "He looked so happy to see us. His eyes were sparklin' so bright and his smile, so big when he first saw us."

"I know," Max muttered, nodding his shaggy blond head. "I hated having to tell him about the Wilson barn and the accusations."

Timmy had fallen asleep on Hope almost the moment they left, and his weight had become painful on the arm supporting him. She shifted his head. "Did you know Joel took his rifle to church a few Sundays back?"

"No, I didn't." Max reined his big roan a little closer.

"At the time," she explained, ducking to miss a low-hanging branch, "I thought it best not to tell Michael that Joel was so irate when Michael returned he was set to shoot him. Or," she qualified, "Joel just could've been tryin' to scare me into marrying him.

I'm not sure which."

"Hope, you're living under the same roof with Joel. I want you to take care. Maybe it would be best if you move back home with your folks."

"I'd truly like to do that, get away from Joel. But I can't. Tilly depends on me for so much . . . and, Max, I truly do love helping her. Your father and I wrote letters to the older Underwood children, explaining that Titus and Tilly would need others to care for them soon, but I haven't heard back from them yet. And at the moment I don't know of anyone else who is free to come take my place. I . . . I wish I did. God hasn't answered that prayer yet."

"Hmm . . . I see. Then stay out of Joel's path. And keep your suspicions to yourself. Promise me."

She smiled. "Don't worry. I will. Besides, Michael already made me promise."

"Tomorrow after church, me and the rest of the men, we'll sort through this mess. With the help of the Lord," he added.

"In the meantime, I'll be sweet and dumb as a newborn chick," she quipped, trying to lighten the conversation.

"I forgot to ask earlier. Did Titus make it home all right?" Max asked as they neared the Underwood turnoff. "He looked all done in after the fire this morning."

"I know. The poor dear is much too old for such hard work. But he just doesn't want to admit it. Ma Tilly and I got all the black off of him, and Joel helped him up the stairs. I pray he sleeps the whole day away. He and Joel were both still asleep when you came by to fetch me. Well, here's my road." She reined in Burns and, shifting Timmy slightly, held out her hand to Max. "Thank you for taking me with you. No need to ride in the rest of the way."

"Let's just hope Joel doesn't give you a hard time for coming with me."

"Don't worry yourself. If I'm lucky, he'll still be asleep and never even know."

Max frowned. "Mayhap I'd better see you to your door."

"Nonsense. Titus and Tilly are there. Everything will be fine."

Riding into the yard with Timmy, Hope saw a saddled horse tethered to a corral post. She didn't readily recognize the brown horse with its one white stocking. Guiding her own mount close to the house, she swung her leg over and carefully brought her sleeping son down with her. Whoever the visitor was, she hoped Tilly hadn't been overburdened trying to be a good hostess.

Just before Hope reached the door with

her slumbering burden, it swung open.

A middle-aged man stood in it who looked familiar, yet she couldn't quite place him. Dressed in a linen hunting shirt over homespun trousers, he graciously stepped aside to allow her entry.

"Hope, dear," Tilly called from a rocker at the parlor end of the large room. "Come in, come in. I don't know if you remember Jude. Our oldest son. He left here a good twenty years ago. He's the one I told you about with the tobacco plantation near Fort Massack. You know, up where the Cumberland joins the Ohio."

Hope stared at him, stupidly, she knew. He had Ezra's round face, and there was still a hint of red in his hair, similar to Joel's.

"Good to meet you," he said just above a whisper as he glanced from her to Timmy. "Ma's been tellin' me all about you." He had his father's round blue eyes.

"That's nice," she managed, fearful of what had been said in her absence, considering she was the one who'd written to him about his parents' need. Besides, she didn't know any more about him than what Titus and Tilly had mentioned. What if he could not be trusted any more than Ezra or Joel? She was starting to regret not having said something to Titus and Tilly before — just yesterday she'd promised herself she would tell them this very day. But now it was too late. "Let me put my son down, and I'll be right back."

Not seeing Titus or Joel anywhere about, Hope concluded they were both still asleep. Climbing the stairs, she stepped softly, very much not wanting to awaken them. She needed a few moments alone with Jude first, to explain that she'd never told his parents she'd written, and hope that he, too, would understand.

With her son tucked into his crib, she hurried below, realizing that, in a way, she was like her father. He'd kept letters from her, and she'd kept the fact that she'd written letters concerning Ezra's parents from them . . . both she and her father doing what they considered was best for others, whether the others liked it or not. To her father's credit, though, he'd at least been up front about it, had not made his actions a secret. Like she had.

Reaching the bottom of the stairs, she found Tilly, with shaky hands, attempting to pour hot water from the big kettle into her pink ceramic teapot.

Hope tried not to look frantic as she rushed to her feeble mother-in-law. "Here," she said, taking the blackened container, "let me do that. You need to be keepin' your son company."

By the time Tilly was easing down into her rocker, Hope had filled the teapot, collected a matching cup and saucer for herself, and brought them back to the tea table. Taking a companion chair to the one Jude sat on, Hope wished he'd been more aware of his mother's condition. She might have scalded herself.

But he'd just arrived, Hope rationalized for him. "It's so nice to have you come such a long way to visit," she said, pouring the aromatic India tea. "If you'd sent us a note announcing your arrival, we all would've been waiting here with bells on when you rode in. Would you care for sugar and cream?"

"No," he said. "Plain's my pleasure."

"My boy don't never need an invite," Tilly said as Hope handed him the cup. "He's always welcome."

"Absolutely," Hope concurred, her own enthusiasm rising. However it happened, the help she sought had arrived. Then she remembered the one who would no doubt try to foil her plan. "I take it Joel and Titus are still upstairs asleep."

Tilly nodded. "I told Jude here all about y'all goin' to fight the fire at the Wilsons' last night, an' how y'all come draggin' in here this mornin' covered in soot an' all wore out."

"For someone who was up all night, you certainly look wide awake, Mrs. —"

"Please, call me Hope. We're family." Taking a closer look at him, she realized that twenty or so years from now he would look exactly like Titus. His hair was already thinning on top, and the red had faded mostly to gray. His expression, too, had that friendly, almost eager quality of his father's. "The reason I'm not asleep was lying in my arms when I walked in. Two-and-a-half-year-olds don't seem to care how much sleep you missed the night before." Handing Tilly a sugared and creamed cup of tea, she took a plain one for herself and settled into the comfort of a pillow-backed chair.

Jude Underwood did the same while he took a sip of his amber-clear drink. "I know what you mean." He sounded quite congenial and, from what she could tell, had not divulged that Hope had sent for him. "Cilla an' me have us a couple of grandchildren about his age, and they keep us all hoppin'." He took a surveying glance around the room. "I'm surprised how fine the old place looks. Crops in, ever'thing lookin' in good repair, and the house never looked cozier."

"The house is Hope's doin'," Tilly said, rocking forward. "She brought the fancy Turkish rug and some of the other geegaws settin' around. She's a real —" Her gaze deserted her son for the stairwell and the sound of padding footsteps.

Someone came down. Joel. His face still puffy from sleep, his feet bare and his shirt-tail out.

"An' here comes my baby," Tilly cooed. "Ain't he grown up into a looker?"

Joel self-consciously raked his hands through a tangle of curls. "I thought I heard someone extra down here." He stopped and stared a long moment, then finally said, "Jude?"

"That's right, baby brother." Jude came to his feet, sporting a grand smile.

The two met halfway, enthusiastically shaking hands, grabbing each other's shoulders, laughing.

"Come on over and sit down, boys," Tilly suggested, her motherly happiness apparent.

"Yes," Hope agreed, although for her the timing of Joel's appearance couldn't have been worse. "I'll get you a cup for tea."

Fortunately, Joel never even glanced her way, he was so glad to see his older brother. "It's been what, seven, eight years since you paid us a visit. What brings you back this way?" he asked as they walked together to the seating area.

Hope held her breath. Would Jude now mention the letters she and Brother Rolf sent?

"Ma an' Pa are gettin' on in years," Jude said, retaking his seat. "Thought I'd better come see how they're gettin' along. Maybe see if they'd like to come an' visit a spell."

Joel dropped onto the settee, looking slightly confused. "Go for a visit?"

"It's way past time. They got a dozen grandchildren they never seen."

Relieved that Jude hadn't revealed her part in his coming, she exhaled, then continued on to fetch a cup for Joel. She'd find a quiet time later this evening to tell Titus and Tilly.

"It purely would pleasure me," Ma was saying, her expression wishful, "to see the young'uns. Yours an' Samuel's an' Mary Martha's. But it's such a far piece. I'm sorry, Son, but I don't think these ol' joints could take all the jostlin'."

"Ma —" her oldest leaned forward in his seat — "the onliest jostlin' you'd suffer would be on the ride from here to the dock at the settlement. From there we'd just float ourselves all the way down to the Ohio."

"La, that does sound pleasuresome." Her old eyes took on a light. "An' I surely would like to see ever'body . . . but we'd still have to take to the trail a-comin' back." Her enthusiasm dimmed, and she sighed. "No, I reckon it just ain't possible."

Returning with the cup, Hope paused. *Please, Lord, give him the right words to convince her. If it's Your will,* she quickly amended.

"I was told by the folks in Nashville that they're expectin' to have one of them newfangled steamboats plyin' the waters within the next month or so."

"You don't say?" Joel sounded duly impressed.

"That's right." Jude turned back to his mother. "Fact is, Ma, once you get there, you might wanna stay on for a spell, what with most of your family livin' there now. Ain't none of us more'n a couple miles from each other. Why, Ma, you might have yourself such a good time, you won't never wanna come back."

Tilly's expression was a mix of emotions as Hope poured Joel his tea. "That's an awful lot to think about so sudden-like an' all."

"Did Mary write an' tell you her Mattie's gettin' married next month?" Jude continued in his effort to persuade her. "It sure would mean a lot to her if you could be there for the wedding."

"Ma," Joel jumped in, "you an' Pa should go. Do it whilst you're still able. Me an' Hope can keep this place goin' whilst you're gone." Grazing Hope with a glance, he cocked an insinuating grin.

Jude and Tilly also turned to Hope. And such anticipation was on Tilly's face.

"Yes." Hope schooled her features to look optimistic and her hands to remain steady as she handed Joel his cup and saucer and moved to the back of Tilly's chair. "It's a wonderful idea. For you, Ma, and for Pa Titus. I'd really like to see him take it easy for a while. He does too much. I worry about him."

"Good." Jude slapped his knee. "Then it's settled. I'll see about gettin' a keelboat made in the next few days, and we can be on our way. And you an' Joel can take care of things here."

"Actually, it would be only Joel," Hope corrected, her fingers clinging to the back of Tilly's rocker for support. "It wouldn't be proper for me to stay here alone with Joel."

A silence followed, thick and heavy.

A full thirty seconds must have passed before carefully, deliberately, Joel set down his cup and saucer and rose to his feet as he eyed first Hope, then his older brother. "Now I understand. You showin' up here out of the blue. You're here to free Hope so she can run off with that barn burner. Hope wrote you, didn't she?"

Jude's features hardened, and he also stood up. He obviously didn't like being caught in the middle. "Yes, but —"

"No *but*s about it," Joel hurled, riding over his brother's words. He lowered his voice, but not the intensity of his passion. "I'll bet Miss High-and-Mighty forgot to tell you the man she wants to take off with is none other than Bantry Flanagan's son. You know, that murderer what got hisself hung up your way. And take Ezra's baby boy with her."

Tilly sucked in a gasp, though she sat very still.

Hope desperately wanted to comfort her somehow, but the damage was done.

Joel's eyes narrowed on Hope, and he took a menacing step toward her. "I'll bet she didn't tell you about Flanagan now, did she? Or that Pa's layin' up in bed right now, half dead from fightin' a fire that Flanagan whelp started last night."

He sparked Hope's own rage, spurring her to Michael's defense. "That's a lie, Joel

Underwood, and you, of all people, know it." Belatedly remembering her promise to be careful around Joel, she whirled away and started for the stairs. Then remembering her manners, she paused. "It was a pleasure to meet you, Jude. But, if you'll excuse me, I think it's best if I get a few things and spend the night at my parents'. There's stew a-plenty for supper. Just needs to be heated."

Jude merely stared back at her, no doubt speechless.

But she wasn't. She swung her gaze to Joel, unflinching. "You'll be pleased to know there will be a meeting after church tomorrow. You can face Michael with your suspicions there. If you dare."

"Oh, I dare, all right." His face red with rage, Joel started for her.

Jude caught his arm. "Let her go. It looks like I got here none too soon." He looked past his brother to Hope, his expression turning hard. "And I'll be mighty interested to see how that meeting turns out."

Chapter Thirty-one

In the last faint light of day, Hope knocked on her parents' door while balancing her son on one hip. She dreaded what her father's reaction would be when he heard what had transpired at the Underwoods'. She would've much rather gone to Gracie's, but it was vital that he be convinced of Michael's innocence before the meeting tomorrow morning.

Her youngest brother, Danny, opened the door. The string bean towhead greeted them with a surprised smile. "Hey, whatcha doin' here tonight?"

Timmy reached for his young uncle.

"Just visitin'," Hope said, relinquishing her son into Danny's arms. "You'd be doin' me a big favor if you'd take Timothy upstairs for a few minutes. I need to talk to Papa."

"Who's out there?" she heard her father call.

She found her parents seated at their dining table, finishing supper. They looked as amazed to see her as Danny had.

"Hi," was the most she managed. "Mind if I get a cup of coffee and join you?"

"Of course not, darling," her mother said, as both continued to stare at her.

"Where's Caleb?" Hope asked, inquiring about her fourteen-year-old brother as she moved to the china cabinet.

"He's visiting at the Spencers'," her mother provided. "It's Bonnie Sue's birthday."

"And what brings you down our way?" her father asked, lifting his napkin to his mouth. His query sounded casual, but they all knew she never would've shown up here at dusk on a whim.

Sitting down at a clean spot, Hope picked up the coffeepot and poured herself a cup. A sigh slipped out. "I reckon you've heard about the fire at the Wilson barn last night."

"Aye." Her father's expression remained noncommittal.

"Then you've heard about Joel's accusations."

"Yes, we did, sweetheart," her mother said with sympathy in her tone.

"And about the game the Wilson kid ran on Flanagan." Noah's tone intimated more.

Hope took a swallow of the lukewarm coffee, then straightened. Obviously her father wanted to believe the worst about Michael. "Do you also know that Joel put Reggie up to it?"

Noah sat back in his chair and stared at her. "Are you sure about that?"

"I overheard them arguing. Reggie wasn't at all pleased with Joel. He thought swindling Michael had cost his family their barn."

"Him and most everyone else I talked to at the store today," her father returned.

"Right." Hope leaned forward. "That's exactly what Joel expected everyone to think. I believe he set the fire for that very purpose."

A frown creased her father's brow. "That's a mighty serious accusation, Daughter."

"So is Joel accusing Michael."

"Bailey said Joel was with you and Titus when you drove to the Wilsons'. Even you can't believe he could be in two places at once."

Her father was questioning her intelligence again. Hope took a calming breath. "Of course not. But, you see, we didn't arrive at the fire for at least an hour after it was first discovered. As you know, we live too far out to hear the church bell. And the only reason I saw the fire at all was because a sound from Joel's room woke me. At the time, I just thought he'd gotten up in the dark and banged into something. Now I think he was trying to sneak back to his room *after* he'd done his worst at the Wilsons' and stumbled into something."

"That's quite a theory, young lady." Plainly, her father was not convinced.

"It certainly makes more sense than your presumption. You tell me, who would gain the most by setting the fire? Certainly not Michael. On the contrary, it places him in the tenuous position of losing everything he came here for."

Noah's expression melted into a grin. "Did I ever mention you would've made one fine attorney?"

"If I were a man," she shot back.

Pushing away her plate, Jessica chuckled. "I made apricot pudding for dessert. Would either of you care for some?"

"Thank you, dear," Noah said. "That sounds delicious." He then turned his attention back to Hope. "This is not just wishful thinking on your part. You truly believe Joel set the fire?"

"Unless it was some bizarre accident, yes I do. And it's vital that you believe that, too. Because I need you to be one fine attorney tomorrow when you plead Michael's case."

"I must've missed something. Has Michael been arrested?"

"No. But after church, Max is going to call for a meeting so you men can get at the truth. And since I'm not a man, I won't be welcome. So I'm counting on you."

Her father shook his head. "This is unbelievable. My defending a Flanagan in an arson case." He barked a laugh.

And Hope knew he'd agreed. Springing out of her chair, she toppled it on the floor as she rushed to him, swarming him with hugs and kisses. "Thank you, thank you. You have no idea how much this means to me."

"All right," he said, chuckling. He caught her hands. "I'll do my best. Now, pick up your chair and sit down so your mother can bring us our pudding."

"Sweetheart," her mother said, placing a spoon and bowl of the spicy treat before her, "arriving this late, I assume you're spending the night."

"Yes, if you don't mind. The atmosphere at the Underwoods' is tense, to say the least. On top of everything, Jude, Tilly and Titus's oldest son, arrived without warning."

"Really?" her mother asked. "Did he bring his wife?"

"No, he didn't. He came in answer to a

letter I sent a few weeks ago."

"This is the first we've heard of a letter." Her father had that dubious look again.

"I wrote, telling him and the others up on the Ohio that I would be marrying someone when my year of mourning was completed, and that I felt Joel wasn't capable of caring for Tilly and Titus. That some other arrangements should be made."

Her father put down his spoon. "I'm surprised, Daughter. That was rather callous of you, attempting to cast off Titus and Tilly as if they were a pair of old shoes."

Why did he always have to jump to the wrong conclusion? "Father, do you really think they'd come to live with Michael and me? I would love to have them, but I would never ask them to choose me and my happiness at the expense of their son's. And Jude seemed to agree. He'd already talked Tilly into going for a long visit. And Joel was all for it until he learned I wouldn't be staying on there after they left. That's when accusations about Michael and me started flying out of his mouth. So I left."

Her mother exchanged glances with her father. "That sounds absolutely horrid, darling. Thank goodness you felt you could come here."

"Oh, I'm fine. It's Tilly I'm worried

about. She witnessed the entire scene."

Her mother reached over and squeezed Hope's hand. "Tilly may be old and weak of body, but she's strong in the Lord. We'll pray especially for her and Titus tonight. And Joel," she added with extra meaning.

"And for tomorrow." Hope turned to her father. "Pray that truth will prevail at the meeting tomorrow."

"Yes, Daughter. The unvarnished truth."

"I do hope the men didn't let Tilly try to fix a big breakfast for them this morning." Hope rode alongside her parents' shay, while her younger brothers rode ahead on their ponies with Timmy. "Her hands always bother her more when she first gets up."

"Stop your fretting," her mother urged. "Tilly isn't a child."

"But she is, Mama. Especially when it comes to her always wanting to please others. I shouldn't have left her last night."

Her mother looked very summery in a new Sunday day gown with cabbage roses on a shell pink background. The subtle hue brought out the color of Jessica's cheeks . . . while Hope's drab black gown did little to flatter her.

"Tilly's not as fragile of mind as you

think," her mother reiterated. "She's merely one of those lovely people who always tries to see the good in everyone."

Her father, wearing his usual gray suit, glanced over at Hope. "Your mother's right. And the Lord is not going to allow any more to be put on Tilly than she can bear. Or you. Or any of His other children. So relax and thank God for this day He has given us, starting with those dark clouds overhead. It hasn't rained in a week."

He was right. She knew he was. Nonetheless, she couldn't remember another day when she'd had so many anxieties trying to steal her peace, foremost being Michael and the meeting after church.

As they turned onto the main street, Hope saw Caleb, fifty yards ahead, ride into the church parking area with Timmy. And coming from the other direction rolled the Underwood wagon. Jude drove for Titus and Tilly; Joel was nowhere to be seen.

Relieved, Hope nudged Burns to a faster trot. She wanted to reach the wagon in time to help with Tilly. She reached them as Jude pulled the team to a halt.

He sent her an unfriendly glower.

Refusing to be intimidated, she dismounted next to them and spoke directly to Titus and Tilly. "You're earlier than usual.

434

Did you have breakfast?"

"I warmed the stew that was left over from last night," Jude answered gruffly before either of them could.

Hope plastered on a cheery smile. "I imagine it's good and fillin' in the mornin', too." Her guilt for running away yester's eve and leaving Tilly to cope alone mounted.

As Jude and Titus climbed down, she stepped up to help Tilly.

"Better let Jude help me," Ma Tilly said. "He's a lot stronger."

"Of course." Hope stepped back, her feelings of guilt multiplying as she wondered if that had been Tilly's true motive for rejecting her help.

"Gramma!" Timmy came running in his blue plaid suit and grabbed hold of Tilly's legs. He looked up at her with his bright innocence. "Caleb ride me."

"He did?" Tilly hugged him close, then ruffled his hair before he ran off to play with the other little ones. There was a great sadness in her eyes. "I'm gonna miss that baby somethin' awful."

Unable to stop herself, Hope pulled Tilly to her. "No more than we're gonna miss you. I promise, after harvest we'll come to see you. And if livin' there doesn't suit you, I'll bring you and Pa right back here to live with me. I love you, Ma."

Even as she held on to Tilly, Hope caught sight of a flash of royal blue. Michael came strolling across the churchyard with the Bremmers, his expression a match for the day — grim.

It was beginning to seem like everyone she loved was being hurt because of her. And here she was, making promises to Tilly after she'd made promises to Michael. But, in truth, she had no idea how many she would be able to keep.

A Scripture she'd learned years before at school came rushing into her memory. *"Ye know not what shall be on the morrow. For what is your life? It is even a vapour that appeareth for a little time, and then vanisheth away. For that ye ought to say, If the Lord will, we shall live, and do this, or that."* And as her father said earlier, *Thank God for the day He has given us.*

"The Lord truly does work in mysterious ways," she said softly to Tilly. "I suppose all we can do is remember, 'This is the day which the Lord hath made; we will rejoice and be glad in it.' "

"Dere is to be a meeting after church," Brother Rolf announced from the pulpit at the close of the service. "It concerns da fire at da Vilson barn. I vant all da men to stay for it."

The mention of the meeting started Michael's stomach churning again. He remembered one such as this when he was a youngster, just before his family had to run for their lives. Sitting in his usual front-row seat today, he'd felt the weight of every eye on him throughout the sermon. And now the time was upon him when every man here would be free to "cast his lot."

Michael stood up with the rest of the congregation, but instead of filing out, he merely turned around, wishing for even a glimpse of Hope. Before the service, they'd managed no more than a passing greeting. Although Joel was absent, as he'd been at the start of last week's service, she'd been occupied by the elder Underwoods and a man of middle years Brother Rolf later introduced as their oldest son, Jude. Michael had been curious to know if he'd come in response to Hope's letter, but there'd been no opportunity to ask.

Once some of the men blocking his view sat down again, Michael found Hope still standing in the Underwood pew, shrouded from head to toe in her usual black. But yesterday, he remembered, she'd given him the profound pleasure of visiting him in the loveliest of lavenders.

She looked back at him, her eyes pools of uncertainty. She mouthed something to him that he couldn't comprehend. But then she blew him a kiss.

That, he had no problem understanding. No matter what anyone else might think about him, her devotion to him never wavered. Their love for each other had survived ten years of separation, a hanging, a marriage, and a war; it would survive whatever was said in this room today.

As Hope left the sanctuary, Michael noticed Titus and Jude Underwood in their usual pew, and near the back, Joel had shown up. He sat with several pals who hung out on the saddlery porch.

With an arm draped over the back of the pew, Joel wore a smug smile as he gave Michael a mock salute.

Michael returned the barest of nods. Then seeing Max and his father returning to the front of the sanctuary, he retook his seat.

As Max dropped down beside him, Howie left the Reardon men and came to sit on his other side.

"Thanks," Michael whispered. It felt really good to have the loyalty and support of friends like these.

Brother Rolf stepped up on the dais and

raised his booming voice. "Gentlemen, I am sure everyone knows about da fire Friday night. Because of God's mercy, all da animals are saved. *Und* da metal tools *und* parts, dey are still goot. But da vooden handles *und* da tack is gone *mit* da ladders *und* ropes, buckets, troughs, *und,* of course, da barn itself. So I am asking every able-bodied man to give one day a veek to helping da Vilsons until ve are ready for da barn raising. Now, are dere any questions?"

Not a single man spoke. But Michael knew they understood and would all pitch in to help their neighbor as the pastor asked. This was that kind of community.

"Now," Brother Rolf continued, "to dis business of da blame. Dere vas ugly talk yesterday morning. Pointing of da fingers. If anyone has proof dat dis fire vas deliberately started, let him speak now. Dis is da place *und* da time."

Tensing, Michael sat stone-still, waiting for the first angry shouts.

However, the cavernous room fairly echoed with the silence as the minister scanned those gathered. A pew creaked. Someone coughed. In the distance, children laughed as they played outside.

Finally, Brother Rolf cleared his throat. "*Na ja,* let this be da end of it. Shall ve go

439

home *und* haf our dinner now?"

"Wait!"

Michael swiveled in his seat to find who'd shouted.

One of Joel's friends stood up. Surprisingly, the expression on his face had a cornered-rabbit look to it.

"You vant to speak?" the minister prodded.

The skinny lad's eyes darted back and forth. "I — uh —" His Adam's apple bobbed with a swallow, and he didn't seem to know what to do with his hands. "Well, ever'body here already knows who did it. I mean, it ain't no secret."

"*Und* who vould dat be?" Brother Rolf pinned him with a stern stare.

The young man glanced around nervously. "Well, think about it. There ain't been nothin' catch fire around here for three, four years; then a Flanagan shows up, an' a barn burns down. What more proof do we need?"

"Hear, hear!" shouted the others in his row.

With an abrupt grin, he sat down, looking pleased with himself.

"I'd like to comment on that hypothesis." Noah Reardon rose.

Michael held firm, though he knew if ever there was a time for Hope's father to rid himself of a most unwanted suitor, this was it.

Chapter Thirty-two

Hope couldn't help glancing back at the church building every few seconds and sending petitions heavenward for Michael. *Lord, he's such a good, kind man. You've helped me to know that. Please help the others to see it, too. And please protect him.*

Still, she couldn't latch on to God's peace. She knew Joel Underwood was determined to convince the valley that Michael had started the fire at the Wilsons'. And another dilemma nagged at her.

That other problem stood outside the church with her and her mother and Belinda, waiting for the men to emerge from the meeting. Although Tilly remained at her side, she wondered if her mother-in-law would ever truly trust her again. Sending for Jude without Tilly's knowledge had been underhanded, no matter how noble Hope's intentions had been.

Nonetheless, she wouldn't desert her again as she had last night . . . not until Tilly and Titus left with their son Jude.

"I do hope the men finish soon," Belinda said, pulling the edge of her baby's blanket up over his head at a sudden breeze. "It looks like we're in for a cloudburst; the sky is so black."

"Yes. Most of the other women are climbing into their carriages to wait. Why don't you go on to your house?" Jessica suggested. "You don't want to get caught in it with baby Mike."

"Only if the Underwoods promise to have dinner with us." Belinda turned to Tilly. "If you're leaving within the week, you simply must come. Besides, I'm sure Rolf will want to do some catching up with Jude. And, of course, you're invited, Hope, and Joel."

Hope was desperately torn. She knew she should walk Tilly to the Bremmers', but she desperately wanted to know the outcome of the meeting. "That's really kind of you, Belinda. You sure you'll have enough?"

Belinda chuckled. "I learned years ago to always fix at least double for Sundays. Rolf or Max rarely fail to invite folks. Today, I'm simply beating them to it. Tell Max I've gone on to start warming the food."

Michael had no idea what accusations Mr. Reardon could possibly make. From what Hope had said, he hadn't even been at the fire.

Noah Reardon turned from Brother Rolf to face Joel and his cohorts. "Barnabas Spencer? That is your name, isn't it?"

The lad who'd accused Michael of arson stared back, looking wholly intimidated. "Aye."

"I know for a fact," Reardon said with the authority of his legal profession, "that one Benjamin Spencer murdered a Horace Wilkes last month in Clarksville. If a dead man comes floating down the river, shall we assume then, as a Spencer, you murdered him?"

The lad sprang to his feet. "That's plumb crazy. I don't know nothin' about no murder up in Clarksville or anywhere else."

"And," Reardon continued, "that also is the full extent of what you know about the Wilson fire, isn't it? On the other hand . . ." He glanced briefly at Michael. "Sergeant Flanagan here might have a very good case against you. For slander."

"What?" the flustered lad cried. "I just said what ever'one else is sayin'." He started pushing past his friends. "Look, I'm leavin'. This ain't none of my business, anyway."

Michael heard a snicker here and there as the lad made his escape.

"T'ank you, Mr. Reardon," Brother Rolf said from the pulpit. "Does anyone else haf anyt'ing to say?"

As he waited, Michael found himself repeating, *Thank You, Jesus,* over and over in his mind. Hope's father had actually stood up and defended him. No one could ever deny Noah Reardon was a just man. Michael would ever be grateful.

After a few seconds Brother Rolf resumed. "No one else has anyt'ing to say? Vell, da Lord does." He opened his Bible. "In chapter six of da Proverbs, da Scriptures say dat da Lord hates: a proud look, a lying tongue, and hands dat shed innocent blood." Glancing up, he made a slow perusal of the sanctuary before continuing. "Da Lord hates a heart dat devises vicked imaginations, feet dat be swift in running to mischief. A false vitness dat speaks lies . . . *und* he dat sows discord among da brethren. I vant all of you to read dis in Proverbs six again tonight in da privacy of your home. *Und* I vant you to search your hearts."

Brother Rolf's voice rose with passion. "Do any of dese sins fit you? If so, you get down on your knees, *und* you ask God to deliver you from dese abominations." By the time the minister finished, he'd become so zealous his face was red, and he was shaking a finger at the men.

Michael, too, felt the burden of blame. Although he felt he wasn't guilty of any of the sins the pastor had read, he knew he'd stubbornly clung to his own great sin. He was no better than those who'd come here today to speak lies about him.

As the others rose to leave, Howie looked down at Michael. "Ain't you comin'?"

"In a few minutes. I have a few amends of my own to make."

The doors of the church banged open, and Joel and some of his friends came charging out. As they trotted down the steps, Joel stopped, stared at Hope for a long caustic second, then took off after his friends, who were already mounting their horses.

The look sent a chill through Hope. He'd no doubt done his worst.

"Where's that boy off to now?" Tilly said, obviously dismayed.

Considering the damage he'd probably inflicted during the meeting, Hope was utterly relieved she wouldn't have to endure his moods through Sunday dinner.

More men came streaming out of the building, every one of them glancing up at the threatening clouds, then rushing to their respective transportation. None gave any hint of the outcome of the inquiry.

But where was Michael?

The first fat drops of rain beat down on Hope's black bonnet. Locating her son playing under a tree with Belinda's Inga, Hope knew she should go fetch them both and start for Belinda's, but she couldn't until she had some answers.

Much to her relief, hulking Max walked out the door, dwarfing Titus and Jude at either side. They headed across the grass toward Hope, her mother, and Tilly.

"Oh, there's your father." Jessica dropped a quick kiss on Hope's cheek. "Everything's fine. You'll see." Picking up her floral skirt, she ran for their shay as the rain began to pelt hard.

"Belinda invited us to dinner," Tilly said even before the men reached them and she started walking as fast as her stiff old legs would take her for the Bremmers'.

"I'll grab Inga and Timmy," Max called and ran in the direction of the tree, while Titus and Jude helped Tilly.

"Wait!" Hope shouted after them. "What happened? Where's Michael?"

Sweet old Titus paused long enough for her to catch up. "Everything is fine. Your papa stood up for Michael right smart. So stop your frettin' an' come on. We're all gettin' soaked." Water was already dripping from his hat brim onto his dark coat. Without waiting for her response, he hurried on.

Her father had defended Michael. She glanced through the rain to the tempting dryness of the Bremmer house.

Max shot past her with the little ones. "Come on!"

But she couldn't leave. Not until she knew for sure if Michael was all right.

Alone in the quiet, Michael gazed up at the simple cross on the wall behind the pulpit. On another cross long ago, Jesus had been crucified, and while His life was bleeding out of Him, He had forgiven the very ones who'd stood before Him gloating over His cruel and unjust punishment. "Father, forgive them; for they know not what they do," Jesus had said. And his Lord asked no less of His own.

Michael sank to his knees. *Father, forgive me. For some time now, I have been shown this great sin in my life, but I've refused to give it up. I now see that I treasured my hate for my earthly father more than my walk with You. As of this day, Lord, I lay down this hate, right here on this floor, and I ask You to give me the strength to leave it behind, sweep it from my mind, that I never, ever pick it up again.*

His eyes closed, he stayed on his knees, allowing the cool quiet of the sanctuary to flow into him as his bitterness flowed out. The peace . . . the Lord's forgiveness replacing his unforgiveness.

When he eventually rose to his feet, Michael felt unaccountably lighter. And happier, incredibly happier. He walked outside into an unexpected rainstorm and couldn't have been more pleased.

Grinning, he spread his arms, welcoming the downpour.

God was washing him clean.

There was something very strange about Michael. He stood on the church landing, his arms wide, his tall hat dangling from a hand, and his face uplifted, as the rain poured over him.

And he began to laugh.

Had it all been too much for him? Had he lost his mind?

Hope made a dash for him.

He must have heard her pounding up the steps. When she reached him, he grabbed her and swung her around . . . still laughing.

"Put me down," she ordered. "Have you gone mad?"

"Anything but," he said, lowering her to her feet. "I'm free. I'm finally free."

"Yes, I heard. Titus said Papa defended you."

"Yes, that, too. It meant a lot. I'm sure your pa and I will be able to work out some kind of friendship now. But that ain't what I'm talkin' about. I just gave my hatred of Pa to the Lord. And I've never felt better in my life. I've never been happier." He grabbed her again and kissed her square on the mouth.

She jerked away. "Please, Michael," she said and quickly scanned the vicinity. "Or we really will cause a scandal."

"Did I hear you right?" Brother Rolf's crusty old voice was dangerously close. He stepped out of the building to face them, his attention on Michael. "You forgive your papa?"

"Yes, sir, I did." The grin on Michael's face told the rest.

Brother Rolf grabbed his hand and started pumping as if both their lives depended on it. With his other, he slapped Michael on the back, splattering rainwater. "I am so proud of you, son. Proud."

"I can't believe it took me so long. Thank you for showing me my sin and keeping after me. Thank you."

Hope could fairly see the old man swell up with happiness. But no more than she felt. Michael had freed himself from the chains of his past. And soon she, too, would be free . . . free to be his wife.

Brother Rolf draped an arm over her and Michael's shoulders. "You haf to come for dinner. Ve haf to celebrate."

"Belinda already invited Titus and Tilly and their son Jude," Hope informed him.

"Goot!" he boomed. "Da more da merrier."

"Fire!"

Hope jolted awake.

Wildly, she glanced around her room and realized she'd been dreaming. Her heart practically pounded out of her chest as she fell back on her pillow.

Her door rattled. Hard.

"Wake up, Hope!" The shout came from the hall. "The corncrib's on fire!" The voice belonged to Joel.

The possibility of such a fire was so remote, Hope instantly became suspicious. Was he using that as a ploy to get her to open her door?

That too was improbable in spite of how surly Joel had been when he came in late for supper this evening. Not only were Titus and Tilly in the house, but so was her brother-in-law.

There really must be a fire!

She leaped out of bed and ran to the door. Ramming aside the lock, she flung it open.

Joel stood there, a candle in his hand. "Quick. The corncrib's a-fire." He glanced past her and frowned. "Since when have you had a bolt on your door?"

"Since you started actin' like a madman," she retorted. "Is there really a fire?"

"As sure as your lover set it."

"Let's go, Joel!" Jude railed as he came out of the room he was sharing with Joel. He was in his long underwear still trying to get his foot in a boot.

The two men raced down the stairs as Hope hurried to find her own shoes in the dark. Slipping them on, she checked to find her son still asleep, then ran out, bumping into Titus in the hall.

"Get on down and start drawin' up the water, gal. An', Tilly," he shouted back into the room from which he'd just emerged, "you take the musket and Jude's pistol outside and shoot 'em. Then reload and do it again. That oughta wake up some of the neighbors."

"Ma can't do that," Hope reminded her father-in-law.

"Stop tryin' to baby me, Hope," Tilly said. "I ain't that far gone."

Reaching the ground floor, Hope saw flames licking up one side of the two-story corn storer. She could hardly believe this was happening twice in one week.

Fumbling around in the dark, she found a bucket and two pails, then ran out to the well.

Jude and Titus each took one and started hauling water from a nearby trough, while Joel shoveled dirt onto the burning wall.

Hope unwound the well bucket. Once she heard it plunk into the water, she started drawing it up by hand, not taking the time to use the crank. Without a stream nearby, water would be much harder to come by.

As she worked, she kept glancing back at the corncrib, wondering how it had caught fire. The rain had stopped as suddenly as it started hours ago, leaving no thunderclouds behind, no lightning to spark a flame.

Pouring a bucket into the trough, she eyed Joel. Of course, the first thing that had come out of his mouth was an accusation against Michael.

But one thing Hope knew for sure. If Michael were so inclined, he would've burned every building in the valley before touching that corncrib. Within the open-ended center beneath the second floor was where she'd found that ear of red corn, and they'd shared their first kiss.

If anyone set the fire, it was Joel. Somehow he must've known burning that building would hurt Hope the most. He'd been a kid of about eleven or twelve when Ezra had invited friends over for the cornhusking party. He could've been hiding up in the loft watching that very evening — he'd always been a scamp.

The musket fired, startling Hope into dropping her bucket as she ran back to the well. She heard two distinct echoes.

Then Tilly shot the pistol. It didn't make quite as much noise, but plenty loud enough to be heard at several of the neighboring farms.

Because of the downpour this afternoon, the wood burned slower than it had at the Wilsons'. If folks responded quickly, just maybe they could save most of this rustic memento of her first kiss.

Chapter Thirty-three

Hope jumped at the sound of the second round of shots a minute or so after Tilly had fired the first out front. Watching the smoke billow from the corncrib with each toss of water she or Titus threw, watching Jude and Joel taking chances with their lives as they tried to beat down the climbing flames, no one caring that they were all still in their nightclothes, she could see what little effect they were having. The smoking, smoldering, spitting blaze seemed bent on outwitting them, leaping and dodging all their attempts in its greedy frenzy.

Please, Lord, she prayed, *let the neighbors hear our gunshots. The four of us will never douse the flames by ourselves.*

Seeing that she and Titus were running out of trough water again, she returned to the well to the even more backbreaking task of hauling up the precious liquid, while her father-in-law scooped up the remains from the hollowed log.

Her concern for him grew. They'd

scarcely started, and he already looked more haggard than he'd been at the end of the Wilson fire. Yet there was no sense trying to get him to stop. If he wouldn't quit at the Wilsons' when there were plenty to take his place, he surely wouldn't now.

While hoisting the well bucket, she glanced toward the road. If help didn't arrive soon, this night might very well kill Titus.

But there was one person she very much did not want to show up. Michael Flanagan. It would be dangerous enough to quench these flames without Joel using them as an excuse to fan his own jealousy and hatred.

"Mama! Mama!" Timmy's fearful holler pierced the air.

The gunshots must have awakened him. Hope swiftly sloshed water from the well bucket into the one beside her and ran to dump it in the trough on her way to intercept her son. With no time to spare for niceties, she scooped him up under one arm and ran toward the house.

He tried to talk, but with his belly bouncing against her hip, Timmy's words spewed out in unintelligible spurts.

Tilly, her white hair glowing orange in the eerie light, came toward her, her own lined face a mask of despair.

"Ma, take Timmy. I can't watch him and work, too." She thrust her son's hand into Tilly's, then started back.

"Don't let Titus work hisself to death," Tilly pleaded after her. "It ain't nothin' but a broken-down ol' corncrib."

They all knew, though, that the roaring fire endangered more than just the corncrib. Sparks could easily ignite the shingles of another building. They could lose everything. The animals in the cages, coop, pens, and barn seemed to know that as well. They made more racket than if a wildcat was on the prowl.

When she returned to the well, Titus was bent over the stone surround, hoisting water hand over hand.

Hope reached in and, while she helped him bring the bucket the rest of the way up, she conveyed Tilly's message. "Ma says it's only a buildin'. It can be replaced." Then added for good measure, "But she says you're the only husband she's got. So don't kill yourself."

The shriveled old man just kept working. "She's a good ol' gal. When the Lord was passin' out wives, He give me the best He had."

His words touched her deeply. "After almost fifty years of marriage, I hope my husband will say the same about me."

"He will, li'l missy," Titus grunted out as he swung the full bucket up and over the side. "You're one of the good ones, too."

He had no idea how much that meant to her, now that he knew of the letter she'd sent Jude.

Suddenly, three riders came galloping around the house — an answer to her prayer. They were off their mounts before they came to a full stop.

"What do you want us to do?" one of them shouted.

With floppy-brimmed hats shading their faces in the darkness, Hope couldn't tell who they were, except that they looked quick and able. "One of you help me fetch water. The others form a bucket line with Pa."

"Where's Joel?" shouted one as he ran to help her.

With his face turned toward the fire, she recognized Benny Moore, who lived across the river. "Joel's at the back, shovelin' dirt on any new starts." She dropped the bucket into the well, hearing its hollow bangs against the stone side as it went down for what seemed like the hundredth time. It was a pure pleasure to watch the big strong lad start hauling it up.

Then a thought came to her. "How on earth did you get here so soon? You live a good half mile on the other side of the river."

"Oh, me an' the boys was just over yonder, fixin' to go coon huntin' when we heard the shots and saw the fire. Lucky for you, I guess."

He poured the water into her bucket, and as she took it to the trough, she pondered the fact that if they'd been close enough to hear the shots, why hadn't she heard their coon dogs?

But what was that old saying? "Don't look a gift horse in the mouth."

A few moments later, Mr. Spencer, the owner of the farm to the south, rode in bareback with one of his husky lads sitting behind, and they joined the bucket brigade.

Then Thompson and his three boys rode up in a cart, bringing more buckets and pails.

Nothing needed to be said except, "Bless you," as they all joined in the fight.

Within a minute or so, the flames started shrinking into a huge, gray, choking mass that shifted with every whim of the gentle breeze. Hope wished she had a kerchief or an apron — something to cover her nose.

"We've just about got 'er," one of the men

shouted from the other side of the smoke.

At that moment, two more riders rushed out of the darkness. Jim Johnson, and to Hope's dismay, Michael.

The instant Michael had discovered the fire glow to the southeast, his primary concern had been for Hope and Timmy. If their house was on fire, they could've been caught in the blaze. He'd ridden hard, overtaking Jim Johnson, who'd also heard the shots and come to help. Michael's relief had been profound as he rode into the Underwood clearing and found the house unscathed.

Then, as he circled around, he caught sight of Hope dressed in a smudged white sleeping gown and her hair in a night braid that hung down to her waist, hauling a bucket of water.

She looked back at him, her eyes reflecting fire and smoke and turmoil, the same as he'd felt so often as a child when he'd witnessed the latest fire that his pa had started, often as not.

Dismounting, his driving desire was to go to her and take away her pain.

"You shouldn't have come," she said as he reached her.

"The fire ain't completely out yet." He

459

took the bucket from her. "You look exhausted. Go sit down and get some rest."

She grabbed his arm, her expression urgent. "Surely you know Joel's blamin' this fire on you, like the last one. Please. Go home. If you stay, I know he'll start trouble."

"Flanagan!" The shout came from behind him before her words scarcely left her mouth.

Michael wheeled around.

Joel sauntered out of the smoke with several of his friends and his older brother Michael had had dinner with today. And there wasn't a welcoming smile among them.

Hope tugged on his shirt. "Go home, Michael. Please! *Now.*"

"I'm sorry, but I can't do that." From the murderous looks on their faces, he wished he'd thought to bring his pistol. "This needs to be settled here and now."

She started forward.

He stopped her. "Go back to the house."

"No."

"Let her stay," Joel said as he and the men closed in. "She needs to see what Benny found. It's time she found out what you really are. Show her, Jude."

Joel's older brother held out his hand and opened it. A plain silver timepiece lay in it.

"Benny found this on the ground behind the corncrib." He turned the pocket watch over.

To Michael's dismay, the initials *M. J. F.* were on its back. The timepiece was his. "How convenient," he stated flatly.

"Do you deny this is yours?" Jude Underwood asked, his words demanding.

Michael picked it up, opened the cover, and examined it more closely. "No, it's mine all right. Since I don't have a clock, I've been keepin' it on my mantel."

"Till it walked itself over to our corncrib." Joel snatched the pocket watch out of Michael's hand, then stepped within inches of his face. "Maybe you didn't leave no proof at the Wilsons', but you slipped up this time."

"This is nonsense," Hope said, trying to barge in between Michael and her brother-in-law. "You're just making —"

Joel shoved her aside.

Enraged, Michael threw a punch to Joel's chin, knocking him to the ground.

"Get him, boys!" Holding his jaw, Joel sprang up. "He ain't gettin' away with it this time."

Suddenly, they were upon him, shouting, grabbing, as he tried to wrench free. He heard Hope screaming, too, and fought all the harder.

"Get some rope. Tie him up," someone yelled.

Unable to budge, Michael finally gave up fighting.

The Underwood brothers and two of Joel's friends had his arms pinned to his sides, while one ran to the barn for the rope.

Another farmer held on to Hope's arm, keeping her back, while a couple of lads and Jim Johnson stared wide-eyed.

Jim stepped forward. "This don't sound like somethin' Flanagan would do."

"I'd expect you to say somethin' like that," Joel railed. "He loans you fellas a few horses to come home on, and y'all think he's a saint." Thrusting out his hand, he shook the timepiece at him. "This is all the proof I need."

"You probably stole it an' put it there yourself," Hope accused from where she was being restrained, her face twisted with fury.

"And set fire to my own place?" Joel finished for her. "When are you gonna wake up, woman? He's trash, just like his pa before him." His expression changed from one of rage to an almost smile. "In fact, I say we take care of him, here and now, just like they did his pa."

Jude Underwood, still holding tight on to

Michael, looked across to his brother. "You mean hang him ourselves? Now? Without a trial?"

"This here timepiece is all the trial we need. Even for the likes of you," Joel flung it at Jim Johnson, the only man who'd spoken up in Michael's defense.

"Yeah," shouted an excited Reggie Wilson, his Adam's apple bobbing wildly. "Hang him for burnin' both buildin's."

"No!" Hope wailed, struggling hard to free herself. "You can't do this." Frantically, she glanced around. "Pa Titus! Pa Titus! Where are you? Say somethin'!"

"I'm right here, child."

Michael swung toward the only calm voice he'd heard.

Mr. Underwood stood a few feet to the side of Hope and the others with a rifle butted up against his shoulder, the barrel aimed straight at Michael and the men holding him. "Joel, you an' your friends step away from Sergeant Flanagan."

"Sure, Pa. Whatever you say." Joel released Michael and stepped back. "I mean, if you'd rather shoot him than hang him, that's all right by me."

The finality of his life hit Michael. Fear gripped him. He was about to die. And Hope? What would happen to her? *Heav-*

enly Father, please help us!

"All of you, step away." Titus motioned with the rifle barrel.

Michael stared at Mr. Underwood. The nice old man was about to shoot him in cold blood.

The others unhanded Michael and moved aside, although Jude Underwood seemed hesitant. "Pa, this ain't like you. Are you sure you want to do this?"

"I been left no choice, Son."

Chapter Thirty-four

"I got the rope!" Reggie Wilson shouted as he came running from the barn. He halted. "What's goin' on?"

Everything in Hope screamed to be freed. Again, she tried to wrench free from Mr. Spencer. "Let me go." She couldn't believe he, too, would be willing to go along with killing Michael.

Even more incredible, Pa Titus stood there, ready to shoot.

"Just step over there by Joel," Titus said, motioning to Reggie with the rifle barrel.

And Michael, who wanted nothing but to have a life with her . . . he stood there, waiting to die. Because of her.

She couldn't bear to look in his eyes.

"Reggie," Titus said, "tie Joel's hands behind his back."

"What? Are you crazy?" Joel dodged away from his friend with the rope.

"Stay where you are, Son."

That's when Hope realized the rifle wasn't pointed at Michael, but at Titus's

465

own son. She heard others mumble their own disbelief.

"Reggie, do as I say," Titus commanded. "Joel set this fire here tonight. And if he'd go so far as to burn his own place, he probably started the one at your barn, too."

"How can you say that, Pa?" Joel asked as he took a few steps back. "I'm your son."

"Stop, boy." He cocked the flintlock. "Don't make me shoot you."

Hope couldn't believe how incredibly calm her father-in-law was.

"Jude, go over and help Reggie."

Jude looked from his father to Joel. "Are you sure, Pa?"

"I'm sure." Neither his gaze nor his aim wavered from Joel. "You see, I couldn't sleep tonight, what with thinkin' about all that's been goin' on the last couple of days . . . your ma an' me leavin' here so sudden-like. Joel, I heard you come sneakin' up the stairs. Then a minute or so later, I saw the fire glow comin' in the window. Just as I was comin' to roust you out, Joel, you come runnin' from your room, shoutin' fire."

"Why didn't you say anything before?" Jude asked.

"I figured to wait till Joel helped us put it out. I reckoned that was the least he could do. 'Sides, I wanted to see what he'd do next. It pains me to know my own son would go so far as to take a man's life to get what he wants."

Mr. Spencer finally released Hope and yelled at his son, who'd ridden in with the other lads. "Barnabas, you get on your horse an' go home, *now.* I'll deal with you later."

Watching his friends deserting him, Joel threw up his hands and started wailing. "Pa, it weren't my fault. I tried to make Flanagan go away peaceable like. But he just kept diggin' in deeper. You know how much I want Hope. I couldn't let him just come in here an' walk off with her."

As Barnabas and the Moore lad backed away toward their horses, stocky Jim Johnson walked over to help Jude truss up his younger brother.

And Hope went to Michael, her knees nearly buckling, her insides shaking like a thousand willow leaves in a storm.

He wrapped his arms around her, holding her so close she couldn't tell if it was his heart or hers pounding so wildly. Nor did she care. He was alive!

"Pa," Joel cried out as the men bound his hands behind his back, "you can't do this. I'm your son."

At this moment, the old man seemed

taller and stronger than she'd ever dreamt possible, as he stood there, rifle still at ready, saying nothing.

"What do you want us to do with him?" Jude asked once he'd finished securing his brother.

"Take him to the toolshed and lock him in."

"Then what, Pa?" Joel's tone had turned belligerent as the two men led him away. "You can't just keep me in there forever."

Sighing, Titus lowered the rifle, suddenly looking very old again. "I know. I'll decide what to do with you later, after I talk to Wilson. I'm sure Reggie had a part in this. His pa is gonna want to have a say in this, too."

The sun was high overhead and burning hot as Hope drove Titus, Tilly, and her son down the grade to the ferry landing. Moored alongside the dock, a large log raft with a cabin built in the middle bobbed gently with the current. Much of the deck was loaded with the barrels and crates of supplies and goods the Underwoods had chosen to take with them.

Jude smiled and waved up to them from the raft. "Ever'thing's ready to go!"

"Hi!" Timmy, sitting on his grandfather's

lap, returned with a shout.

Next to Jude, Joel slouched beside Reggie Wilson, watching the wagon rolling slowly toward them. But no smile graced Hope's freckle-faced brother-in-law. Being aboard was the start of his punishment. He'd been forced to make an unhappy decision . . . either be taken to Nashville in chains for trial or travel with his family up north to Fort Massac and enlist in the army. He'd chosen the army.

As Hope pulled the wagon team to a stop, she couldn't help smiling. Instead of her leaving for army life with Michael, Joel was going. And so was Reggie Wilson. Both their fathers felt they needed that added measure of discipline.

"It's all for the best," Tilly, beside her, sighed.

"Are you sure, Ma?" Hope asked. "With Joel heading off for the army, there's no reason we can't just go on as we have until Michael and I get married."

Tilly's paper-thin skin creased in myriad places as she smiled, though her eyes remained sad. "Pa's gettin' too old to run the place. It's time he took a rest."

"You sleepy, Grampa?" Timmy asked, twisting around to look at the old man's face.

"Yes I am, li'l man. And I'm gonna take myself right down there to that room an' take a nap." He pointed to the cabin on the raft, then sent Hope a teasing wink. "Let's you an' me go in there an' take us a long nap."

Timmy's excitement turned sullen. "Me not sleepy. Play wid Inga."

"Well, if you'd rather play with Inga than sleep with me, then I reckon that's how it's gonna have to be. But first . . ." Titus pulled a fold of paper from inside his brown vest pocket. "Here, Hope. Keep this safe. I've signed the property over to Timmy. It's yours to look after till he's old enough to take over."

"But, Pa, what about Joel? You were givin' it to him."

"Joel showed me how little he cared about the place when he put a torch to it." He handed the tot over to Hope. "Come on, Gramma, let's you an' me go take us a nap."

"Wait. Not yet." Hope reached for Titus and Tilly with Timmy caught in the middle. "I love you."

Tilly gave her a shaky kiss. "We love you, too, sweet girl."

"We'll come see you right after harvest," Hope promised.

"You should be startin' your honeymoon

then," Tilly said, patting her arm. "Come see us next summer after spring plantin'. An' in the meantime, we'll have us a whole slew of grandbabies to keep us busy. Ain't that right, Pa?"

Hope glanced to the balding dear with his patches of white fuzz and saw his eyes rimming with moisture. All he managed was a nod while clearing his throat. He started off the side.

Taking a deep breath, Hope swiped at her own tears.

"Night, night, Grampa, Gramma," Timmy said as Titus reached up for Tilly.

Reluctantly, Hope watched them go. Logic told her it really was for the best, but that didn't stop her heart from aching. They were too old. She might not see them ever again.

And she hadn't seen Michael since the night of the fire. Though she knew it would have been more than awkward for him to drop by the Underwoods' after the events of that night, she'd been left with a hollow feeling. Would he — or any man, for that matter — continue to think she was worth the effort, after coming within seconds of being hanged because of her?

Max and Rolf Bremmer came walking alongside the wagon, passing her to reach the Underwoods.

Sitting up on the driver's bench with Timmy, she watched them help the couple board the raft, then exchange handshakes with all the men and hugs with Tilly. Then, too soon, Max unlooped the mooring line from a dock post, and the raft slowly moved out into the water.

With arms around each other, Titus and Tilly waved good-bye.

Abruptly, Timmy jumped up onto the seat. "Go! Go! Me go!"

Holding her son in place, Hope's tears came in earnest, spilling down her cheeks. "We will, sweetheart. Next summer."

Feeling the wagon lurch forward, she grabbed for the reins.

"It's all right, Hope. I'm just turning you around." Max had hold of one horse's bridle.

Hope wiped away the wetness on her cheeks and took a last look at the departing raft while Timmy continued to fight to free himself.

"Oh, by the way, Timmy," Max said, glancing up at their struggle, "Inga is waiting for you to come play with her. And while you're at it, y'all might as well eat with us. The noon meal should be ready about now."

"Taters and gravy?" Timmy asked, his attention now diverted.

"You bet. But only if you'll give me'n my pa a ride on up the hill."

"Yes! Yes!" Timmy bounced up and down as the two big men climbed aboard.

Once the men were settled and Timmy had hopped onto Max's lap, Hope slapped the reins over the horses' backs, and the two leaned into their traces for the haul up to the street.

"So, you'll be staying *mit* your folks for a while, *und* Joel is going into da army," Brother Bremmer mused, hanging onto the front board as the wagon lurched up the hill. "Ve pray da army makes a honest man out of him. Like your Michael. And, speaking of Sergeant Flanagan, he says he still vants to stay in da valley. Even after dem boys try to hang him. Goot. He's yust da kind of fellow Reardon Valley vants. A hardvorking man dat fears da Lord. *Ja,* he fits in real goot."

"Yes, he does," Hope agreed. *At long last, yes, he does.*

Reaching the Bremmers', Max helped her and Timmy off while the elderly Rolf lumbered down.

Timmy immediately ran onto the porch, yelling, "Inga! Inga!" He raced through the open door before Hope and the men had even reached the gate.

"He does love Inga," Brother Rolf mused

with a grin lifting his heavy jowls as he followed.

"Except when they're pullin' each other's hair," Hope quipped.

Max laughed as he waited for Hope to precede him up the walk. "Just a lover's spat. Reminds me of Junior Smith and Mary Jo when they were little."

She glanced back over her shoulder. "That's right. I'd forgotten. And here they are gettin' married on the Fourth of July with all —"

Michael!

He rose from a chair on the porch, watching her and Max approach.

"Oh, I forgot to tell you," Max said right behind her, a grin in his voice. "We invited Mike to eat with us, too." Moving past her, Max climbed the steps and disappeared inside, his father right behind him, leaving her standing there, staring up at Michael. Her heart did a crazy flip-flop.

Waiting at the top of the steps, he stared back at her, looking more appealing than she could've imagined in his white shirt and buff breeches.

Becoming aware that she was just standing there, searching his eyes, she lifted the hem of her black skirt and started up to him.

Before she reached the top, he offered a hand.

She slipped her much smaller one into his and let him assist her the rest of the way.

He didn't let go but pulled her close. "You don't know how many times I wanted to come see you." His breath feathered across her hair. "To find out how you were doin' this week."

"Me, too." She reached up, touched his face. "After you almost lost your life over me, it means everything to know you're still here —" she looked down — "and still holding my hand."

He took her other one and brought them to his lips, brushing across her fingers. "I know I never deserved your trust again after waiting ten years before coming back. But you gave it. And when I said I wouldn't ever leave here again without you, I meant it . . . for better or worse, in sickness and in health." He caressed her with a smile. "In-laws or no in-laws."

She, too, smiled and twined her arms around his neck. "And outlaws or no out-laws, till death do us part."

Then, just before his lips came down to claim hers, he whispered, "Not even then, sweetheart. Not even then."

A Note from the Author

Dear Reader,

I'm sure you noticed that this novel's spiritual theme was about Christian love and forgiveness. The theme was inspired by a hope I have that all the children I work with at my church will come to experience the fruit of the Holy Spirit in its fullness. I was made particularly aware of the need to stress love for others one day when I told a group of kids a story about a sister who came to see her brother with more loving eyes — no easy feat, considering sibling rivalry. At the conclusion, I asked the kids to look at the person sitting to their right and told them that Jesus commands them to love that person as they love themselves.

I know they'd heard the commandment before and hadn't questioned it in the abstract. But when they were faced with an actual person to love as much as themselves, they were caught completely off guard. To them, that didn't seem remotely plausible.

But then, selfless love for a neighbor is

rarely something that comes naturally. And forgiving someone who has grievously harmed us is even harder. In the natural, a person feels completely justified in his unforgiveness, even though Jesus told us to forgive those who trespass against us. My prayer is that the kids I teach will come to understand that, by living in faith and obedience to their loving heavenly Father, He will give them an overflowing of love and forgiveness for others they never thought possible.

My wish for you is that, as you took your journey with Hope and Michael, you, too, were reminded that there is only one place to find that fullness of love and compassion . . . as a Galatians 5:22–25 child of the living God.

Dianna Crawford

About the Author

DIANNA CRAWFORD lives in the Sierra Nevada Mountains with her husband, Byron. Although she loves writing historical fiction, her most gratifying blessings are her husband of many years, her four daughters, and her grandchildren. Aside from writing, Dianna is active in her church's children's ministries.

Dianna's first novel was published in 1992 under the pen name Elaine Crawford. Written for the general market, the book became a best-seller and was nominated for Best First Book by the Romance Writers of America. Three more novels and several novellas followed under that pen name.

Dianna much prefers writing Christian historical fiction, because our wonderful Christian heritage is commonly diluted or distorted — if not completely deleted — from most historical fiction, nonfiction, and textbooks. She felt very blessed when she and Sally Laity were given the opportunity to coauthor the Freedom's Holy Light series for Tyndale House. The books center on fictional characters who are woven into many of the real-life adventures and miracles that took place during the American Revolution.

The Freedom's Holy Light series consists of *The Gathering Dawn*, *The Kindled Flame*, *The Tempering Blaze*, *The Fires of Freedom*, *The Embers of Hope*, and *The Torch of Triumph*. Dianna has also authored two HeartQuest novellas, which appear in the anthologies *A Victorian Christmas Tea* and *With This Ring*. She has written a novella, "November Nocturne," in the anthology *Autumn Crescendo* (Barbour Publishing). She is the coauthor with Rachel Druten of the novel *Out of the Darkness* (Heartsong Presents).

Her first HeartQuest series, the Reardon Brothers, consists of *Freedom's Promise*, *Freedom's Hope*, and *Freedom's Belle*. This current HeartQuest series, Reardon Valley, includes *A Home in the Valley*, *Lady of the River*, and *An Echo of Hope*.

Dianna welcomes letters from readers written to her at P.O. Box 80176, Bakersfield, CA 93380. A stamped return envelope would be appreciated.